KILL-GRIEF

KILL-GRIEF

Caroline Rance

First published in Great Britain in 2009
by Picnic Publishing
PO Box 5222, Hove BN52 9LP

A catalogue record for this book is available from the British Library.

ISBN: 9780955861345

Printed and bound in Great Britain by the MPG Books Group
Designed by SoapBox, www.soapboxcommunications.co.uk.

CHAPTER 1

CHESTER, 3 JANUARY 1756

Narrowed eyes watched her from across the street. High up in the confines of Eastgate Row, she gripped the oak railing and returned the stare.

Rain gusted into the walkway and numbed her lips. The eyes narrowed further, as if she were the first darkenings of a horizon, and her knuckles whitened on the rail.

Mary feigned distraction at the drunkards who laughed and slid on the mud below. Squawks of geese grated in her ears and the sulphurous stench of the gutters surged and ebbed with the wind.

Tightness gathered in her stomach. The man did not move. Slumped against a shop wall, he rested his stubbly head on the bricks, heedless of the people who skirted round his legs.

Hark at you – gawping at a scabby beggar! Mary took up her bag. A few more days in the city and she'd ignore him like the rest of them. She hurried on.

Cursing drivers, bellowing poultry hawkers, beer-fuelled brawlers – the city seemed made of gaping mouths. Stumps of teeth as rotten as taters, gums mashed by scurvy, noses crumpled by the pox. Mary squeezed round a horde of men outside a tavern, their armpits level with her nostrils. Beyond their oniony heat and the blast of ale fumes, the air chilled her face.

1

Then she stopped and looked back. The beggar's gaze had followed her, as folk always said of portraits. She blew out a long sigh. Sometimes the tangle under her ribs writhed so hard she thought of cutting it out with a knife. A church clock tolled close by. Eleven. *Damn.* Late already for her new job. She had sat in the inn worrying about it for too long.

Down on the street, away from the shelter of the Row, muck splashed her stockings and seeped through to her legs. The beggar shoved back his sleeves and thrust his arms into the rain, wringing his face into a grimace. Scabs and weeping blisters pitted his skin.

She'd have to deal with worse than him. His stare made Mary's neck itch. The uneven cobbles made her stumble and swear. The man showed his teeth in a yellow grin, then dragged himself up and strolled towards her. Mary clattered up the steps of the Northgate Street Row, her breath quickening. She had nothing to give him – he must be able to see that. Why did he not follow that gentleman with the gold-threaded hat, or grab watches from the waists of the vast petticoats that blocked the walkways? But then she felt for her pocket. The lump of coins was still there, from the pound *he* had given her.

This second storey of shops looked smarter. Too smart for her. She hesitated.

Do you think yourself better, Mary?

But she slipped into the nearest doorway and waited for the beggar to pass. He scratched his hands as he walked, his nails dislodging scabs.

'May I help you, madam?' The shopkeeper's world-weary tone carried no welcome. His shop, distanced from daylight by the covered gallery of the Row, was brightened by lanterns.

'Might I stand here a moment?' Mary said. 'There was someone . . .'

But she broke off. Bolts of cloth formed ranks along the counter. The shopkeeper glanced heavenwards.

'Funny thing, eh, to find in a silk mercer's? Silk?'

Mary scanned the neat rolls. Silks as vivid as sunlit seas, some red as the sand at home, some as pale as silver-birch bark. Silks printed with flowers, stripes – even birds. And, at the end, its edge frayed into a cobweb of threads, sat a bolt of silk of vibrant blue. Its weft crackled under her rough fingertips.

'Where did this one come from?' she asked.

The shopkeeper eyed the bedraggled hem of her topcoat. 'From a merchant. Cost a fair penny. Too fair a penny to warrant letting folk finger it unless they mean to buy.'

Mary shifted aside to let the light fall better on it. A trace of green played through the weave, as algae might blossom in a pool. No. Pain and relief bunched in her chest. She drew her hand away.

'I can't afford anything,' she said, smiling. 'I just need to escape someone.' The shopkeeper's expression softened when Mary described the man.

'Some blasted vagrant,' he said, looking along the Row. 'No shortage of them in this town.'

'He in't down on the street, is he?'

Scorn leapt back into the mercer's eyes and he laughed. 'Do you think I were washed up with the tide? You'd pike with all my ribbons before I could even shed a tear for your sorry plight.'

'I'm no thief!' Mary said. The mercer made a mocking bow and gestured at the door. 'All I asked was to stop here a minute when I might else have been murdered.'

The shopkeeper snorted and a dash of spittle alighted on Mary's neck.

Well, there was one enemy for her. Perhaps the city was not so different after all. Mary hastened past the Exchange and the cathedral, her feet unsteady on the slippery ground. She kept her eyes from the building ahead.

The Northgate Gaol glowered over the street like a cat examining a gap in the floorboards. Silence surrounded it – an atmosphere so dense that it muted the shouts of the drivers who fumed in the queue to pass through it on to the road north. People said the dungeons were roots, branching under the whole of Chester to the limits of the city walls. A hundred years ago, they said, parts of them were bricked up, prisoners and all, when the stink got so bad the gaolers couldn't go in.

The innkeeper at Foregate Street had sworn it was true. Mary had told him not all country girls believe everything you say. But she had not told him the place was the reason she was in Chester at all.

Inside the gate's passageway droplets of damp settled on Mary's eyelashes and the odour of urine stung tears from her. Moisture swooped into her lungs, igniting an echoing cough. The busy street behind hid the beggar, at first. Then his white, shaven head broke above the waves of hats and straggly locks. He must have doubled back, in search of her. He must not be able to see her, in the gloom of the passageway, and yet his gaze seemed able to slice the darkness and leave her visible, like a spy discovered behind a tapestry.

Not far beyond the Northgate the cobbled terrace of the Blue Coat School offered refuge; Mary trailed mud to the door of the north wing. The gaol towered behind her. What if the innkeeper told the truth about cells the size of coffins and cockroaches the size of mice? She could not afford to be frightened. That wouldn't help the man in there who needed her to get him free.

Outside the railings the beggar stood dragging his fingernails down his raw arm.

'Mary.' She shrank back into the porch. 'Is you, ain't it?' He paced the school's boundary, his tread even and firm. He waited a long minute, then chuckled and headed back towards the Northgate, squinting up at the turrets of the gaol before he disappeared into the passageway.

Sweat beaded under Mary's stays. She knocked too lightly for anyone to hear. She must only have imagined him saying her name. It must have been a distortion of the jangle of a harness, or the bark of a dog, or another man calling to his wife. She smeared the rain from her face and opened the door.

'Excuse me.' Her voice fled into the whitewashed walls. 'It's Mary Helsall . . .'

There'd been a cook in the kitchen the previous day – a big woman who pretended not to listen to the matron's questions and Mary's hesitant answers – but now the room was deserted, its fire a snowy mound

4

of ash and its kettle empty on the tiles. All the blood had left Mary's fingers. She pinched them, and they were numb, and when she stretched them towards the cinders, the last of the heat bounced off them and they buzzed.

No use wishing she had not come back. What else could she have done? Stayed at the inn until the money ran out? Then what? Food and a bed and four pounds a year – not that she would be staying that long – would suffice until the situation changed.

Footsteps shuffled outside. Mary neatened her kerchief.

The man at the door stood and observed her for a moment, as if uncertain what to do with her. He frowned and fiddled with the thread of a missing button on his jacket.

'You the other nurse or summat?'

'Yes. I did knock, but—'

'I was upstairs,' he said. A smile, weary but not unpleasant, stole across his mouth. 'Suppose I'd best show you to Mrs Seward's *parlour*.' He affected a high-and-mighty accent for the last word. He lifted her bag and led her up a staircase, taking the steps two at a time.

'Are you the porter?' Mary said.

'Aye. Run errands and such-like. Mind the doors.'

'Mrs Seward talked of you yesterday.'

He shrugged a laugh. 'I bet she whinged her shrivelled guts out, an' all, didn't she? Did she tell you not to look at me, lest you turn to stone?'

The porter would not enter the matron's parlour, such as it was; he propped himself against the door frame – his messy sandy hair almost brushed the top of it – and indicated to Mary to sit on one of the austere chairs. 'I an't noticed you in Chester before.'

She met his eyes. Grey. 'No one notices me.' His expression changed. A half-amused, searching look. 'I'm from a village, on the coast. Don't know if I'll be here long.'

'Me neither,' he said. 'I'm off to London soon as I've saved enough.'

The idea sounded decisive and unchangeable. What would it be like, to get into a coach and go? To go to London, to York – anywhere

5

– by herself? She could escape. But she had no business letting herself think about such things now.

'What do you want to go there for?' The words sounded more terse than she meant, and she smiled to soften them. The porter's unblinking gaze discomfited her. Drink infused it, and yet there was something else. Something she had seen before, in green eyes. Streams of air flowed through the window frame, touching her neck, and she shivered. He broke the stare.

'That's where there's a future,' he said with a shrug. He swayed as he pushed himself up from the door frame. His feet made empty sounds, two steps to each grind of the pendulum on the clock at the top of the stairs.

It still didn't seem possible, that she was to be a nurse in an infirmary. She'd have to be kind to people. The innkeeper had been puzzled when she told him. 'What infirmary's that, lass?' he'd said.

One that didn't have any patients yet. One about to open in an empty part of a school, cramped into a few rooms even the likes of teachers didn't want to use. An infirmary for people like that beggar and his scabby arms. People who would puke and swear and need their pots emptying. People undressed, issuing invalid-breath.

A different, harsher tread sounded on the landing.

'Good morning, Miss Helsall.' She stood up and tucked a stray strand of black hair behind her ear. Mrs Seward assessed her through round wire spectacles. The filth on Mary's skirt made her smile with satisfaction. 'You have other clothes, I take it? You can't mean to begin your employment looking like that.'

'I have . . .' Mary's throat stuck. 'I have a bed gown and a quilted petticoat, aside of these.'

'Clean?'

'No, I . . .' She checked her words. 'Yes, madam.'

'Wells!' Mrs Seward's shout echoed through the silent building. The young man took his time to climb back upstairs. 'Carry Miss Helsall's bag.'

His fingers brushed Mary's when he took it. She flinched her hand away and followed the matron, each step jerking her heart lower, rib by rib.

CHAPTER 2

Icy air rushed from a doorway. Mary peered past Mrs Seward and saw a bedroom – sparsely furnished, dim and filled with Fore-Northgate Street's noises, borne through the window on the smell of wet manure. The porter dumped the bag down on the bed, showering crumbs of dirt on to the linen. Mary hastened to brush them away, but her boot muddied the hem of the counterpane and a sigh hissed from the matron's nose.

'Oh, for goodness' sake.' Mrs Seward's gaze fell to the powdery tide-marks of dried salt water on Mary's cape, and the creases in her forehead deepened. 'I vowed to tolerate neither sluttishness of dress nor excessive prinking, but I fear between you and Nurse Hewett I shall be forced to suffer both extremes.' She called for someone on the landing. 'And mind you do not neglect the doors this afternoon, Wells. Mr Crane told me you were not there when he arrived yesterday. Anyone might have walked in. Thieves and all sorts. And it would have been your fault.'

The porter folded his arms. 'You bid me take a message to Barnston.'

'You mean *Mr* Barnston.'

Wells rested against the cupboard and gave an insolent laugh. 'Trafford Barnston *Esquire*.'

'Enough! Impudence will not save us should a murderer sneak among us.' Mrs Seward slammed the window. 'Miss Helsall, you are

7

advised to have as little as possible to do with him. He is a worshipper of the gin cup.'

Wells raised his eyebrows. The drink seemed to have lifted a little, and more colour had risen to his slender face.

'No worse than worshipping round a cauldron,' he said. Mrs Seward made no other response than a glare. Instead, she nodded towards the door.

'Here is Agnes Hewett,' she said to Mary. 'I trust you will make every effort to share this room in harmony.'

The girl fiddled with her conker-shiny hair and gave Mary a friendly smile. Her face and hazel eyes were as round as apples, her handshake soft and her skin almost unblemished. A modest strip of lace trimmed her cap.

'Miss Helsall at least does not count vanity among her faults,' said the matron. 'Perhaps I failed to make myself clear when I told you lace and other such ornaments are improper for your station.' Agnes Hewett touched her cap and the smile glinted deeper in her eyes.

'I'll unpick it later,' she said. Her tone was blithe and free of any apology.

'Immediately after you have shown Miss Helsall around the infirmary.'

'Yes, madam.' She stifled a giggle until the door to the supposed parlour swung shut. 'She hates me,' she said, flopping on to the bed. 'She'll hate you too, I expect. She hates everyone, doesn't she, Anthony?'

'Not so much as I hate her.' The porter's fist thumped away along the wall of the corridor.

'You must be hungry,' Agnes said. 'It's nigh-on twelve.' Even anxiety no longer subdued the rumbling of Mary's stomach and she was glad to go back to the kitchen. Agnes stoked the fire and cut slices from a loaf. She wore a pretty green cotton gown, her petticoats spotless at the hem. 'I'm terrible relieved you're so young, too. Mrs Seward keeps saying I'm not old enough. I'm twenty – I'm not such a child that I'll do anything silly. But I was expecting you to be some ancient widow who'd gossip with her about me.'

Traces of warmth lingered in the centre of the bread; Mary could have eaten the whole loaf. 'I feel ancient enough sometimes,' she said. 'But I promise I won't go fishing after scandal.' Well, how could she? She'd known enough of that herself.

Agnes's round cheeks flushed. She rolled a crumb of bread into a doughy ball.

Efforts of light washed on to the floorboards of the infirmary's deserted ward, and cobwebs drifted on every beam in the ceiling. A dead pigeon spilled, soot-ridden, from the fireplace and the sickliness of decaying flesh made Mary wrinkle her nose. Dust rested everywhere – a choking layer that wisped up and speckled her arms.

Twelve beds, Agnes told her, would fill the room – there would hardly be space to walk between them. But the governors hadn't even contracted with a carpenter yet, and it must have been six months since they first thought of it.

Even home was clean next to this. Even the grime in the carving of the bedposts would have been easier to wash away. Outside, gulls mewed, raising their wings to balance themselves on the ramparts of the Northgate Gaol. No more than fifty yards away the building struck out into blind clouds. No one could ever hear the shouts of the prisoners. The walls were too thick. Mary clutched her thumbs in her fists. Fatigue descended on her and she steadied herself on the windowsill.

'You're not ill, are you?' Agnes touched her shoulder. 'You look dreadful pale.' Mary shook her head.

'Only tired,' she said. 'I didn't sleep much at the inn.'

'Oh, they're terrible places. I stayed in one once and a terrier walked around on me all night and—'

'I might just take some fresh air a minute.' Mary ran down the stairs. Outside, the cobbled courtyard seemed wide; the gate stood part open, inviting her to keep running.

Damn it – why didn't she stay at home? She could have made the pound last, with only herself to feed. She could have kept herself to herself and blocked her ears to gossip. Bryce wouldn't have let her starve. She should have seen him again, before she shut the cottage gate and walked away from the scent of the sea. She should have tried to make him explain.

The door clicked. Anthony Wells hesitated when he saw her. She smiled, but his jaw tightened in indignation. 'What are you laughing at?'

She fought down a wave of anger and confusion. Did he hate her for smiling? Even less than the rest of them hated her for. 'I only meant to be friendly. But I'll always frown, if you like it best.' Damn his buttonless waistcoat and his sleeves too short for his arms and his wild hair and his soft grey eyes.

'I thought you were laughing at me,' he said at last.

'Well, I wasn't.'

He gave a brief nod of acceptance. 'Why d'you stand in the rain without a hat on?' Droplets sparkled on his greatcoat. He chewed his thumbnail, then displayed the beginnings of a grin and held out his own battered hat to her. She did not take it.

'I don't know. Why shouldn't I?'

Noise filled Fore-Northgate Street. Axles creaked, horses snorted, feet splashed. The mustiness of wet straw caught on the wind; a farm cart stood, piled high, in the queue to pay its toll. Her gaze darted to the driver. An old man, with a grog-blossomy nose. No one she knew.

'Wanted a bit of quiet from Agnes?' Anthony Wells smiled. 'You won't get that.' Listlessness lifted from his eyes and left a strange gleam. Of a joke, perhaps – too unclean to share. A bead of rain scurried under Mary's kerchief and she hugged her arms.

'I don't mind her talking a lot. Saves me having to. She's been very welcoming.'

He pulled his coat closer round his shoulders, the tips of his long fingers pressing hard into the cloth. 'And I haven't,' he said. 'I'm sorry. I must've seemed rude.'

'I'd best get in.'

'Miss Helsall.' The softness of his voice filled her with unease. 'Why are you here? Someone like you shouldn't have to work here.'

Heat inched up Mary's face. 'I was hasty, that's all,' she said, keeping her voice steady. 'The feller at the inn said there was a job, so I saw Mr Barnston about it, at his house. I feared the chances of finding anything else.' She smiled. 'Any end – someone like me? What about Agnes? She ought to be a lady's maid, not a nurse.'

He picked at the loose threads on his coat. 'Aye, well, she was. Fell out with the mistress or summat. Wouldn't vouch for her character. Here they don't ask – they take who they can get.' He paused, and one corner of his lips almost tapered into a smile. 'Like me. Still, I was just going out.' He sloped off towards the gate, then looked back at the upper windows of the school's north wing. 'Tell Mrs Seward you haven't seen me, if she asks. But mind she don't put a curse on you. She's jealous of anyone pretty.' He smiled, and she smiled back; then he skirted round a carriage, avoiding the restless horses, and she lost sight of him before he reached the Northgate.

Cold numbed Mary's face when she awakened in the early hours of her first night in the infirmary. She turned her half-closed eyes to where the embers should be, stretched her toes to the footboard of the bed, peered up towards the canopy. The cellar would be emptied today. Bryce would send the waggon. Then the clean scent of the pillow stamped a frown on her face: the canopy was not there, diamond-shaped window-quarrels broke the wall where there should be shutters; and her eyes opened wide and flooded with tears.

But it was not dreams, or cold, that woke her. Someone moved on the landing floorboards, stopping at each creak. She blinked the tears away and listened.

'Agnes, are you awake?' The door hushed open and Mary gripped the counterpane. The sheets beside her lay empty. Agnes's silhouette passed by the window. 'Where've you been?'

Agnes nestled under the blankets. 'Downstairs,' she whispered.

'Why? It's pitch dark.'

'I know.' Agnes giggled. 'I was *downstairs*. You know – in Anthony's room.'

A long pause cranked the air taut.

'Oh.'

'Oh, Mary, don't say you're the sort to think ill of me. We're only here 'til we've saved up enough to get married. We might go to London. I know it looks shameful, but I swear it won't be long now 'til we're wed.' Mary stared into the dark. She ought to have guessed. Besides, what could it be to her? 'Mary . . . you won't tell anyone, will you?'

'No, 'course I won't.'

What sort of place was this? No wonder he'd asked her history. A place for girls with no chance of a respectable situation? No wonder his eyes had hinted at laughter. Mary huddled up small. She willed the rhythm of the clock to deaden her unease, but the feeling spread, biting into her flesh. At last she slept, and dreamed of seaweed growing through her hair and twining across her mouth.

Damp oozed out of every wall of the empty infirmary and brought to Mary a sense of sickness and gloom. The odour of the decaying pigeon flowed, noisome and unhealthy, on the draught from the ward's open windows. Mary and Agnes swept hard all morning, raising a fog of dust that made Mary cough until tears brought some small relief to her smarting eyes. Spiders fell from the beams and scurried for their lives over the floorboards. The thuds of Agnes's broom made them roll and curl, their legs folding in like evening flowers.

Anthony Wells didn't get up until about half past eight, when the matron hammered on his door. She sent him out on an errand: from the ward windows Mary saw him slink to the gate with his shoulders hunched in his greatcoat and his hair suppressed by his scruffy hat. He took long strides, as ungainly as the spiders'. When he returned he sat on an old dining chair by the main door, tipping it up on two legs and planting his feet on the opposite wall. He seemed to doze.

''Scuse me.' Dust tasted dry in Mary's mouth. It made a changing landscape in the box she held before her. It was her turn to lug it to the night-soil midden at the back of the school.

Anthony stretched up from his chair.

'I'll take that for you. I'm meant to carry and such.'

'I can manage.'

'Did you sleep well, your first night?'

'Tolerable, 'til I was disturbed.'

Outside, mud glazed the cobbles nearest the street, and sloshed under cart wheels. Just as it had under the potato-cart that had brought her the last few miles. The potato man had warned her to be shy of folks offering work to a lass – you never knew what sort of place it could prove to be. And now, well . . .

The matron, Mr Barnston – even Anthony Wells – they must all think she was just the type to fit in here. Couldn't she spend even a few days in Chester without folk rooting for gossip? She spun round; Anthony leant on the doorcheek, watching her.

'Yesterday,' she said, 'when you asked me why I was here, and you said Agnes hadn't a character – well, you must have thought I haven't either, and it's not . . .'

He glanced aside at the Northgate. 'I didn't think that.'

'I mean people always say things about me – well, they aren't true.' Raindrops made pits in the dirt in the box.

His expression darkened. 'I thought the opposite.' He made a controlled fist. 'I thought someone like you would be somewhere better, that's all.' The noise of the carriages faded. 'I'd no thought to upset you.' Red crept up from his collar and over his tense chin.

'I know,' Mary muttered. 'I'm sorry.'

She hurried through the archway to the back of the school, where almshouses sat, squat and dreary in the puddles. She flung the dirt on to the night-soil, scrunched her eyes tight when it blew back at her, and cursed herself.

Exhaustion weighted her limbs when she climbed into bed. Dust had compacted itself in the back of her nose and made her sneeze. The washing water had turned to mud, at first, on her face. Agnes said mud made your skin soft.

'Have you got a sweetheart, Mary?' She plumped her pillow and flumped down.

'No,' Mary said. ''Course I haven't.'

Raindrops, huge and intermittent, smacked the window. A beginning storm.

'Oh, I bet you have. I swear I won't tell a soul.'

Mary didn't answer for a moment, listening to the drops gathering urgency on the glass.

Feet splashing, cart-wheels rolling to the tops of cliffs, lanterns casting orange beams on to sand. Water in her lungs and yellow eyes sneering at her shivers.

'Honest, I haven't.'

The rain increased rapidly until the barrage of noise almost drowned Agnes's voice. 'Then I'm sure you'll find someone now you're settled in Chester. I swear you will – you're so pretty.'

Mary tried to laugh. It was only a storm. 'No I in't.'

'Don't be daft. I'd give an arm for my hair to be so smooth. Everyone always thinks my mind is as frizzly as my head, and they might be right for all I know.' Mary touched the dirt and grease on her own hair. Her scalp itched and her eyes felt as puffy as a frog's.

Lightning flashed. Agnes sprang up and darted to the window. 'Oh, come and look!'

Mary heaved her weary limbs from the bed. Rain pummelled the almshouses and the courtyard, exploding back from the ground and cracking on the glass like fistfuls of gravel. She grasped the windowsill. Water veiled the cobbles. She watched it, wide-eyed, her ears inventing screams. Agnes laughed beside her. Lightning branded the sliding shadows of the rain on to her shift.

'You look so frightened. You're not one of those girls who affects to be scared of everything, are you?'

Mary sank back into bed. 'I'm not scared. It's nothing. I don't like storms much, that's all.'

Thunder fractured the sky and she dug her nails into her palms. She tugged the blankets over her head, but the rain carried the crashing of waves, and the creak of distant trees conjured the sound of timbers groaning and splintering far from the safety of shore.

CHAPTER 3

'Can you believe it, my love? Mary says she isn't stepping out with anyone. I'd say she must have an admirer, and she plays the innocent country maid, who pretends to think herself plain – don't you think so?'

'Agnes . . .' Mary rested her forehead on her hands. The cracked skin between her fingers smarted as though she had plunged them in vinegar. Days of sweeping had made her shoulders ache, and even the warmth of the kitchen and Mrs Seward's absence could not lift the weariness from her.

'Don't you think she must—'

'She likes not to say.' Anthony drained his cup and the bottle glugged as he poured another. 'Let her alone.'

Let her alone?

He pushed the gin across the table. Harsh vapours sidled over the rim of the cup. So different from brandy, and yet it reminded her. No sweet mask of refinement, and yet the scent rasped her nostrils in the same way. The cramp in her stomach writhed harder, daring her to still it.

'Oh, don't feed her that evil stuff.' Agnes lifted the cup away. 'He made me drink this once – and the next morning I thought I was looking out of a dog's backside.' She kissed Anthony's cheek and giggled. 'I'm sure Mary's never been drunk in her life. They don't do such things where she comes from.'

'Leave her alone, I said. She in't here to be plagued by you.' Anthony smiled at Mary, in a crafty way that unnerved her. Almost as if Agnes were the subject of a joke between them. 'You'll drive her away and she'll have to freeze in bed all evening, by herself.' Tallow-light defined the contours of his face and threw his light brown stubble into relief.

He drank until the bottle was empty, and by then his eyes were hot and his skin colourless, but his stories made Mary and Agnes laugh, and the evening passed quickly. He told them of a place in Cow Lane, where he had friends, and of the pranks they would play on one another. And he told them of his two years at school in the other side of the building and of everything he did to try to make them throw him out. Once, he said, he hid his uniform in the roof during the night and claimed it was stolen by goblins. He described them: their sinewy legs, the way they hopped like a mountebank's monkey, their saucer-eyes as white and glowing as bleached bones. Agnes pulled her shawl together at the front.

'Like the hounds,' Mary said. 'Black hounds. I used to see them round my bed when I were little. They had eyes like that. The ones as had heads, any end.'

Agnes looked towards the window. 'You might summon things if you talk on them so.'

'Trouble is,' Anthony said, 'they come whether you summon them or not. Don't they?'

The length of time that he regarded her made her heart curl in on itself like a letter in a fire. The grain of the table ran like lines of script, all of them reading, *Don't start, Mary. Don't start that again.* But when she looked up, his grey eyes were all she saw.

Two weeks after Mary's arrival at the infirmary Mrs Seward inspected the clean ward. Her air of disappointment flowed into every corner of the room, settled on the surfaces and dulled the gleaming windows. She could find no fault with it. Agnes and Mary might have a few hours' holiday, she said, but they must be back by five.

Mary stood by the bridewell opposite the Blue Coat School. The Northgate loomed close, light forming an aura around it as if too revolted to fall on its surface. She paced to the door on the right of the passageway, took a lungful of air and held it until she went dizzy, then raised her knuckles.

No, she would walk round the walls first. Clear the indoor-fuddle from her head. The circuit would bring her back here: it would only take half an hour. Just enough time to let her think.

She could think of nothing, though, but the lulling tap of her boots on the paving stones and the stinging of her ears in the wind that rushed across the Rood Eye racecourse. When she reached the Castle she paused to look down at the river. Small boats lay moored at a jetty, ropes purring against their furled sails.

Mary approached the Eastgate sooner than she expected, her circuit of the city already three-parts done. She went up Foregate Street, past the inn where she spent her first lonely nights in Chester, and back again. She pretended, at first, to ignore the turning on the right. To pretend she just happened to be passing by. Cow Lane – she had walked by it often enough while staying at the inn. Perhaps she had walked past Anthony too, without knowing. It would take her back a different way. A change of scene.

Mary hesitated, too far in to turn back. Cow Lane stank, and its mud glistened like grumous blood. Scornful eyes swivelled towards her; every window framed a lank-haired face. A pair of scruffy children laughed at her, slime oozing between their toes. Buildings slanted over the street, teetering on pillars of stench, and moisture hung over the houses, lending a pallor to the grubby afternoon light. Mary raised her chin, kept her nerves still and strode forward.

Six thick-set, square-arsed cattle ambled ahead. Their breath steamed up in clouds and their drover aided his trudge with a hazel staff. He tipped his hat at her when she overtook him. Imagine – a man noticing you like that. It might be more proper to blush and pretend to be cross, but she gave him a smile. What a difference, in the city. You'd almost think you didn't have to beg, here.

Cow Lane widened, its houses shrinking back from the debris piled in its gutter: waves of watered-down manure, rotting vegetables, slimy remainders of rats. Outside the houses lay toppled barrels and bundles of straw, washing hanging from windows and clinging to the walls below.

People. A row of them, slumped against a house.

Two weeks had persuaded her she had been frightened for no reason. Two weeks of hard work in the daytime, and of pleasant evenings in the warm kitchen. Of nights awake in bed with her cloak flat over the blankets and the moon traipsing a dogged path from one window-pane to the next. Too many thoughts about more important things than scab-encrusted beggars. What do you expect in the city?

But if she were to see him anywhere, wouldn't it be somewhere like this?

Two boys rested back on the wall, their noses snotty above fish-like gaping mouths. An old woman in layers of shawls searched the coat of a man who slept on a pile of straw. But it wasn't the beggar. It was Anthony. The woman found nothing. Anthony's hand strayed to his pocket, but he did not open his eyes.

Mary retreated into the shadow of a house and watched him. He would be all right. He would make his own way home, late at night. He must come here every day; he would not thank her if she interfered. The crone's skeletal fingers closed round the cup in Anthony's hand, but he tightened his grip. Mary crossed the street.

'Anthony, wake up,' she said. The old woman laughed and elbowed him. Mary shook his shoulder and he dragged his coat-sleeve across his face.

'I am awake. Leave me alone.'

'Ah,' said the old woman. 'Go along away with tha missis, lad.' She hummed without a tune. Two men watched Mary from a glassless window.

'Come on,' Mary grabbed Anthony's elbow. 'You'd be best to come home and go to bed.' One of the men muttered to the other, and they laughed.

Anthony drained off the last of the drink and let the cup tumble to the ground. The old woman sang, her face turned upwards as if towards the sun. 'Come back, sweet love, come back to me . . .' She paused and chomped, toothless, on the reeking air. 'Didst think he'd come back? Needn't have frit hisself so bad, when it were soon to die.' Anthony retrieved a bottle from behind the straw. The woman's face crumpled. 'She'd have been older than you, lass!' Mary stepped back from the jab of her finger. 'Kill-grief! It don't fill the gap, lass, but it numbs the edges. Give it to me – you young uns don't need it. Give it to a poor old woman.'

'Help me up.' Anthony's clasp was uncertain and clammy. He stumbled forward and they made their way towards the northern end of the lane. 'Don't heed Widder Wiggins – she's barmy.'

Mary grabbed the cup from the handle of Cow Lane's pump. 'Have some water. It'll wash the drink away.'

Anthony scowled at the contents. 'I in't drinking that.' The water hit the ground in one splash, bouncing a spit of muck on to Mary's petticoat. She snatched the cup back and refilled it.

'Yes you are. Don't be stupid.'

The vagueness in Anthony's eyes sharpened into fleeting surprise. He drank, making a face at the taste.

'More,' Mary said. 'As much as you can.' The water flooded into his neckcloth. He clutched the pump handle for support. Laughter burst from the houses: even the old woman chuckled. Mary took his hand.

'Please,' she whispered, 'let's get away from here.'

She marched him out of Cow Lane and into the Kelyards orchard, where the massive shadow of the cathedral dimmed the trees.

'You mustn't think it's always like this.' Anthony talked at the ground. 'I don't get drunk that much. Just bad luck that you should walk past the one time I don't want to see you.' Sweat sheened his face. He stumbled to an outcrop of ancient stones at the foot of the city wall and sank his head to his knees. 'You should've left me there.'

Mary breathed spectral shapes in the bitter air. Mist rose from the leaf-litter under the apple trees and seeped into her bones. 'Anthony.'

He sat up, closing one eye, and looked down at her hand on his shoulder. His slim face was pale – almost ethereal – and his eyes held her tiny, hazy reflection. 'It's naught to do with me, I know. But it won't be much of a life for Agnes if you don't leave it off.' Confused by the way he studied her, she pulled her hand away.

'What?' His gaze fell to her lips.

'Gin.' Mary prised the bottle from him, and his fingers quivered. 'How will you afford to set up home? She'll get tired of waiting.'

Anthony frowned. 'What d'you mean?'

A bird took off from a branch and a shower of droplets pattered the wet leaves.

'She's excited to be getting wed, but . . .'

Anthony stared at the forlorn trees ahead of him and gnawed his thumbnail. 'Oh, good God,' he said.

'What's wrong?'

He searched for the bottle. Mary tucked it between the folds of her topcoat and it weighed in her pocket.

'Nothing.' He breathed heavily, running his fingers under the hollows of his eyes, then swore and lurched to his feet. 'I must get back and speak to her. I didn't mean her to think . . .'

Four clock-chimes rang in the distance and the cathedral bells boomed so close that Anthony flinched and held his head. Twilight grew under the shadow of the wall and the moisture in the air released a fungal scent from the soil. Beads of dew gathered on Anthony's tousled hair. He staggered up the Kelyards steps to the paved pathway at the top of the city walls.

'Help me.' He slid his arm round her shoulders, and her heart beat hard. 'I can go faster if you help me.' She imagined amusement, sly and suppressed, in his voice. Was he mocking her? He would soon find out she was wise to such things. He was so close that she could smell the mist-damped wool of his clothes, and the sweet warmth of straw, redolent of summertime, and a touch of musky sandalwood. The knot of nerves and excitement tunnelled deeper in her stomach.

Daylight ebbed from the sky. They turned the corner and the Northgate Gaol appeared ahead.

'They've nowt to eat but rats in there,' said Anthony, lowering his mouth close to her ear, as if to impart a secret. 'That's if they can catch them, with the fetters an' all. They have to catch them and rip their heads off and eat them raw, else they'd starve.'

'I don't want to know. '

'There's some places in there,' he whispered, 'places right down in the ground, where even the rats are too feart to go.'

'Anthony—'

'That's where they put the murderers, so's they beg to be hanged.'

'Anthony, don't!'

'Didn't mean to fright you,' he said softly, and fell silent.

Their footsteps echoed from the stones. Twilight and the vapour of water magnified movements as well as sounds. The changing pressure of his hand on her shoulder; the movement of his body, warm against her side. The lanterns of the carriages in the street below, bobbing like the lights of ships in restless waters.

As they reached the Northgate the way he leant on her changed. At first he touched her so gently that she mistook the sensation for the mist on her neck. But then he traced his finger down her skin, and made her shiver.

'What are you doing?' she asked. He regarded her intently in the orange light of the Northgate's lamp.

'Mary . . .' He half-laughed. 'Don't pretend you don't know.' He took her chin between his thumb and finger and she looked up at the lamp's reflected glimmer in his eyes. 'You know what I'm doing. You know it in't Agnes I'm after. It's you.'

Water ticked, faint and repetitive, from the Northgate's eaves. Mary tried to smile. 'You don't mean that,' she said. 'You're more fuddled than I thought.' She pulled back, but the pressure on her face tightened.

'No.' Anthony spoke close against her lips. 'This is what I mean. Mary, whatever it is . . . What you're looking for. It's the same. We could find it.'

His hands no longer shook, but drew her against him. His lips were soft and cold, warming against hers. When she stretched her arms round his neck the damp on his coat chilled her wrists, and the trees in the distance hissed like gossip through the thud of her heart.

Don't you start on him, you selfish witch. Don't start.

But it was too late.

Thurstaston, Wirral, Autumn 1755

Night-creatures skitter through the gorse; a breeze flutters strands of mane across Mary's hand. She holds the pistol awkwardly, so its barrel points far away from the pony's head and into the cushions of heather beside the track. It becomes heavy; the bones in her wrist drag. Thank God the track is silent. So silent that the end-of-summer movement in the air takes on a faint sound of its own, whispering below her tricorn hat and skimming her ears.

She listens hard. If the sound of hooves comes now, it will finish her.

Mary wills the motion of the pony to lull her nerves, but every step makes her veins jitter.

Two years. Two years she's been doing this and not once has she come near to being caught. Perhaps the Customs man is stupid, and thinks the invitations to dine with Bryce are made out of esteem for his company. Or perhaps he knows everything and finds it worth his while not to interfere. After such a length of time – and she tuts in disgust at herself – she ought to be more carefree as she rides along the low cliff, more nonchalant at handling the pistol, and a little less terrified at every sound under the moonless sky. She tucks the numb fingers of her rein-hand between the saddle and Jakey's withers.

'Where's this boat, then?' she whispers, but Jakey doesn't listen, his attention yearning towards the other horses down by the shore. She bends forward, her stays digging into her, and breathes in his calming, dusty scent.

Murmurs rest on the air, from the group of women gathered on the sand. She hears her name, and a quiet laugh. A horse shakes its head;

the jangle of the bit reverberates up the cliff. Mary forces every remnant of air out of her lungs, but the clamp of agitation stays.

At last, the flash.

Instantaneous, it streaks from somewhere across the water, and she rides to the top of the cliff-path, Jakey's flanks warm on her stockinged calves. In the blackness she makes out the deeper blackness of a human shape.

'Ghost may walk,' she says, and the words come out harsh and clogged, making her cough and say them again. The boy scrambles back down to the sand. A second flash sears the darkness, this time from the land, and a flicker of excitement overtakes her fear. The boat is pulling in.

Chapter 4

The sound of their feet rang hollow in the Northgate passageway; the bottle in Mary's pocket bruised her leg with each step.

'Quiet,' she said, her hands unsteady on the infirmary door.

The cook laughed in the kitchen. Then came Agnes's voice, too – gentle and fluting and happy.

Anthony fumbled for the key to his room – it chimed on the tiles and the sound rattled Mary's nerves. 'Come in with me,' he whispered. She stepped away.

'It wouldn't be right.'

He grinned. 'Nor's anything I do.'

Light rushed from the kitchen, carrying the sizzle and smoky aroma of roasting meat. 'Best to pretend nothing's happened,' Mary said. Her head felt light as she went up the stairs.

Mary took the bottle of gin from her pocket. The last remnants of daylight drained from the sky. Nothing broke the walls but the criss-cross pattern of the windowpanes, and nothing eased the silence but her own whispered curses.

Disgust would come first, when he woke up. Disgust at the power of gin to make some freckle-faced, black-haired girl seem worth kissing. Fear would follow: fear that she might tell Agnes, or that one kiss would be enough to turn her head and make her go silly over him. To make her cause scenes. She paced to the window, the bottle in her hand. Then, after disgust and fear, worse. Laughter. Everyone at that crumbling gin shop would soon know how he'd kissed her for a lark, never thinking she'd be such a forward trossle as to kiss him back.

A candle in one of the almshouses shed out a few faint rays, lending a sheen to the cobbles. Mary held up the gin bottle, just able to discern its shape against the clouds. Such dimness held familiarity; how often had she dreamed of moving at the edge of night, fumbling at some vital task and unable to open her eyes?

What if gin were like brandy?

No one ever took so much as a sip of gin back home. Why glug such rot-gut stuff when there was something better?

What if gin could wrap you in feathers and warm you like a smile?

A dainty cork stopped the bottle. The cracks on her knuckles opened and hurt when she tugged it out. Fumes stung her nostrils and she blinked. The gin nettled her chapped lips; scraped down her throat like a cat down a curtain. She gasped, her tongue numb.

Mary took another swig from the bottle. Then another. Then she stashed it in the folds of her bag in the cupboard. For a while she concentrated on the candle in the almshouse, watching its flame waver in the draughts. Her breath slowed and deepened, the stinging of her raw hands subsided and the snarl of nerves slowly unwound. Across the courtyard the flame guttered.

This was gin, then. Just like brandy, it worked.

Only the uncontained first chirrup of a blackbird signalled morning. At first Mary snuggled under the blankets, unaware of being anywhere other than at home.

Anthony. Wakefulness stabbed her.

Gin.

She smothered her face in her pillow, a scarce-suppressed groan hurting her throat. Agnes breathed softly beside her. Dreaming of weddings?

What if Anthony had left during the night, unable to face either of them? What if he were dead? Someone at Wallasey, people said, once bezzled off a pint of gin in a single go and fell dead as a nit right there on the hush-shop floor. She padded to the washstand and scooped up palmfuls of icy water.

One kiss. No one need know. Anthony would not remember it; she would do what she could to forget it. The clock struck six and an anguished wail rose from Agnes's side of the bed.

'Oh God. Outpatients.'

Trafford Barnston strolled into the infirmary at around half past nine, just as Mary finished mopping the floor. He shook the worst of the rain from his hat and handed it to her with a smile; drops glistered on the felt, and powder speckled its rim. Mr Barnston adjusted his peruke, his hands as clean as the cuffs of his shirt. Traces of cologne fought the stark smell of soap from the corridor tiles.

'Do you settle in well, Mary?' His voice was calm and cultured. She pictured his house – as big as the whole of the Blue Coat School, with five windows to every room and servants in bright aprons smiling at their work.

'Yes, sir,' she said. Mr Barnston picked some fluff from his sleeve.

'I see young Wells is absent again.'

'Oh, no, sir. He's here – I only happened to be passing when your chairman knocked.'

Perhaps Mr Barnston's eyebrows raised a fraction, but he only asked for some coffee and sauntered towards the board room. As he passed Anthony's room a stream of muted curses accelerated and died. Mr Barnston paused, and then walked on.

When Mary set the tray down on the table Mr Barnston squared the papers in front of him into a perfect pile. Mary shot some coal from the scuttle and stoked the flames.

'I fear Anthony Wells passed an intemperate evening – again.' Mr Barnston took a leisurely sip of coffee. Its bitter scent stirred Mary's stomach. 'I will not tell the rest of the Board at this stage. But if he maintains this degree of drunkenness, it is unlikely we will suffer him to remain long in the infirmary.' She hadn't left the bottle out, had she? Agnes had made the bed – it wasn't under the pillow? No, she remembered stowing it in the wardrobe. She would get rid of it today. 'He's a good lad at heart – but that's a weak defence against depravity these days. I'm loath to see him turned out, but there'll be no other option if he continues drinking. Would you have a word with him about it for me?'

'I don't know he would listen to me, sir.'

'Perhaps not,' said Mr Barnston, with a faint smile. 'But I imagine you have a better chance than Mrs Seward.'

Mr Barnston's suit was the colour of port-wine, his neckcloth so white that the wall behind him took on the tinge of new milk. Gold thread trimmed his cuffs and patterned his waistcoat. He preened his pen, his pale fingers slowly smoothing the fronds. 'It's not too harsh for you, is it?' he said quietly. 'Living here?'

Mary felt sick. 'No, sir.'

'You haven't told anyone? Our agreement—'

'I gave you my word.'

'That does not count for much. Have you seen him yet?'

'I—'

'Good morning, Mr Barnston.' Mrs Seward curtsied low. 'I hope Mary has not been neglecting the fire.' Flames took hold and bolted up the chimney.

'No, indeed,' said Mr Barnston. 'I am well looked after.' He returned his attention to the papers and Mrs Seward's expression hardened. Her tense, thin lips radiated little lines, like those on a withered apple. She ushered Mary into the corridor.

'Go and wake Wells,' she said. 'Get him out of his bed. He is not to behave like this when the governors are here.'

Mary looked towards Anthony's door, flustered and uncertain.

'What's the matter?' the matron asked.

'Do you mean me to go into his room?'

'I hardly think he will be persuaded to surface unless you throw some cold water at him.'

29

'But he might be undressed.'

The matron's eyes widened to the limits of her spectacles, and a laugh broke between her yellowing teeth. 'Indeed he might. As will hundreds of patients. Modesty and virtue are admirable qualities but they are not compatible with nursing.' Mary's face smarted. 'You and I both know very well that Mr Barnston would not have recommended to this situation any woman whose character he held in high regard. Do as you are told.' Mrs Seward's mouth twitched in triumph. Mary looked back at the board room door. She heard the shuffle of papers and the chink of a coffee cup. A dull weight of shame sank through her.

Bleak daylight fell without vigour on Anthony's bed. Anthony lay under a mess of blankets, his face the same colour as his pillow. 'I need summat to drink,' he said.

She fetched him some water from the kitchen. He didn't remember, then. He would have said so straight off, if he did. Or, mayhappen he did remember, and would never mention it. Write it off as a dream – a bad one, perhaps, for him – or a mistake to be added to the file of experience. Just as well, in the circumstances. No use putting another tangler on things.

'What did you do with my gin?' Anthony's breathing was shallow.

'I threw it away.'

He turned his head sharply, and winced. 'Aye, well,' he said. 'Thank you.' He dragged himself up on to one elbow and raised the cup to his mouth, a tremor invading his hand. His shirt bagged open at the neck; sweat glistened along his collar bone. He must taste of salt. Mary looked away. 'Best off without it.'

So, he wasn't going to mention it, then. Not worth remembering. Just as well . . . He slammed the cup down and the water slopped on to the night-table. 'Mary, I'm sorry,' he said, 'if I offended you.'

She glanced at the open door. 'I didn't think you'd remember.'

'It'd take a deal more drink than that to make me forget how you kissed me.'

'I didn't mean to. And you kissed me first.'

'Mary—'

'Will you take some breakfast?'

'I can't.'

Talking and laughter came from outside. Patients. And no porter to keep them in line.

'Best sleep, then,' she said.

'Mary—'

He swore as she shut the door behind her.

Agnes stood in the porch and eyed the line of patients in the courtyard. Mary and Mrs Seward took turns to accompany them to the board room for the governors to accept them, and then to the treatment room to see the doctor and surgeon. The patients shared wariness in their expressions: they looked back over their shoulders at the outside world, or stared blankly ahead, chewing their lips. One man had just marked the thirty-sixth birthday of his leg ulcer; another's hands wobbled such a deal he could pick nothing up; another brought his severed thumb with him, brown as a raisin and swaddled in a hand-kerchief. 'Might as good give it the bloody dog,' he said, when she saw him out with his hand bandaged.

Stale sweat pervaded the corridor, footprints overwashed the floor and Mary's shoulders ached as she trudged back and forth. By midday hunger growled in her guts and a dry pain burrowed through her fore-head. Agnes took to resting on Anthony's chair when Mrs Seward was not looking. Each time Mary brought a patient out she dragged herself to her feet and scowled.

'Why is it me who must do this?' she said. 'She ought to let us take turns.' Mary's patient hobbled out to a trickle of applause and ironic cheers. 'Did you see that one with his nose poxed off? His face was melting off his skull. He shouted stinking fumes all over me when they wouldn't let him in – as if it's my fault he must go running after filthy whores. I bet he was meek as anything to the Board.'

31

'Look at it a-this-n,' Mary said. 'At least the surgeon's not after grop-ing you.'

Agnes made a face and ushered the next patient in. His bulk blocked the light. Agnes shrank back, her forehead creased. The man rested his hand on the wall and took a good look along the corridor. Raw scratch-lines furrowed his skin, angry against the white paint. If he remembered her, he betrayed no interest. Unhurried, he followed her, his ragged shoes flopping on the floor – uppers gaping from soles like hungry mouths. Mary took slow breaths and counted her own quick-ening steps. Then his shuffling stopped, and she turned to see him looking into the apothecary's store. His shoulders spanned the door-way and his fingerprints begrimed the clean frame.

'The apothecary . . .' She swallowed the words. '. . . Mr Crane must have stepped out. He'll be back in a minute, and if the doctor says you need physick you must go there to get it.' He smeared snot over the back of his hand. 'You must have your recommendation letter ready. The governors won't see you without it.'

He waved a crumpled piece of paper.

Heat struck Mary's face and stripped the moisture from her eyes, making them itch. The gentlemen nearest the board room fire sported blooms of perspiration on their foreheads. Ten of them sat round the oak table, exud-ing musty odours of tobacco, powder and rain evaporating from woollen coats. Old-man breath formed a miasma around their perukes.

Mr Barnston held out his hand for the letter. Stains smeared the dog-eared page.

'Ah, yes,' he said. 'William Hartingshall.' He glanced at Mary, but at once averted his gaze. *William Hartingshall.* The name meant noth-ing to her. The scrubby hair, the vein-threaded eyes, the scratched arms – nothing sparked even a hint of recognition. The gentlemen of the Board pushed the letter from one to the other, their fingertips seek-ing islands in its map of filth.

'This man is one of my recommendations,' Mr Barnston said. A mumble of disapproval circled the table. The man nearest the fire slid his handkerchief under his peruke.

'Sir,' said a man with jowls like panniers. Mr Barnston displayed a firm smile.

'You wish to comment, Mr Hesketh?'

Mr Hesketh held up the recommendation letter by one corner, his little finger extended in a straight progression of his lace cuff. 'Gentlemen, I avail myself of this opportunity to remind the Board that the purpose of this charity is to afford relief to the respectable poor.' Several of the wigs bobbed. 'Wanton destruction of the proper papers does not, to my mind, permit one to infer the respectability of the destroyer.'

William Hartingshall rested his fingers on the table, his face impassive.

'I am a life subscriber like you, Mr Hesketh.' A complete absence of aggression chilled Mr Barnston's voice. 'I shall make my recommendations where I see fit.'

'The Statutes, sir . . .'

'I am well acquainted with the Statutes,' said Mr Barnston. 'Nothing in them advocates abandoning a man to his misery when he might derive benefit from our care.' He poised his pen over the inkbottle. 'I propose that this man be admitted as an outpatient.' His tone radiated finality.

'Seconded,' said the man nearest the fire. Mr Barnston wrote in the minutes book and nodded dismissal.

William Hartingshall scratched his arms before he left the board room. He brushed past Mary in the doorway. When he spoke his breath made her blink.

'Here you is, then,' he said.

CHAPTER 5

William Hartingshall chuckled to himself, but the hostility in his eyes was untempered by laughter.

'What's your business with me?' Mary asked. Hartingshall scratched his scalp. Dandruff snowed on to his shoulder.

'You don't see the likeness, then?'

'I've never seen you. Not before that time you followed me.'

'Never looked.'

Dr Tylston hummed a cheerful tune while he inspected the pustules on Hartingshall's arms. The surgeon, Mr Racketta, leant on the sideboard – where tarnished instruments lay cushioned in napless velvet – and studied the front of Mary's kerchief.

'The itch,' he said. Grooves parenthesised his mouth. He caught Mary's eye and his lips spread into a smile.

'Aye, thank you, Mr Racketta, for your matchless powers of observation,' said the doctor. He patted Hartingshall on the shoulder. 'Well, man, you've the distinction of having the worst case of the itch I've seen this side of the Rebellion. It'll be a tricky thing to bring off, but we'll do what we can for you. Mr Racketta, perhaps you'd be so good as to write the fellow's name in the book.' The surgeon showed no inclination to move. Dr Tylston fiddled with his spectacles.

'Can you write, dear?' he said to Mary.

'Yes, sir.' But Mr Racketta prised the pen from her, his fingers moistening her hand. Fumes of tobacco and sweat wafted from his clothes.

'At this stage of the disease,' said Dr Tylston, 'you're lucky the blood isn't corrupted. You must have been putting up with this for quite a time. Why didn't you come in before now?'

'Travelling,' replied Hartingshall. 'No doctor.' He spoke like a foreigner.

'Bleeding's the only efficacious thing for it,' said the surgeon, turning to the instrument cases. Mary shifted uncomfortably and rubbed her neck. Pain drilled through her head, driven by the stuffy, salty heat of a morning of unwashed bodies. Mr Racketta plucked a knife from a case, pressed the point into the table and ran his fingers down the handle.

'Don't be alarmed, now,' said Dr Tylston as Hartingshall rose from the chair. 'There's nothing to it. It'll draw off the pollution of the serum – let out the impurities if you like – and effect a cure from within.' Hartingshall rolled his sleeves back down.

'If you ain't giving me anything to put on it, I'm off.'

'We'll certainly prescribe a topical application for you. Flowers of sulphur, I think, which you can take inwardly as well, but I really would advise you to stay and submit to a small let of blood. The advantages will be immeasurable, and the anticipation of it is always worse than the reality.'

Hartingshall screwed up his face, parting clearings in his stubble. 'Will it stop the itching straight off?'

Dr Tylston's old-fashioned wig swung at the ends. 'Within a very short time.' The rounds of his cheeks shone pink and healthy when he smiled. Hartingshall slumped back into the chair and the physician poured him a glass of hospital wine. 'This'll cheer you up. Must be the last for now, though. No wine, certainly no spirituous liquors, and even strong beer is best avoided – at least until the pustules have dried up.'

The surgeon handed a round pewter bowl to Mary. Pomade weighed his shabby peruke, the scent of it sickly and redolent of oil.

A crust of food smudged his waistcoat. 'Tell me if you're like to faint,' he said, 'and I shall catch you.' She narrowed her eyes at him and his lips twitched.

Hartingshall looked away as Mr Racketta tightened a strip of linen around his arm. When the arm reddened, his face paled and he raised his eyes to the ceiling.

'I see you're not a native of Chester,' said Dr Tylston.

'London,' Hartingshall said.

Mr Racketta drew back the tortoiseshell covers of a lancet and held the blade to the light.

London. Mary had never seen anyone from so far away. Did all London folk have such hatred in their eyes?

Blue veins bulged in Hartingshall's arm. Mr Racketta pressed his thumb over the largest and it stopped up and swelled as though a pulpy grub lurked under the skin. He poised the lancet before it, looked up at Mary and winked.

'London,' said Dr Tylston. 'A fine city, though I'm one for preferring the country, myself.'

Globes of sweat dampened Hartingshall's face; his hand contracted round the chair arm and he closed his eyes. Quick and sharp, the lancet split the skin and Hartingshall swore. Blood pooled around the incision, then rolled in a thin and uneven stream through the hairs on his arm.

'In perfect as always,' said Mr Racketta.

Droplets hit the pewter, then the surgeon loosened the linen strip and the blood flowed more readily, a metallic tang spiralling into Mary's nose. The surgeon's breath fell hot on her neck. 'No,' he said. 'Like this.' Dingy grey shirt-cuffs flopped over his hands as he closed them around hers and tilted the bowl. Mary inched forward, but the heat of his body surrounded her. She ground her heel into the toe of his shoe.

'Mr Racketta,' said the doctor, peering over the top of his spectacles, 'I'm sure the nurse is quite capable of holding a porringer.' The surgeon flitted one hand across her back and moved away. Mary smiled at Dr Tylston and he cleared his throat. 'Well, now. Well.' He wrote out Hartingshall's prescription, the pen scritting like a rat. 'Do you plan to reside in Chester permanently?'

Hartingshall grimaced. 'Just visiting.' The grimace became the rudiments of a smile. He held Mary's gaze, his eyes dark as flies in a web of inflamed veins, and the knot tightened in her stomach. 'Visiting a man named Selwyn Jones.'

The pewter bowl clattered against the chair.

Hartingshall clutched his bandaged arm and fired a dirty look back at the treatment room door. Mary glared up at him. 'What do you know of Selwyn Jones?' she asked.

He shrugged and inspected the bandage, prodding the bulge where a compress covered his wound.

'That fat bugger likely cuts everyone for a laugh, don't he?' The empty sleeve of his jacket swung forward and back in time with his steps. Mary caught up with him and jabbed him so hard in the back that he swore and raised his fist.

'Tell me!'

Hartingshall regarded her through swollen eyelids. 'All I know is, he deserves the gallows, and so do you.'

Blood rushed to her ears, as loud as the growling of waves.

Distant shouts, closer screams, the gurgle of blood, water weighting her clothes and numbing her skin.

Bryce. He was the only one who might dredge up some London heavy to keep her quiet. To try to scare her. 'You work for Mr Warbreck?'

He shook his head at once. 'We've met, but I wouldn't work for a crook like that.'

Mary flinched. It was like a punch – a stab even – that forced the breath from her lungs. 'He in't a crook.' The tiled floor magnified her voice. Agnes sat just inside the main doors, watching them. 'She sees us. Move along.'

The apothecary avoided touching Hartingshall's skin when he took the doctor's note. Herbal scents spilled out into the corridor, a clean oasis in the patient-tainted air.

'Tell me why you're here.' Mary hurried to compete with Hartingshall's long stride. He moved with a deliberate gait, his feet landing apart as though the floor rocked under them. He held out his diseased arms.

'To get this seen to. Why d'you think?'

'I mean, what brings you to Chester? Don't they have hospitals in London? What's your business with Selwyn, and me?'

Agnes rose to open the door. Hartingshall grinned, and gave her a polite nod. The usual weary cheer came in from the courtyard, where rain collected between the cobbles and dripped from the brims of the patients' hats. Hartingshall brought his crooked mouth close to Mary's ear. 'Ask my arse,' he said. Then he wandered to the gate with his bandaged arm cradled to his chest.

'Surely the treatment room cannot be clean already?' From the way Mrs Seward's mouth puckered and her eyebrows gathered closer together, she was secure in the answer. Mary leant on her broom. The pain in her head had lifted. No more patients till next week. She looked aside when she spoke, lest her breath carried traces of gin. It had only taken her a moment to creep up the stairs and drain the bottle.

'Mr Racketta won't go home, madam.'

The surgeon sat by the sideboard, sipping hospital wine, his waistcoat taut round his paunch.

'For goodness' sake, Mary,' Mrs Seward said, 'he's only a surgeon. Sweep round him.'

Mary opened the door as far as it would go and scuffed her broom over the dried mud on the floor. Splashes of blood leached into the tiles.

If Hartingshall were not, as he said, one of Bryce's men, might he be a dismissed worker? A warehouseman, perhaps, who stayed in Chester? Then there would be no reason for her to have seen him, back home, and every reason for him to be bitter enough to call Bryce a crook. The drips of blood moved before her eyes; the broom handle rested against her cheek.

'Forgive me.' She put her broom to work again, and paid no outward attention to Mr Racketta's observation. 'I've had the pleasure of your company all morning, and I've not had the courtesy to ask your name.'

'Mary Helsall,' she said, without looking up. Dust obscured the blots of blood, and then the broom caught a rainy footprint and darkened over them.

'Mary,' said the surgeon. 'Pretty, that.' The base of the glass grated on the sideboard. 'And how long have you been at the infirmary, Mary?'

'A fortnight.'

The chair legs scraped round and Mr Racketta sat forward, his second chin oozing over the top of his neckcloth like broth boiling from a pan.

'You're a mite young, are you not, to be a nurse?'

'Am I?'

'Aye. Liverpool infirmary has a coven of hags, Shrewsbury not much better, whereas you're – what? Eighteen?' He wetted his lips. 'Seventeen?'

'Two-an'-twenty last September,' she said.

'Oh.' Mr Racketta swilled the wine round the glass. 'Still. I expect it's the fresh air and honest diversions of the countryside that have contrived to keep you so pretty, eh?'

Hartingshall's blood still congealed in the bowl. Mary set down her broom. 'Excuse me. I must go and empty that.' But the pewter base spun from her grip and collided with the instrument cases; puggy fingers crushed her hand.

'Later,' said the surgeon. 'Sit with me awhile first.'

'No.'

He rubbed his thumb across her palm. A web of dirt-filled cracks covered the inside of his knuckle. 'Mary, my dear, I only want you to come and talk to me. Tell me why Chester has such uncommon comely nurses, eh?'

Mary cast her gaze over the sideboard. Porringer of blood, instrument cases – all open – crumpled cloth, wine bottle and glass, *lancet*.

'Let go,' she said. He stroked her wrist, and his breath quickened as he traced the paths of her veins.

'You're wicked, Mary,' he said, 'to pass a morning forcing a man to think improper things, and then not to delight him with a minute or two of your company.' He slipped his hand round her buttocks. 'You know we don't get paid for treating patients here?'

'That's nowt to me.' Strange calmness washed over her.

'You don't think you had like to look after me, my dear? To see I get some recompense for my time?'

'I'm not like that.' His grip strengthened and pain shot up her arm. Mr Racketta's stomach wobbled when he laughed. His shoulders shook as he pressed his moist lips to her wrist, and stilled abruptly when he saw the point of the lancet an inch from his face. 'I *said* let go.'

Alarm darted through his eyes. He looked down at the dry brown blood on the blade, loosened his grasp and forced another laugh. Mary backed away, holding the lancet out in front of her. 'Hand it to me, sweeting, it isn't a plaything.'

She did not move. The case-lids slammed shut.

'Please yourself, then,' the surgeon said, 'you heckle-tempered bitch.'

She threw the lancet after him as he left the room; it hit the wall and a splinter of tortoiseshell spun over the tiles.

What sort of place was this city, where men tipped their hats at you in the street and a surgeon could lie in wait, like a slug on a pump handle, to slime your fingers? She scrubbed away the smell of his sweat. The thought of his mouth on her wrist made her retch. The stench of tobacco and armpits lingered in the room.

Kissed twice since this time yesterday. Where were the men who shrugged when you smiled at them, who flinched when you touched them, who had you thrown out into the mud?

Ribbons of light quivered in the hospital wine and the rim of the glass chattered against her teeth. Sweet as a blackberry, syrupy and strong, it flowed easily down her throat. The pain between her eyes had returned – some use that gin had been. The friendly warmth of the wine promised to still her shaking hands.

The sound of feet outside made her drain off the second glass and grab her broom. The gritty taste of dust cancelled the sweetness. Anthony rested his head on the door frame, his face as grey as his eyes.

'I see you feel better now all the patients have gone,' Mary said.

'I don't.' He pushed himself up from the frame and closed the door. 'I won't feel better 'til I find out what you'll do.' His hair was clean and damp, but already springing back to its natural wildness.

'What d'you mean, what I'll do?'

He smiled – a slow, hung-over, languorous smile. 'When I kiss you again.'

No one would know. She turned back to her sweeping, hiding the flush of heat on her chest. 'Nothing. Besides, how do you know you'll have another chance?'

'I don't.' Anthony took the broom from her and set it aside. 'So I'd as good take this one.' He grasped the back of her neck and drew her to his lips. Outside, a mop sloshed and trickled, over and over. Poor Agnes. Mary tried to pull away, but he strengthened his hold, deepening the kiss, and she felt her body heat and soften, giving in to her own eagerness. She let her hands slide under his jacket, exploring the contours of his back. Gently she inched up his shirt and ran her fingertips along his warm skin, as if they could taste him.

'Is this to be my only chance?' he whispered. She shook her head, resting her cheek against the coarse wool of his clothes. Out in the corridor Agnes's bucket clanged.

CHAPTER 6

'Wouldn't it be lovely to have a new gown to be married in?' Agnes tiptoed to view herself in the looking-glass above the empty fireplace. 'I would have the softest pink, with tiny flowers, and lace round the sleeves. Wouldn't that be lovely?'

Mary picked at a loose thread on the hem of her jacket and twined it round her finger. She kept her eyes down. 'I suppose it would.'

He doesn't love her anyway. Better for her to cry now than to live in a loveless home.

'You sound so sad. I'm sure you'll get married one day, too.'

Mary rolled the thread into a ball.

Feel guilty and don't do wrong, or do wrong and don't feel guilty.

Agnes giggled. 'You'll get over him eventually.'

'*Who?*'

'Whoever you came here to forget. Whoever it is you think about when you stop and gawk at the fire, or rest your cheek on your mop-handle and let the dirt dry in streaks.'

Damn Agnes, with her shiny curls and her pretty eyes and her laughter. What choice could it be for him, between a bucksome, cheerful girl and a green-eyed, solemn, skinny creature with a gift for making people hate her?

'I don't think of anyone.'

'Was he as handsome as Anthony?'

'No!'

Silence could have chilled the room; the humour in Agnes's eyes could have changed to confusion or anger. But she laughed, thank God.

Mrs Seward waited at the bottom of the stairs, her Sunday gloves disguising her dry hands. Anthony stood further down the corridor, nibbling his thumbnail. He cast Mary a wily smile.

A false notion of spring wafted in the January air. Patches of dryness spread over the cobbles and a stronger scent of manure hinted at hardening ground and lengthening days. A gust of wind chased the warmth back into the shadow of the gaol, and Mary rubbed her fingers and wished they could be enclosed in his. He walked beside Agnes, more than a head taller than her, his hair sticking out of the sides of his hat.

Then, with Mrs Seward hurrying on before them, Agnes took hold of Anthony's hand.

The gash of jealousy shocked Mary in its intensity. He looked back at her, and smiled, and however long she had with him – a threeweek? a month? – was not like to be enough.

'Remember, Wells,' said Mrs Seward at the door to the chapel in the south wing of the Blue Coat School, 'this chapel has been the final stop of many a notorious felon on his journey from the Northgate to Boughton, and thence to hell. And most of them no doubt began their careers with idleness and frequent drunkenness, so let that be something for you to ponder upon.'

Anthony only stepped back to allow the matron to go ahead of him. 'No, it's the Bear's Paw,' he said.

Mrs Seward spun round, her crinkly skin greyed by the shadow of her hat. 'What?'

'Their last stop. It in't here, it's the Bear's Paw in Foregate Street. They halt there for a mug of ale before they reach the gallows.' He grinned. 'The ale's free, an' all.' He stole a touch of Mary's hand as the matron turned from him in disgust. The Northgate's shade blackened the cobbles beneath their feet. Mary forced a smile.

They were the only parishioners in the chapel other than the Blue Coat boarders and their masters. Anthony slumped into a pew with his head in his hands, and the matron jabbed him with one gloved finger.

'Sit up!'

'I'm praying,' he said.

'Well!' Mrs Seward puckered her mouth. 'I'm sure God has more sense than to give you the sorts of things you would pray for.'

Mary snuggled into her cloak. The boys behind her stifled laughter and kicked the backs of the pews. She would go to bed early that night. So early it would scarce be dark, and she would sleep and sleep for twelve hours and more. Nothing ever happened in the infirmary on a Monday, other than the laundry maid coming in. She would be able to sit by the fire and sew the bedding for the ward. A whole day of being warm.

An elbow thumped her ribs. She jerked awake with a gasp and Mrs Seward hissed close to her ear. 'Pay attention.'

He injures not only himself, but also his family, his friends – the very society in which he subsists.

Anthony stared ahead, as if affected by the words. But he rubbed his shoe against Mary's ankle, slowly and hard. She shifted closer to him. Through her layers of petticoats she felt the warm pressure of his leg.

Everything of a virtuous nature becomes to him as water to a mad dog.

Mrs Seward fixed a tight smile. 'Indeed,' she whispered. A hushed woof and a ripple of sniggers came from the pews behind.

Let not yourselves become ensnared in so unpardonable a sin, but learn to quake at the example of the dissolute generation that plagues the streets of our city!

'Quite.' Mrs Seward leant forward and raised her eyebrows at Anthony.

Their minds are intoxicated and disordered by violent passions; they crave only bodily satisfaction. They are mired in the temptation of sensual indulgence . . .

More stifled giggles. To Mary's right, Mrs Seward's nostrils flared. To her left, Anthony's lips curled into a mischievous smile. Mary fleetingly touched his knee. He tensed beside her; she leant against him hard enough to feel the rhythm of his breath quicken when she wrapped her foot behind his ankle. He drummed his fingers softly on the pew, and then slid them beneath her thigh. She stared ahead, biting the inside of her lip. Then she took a glance at him. He seemed intent on the sermon. Only the slight colouring of his cheek and the sparkle of his eye betrayed him. She touched one fingertip against his leg again, and he took off his hat and held it in his lap.

The scandalous intemperance of today's young people hurls them over a precipice of moral disintegration. It is a canker to both mind and flesh, a propagator of the pox and the melancholy, a direful antagonist to faith and charity and – mark it well – a most fearful peril to the soul.

Mrs Seward knelt, and three deep lines imprinted themselves in her forehead as she lowered it to her clasped hands.

By dinner time Anthony had turned to fidgeting, his concentration diverted from Agnes's unbroken chatter. He ate little, but jumped up often to stab the poker at the fire or refill his mug with strong. He drummed one finger on his plate, tap-tap, tap-tap. The sound strung Mary's nerves tighter.

How could Agnes be so oblivious? She stopped talking for nothing – not the scraping of the point of his knife on the table, not the gurgle of the ale-jug, not the shriek of the chair-legs or the rustle of the fire. Mary watched her as she talked. No answer required, no breath necessary. Sound surrounded her, like cuckoo-spit shielding the creature inside it.

'Oh, Anthony, look!' Agnes stroked his hair. This time the streak of jealousy did not take Mary by such surprise. She wrestled it down, concentrating on her plate. 'Your hair's like a nest. It's so adorable. Look!'

Anthony ducked away. 'How'm I to look at my own hair, for God's sake?'

Agnes laughed. 'Well, then, I mean for Mary to look. She ought to laugh more.' But Mary did not trust herself to exchange a glance with him.

Leave him be.

'Ah,' Agnes said. 'We shouldn't tease.'

Anthony's knife crashed on the table and bounced to the tiles. 'Don't, then.' The knife hummed on the floor and at last stilled. Agnes's chin wobbled. She looked away through the window to the hurrying clouds.

Mary listened to the crackle of the fire and fought off an inkling of triumph. Agnes started at Anthony's sudden movement when he turned to her.

'Will you go for a walk with me?' His tone said everything. Tears brimmed in Agnes's eyes as she hurried to the door.

'I'll get my hat.'

Anthony clasped Mary's fingers across the table. 'I don't hate her,' he said. 'I don't want to be cruel.' He brought her hand to his lips and she smiled. Anger vanished from his eyes, leaving them vibrant and warm. 'See,' he said. 'Kissing you is like drinking gin. I can face it now.' Mary laughed.

'I an't been called gin before,' she said. 'D'you mean I'm fiery, and like to give you a headache?'

'I must have more of you to find out.' He kissed her again, but when a movement of the fire made her look quickly at the doorway he became serious.

'What should I tell her?'

'Don't say it's on account of me.' Because it wasn't, really. It would have to happen sometime, with or without her. She was no thief of men: they must choose for themselves. 'Tell her you don't love her. If it's true.'

'It is.'

'Well, then.'

The windows of the Blue Coat School reflected the ramparts of the Northgate, their outline softened by fleeting images of clouds. Mary could not tell whether the matron stood behind the reflection, watching her skulk at the foot of the gate. Whether she knew that concealed under Mary's cloak was a loaf of bread, whether she lifted up her spectacles and glowered out from under them at the sight of a hospital servant walking purposefully into the gate's dark passageway.

Mary struggled to heave open the door; it thudded shut behind her. At once moisture condensed on her face, robbing it of heat. Grasping the loaf of bread, she took two steps into the Northgate Gaol.

It was dark.

She gained an impression of a narrow tunnel stretching away from her – drips of water echoed somewhere ahead – but she could see nothing. The heat of her breath dissolved into the chill. Her fingers met a slimy wall; she recoiled and, in sudden panic, hauled the door open again. Even the raw January breeze brought in a trace of warmth. Wintry light allowed her to make out the hinges of an inner door. Her knuckles made no impression on it – all the sound drained away into the ceiling, which loomed no more than a foot above her head. Warmth ebbed away through the soles of her boots and her toes became numb. She let the heavy door-ring fall against the wood, and this time a boom reverberated down the passageway. Her fingers tightened and she caught the friendly, warm scent of the bread.

A man opened the door. An ordinary-looking man, dismal-eyed and sporting a couple of days' growth of beard. Not the growling, bull-necked lummock she might have expected a gaoler to be, had she known what to expect at all. His peruke listed to the right and he was hardly any taller than she was. Mary fixed a scowl.

'I want to see Selwyn Jones,' she said, deepening her voice, and the gaoler's eyes took on a glint of amusement.

'Do you, now?' He held out his palm.

'Oh.' Mary rummaged in her pocket. 'I don't know how much . . .'

'How much you got?'

Mary felt through the remains of the pound in her purse. 'Tuppence,' she said. The gaoler rolled his eyes.

'That'll do, if you give us a smile.' She did, and dropped the coin into his outstretched hand. 'Mangham!'

The shout ricocheted from wall to wall and then died, and the drip of water again became the only sound. Mary pulled her cloak close around her. Lanternlight draped on to the floor, exposing a mess of uneven stones. An old man ambled towards her, the lantern in one hand and a gnarled stick in the other.

'Wants to see Jones,' said the gaoler. He put his hand to his throat, widened his eyes and lolled out his tongue, and the old man chuckled, revealing a muddle of teeth. But then he held up the lamp and squinted at Mary, and his laughter subsided.

'You sure, lovely?' His scrawny face and bulbous eyes held nothing to frighten her.

'Yes,' she said, proud of her firmness. Mangham pushed his lower lip out and nodded sombrely.

'You'll want this,' said the gaoler, handing her a rag. A sharp acid tang filled her nostrils.

Mangham led her to a gate and sorted through a bunch of keys. The hinges rowled and the gate echoed shut behind them. Ahead, a flight of steps stretched beyond the limit of the lamplight. Water stagnated in the foot-hollows, exhaling a dank odour that rose to meet the shouts and howls from somewhere above.

Mary hesitated and looked up at the point where the steps melted into darkness. They narrowed to nothing, like the staircases in her dreams.

Mangham looked back at her. 'You don't have to, lovely,' he said, with gruff kindness. 'This is no place for such as you.'

No place for anyone. But she could leave, when she wanted to. What an affectation – what feebleness – to show fright, when Selwyn had no choice but to stay. She kept her gaze within the circle of orange lamplight and pressed her nails into her palms. Her petticoats brushed the walls on either side.

The steps ended in another wailing iron gate and, beyond that, a long, draughty room filled with grunts and dim lights. Mary clamped the vinegar-sodden rag to her nose, her eyes smarting.

Like bundles of clothes taking demon-forms in wakeful early hours, the prisoners were no more than shapes in the dimness. A grille segregated them from her and Mangham. Cross-shaped openings in the sandstone allowed a ration of daylight to leak in, but rushlights gave most of the illumination, their long flames guttering in the draughts. Bodies and a series of small fires made the place seem warm at first, but it was a transient heat that leached away into the walls.

Hands grasped at her petticoats. Mary shrank back. Mangham's stick clashed between the bars. 'Leave her be.' His kindness had fled. 'Where's Jones the Hatchet?'

'Down the end.'

They passed through three more patches of light from the window-crosses and there he was, fettered and shrunken, his head resting back on the bars.

'There's a girl to see yer,' said the turnkey. 'God knows what she wants with the likes of you.' Mangham hung up the lamp and turned back to Mary. 'I'll be at the end when you want to go.'

The terror in Selwyn's eyes scratched her heart to pieces. Dirt matted his hair and a beard covered his sunken cheeks. He missed a front tooth. But his eyes had changed the most. They retreated into his skull, as if forced by horror to hide. 'Mary.' His voice was a dry croak. Tears spilled hot down her cheeks and she hurt as though a claw scooped out her heart. 'Have you brought me some food?'

Her mouth opened against the rag. Eagerness brightened his eyes and, as always, it was not for her. With a flick of her wrist she threw the bread at his feet, and he scrabbled for it in the filth.

'What d'ye do that for? You've grubshited it now.'

The vinegar stung out more tears. 'Must I magic myself into a side of roast beef for you to heed me?' Muffled by the cloth, her words provoked no reaction. He stuffed the begrimed loaf into his mouth. Other hands stretched between the bars. Eyes shouted hunger; Mary bowed her head. 'I'm sorry.'

Selwyn reached through, as far as the manacles would let him, and took her hand. He could still enfold it within his, but his fingers were bonier now, and weaker.

'Where've you been?'

'I got to Chester a few days ago,' she said, avoiding his gaze. 'I've found work at the new infirmary – but fifty yards from here. Bed and board.'

'Christ alive, Jones.' The words grated from somewhere in the gloom. 'Tha never said she were as tipping a bit as that.' Indistinct shapes moved under the glow of the rushlights. 'This is your little Mary, eh? I tell thee, I'd kill someone, too, if it bagged me an hour with her.'

Selwyn hauled himself up, his chains dragging over the floor. He stooped like an old man. 'Won't you kiss me, Mary?' Sickness weighed in her stomach. She took the cloth from her mouth, but the foulness of his breath made her recoil.

'They put a fetter on his arse an' all, that he mun fart through his chops.' Harsh laughter surged and just as quickly died. Mary breathed in the vinegar but the sour heat of his mouth and the stench of the beshitten floor had pervaded the cloth. Selwyn's face clouded, and then his fingers contracted round hers and he jerked her towards him. She staggered forward, but weariness entered his eyes and at once he let go. The vinegar-cloth wore a thick line of grime where it had met the bars. She gave up on it and breathed through her mouth, nauseated by the taste of the air.

'What happened,' asked Selwyn, 'after I left?'

'I took the blue silk to Bryce – Mr Warbreck – and he gave me a pound.'

Selwyn thrust his face between the bars. His black eyes caught the glimmer of the rushlights with such coldness that she stepped back. 'That all?'

'I didn't know if it were a good price. It looked such a lot—'

'I mean was that all he gave you? You go to see him, and five minutes later he turns up in Chester with a pair of bull-beefs and a warrant to arrest me. Did you tell him over the pillow where I'd gone?'

Mary hurled the cloth at his head. 'Is that all you can think of me?' It smacked his face and flopped into the dirt, and a raucous laugh rose up behind him. 'I told him you'd gone to Liverpool.'

Selwyn's eyes seemed to sink deeper in their sockets. The lamp defined every scratch and blemish on his face. He still wore the old shirt he had gone away in, and the neglected hem of his jacket sagged undone. She had meant to sew it up.

'Listen,' she said. 'Do you know of a man named William Hartingshall?' Selwyn's dark eyebrows lowered.

'Hartingshall? That was the name of the dead man.'

She fought a sudden, irrational fear of ghosts.

'Well, this one's alive. He came to the infirmary with a badness in his skin. He followed me when I first went there. Knows who I am, and said he wants you hanged.'

Selwyn cursed. The glistening dirt on the floor stirred and changed.

First went there? Near three weeks ago. How could anyone have traced the dead man's kin and got him up from London in so short a time? Her skin chilled. Her eyes adjusted to the movement on the floor, and she recognised the tiny curved shells of hundreds of lice.

'Find him,' said Selwyn. 'If he's the one bringing the case make him drop it. Any money left?'

'Ten shillings.'

'Give it here.' Filth gloved his palm.

'Why? Do they let you out to the shops once in a while?'

Selwyn sat down heavily on a crate and buried his face in his hands.

'I'm sorry. Here.' Mary handed him a shilling.

'Mangham,' he said. 'He gets us gin. Has a barrel in his room – keep it quiet. You understand, don't you?'

'I must go,' Mary said.

Wild light rushed into his eyes. 'Don't leave me.'

'I must. I'll come back, I promise.'

The turnkey waited at the top of the steps. 'You his wife?' Mangham's keys jangled as he crunched the gatelock open. Mary nodded sadly. 'Thought so. You look too sweet for a whore.' She followed him in silence, lifting her petticoats away from the standing water on the steps. 'Y'ought to find yerself a decent feller who'll look after you.'

Fetid vapours filled her head, poisoning her brain and needling the backs of her eyes. She could have vomited at the foul taste in her throat. Each step made the empty gin bottle thud against her thigh.

'I heard someone say there's a hush-barrel here.'

Mangham stopped and looked back at her, his eyes widening.

'Oh aye? And what'd it be to you?'

The passageway at the bottom of the steps was only gloomy now, not black. Mary could make out the rough blocks of the ceiling, so close overhead, and pick her way more easily over the uneven floor.

'I'll not tell anyone. Only I've a friend – someone I work with – who asked me to get a bottle filled. I'll have to walk to Cow Lane else, and it frights me to go there.'

Mangham's crooked teeth jutted beyond his lip. 'Gi's the bottle,' he said, and then he went down another flight of steps, and the lamp-light joggled and faded and left her in darkness.

Buoyed by the weight of the bottle when he handed it back to her, she smiled, and an unpractised grin spread around his rabbit-teeth.

'How much is it?'

'Tuppence to you, my love.' He scratched his wigless head. A bloom of peppery short hair accentuated every bump and dent of his skull. 'I'm a soft old get, aren't I? Don't you tell anyone it's here.'

Mary blinked in the light of Northgate Street and breathed in great mouthfuls of its sweet-tasting air. But then she looked down at the tide of green on her hem, and spread her fingers out in disgust at the filth on them, and the air lost its freshness. Gaol-stench clung to her – in her hair, in her cloak, on her boots. Something crawled under her kerchief: she batted it away and shuddered.

All Mary could hear on the walkway of the city walls was the tap of her feet. Gusts of air scudded over Lady Barrow's Hey. Far below her, clumps of scrubby grass bent away from the wind and stocky cattle chewed mournfully in the lee of a bank of gorse. Mary sheltered in the half-moon ingress of the Goblin Tower, freed the bottle from her pocket and let the liquid rasp away the taste of gaol air from her tongue.

Mangham did nothing to sweeten his gin. Mary coughed and retched, and fire flooded her face. She sniffed her cloak. Weaker now, the odour battled with the spirituous fumes.

Selwyn. Selwyn Jones: coward, cuckold, murderer. Like oil in a lamp, the gin fuelled a flame of bitterness. She could have smashed the bottle on to the wind-dried stones. Instead, she tilted it to her lips again and begged it to quench the flame.

Might Anthony be back at the infirmary now, thinking she was his? She covered her face with her hands and groaned aloud. Nothing had been real, until today. Must it be so very wrong? Mary looked up at the Goblin Tower's stone ceiling. An eternity of hellfire for just a few weeks of passion? Would not repentance be enough, afterwards?

This time, its path forged, the gin's coarseness did not hit her. She looked across the Hey at a clump of silver birches, leafless and fragile. The city clocks struck a distant half-hour. And, inchmeal, her thoughts fell into order.

Not loving your husband is not the same as wanting him hanged.

Freedom from such a gaol must be enough recompense for betrayal.

And by the time Selwyn was free, Anthony would long since have moved on. Another glug of gin quelled the ache borne by the thought. Warmth cushioned her mind, and everything seemed clear.

First, she must find William Hartingshall.

THURSTASTON, AUTUMN 1755

This is the time when they will descend, if they're watching. The time when a rumble of hooves will close in. There'll be shots, screams – hers, probably – and the pony might gallop, or he might not.

Mary rides along the cliff and back, too agitated to keep still. Jakey raises his head when she asks him to trot, putting his ears back in protest. Some getaway they'll make, if the patrol comes. She bites on the hard skin of her lips.

You're the best rider, the other women say, their mouths curling in the dim lanternlight. Oh! You're by far the best shot! So she always has to stand alone with Jakey at the top of the cliff, while they snipe together further along the shore. Sometimes she hears them as she rides away. Whispers designed for an audience; darkness concealing sideways glances that shard her skin like sleet.

We'll have time to get away while they take her.

Lover-boy will see she is freed.

She'll let the officer make free with her if he promises to let her go.

The devil will whisk her off from the gallows.

She's the best one to send, for she has no children to miss her.

With care, she moves the pistol into her other hand, then drops the reins and shakes her tired wrist. However much the prospect of dining opposite Jessica Warbreck might appeal to the patrolman, there must come a time when something is going to go wrong. Perhaps he will come home early, to his white house on the limit of the shore; take a glass or two less wine than the Warbrecks offer him; get a bigger payment from his boss than from Bryce; get some other men to keep watch while he fills his face. Perhaps Jakey'll gallop when it comes down to it, perhaps not. But it is Mary who will first face a bullet or arrest. And she knows – though Selwyn calls her a soft bugger for it – that she would never be able to fire back, for fear of hitting a horse.

The fishing boat is in. It slid up to the shore in silence, the ropes of the sails – lowered, because the men have rowed – lashed quiet to the mast. At last she can ride down the path, letting Jakey place his feet where he will, and undo the hidden straps from under the saddle-flaps.

Selwyn's bulk is easy to make out when he blocks the stars that flash in the cloud-windows. Other women's husbands talk to them quietly; Selwyn remains silent while he loads up his part of the haul.

One by one the group walk their horses up the path and back to the village. In the dusty shelter of the stable Mary unsaddles Jakey while Selwyn lifts the goods down into the cellar.

'Next time it won't be for him,' he says, and she is not quite sure what he means.

The sea growls in the distance. Softer now is the feeling that swathes her; warmer and safer. It is done, and the next time the ghost is due to walk – well! That's a whole fortnight away. Ages.

Selwyn replaces the barrels of apples over the cellar's little cellar, then goes off to Kate's tavern with the others, and the terror lurks in a corner until the sounds of his voice are far enough into the night. Then it sneaks back, its skeletal fingers spidering up her spine.

Mary lies awake for hours under the low, wooden canopy of their bed, pressing her fist against her chest. She jumps at every splash of a foot outside, starts towards the pistol at every whisper of the breeze under the shutters, waits for the crack of a fist on the door, until it's no good; she has to get up and take some brandy from the cupboard. Just enough to make her scoff at the night-sounds, and enough to make her heart fold into sleep like a weary moth.

CHAPTER 7

Three o'clock on a Sunday afternoon proved a cheerless time to trudge about Chester looking for a scabby Cockney. Eastgate Row was bereft of the body-heat and bustle that had crowded Mary when she first saw William Hartingshall. In place of the tread of feet behind her, the wind scuttled pieces of straw along the walkway. No one slumped on the wall on the opposite side of the street. A pair of riders passed at a smart trot; a cart rambled westwards, its horse's crupper twisted. Two small boys waved up at her from the cart-bed, and she smiled and waved back. A sheet of newspaper tumbled and drifted and plastered itself into a puddle.

But William Hartingshall was not there. One more turn along each of the main Rows, and then she could say to herself she had tried.

Pale patches tipped the grubby cobbles in front of the Pentice. The sight lightened Mary's mood. Every year that change in the ground's colour betokened spring; those patches of hope in a landscape of sludge. And yet the first half of January was scarce over, and there must be more winter to come.

Mary's shoulders ached and the glow of gin turned to dull tiredness. Her thoughts slowed to nothing, like the wheel of a capsized cart.

Mr Hartingshall, I beg you not to let them . . .

Selwyn asked me to . . .

He is innocent and it would be a grave . . .

Would he not just laugh at her? Get violent? What chance would a diseased beggar have, any end, to influence the courts?

Worn stone steps led up into Watergate Street's North Row, a passageway of hollow boards and low rafters, where the breeze stilled. Barrels and heaps of sacking spilled into Mary's way below the wormy, uneven beams. The scent of sawdust mingled with wafts of beer and rancid meat and quiet threat. Scurrying sounds came from the rafters.

Here, they said, Bryce brought the goods. He, of course, would never say. Perhaps, though unknown to her, this place might be known to him. Perhaps he had walked where she placed her feet now. Facing away from the deserted shops, Mary took another swig of gin. Then she made a fist, kept her mind blank and continued over the carpet of food scraps, sawdust and rat droppings. Past the alleyways that led to somewhere behind the buildings, past the well-dressed man who dipped his gaze over her and winked as he waited outside a house, past a thick double door with a padlock. Footsteps sounded behind her. Hartingshall was just disappearing down a flight of steps.

He had acquired a coat, and his left sleeve bulged at the elbow. He shielded his arm with his other hand. From the Row Mary watched him walk down the centre of the quiet street, and then she ran down the steps. Mud slowed her, but she caught up with him at the Cross, her stomach twisting.

'Mr Hartingshall!' No surprise showed on his face when he turned. 'I've seen Selwyn. I must talk to you.' Hartingshall strode on past the shop where he had sat begging, past Mr Bagnall's tea warehouse and towards the Eastgate. Keeping pace made her cough. 'You're his kin, aren't you? The dead man's.'

Hartingshall trudged up the Eastgate steps on to the city wall, the holes in his woollen stockings exposing patches of grimy, hairy skin. 'Not much gets past you,' he said, without looking back. Up on the walls the crisp wind whirred the brim of Mary's hat. 'A fine pair we make, eh? Promenading with the swells. Me shedding like a snake, you half-seas-over like a tupp'ny trull.'

'I am not.'

'Some swain buy you perfume that smells of gin, then?'

Mary pulled a face at his broad back. 'Did Bryce Warbreck send for you from London?'

Hartingshall laughed. In the shelter of the cathedral, he pulled up the collar of his coat. 'Bloody cold here.'

Didn't they have winter in London? 'Why are you here, then, if you like it not?'

'As I said, ask my—'

'Oh, to hell with your arse. Tell me.'

Two passers-by skirted along the other side of the walkway. Disgust and wariness flitted across their faces.

'Here to see Jones scragged for killing my brother. That's all.' He observed her closely.

'I'm sorry,' she said. The wind snatched up her words and wheeled them away.

'Well, so'm I,' said Hartingshall. 'So, I bet, was Jem – to survive a shipwreck only to have his head cut off by some thug.'

'That's not what happened.'

'Oh, ain't it?' The veins in his eyes burned red. 'Give me a laugh, then. Let's hear what you've come up with for the courts.'

Mary steadied her hand on the wall's coarse sandstone. She should have taken more gin. Made it easier to blurt out the story without the words getting stuck between her dry lips. 'Night of the wreck,' she said, 'we went to the shore to seek spoils – that harms no one, does it? And we pulled a great ark out of the sea. Selwyn smashed the clasp and were that eager to see in he threw the hatchet aside to free his hand. The next thing I hear screams, and Betsy Roberts is crying, "Murder! Murder!" And there's a man lying there, dead as a rat.' Hartingshall scratched his cheek and looked up at the cathedral roof. Herring gulls perched on the lead. Gargoyles stuck their tongues out and picked their noses and widened their devilish eyes. 'He'd washed up dead, but from where Betsy stood, it looked as though the hatchet struck him. She's always hated us. That night she'd thrown me in the water – that's how much she hates me – and she were jealous I barleyed first spoils.'

Sulphury smells drifted off Hartingshall's skin. Brown holes riddled one of his front teeth. 'And Warbreck?'

'He says he has evidence that'll get him a hundred pounds if Selwyn is convicted. That's enough of a reason for him to press the case, even if it weren't for other things. He'll tell you anything to make you think Selwyn is guilty.'

'You mean that crook has framed an innocent man?'

Hartingshall's attention was on her. Suspicion still filled his eyes, but he listened. What if, this time tomorrow Selwyn was free? Going home. Walking aside her past the infirmary. Anthony watching from the window. 'That's what I mean.'

Hartingshall spat into the cathedral grounds. 'And my arse is a bloody pomander,' he said. 'Lend me a wiper for me single tear.'

'It's the truth!' Her ferocity made him blink in surprise. But then he laughed – a grating, humourless, weary laugh.

'Don't ever give up puke-scraping to go on the stage, will you?'

Beyond the apple and pear trees in the Kelyards orchard, the backs of Cow Lane's houses squashed together, the wall under every window encrusted with slop. Hartingshall adjusted his sleeve, his face tight with discomfort.

'Does your arm hurt?' Mary said. He clenched his teeth.

'Of course it bloody hurts. Some fat bugger stuck a knife in it – of course it hurts.'

'Let me have a look.'

Hartingshall shielded the bandage. 'Why? Does getting felt up by a surgeon lend you the power to cure gammy arms?'

'I've seen a fair bung of wounds this past few weeks and I know a healthy one from a bad one.'

He eased his elbow, bit by bit, out of his sleeve. He shivered as he peeled back his filthy shirt; the wind buffeted the gulls on the cathedral roof and whipped up a volley of cawking and flapping that gave Mary an uneasy memory of the shore. She looked up at Hartingshall and he nodded, so she pulled the ends of the bandage knot and unrolled the linen. The compress fell away, flattened and stained by a tidemark of brownish-yellow. The lips of the cut curled away from each other, purple at the edges, exposing pale, ragged meat. Fear darted through Hartingshall's eyes.

'Come back to the hospital on Tuesday,' Mary said. Hartingshall's face grew whiter.

'I ain't going anywhere near that place,' he said. 'I know what'll help this.'

Gin. The bottle hung safe between Mary's petticoats. Help him, and he might take pity on Selwyn, for her sake. She worked her fingers into her pocket. Perhaps the strange comfort of having a full bottle would be crushed.

'I've had some stuff before,' Hartingshall said. 'In London. Laudanum. I saw it on your gallipot's shelves. The label said tinctura thebaica, but I seen the words often enough: it's the same. You'll get it for me, won't you?'

The bottle stayed in its pocket. The relief was almost like gin itself. But Mr Crane would not hand out medicines just like that for someone who refused to attend the hospital.

'No. I can't just take things.'

Hartingshall yawned. His shirt-sleeve fell on to his wound and he flinched as if burned. 'You see, the thing about laudanum is that it clears your mind. Makes it obvious what to say. Might help me – if you understand – think about things. This hurts too much to think. You understand?'

Mary hesitated. 'I don't know.'

'I could think about whether to believe what you've told me.' Pain wrung his face. His dark eyes sat in grey sockets, like berries in a bowl. Like Selwyn's.

'When?'

'Tomorrow,' he said. 'Round by the Northgate, between two and three.'

'Give me 'til Wednesday.'

He concurred. Then he rolled undone the last coils of the bandage and flung it into the orchard. It caught on the branch of an apple tree and twisted in the wind. Wafts of foulness drifted back over the wall. Hartingshall strolled off towards the Eastgate, examining the wound, his coat still hanging off his arm.

Creaks rose from the floor of the empty ward. Mary shook out her cloak, pattering specks of dirt on to on the boards, then hooked it on the window-handle to air and paced the length of the room. Sobs crossed the corridor and invaded her tense silence. Dust already coated the floor and the mantelpiece. She ran her finger along it and it gathered into a line of beggar's velvet. She wrote a hesitant 'A', and then scrubbed it out.

The sobs grated on her nerves. Each gulp of air accused her. An innocent person, of course, would go in and be of comfort.

Oh, perhaps it's for the best. Imagine living with him! Never knowing what mood he'll be in. Never knowing who was winning: you or the gin.

Mary raised her gaze to the rafters, where new cobwebs floated, collecting their own burden of dust.

Perhaps there's a good, honest, sober, dull fellow just waiting for someone as pretty and cheerful as you.

Perhaps Agnes would refuse to let her in.

The enclosing walls of the landing exaggerated the sobs. Mary tapped one finger on the bedroom door.

Even the dimming light could not hide Agnes's face, a red mess of tears. She sat on the bed with her knees pulled up to her chin, her stays discarded, her curls straight and sodden about her face. Sprawled on the floor in front of the fireplace, her cap lay limp and white. A gush of cold air iced Mary's cheeks – the window swung open, bashing into the frame.

'What's happened?' If the daylight were full broad, she would not have the nerve to speak at all.

'He doesn't love me.' The words came out broken. 'There's someone else.'

Mary secured the window, trapping the coldness in the room. She mumbled how sorry she was, picking up Agnes's cap and the shoes strewn on the floor. Efficiency and bustle. She stowed her gin bottle in the cupboard and brought out a pocket-handkerchief. Then she put her arm around Agnes. As a real friend might. 'Who is she?'

'I don't know,' Agnes said. Mary breathed deeper. 'He said she was beautiful – more beautiful than me, in other words—'

'Well, that's daft.'

'And he's fallen in love with her and it doesn't mean he hates me. Would you believe that? I'm not even worth hating. He said he'd never love anyone else but her – would you believe that?'

Mary squeezed Agnes's shoulder. 'No. I wouldn't.'

Agnes pitched her pillow at the wall with a scream so loud that the silence, afterwards, hummed.

'If I ever find out who the bitch is, I'll steal poison from Mr Crane's shop and go to whatever damned bawdy-house she lives in and stick the whole lot in her gin and hope it takes her a week of agony to die.'

Whether, in taking the handkerchief, she noticed the tremor in Mary's hand, Mary could not tell.

She found Anthony about to open the door of his room. He hummed to himself, out of tune. The last smatterings of daylight cast a hazy glitter in his eye. 'I did it,' he said, clasping her waist. She listened for feet on the stairs. 'I'm yours.'

The words punched a hollow in her chest. 'She said . . .' Half-light shadowed his angular face. He gave a crafty smile that near stalled her heart. 'She said you told her you'd fallen in love.'

He laughed softly. 'Over topteels.'

'Why?'

Anthony followed her to the kitchen, where the smoky glow of red embers was the only light. He watched her build up the blaze; she felt his gaze on her face like the changing heat of the fire. 'Is something wrong?'

'You can't love me,' she said. 'No one does.'

He touched her cheek. 'Well, I do.'

Anthony lit a candle, scavenged in the pantry for food, then took a bottle of gin from his pocket as he sat down.

Why must men say such things? Give it a month, and he would be saying it to someone else. And, for all he was aware, she did not know any better. She might believe it. Go all funny. It was cruel. He smiled and offered her some gin, and the familiar fumes blended with the smoke and the fresh scent of flour.

The gaol gin had long worn off, its legacy weariness. Mary drank gladly, and the fire's heat hastened the drowsy comfort that spread through her limbs. She stretched her feet towards the flames. Anthony must have thought she didn't notice when he glanced at the inch of stocking between her boot and her grubby hem.

'Mr Barnston asked me, the other day, to speak to you,' she said, and his face clouded. 'Don't be cross at me – I'll only tell you what he said and have done with it. The Board are like to throw you out if you keep getting drunk.'

Anthony's jaw tightened. 'Well, I've no mind to heed a prinked-up gorger such as he.' He refilled his cup, the bottle-neck clouting the tin. He shoved it across the table, and she drank.

'He wouldn't dismiss you,' she said, and coughed as the gin caught in her throat. 'But the others would. That's why he asked me to warn you. He's a good man.'

'So would I be, if I had nowt to do but watch people sew gold thread on my waistcoat.' Anthony swivelled the cup round and round. A drop splashed out, like spray over a sea wall, and he smeared it up with one fingertip and dabbed it to his tongue. 'He's like some great fish that drifts through the river with scarce a flick of its tail, while all else thrash not to drown. I drink gin alung o' liking it, and I'll not account for it to him or anyone else.' Specks of candlelight burned in his eyes.

'He's concerned, is all—'

'Aye – they're all concerned, aren't they?' he said. 'Concerned that civilisation will fall because I take the odd sip of gin. Concerned enough to spend hours at table bezzling gallons of port-wine and keening over the times and oh, when they were young you could leave your door wide open and the gaols were empty and folk doffed their hats like they ought, and look at it now. It must've been him as paid the parson to rant on it this morning.' He wiped his mouth on his sleeve. 'Vice and sin, sin and vice. Well, I say it'd be a damn sight less of a sin if I were twenty year older and had a guinea or two in my pocket.' The screech of his chair made Mary's teeth hurt. He shot a tumbling mass of coal on to the fire, damping the flames. When he sat down again, he reached for the bottle, but Mary took his hands.

'I just want you to stay here with me, not to have to sleep out in the cold.'

'I can't stop them throwing me out if they choose.'

'You could leave off gin for a week or two – show you can, and then—'

'I don't need to prove anything,' he said, his cheeks flushed. 'Don't they think if I could turn anywhere without hearing my sins and vices numbered and gloated over – don't they think I might not need a few sips of comfort, a few hours of forgetting how much everyone despises me? And don't they think they wouldn't imagine such a harbouration of drunks about them if they weren't seeing double themselves?'

She went to him and held his head close against her chest. 'I don't despise you.' Even through the double layer of petticoats his hands warmed her thighs. The firelight glinted on his hair, lending it rust as deep as the rich red sand of Irby Heath.

'How can you say that,' he said, 'and puzzle at why I love you?' She kissed him, then freed herself from his grasp.

'I must see how Agnes fares,' she said.

Condensation misted the windows in the corridor. Anthony's soft footfalls caught up with her at his bedroom door.

'You mustn't come with me,' Mary said. 'She oughtn't to see you.'

He took the candle from her and set it on the floor. Cold flowed from the whitewashed wall into her shoulders; his body pushed, warm, against hers; gin heated her veins.

Upstairs, sobs still broke the silence.

His hands firmed up her sides, creaking her stays. She took a sharp breath, felt his cheek rough against hers, and his lips smooth on her neck. She looked back at the stairwell.

'Leave her be,' Anthony whispered. 'No one will miss us a time.'

And they wouldn't. Agnes would stay upstairs. Mrs Seward might come back, but she would pass Anthony's room and go to her parlour. She would suppose Anthony was out drinking, and tut and humph, and enjoy hating him for it. But she would not go into his room.

And Selwyn.

Anthony took the key from his pocket, and its clink in the lock made the pulse clamour in her ears.

Selwyn could not know. And when he got out, well – that would be it, for ever. This might be her only chance. A man who wanted her. *No one would know.*

Anthony pushed back her kerchief and his fingers slid over the glow of sweat on her skin. She was not sure what it meant, the unnatural glimmer in his grey eyes. Except that, until she blinked the thought away, she imagined them blue.

CHAPTER 8

The clutter in Anthony's room made Mary smile to herself. Bedclothes sprawled over the side of the mattress, and the candle cast a gleaming line on to another bottle on the night-table. Anthony smiled at her, and she smiled back, and it struck her how many other girls he might have smiled at in the same way, and she hesitated on the threshold.

Then he stumbled. The crack of shin and table made Mary wince. The candle dipped. Anthony spun round, his face scarlet with rage. 'I can't even walk any more!' For a moment Mary did not know what she expected. A joke? But the moment vanished. He swiped the bottle from the table. It chinked and trundled over the floor.

'What? Anthony . . .' Mary's voice rose at the slam of his fist on the wall. 'It doesn't matter. Please . . .'

The door key sailed through the air, hit the glass above the wash-stand and chimed into the bowl. Mary backed into the corridor.

'It *does* matter. It gets to matter when it's every day. When lifeless things have to remind you every day how useless you are. If I could just have one day . . . I can't . . .' Confusion infected his eyes. Even the pinpricks of reflected candlelight shone wild and vague. Mary touched his arm; it quivered like a dropped coin.

'Anthony, don't. I don't understand what's happened. A moment ago—'

'Aye, a moment ago I let myself see a glint of happiness. Let my guard down – for one second – but it was enough for them to see their chance and dash it. To keep me in my place.'

'Who?'

He gripped her arms and she gasped at the pain. A glaze misted his eyes. 'Things,' he said, his hair falling across the sweat on his forehead. 'People are one matter, but lifeless *things* . . . every day . . . they judge and judge. All the time, and it must be true because a bloody table can't lie, can it?'

'Don't shout at me.'

'I'm not shouting at you.' The force of his voice rang in her ears. Water welled in his reddened eyes. 'I'm shouting at myself for being such a damned waste of air.'

'Let go,' she said.

His eyes widened and the glaze sharpened. Hushes of breath fell, heavy and rapid, from his nose. His hold loosened and an ache spread through Mary's bruised flesh.

'I'm sorry,' he mumbled. The door slammed hard behind him. Then it opened and slammed again, and opened and slammed again, and again, until it bounced back after each slam, and smashed into its frame. Light flashed; the candle hurtled past her shoulder; and she screamed. Then darkness. Streams of candle gas threaded their charred scent all around her. In the room, glass chattered on to the tiles.

Mary ran and shut herself in the kitchen, where the firelight reflected from the gin bottle on the table.

She stared at a candle for over an hour. Her swollen eyes stung, and to stare allowed the only relief from crying. She poured cup after cup from the bottle, until thought dimmed and slowed and ceased, replaced by sips and stares. Then that was it, gone, and it served Anthony right.

Embers glowed in the fireplace. When she stood they drifted in front of her eyes. Sickness bubbled through her; she slumped down with her head in her hands.

'Oh God,' she whispered. *Oh God, I didn't mean it. Only make it stop, make me well in the morning, and I'll read the Bible every day, I promise.*

Thousands of tiny fists clenched inside her aching back. Hunger lightened her head, but the thought of food churned her stomach. Then the latches of the main doors clanked.

Mary pushed the light away, and hid the gin bottle on the chair beside her as Mrs Seward filled the door frame.

'Oh, just you, Mary?' said the matron, displaying more jauntiness in her manner than usual. 'Where's Agnes? And the family drunkard? It would surely be too much to hope for that the pleasantness of my afternoon might be continued by his absence.'

Heat rushed to Mary's face. Mrs Seward removed her hat and straightened her cap over her grey-streaked hair. She did not seem to expect an answer, but fetched herself a candle and tutted at the condition of the fire. She stabbed the coals with exaggerated efficiency until yellow flames burst through.

'Out drinking now, is he? Leaving the doors unlocked so anyone might walk in. We might all be murdered, but what is that to him compared with the lure of the bottle? Such a waste. It makes him more of an idiot by the day.'

Mary breathed faster. Only a few more minutes, and Mrs Seward would go to her parlour. Just a few minutes, long though they might be. She waited for Mrs Seward to say something worse.

'Perhaps he will topple into the river and give us all something to rejoice in.'

Mary's fists hit the table. '*Don't* you speak about him like that!' A drop of hot wax dashed on to her hand.

At first Mrs Seward became unnaturally still. Mary's sobs shuddered through the quiet room. She lowered her head to her arms and cried tears that could have been bottled and sold from a grim shop in Cow Lane. Mrs Seward sounded distant and distorted.

'May I remind you,' she said, 'that you had like to treat me with civility and respect as the matron of this house.'

Mary clasped her hands around the back of her head. Wet strands of hair hung in front of her face.

'Hysterics will not impress me, Mary. I'll leave you to compose yourself, but any more of this and the Board will be obliged to enquire after a new nurse.' She expelled a terse sigh. 'I told Mr Barnston at the beginning that we must employ sensible widows, but he insisted on taking you on. And whilst there are few things in which I would fault him, he does have a tendency to overexert his natural sympathy on the least deserving of objects. Stop making such an idiot of yourself, Mary. When we receive inpatients I fear you are like to hear far worse insults than you imagine you suffer from me.'

Mary closed her arms more tightly around her head. The scent of the table comforted her; she breathed in the richness of the oak, the powdery traces of flour, the fatty tallow.

'Don't fool yourself I can't see what's going on,' said Mrs Seward. 'You and Anthony were not exactly the pinnacles of discretion this morning.' Mary looked up, supporting her heavy head in her hands. Mrs Seward raised an eyebrow. 'Oh, you imagine I didn't see you sidling against each other? Exchanging looks? That I didn't notice you touch his leg with the design of provoking him to impure imaginings? In church! I'll not have you two withering the reputation of the hospital by embarking on some sort of passionate misadventure that will soon become the talk of the subscribers.' The matron regarded Mary acutely. Candlelight deepened the wrinkles in her face and danced in her spectacles. 'Listen, Mary, I shan't profess any perfection of my own, but I've ended up in charge of an infirmary and I am obliged to maintain certain standards. As far as I'm concerned there must be no carrying on in public, no babies, and work must be done properly and on time. Other than that, I don't give a damn how much you break each other's ridiculous hearts. If you're fool enough to fall in love with a drunk, so be it. But when it ends in tears – which it will – then there must be no effect on the smooth running of the infirmary. Keep it quiet and I am prepared to ignore it, but I won't tolerate any hysterical idiocy.' She huffed in disgust. 'Well! That's my enjoyable day successfully ruined.'

Her footsteps halted in the corridor. Mary heard the chink of the broken candle holder on the floor. A stifled cry might have followed it, but Mary sank her head back to the table and passed out.

She awakened at the scrape of chair legs. Cold sweat covered her forehead. Only the embers showed the silhouette of Anthony's unruly hair and lean shoulders. Mary's head pounded so hard that she gasped. Anthony bit his thumbnail; his teeth nipped together, overloud in the darkness.

'I'm sorry,' he said. Hot nausea streaked through Mary's stomach. Anthony pushed his fingers through his hair and it remained standing, like barley slanting in the wind. 'A fortnight, you said?' He reached for her hand, but she pulled it away.

'What?'

'If I threw off drink for two weeks – not for Mr Barnston, but for you – would you forgive me?'

Mary shrugged.

'Would you believe I love you?' he said.

He couldn't do it. Within two weeks that would be it. The shortness of the time did not sink in. But, two weeks or two days, he could not do it. Not for her. Mayhappen for someone beautiful, and vivacious, and kind, but not for her.

'I might,' she said. Everything smelled of gin, tasted of gin, hurt of gin.

'I will, then. I promise.'

Three o'clock struck. A pattern of stars circled in the square of the window, and the movement was strangely soothing for a second. Then Mary caught her breath and gaped at the moving belt of Orion through the diamonds of glass. Air turned to gin and scalded her throat. Her heart descended and rose like the arm of a windmill in the heat. Nervous fingers seemed to drum the inside of her chest. Not a proper rhythm, for a heart. It must be how people feel before they grasp their chests and turn blue and fall. She would die. *Oh God! At two-and-twenty!*

Pains hammered through her eyes when she stumbled to the wash-stand. She drank straight from the jug and the water collected heavily in her stomach, and when she used her pot and lowered herself back to the bed every inch of her skin quaked.

Selwyn's name repeated itself in her mind until she blacked out and dreamt of stairs.

Swimming stars meant night, and night meant staying in bed. The paling blue of the window on her next awakening terrified her. She rubbed her eyes and thought, oh God! Any other thoughts were too big to go through her mind without injuring it.

'Are you awake?' Agnes looked pale and blotchy, her eyelids inflamed. Mary's mouth felt as dry as the rat-shitten sawdust of Watergate Row.

'Mmm?'

'What happened? Last night?'

'Last night?'

'I heard Anthony shouting at you. I was too frightened to come down. I swear I thought he was killing you.'

Did she think he would ever kill someone? Indignation clawed too sharply, making Mary's eyes throb inside. 'Well, he didn't.'

'Was it . . .' Tears spilled over as Agnes spoke. 'Was it because he was upset about me? He regretted what he said?'

Mary's stomach cramped so hard that she drew her knees up to her chest. 'No.' The warmth of her hands round her toes brought fleeting comfort. 'He was angry. Not about anything, just angry. He'd been drinking afore he came home.' Mary wiped her clammy forehead. The blankets grated on her skin and the clamour of gulls outside battered in her head.

'Is something wrong? You look alarming sick.' Agnes smoothed greasy strands of hair away from Mary's face. 'You're dreadful cold.'

'I was afeard of his raging, that's all. I've lain awake all night.'

'Well.' Agnes rose from the bed, and the change in the lie of the tick made Mary fight not to vomit. 'Mrs Seward ought to throw him out, for getting us both into such a state. Let him run to his tragwalleting hedge-whore and let's see if her supposed beauty is enough to keep him in gin, eh?' Water crashed into the wash-bowl. 'And when he jilts her for some other clap-infested maukin I hope she dies in a ditch with a broken heart, and festers in the lowest hole of hell with all the other man-stealing whores.'

CHAPTER 9

Life became a window, its funeral-card frame filled with swathes of grey rain. This was not like drinking too much brandy. No sticky feeling of distance from the world, no dull ache or queasy trembling. Instead, agony. Fissures opened in Mary's head. Each stair brought a new world to adjust to; a darker one, like a hell where the flames took turns with shards of ice. Mary imagined her veins black and shrivelled, and her flesh as pale and dry as ashes.

Concern flooded the cook's face. 'Sakes alive!' Mrs Stout said. 'You're like the ghost I saw at Burton when I was but thirteen.' She plonked a plate of eggs and ham on the table. Mary sank to the chair and the change of height brought out sweat on her neck. 'Where's Agnes? Not lying abed still, is she? And our handsome lad.' The cook made a show of fanning her expansive chest with her hand. 'Oh, I tell you, if I were thirty year younger!' Mary knotted her forehead, but the action pulled her scalp too hard, seeming to peel it away. The eggs glistened and wobbled; Mary gagged.

'Poor mite,' said Mrs Stout. 'Is it your monthly time?'

Mary groaned. 'I don't know what it is.'

'Oh! There in't some youth you been carrying on with? You in't . . .'

'No!'

Mary prodded the eggs. Yolk streamed out like pus and she had to close her eyes and keep still and concentrate. When she put her palms

73

to her mouth, their clamminess smelled not of sweat but of gin, oozing through her skin.

'Oh God. Why . . . ?'

'Ah,' said Mrs Stout. 'Drink.' Mary shook her head but her brain did not keep up with the rhythm and smashed against the walls of her skull.

'Please may . . .' A surge of nausea made her hold her stomach. 'Water.'

Mary drank it all in one draught and a renewed flush of sweat sprang out, as though the water fled, cowardly, from the evil of gin. The cook chuckled.

'Dear me, you won't take that stuff again in a hurry, will you? I remember getting myself a-that-n once. Only once, mind.' Mary nibbled at the ham and a knifish pain gouged through her teeth. The stirring of the fire scrunched in her head like a thousand pieces of paper. 'Don't fret – I were fine after a week. And it didn't do my boy any mischief either, for he was a great pudding of a thing when he was born.' She tapped Mary with the back of her hand. 'Nine month later, that was! Got myself a right pinnyful there.'

Mary shoved her plate away, lowered her head to the table and listened to the rhythmic gasp of her breath. Her stays dug into her stomach. Mrs Stout talked about the board room wanting a fire. Mr Barnston, she said, was to come and write letters with some of the other gentlemen, to the subscribers who hadn't paid. Coffee and more coffee, they'd want, as if you could scrape it off the street, and for all Mrs Stout could tell from its taste, you might as well.

'Yo' bin late, my love,' said Mrs Stout, and her knife slipped on the ham, hit the board and shot a bolt from one side of Mary's head to the other. 'Poor Mary's the worse for gin, so don't gabber too loud.'

Cutlery crashed close to her ear. Anthony tucked into the ham and eggs, then he yawned and stretched his long legs out under the table. 'Ready for my own breakfast now.'

'That's my lovely lad,' said the cook. Under the table Mary's fingers trembled in Anthony's hand. His indulgent grin made her scowl, but when he touched her hair she closed her eyes, the soothing stroke nudging her towards sleep.

'Oh!' The cook's cry made Anthony pull his hand away, but Mrs Stout chuckled as she placed his plate in front of him, and said he might very well go pink – for she could see what was going on and it ought not to have surprised her, 'what with the bunge of you in the same house, and so young'. She winked at Mary and fanned herself with her hand again, and Mary curled up inside.

'You'll not tell anyone, will you, Mrs Stout?' A cheeky smile threaded through Anthony's voice.

'Of course not, my love. I don't want to set off any fights. I don't want to see Mary and Agnes scrapping like a pair of terriers after a rat.'

'I must . . .' Mary stopped to steady her breath. 'I must do the fire. For Mr . . .'

'Well, don't you go letting him see you in that state,' said Mrs Stout. Standing up made Mary's legs shake. Black prickles gathered at the rim of her vision. 'Mind, it wouldn't gloppen me any if he were fond of a spot o' port-wine himself.'

'He likes brandy,' Mary said. And then she jolted fully awake. Mrs Stout laughed and flapped her with a dishclout.

'Oh, he told you that over high tea, did he?'

Anthony paused with a morsel of ham halfway to his mouth. Mary held on to the door frame. 'I must have overheard him talk on it,' she said.

Her blankets cried out to her each time she passed the stairs. And the pillow – the soft feather pillow such as she had never had at home. Each time she passed, she also passed Mr Crane's room. She had a vague image of the rows of bottles and paper packets, all lined up, their labels facing the front, and of one marked laudanum. She imagined it large, as big as the gin bottle, and the empty space it would leave, as plain as a missing tooth.

Mary was only half-aware of Anthony helping her to bring a shovelful of fire from the kitchen. He tried to kiss her, and then Mrs Seward shouted for him and she was alone once more in the board room, the first glints of fire scurrying from the old coals over the new. Sickening heat washed through her body and she lowered herself to the floor.

Mrs Stout was right – she would never drink gin again. If she ever even smelled it again in her life she would be sick. No amount of worry could be worse than this.

Cold flooded through her clothes. She turned her forehead to the tiles and the sickness subsided. Everything – the chill of the floor, the splash of feet in the lane outside, the sputter of the fire – brought a momentary change and comfort. But the moments proved short, and the return of misery rapid and intense.

Birds sang just outside the window; the sound soothed her, making her think of spring. She closed her eyes, and the clear notes became all that existed. Then people spoke in the corridor. Mrs Seward, and a man. Not Anthony.

Mary stood, pain biting through her head. Mr Barnston did not seem to see her brush the dust from her sleeve. He raised the lid of his document-case, his fingers neat and clean against the leather. The case was spotless too, like the rich green velvet of his suit.

'Well, Mary,' he said, and he took out a bottle of ink. 'How many of our dedicated governors do you think will attend today?'

What reply would be proper for a servant? To give an opinion? Say nothing? Suggest the most desirable outcome, and be wrong? Warmth flared behind her and she looked back – a single tall flame threaded from the coals.

'Not one, I should think, sir,' she said, and he laughed as he took two pens from the case and set them on the table, about an inch apart. And Mary thought, no – it wouldn't be about an inch. It would be an inch exactly.

'Mr Hesketh, Mr Racketta – even Sir Richard – have given their absolute promises. I suggest you bring coffee for one.' He smiled, squaring a pile of papers into a stack. 'As for the subscribers, I fear we shall be obliged to employ a surgeon solely to extract the money from their pockets.' He looked at her directly for the first time, and concern lowered his eyebrows. 'Mary, are you quite well?'

Mary clasped the back of a chair. 'Aye, sir. Thank you.' Through a narrowing tunnel of speckles she saw him put down the bottle of ink, and its muted thud reached her after a delay.

'You have been to the gaol?' Mr Barnston asked. The lines of gold embroidery on his waistcoat writhed like worms. 'I advised you not to.'

Mary hung on harder to the chair. She pulled it out a fraction; Mr Barnston completed the movement and she sat down.

'I had to,' she said.

'You do not appreciate the danger. What if you have brought some virulent disease into the infirmary? Gaol fever, the smallpox . . . the physicians are so vigilant about excluding such patients, and yet you wander freely in and out of that dungeon of filth.'

Mary shivered, but her face grew hot. What if that was it? What if it were nothing to do with the gin? Because there had not, after all, been that much in the bottle, and the way her heart quavered and dipped must be akin to the ravages of a fever. She touched her face, dreading to find it covered in clusters of spots. The strange prickles danced with greater glee between her eyes and the golden threads.

'I'm sorry.'

'How does he bear up?'

'Desperate bad.'

Mr Barnston frowned. 'Perhaps I misjudged sending you here. I will speak to Mrs Evans this afternoon, and we will find work for you in my own household – there must be something she can set you to do.'

If only he had said that at first. 'Please, I would rather stay.'

Mary concentrated hard on the chirrup of the birds. Pure and cheerful, the sounds pushed everything else out of her mind. They seemed the only things to cling to – a way to force the sickness aside and contain it. Mr Barnston waited until she looked at him again.

'Why?' He knew. The throb in Mary's head quickened. 'Because of Wells? What there is to choose between a murderer and a drunkard I could not presume to judge, but you can't have both of them, Mary.'

'He's no drunkard. He's given over drinking.'

'Since when?'

Mary lowered her eyes. 'Yesterday.'

Mr Barnston smiled. 'We will want some coffee.'

'You could get Selwyn out,' said Mary. 'You could tell the judge. All you would have to do is speak to the judge and make him tell the jury what to say. Or . . .' A small swollen pressure rasped in her throat. 'Or you could speak to Bryce.'

Mr Barnston went back to his document-case. 'I am not inclined to do so,' he said. 'Bring the coffee.'

The cups chattered on the hand-board. Muddy wisps of steam slid down Mary's throat and gathered into a poisonous fug in her stomach.

Mr Barnston sat nearest the board room fire, the scratch of his pen loud and grating on the printed forms.

'Flintshire again,' he said to himself as Mary set the tray down. 'They are far quicker to send their poor for treatment than they are to send their money.'

Mr Racketta grunted assent. He lounged in his waistcoat and shirt-sleeves next the window, a pile of untouched letters before him. Smoke curled from his nose. He winked at Mary and drew the slender clay pipe from his lips, stretching them into a lubricious smile.

The odour of tobacco ended Mary's composure. She staggered out and fell to the corridor floor.

Through specks of mist she saw nothing but distorted movements above her, and sensed only watery sounds. A door opened. Footsteps moved close to her ears. Hairpins dug into her scalp. She turned her head aside and the coldness of the floor shocked against her cheek. Someone shouted Mrs Seward's name. Tobacco fumes choked her, warmth sidled against her and fingers pressed the side of her neck.

She pushed them away and someone said, *Come now, don't be a silly girl – I must take your pulse, mustn't I?* The pressure made her retch. *Right swift and unsettled.* Hot breath fell on to her cheek. *Very erratic. And your lips – too pale.* A rough-skinned thumb stroked them. Then, abruptly, the fingers released her throat and brushed under her kerchief.

'Good God!' Mrs Seward said. 'More hysteria? Up you get.' Hands helped her to her feet. Shadows and lines defined the stairs; she gripped the end of the banister, afraid to fall.

'May I offer my services, Mrs Seward, and carry the wench to her room?'

'She will be quite all right, Mr Racketta,' said the matron. 'We shall consult the physician in the morning if she has not slept it off by then.'

A humming noise droned through Mary's ears. Agnes and Mrs Seward helped her undress, and made no comment when she vomited into her pot, and then the bed-tick embraced her shaking limbs.

'Mrs Seward, look!' said the cook. 'Here is Anthony, drinking nowt but water! What do you say to that, now?'

Uncomfortable heat stifled the kitchen. Steam blanked the window and a bloom of sweat shone on the cook's cheeks. Mary's ankles itched in their woollen stockings. The night had not effected a full recovery, and her hand still trembled on her knife.

Mrs Seward snorted a laugh. 'You are too inclined to believe in miracles,' she said. 'Only take a sip of it, and you will be assured it is not just water.' Mary's fist tightened. Anthony simmered next to her; the air itself stiffened and seethed. Agnes studied her uneaten breakfast.

'No, indeed, I poured it myself, from this very jug,' said Mrs Stout, and Mary vaguely heard Mrs Seward say, 'What is this? Wells, you cannot be seeing sense at last – I cannot believe it.' Anthony shuddered deep inside himself, and Mary was not sure if anyone could see it but her.

'If you were to go a day without being drunk, I should prod my eyes out with a knitting needle,' said Mrs Seward. Then Mary caught his gaze and tried a smile, but he only ran his fingers under his eyes and focused on the table.

'I have known of drunks to do this before,' continued the matron. 'They throw it off for a week, or a month, or for Lent – two years even, and oh! I do not deny they are often capable of managing it, but at the last they drink again, and it captures them as if they had never left it off. Myself, I pity anyone who has the least thing to do with them.' She looked narrowly at Mary, and Mary squeezed her fists tighter under the table.

'Oh, bless his little heart,' Mrs Stout said. 'We're only teasing. Would you like some more *water*, my lovely boy?' And she ruffled Anthony's hair. He jerked his head away.

'No I wouldn't,' he said, strung tighter, like a rope stretched by a travelling acrobat between Eastgate Street's Rows. Agnes flitted her fingers across each eye.

'Well,' said Mrs Seward, 'I hope you are turning out for the better, though I have to say I doubt it. Give it only until five o'clock this evening, and you will be as drunk as ever, I am quite certain of it. There is never much that can be done when it gets to that stage.' Anthony bit the side of his thumb, his cheeks hollow. 'It gets into their brains, Mrs Stout, like maggots into a carcass, and then there is nothing they can do to stop it. I warrant he will be drunk again by five, for all the water he might claim to sup now.'

Anthony set his spoon very straight upon the table. Agnes sniffed and pulled a handkerchief from her stays.

Mrs Seward was not teasing. Her gaze fell hard on Anthony's crimson cheek. 'You are a drunk,' she said, her nose wrinkled. 'Through every muscle and every vein; and all you will ever find the wherewithal to do is hurt people.'

Mary shrank into herself, cold, and Mrs Stout sneaked her an uncomfortable look. Without a word the cook returned to washing the plates.

Anthony did not speak as he left the kitchen. The main doors slammed and she pictured him with his hands in his pockets, fuming on his way across Northgate Street and through the building works by the cathedral, through the Kelyards Gate and the orchard, to the bundle of rotten straw and the crazed old woman in Cow Lane.

'Well, there he goes,' said the matron. 'To a dram shop, as I might have predicted.' Her face tautened into a satisfied smile.

Mary stood at the main doors and looked out across the courtyard. The only reason he would not drink now was if he loved her. That was the end of that, then.

She gazed up at the Northgate until the glare of the sky around it hurt her eyes.

THURSTASTON, EVENING, 27 DECEMBER 1755

A long evening, and Selwyn Jones is annoyed because the turmoil of the sea prevents the boat going out to Hilbre, where a stash of Manx beer waits in the cave. Mary is glad; she has no desire to ride along the scrubby mounds of cliff, pointing the pistol into the heather, trying to catch what the others say about her. A peaceful night.

'Happen it'll be calmer tomorrow,' she says as she finishes rinsing the plates, and her voice rings over-loudly against the cottage walls. The shutters rattle, first at one window and then at the other, a sound that makes her heart spring. A storm. The wind growls in the clump of oaks by Thurstaston Hall. Selwyn is engrossed in the flames. 'I said, happen it'll be calmer tomorrow.'

'Happen.'

The back of his neck still holds the brownness of summer. It reminds her of taking bread and ale to him in the dusty fields. She had almost felt contentment then; affection, a remembrance of how they had been as children. Enough to make him notice her smile, and smile back after he had wiped his mouth on his dirt-speckled arm.

Perhaps it's love. She stands still with the dish-bowl in her hands. To be so familiar with someone – to know the imperfections of the curve of his ear, the hard tags of skin around his nails. Perhaps this is all it is; perhaps she was mistaken in expecting something else. This – what is it? – tenderness – that's it. Well, that's enough. That's all most women have to go on. She makes herself smile, but incompleteness buzzes around her. Always waiting for sunrise, waiting for love to struggle over the horizon and disperse the chill. Perhaps if they'd been able to have a child. But that's life.

Outside, the wind buffets the spikes of rosemary by the picket gate, and the moonlight struggles through surges of rapid grey cloud.

Mary throws the water away, looks back at the door and unpins her cap. She takes the wires from her hair one by one. Tresses lash against her neck.

Light comes from an opening door and water sloshes on to the mud. Betsy Roberts, throwing out her dishwater – perhaps, if the clouds have once again exposed the moon, seeing her and standing with her hands on her hips, and slowly shaking her head. But Mary cannot tear her face from the touch of the storm. She grasps the picket-gate, sensing the tiniest, most short-lived lull in the wind, as if it is recruiting strength.

Then a great rush of air pummels the breath from her, whips her hair into a turmoil of black snakes and leaves her open-mouthed like a fish on the sand.

Whether Betsy Roberts can hear her gasp through the wail of the wind she doesn't know, but if Betsy had nothing to cant about she'd invent something anyway.

The Roberts's door slams and Mary shivers. Although the light of her candles is dim, it makes her narrow her eyes as she goes back into the cottage. Water drips from her fingers and her hair clings to her cheeks. She takes off her topcoat and jacket, fetches her shawl from the bedstead and stands before the fire.

'D'you ever think how it would be, to be in the sea?' she says, tasting salt on her lips. When Selwyn looks up, he appears baffled.

'Wet,' he says, his eyebrows lowering. 'Cold. You know what the sea is like – you've been in it often enough. What are you going on about?' He peers at her. 'What are you standing there half nekkit for?'

'No, I don't mean to be wading in the sea, or swimming in it. I mean to be in it. To be in it. To be part of the water – not a thing floating on it, but part of it, without skin keeping it out.'

Selwyn screws up his nose and rolls his eyes sideways. 'What?'

'It would be quiet, wouldn't it?' Mary keeps her voice soft. 'Even on a night like this, it would be silent, under the surface. It would roll *you back and forth. Awake enough to be aware of things, and asleep enough not to mind them.'*

'No, it wouldn't. You'd be dead.'

'No, that in't what I mean.'

He regards her steadily. The tiniest indication of a smile grows on his lips. 'What's happened to your hair?'

Hesitating, she is afraid any words will chase the smile away. 'I let it down,' she says. 'To feel the storm go through it. It was like fingers.'

A proper smile now; and yet she is still not sure whether it's one of affection, or of amusement. 'It reminds me of how you looked, that time . . .' he almost laughs, 'that time you tipped a bucket of slubber over my head.'

It is such a pinprick of warmth, the faintest glimmer of together-ness, and yet it lights her with happiness and strength. Holding her breath, she tries to prolong the moment of affection. Speaking, she thinks, must shatter it, so she only smiles.

'I was awake for nights after, worrying I'd swallowed some and'd get taddies wriggling about in me.' He shudders, but his laugh fills the room, pushing the storm-sounds away into the night. 'You were a devil! Your hair was all over the place, just like now, and your nose was all scrunched up as you giggled.'

'My ma had a duck egg when she found out.'

'Mine stuck my head in a barrel and scrubbed it with a bloody washing-brush. Near took my ears off.' He rubs his ears violently and chuckles, remembering, and to see him do anything other than sit and frown makes hope twist into her. If this were how it could always be she would be content. 'Mary, we oughtn't to have any secrets, ought we? Not as husband and wife.'

'No,' she says, anxiety worming back into her. 'We oughtn't.' He ripples his fingers on the chair arm.

'The beer, in the cave. It in't part of the scheme.' Mary questions him only with a look. 'I've been putting by a bit of money. I bought the beer myself and brought it over on the last trip we did for Warbreck. I'm going to sell it and keep the profit for us.'

Whenever he says that name he has a habit of observing her. Waiting for the usual rise of colour.

'What if he finds out?'

'What if he does? The profit'd be enough to buy another load. We could be independent. Think of it, eh? We could buy this house outright, or a better one, even.'

'He'd take the horse and cart back from us.'

'We'd buy better. You wouldn't have to ride decoy any more.'

That thought starts to thaw her discomfort. 'We could move away. Further up the coast, nearer Hilbre. Get away from—'

'Warbreck.'

She was going to say the gossips. The ones who never could accept that Bryce had only kissed her. The ones who called her a whore, and didn't wonder at her barrenness, for no God worth his salt would give children to such a mother as she would make.

'Yes. Get away from him.' *She pauses.* 'Shall I fetch you some ale?'

He thanks her cheerfully when she brings it, and doesn't recoil when she lays her hands on his shoulders. She rubs the tired muscles, feeling him sink back in the chair and rest his head against her body. Perhaps tonight. Perhaps this time. His cheek feels rough on her lips.

'Is there owt else you'd like me to do?' *she whispers. His near-black eyes look up at her warily.*

'I . . . I don't mind,' *he says. Mary drops her hands from his shoulders and tears burn into her eyes.*

'I'll go to bed, then.'

It's a wakeful hour on the straw tick, with too many things to think about and nothing to see but the shape of his feet against the embers. He does nothing but sit there, sometimes letting out a single snore, but she is still awake when he makes the fire safe, goes out to the privy and at last crawls into bed.

He does his best. She wishes now she had pretended to be asleep, but still. After two years perhaps this will be the time. She can always think of something else. How she used to try not to, at first!

CAROLINE RANCE

But now she summons visions, and it is not Selwyn she kisses, and not his hand rumpling her shift up over her thigh.

How smooth his cheek would be against hers; how his lips would linger on her skin. Bryce. How strong his heart would beat on hers, how candlelight would sparkle in his blue eyes. Come on, Selwyn, get on with it.

Bryce, Bryce. She'll say it aloud one of these nights, and then there'll be trouble. Bryce. The name mocks her, tries to escape from her lips. Her heart bubbles and flutters and hurts.

Selwyn's bulk crushes her. It's always like this; grinding his hipbones into her, and he isn't even inside her yet. At least, not as far as she can tell. Encourage him. A gasp, a moan of conjured pleasure, a hungry kiss.

He swears and rolls away and she pulls her shift back down.

'What have I done wrong?' she says.

'You were thinking of him again.'

'No!'

Clenched teeth. Resentment fighting through them. 'For God's sake, Mary, you think of him all the time. I see you stop what you're doing and stare at the floor, or nod at what I'm saying without hearing me. He kissed you once and thought no more of it. That's it. And I have to go through every day and night knowing my wife doesn't love me, and she'd rather someone else lay next to her, and not me.'

'I wasn't thinking of him. Nor of anyone but you.'

'He's got everyone in this damned village by the bollocks, and he laughs his arse off every time we risk our necks to keep him in silk hanketches. Pox take him – I'm bloody sick of him.'

Selwyn grunts, and the remnants of the fire glower red, silhouetting his shoulder as he snatches the blankets over it.

CHAPTER 10

Elixir of Aloes, Sarsaparilla, Antimony. All sizes and colours of packets, tins and bottles. Labels inscribed in sepia ink in a minuscule hand. Guaiacum, Wormwood, Cream of Tartar. Behind the partition of shelving Mr Crane coughed. Stone ground upon stone. Then three sombre taps, the chink of glass, liquid pouring. Elderflower Water, Spirit of Hartshorn, Syrup of Violets. Just more than an arm's length away.

A calf-bound ledger lay open on the narrow counter, its rows and columns all delineated in the same watery brown. Asa Foetida, Nitre, *Tinctura Thebaica*. That was it – it was what Hartingshall had said. Down the corridor Agnes opened the doors, and slow applause pattered in on the draught. The smell of quicksilver drifted over the partition, then hints of rosemary. An image of soft blue flowers came to Mary so strongly she shivered. She was no thief. Hartingshall could steal his own damned laudanum. Or let him face the doctor like a man and ask him for the stupid stuff.

But through the high window a dark triangle jutted into the sky; a tern stretched its wings on the pinnacle. They said the condemned cell lay so far underground that no air could get to it but by a pipe. Deeper than a tomb, and as black and cold.

Dead leaves scurried up the corridor towards her and she hugged her arms. If Hartingshall, the man's own brother, pleaded for Selwyn, what could Bryce do? Bryce, who relied on nasty old besoms like Betsy Roberts and Liza Mobbett to tell what they saw. But the man's own brother . . . Crab's Eyes (Whole), Oil of Juniper, Myrrh . . .

The echo of Agnes's feet brought with it a smothered sob. Mary backed away from the apothecary's store.

'He's back,' Agnes said, her chin wobbling. 'Sober.' Tears damped Mary's shoulder. 'You know why it is, don't you? It's for her.'

Mary's arms rested, cold and still, around Agnes, and her heart squirmed like a maggot.

Anthony paced in front of the door all morning. She could talk to him only with looks. Patients eyed him warily, with his ashen face and dishevelled clothing, and the blood that smeared the side of his thumb.

'Only walked round the walls,' he said, grabbing her arm. 'Don't think I'd go and drink. Don't think that.'

Eleven o'clock passed and Mrs Seward emerged from the kitchen with a tray of food for herself. Mary had lost all appetite when she saw the patient who now accompanied her to the board room. He edged along using two bristleless brooms as crutches, his breath rasping out as rank as if he had been chewing a corpse. His mouth was a dark lesion in his yellowish face, showing teeth so rotten they were almost eaten up by his swollen gums. Every few steps he spat blood on the floor.

'You haven't got the pox, have you?' Mary said. 'Because they won't let you in, no matter how much you beg.'

The man wore only one stocking; on his other leg, just below the cuff of his breeches, was a mushy wound. A mass of flesh mushroomed out, as though someone had sewn a piece of liver into the skin.

'How am I to have got a pox at sea?' he said, his voice muffled and hardly understandable. 'There weren't any of your sort on board.'

'My sort? Well, that's—' She broke off when the man suddenly turned towards the outer doors, his fetid mouth open to aid his listening.

'Shilling on the short bugger!'

The shout came from the courtyard. The matron's pattens halted on the stairs. The bright rectangle of the doorway showed a segment of cobbles and the red brick wall of the chapel wing. More shouts rose. Feet scuffled the stones and shadows flitted over the doorstep. The patient hobbled as fast as he could out of the infirmary. Mary's shoes smeared his smatters of blood and spittle, then she heard Anthony's voice, loud and unnatural. The gin-pain in her head thumped back.

'I don't give a damn how long you have to bide there.' Gleeful jeers swelled through the queue, which disintegrated into a milling ring around Anthony and the stocky, pock-faced man whose jacket he grasped in his fists. 'Go home if you don't like it.' Between the hats and shoulders Mary glimpsed his white knuckles on the collar, his unkempt hair, the tight sinews on the shorter man's neck. Clangs of the gate brought more people in from the street; others climbed the railings to see. 'Go home to your stinking hovel and suffer, if your thankless arse thinks we in't good enough.' A wave of red flooded up the man's neck. He jabbed Anthony in the chest and Anthony knocked his finger away.

'Mek a bloody spectable of yourself if you mun. All I want is to see the doctor and be on my way.'

Mary wriggled through the crush of bodies. Mrs Seward shouted her name, but the sound faded in the sweaty closeness of the air. Damn him, why couldn't he just ignore them?

'Anthony!' Someone jostled her aside. She lashed out, her fist meeting an arm, and the owner of it put up his palms. Anthony shoved the patient away and a lively bellow reverberated in Mary's ears.

'Wait, then, and keep your shovel-fed gob shut.' Disappointment rumbled across the courtyard. Anthony stalked back towards the building, where Mrs Seward stood in the doorway, her face purple. The pockpitted man straightened his coat, resumed his place at the front of the queue and folded his arms.

'Get back inside.' Mrs Seward pointed behind her, but her eyes betrayed a glimmer of uncertainty that he would obey. Mary reached

Anthony's side, and the anger in his face did not frighten her. Instead it seemed to flow into her, until her own fists tightened at the sound of the patients laughing.

'His ma was that drunk, she kept the stork.'

She lunged for Anthony's arm but he wrested his sleeve away and the wool burned her fingers. The man grunted at the collision of head and wall and Mrs Seward screamed.

'Why don't you tell everyone what's so funny?' Anthony shouted. 'Why don't you tell 'em all, eh?' A blob of blood descended from the man's nose.

'They've seid that for theirsels,' he said, a powerful sniff retracting the glutinous flow. 'If they anner turned to bloody skellingtons waiting.'

Anthony slammed the man against the wall and the cluster of people ahhed a collective wince.

'Nowt I do can be good enough, can it?' Veins stood out in Anthony's neck. 'Well, I'm sick to my grinders of the lot of you.' The man's eyes glazed more with each collision of skull and brick. Thud. Thud. 'Sick of your whinging, sick of your gurning faces laughing at me, sick of the damned lot of you scraping the barrel for every last reason to hate me—' Hands seized his arms and dragged him away, and the pock-faced man slithered to the ground. Anthony struggled and kicked, his face red and feverish, and the two men who held him seemed about to wrestle him down.

The matron's screeches became muted, overcome by the rushing of blood in Mary's ears. They were not going to hurt him. She would kill them if they tried. People stepped out of her path, washy figures at the brink of her vision.

She reached the biggest man first. Her fist resounded on the barrel of his chest. 'Leave him! Leave him be!'

Laughter swelled behind her, and the man looked down and grinned and said, 'What, or you'll clapper-claw me, little'n?'

The bricks, the cobbles, the Northgate, the carriages beyond the railings, juddered before her eyes. She sank her nails into his throat, his stubble rasping her fingers. His face twisted like a wrung-out cloth. 'Let him go.'

The big man choked, his eyes round. A murmur circled the court-yard and he loosened his hold on Anthony's arm. Warily his companion did likewise, and Anthony staggered upright. Crescents of blood welled on the man's neck. He dabbed his fingers to them, stud-ied the red smears on their tips and wiped them on his coat.

Anthony breathed heavily, his fists slowly loosening. Sounds lost their muffled quality and came back to Mary. Eyes observed her from every side. Anthony bowed his head and his long limbs trembled.

Whether or not Agnes was watching she did not know. She took Anthony's elbow and guided him back to the infirmary – past the star-ing people; past the pock-faced man who lolled, sparky-eyed, with his back to the wall; past Mrs Seward's silent and powerless anger; and past the cook, who clutched a shawl around herself and shivered like a foreigner newly arrived from the hot country of the kitchen.

'Go in your room,' Mary said. Anthony fumbled in his pocket for the key. 'Keep least in sight 'til they've gone.' He stumbled towards his bed. Guilt made her hesitate. But it would be for the best. In the last second before the door clicked shut she saw him spin round, his eyes flaring, and then she turned the key and retreated from the shudder of his fists on the door.

Mary took one foot, Mrs Seward the other, and the big fellow with the blood on his neck took the shoulders. The man with the pitted skin was conscious enough to shake a weak fist towards Anthony's room. 'Bloody maggot-yed.'

'At least you've got in faster,' Mary said, and Mrs Seward glared at her. They took him straight to the doctor, the matron exercising her power to admit emergencies without reference to the Board. She told the big man he could go to the front of the queue and would be treated next, but he said 'not likely,' and left, with a frayed bit of cloth pressed to his neck.

Agnes had heard the commotion from the treatment room. The sight of the man's grey face made her look questioningly at Mary. 'I heard his voice,' she said. Mary did not answer.

Warmth and the smell of patients pervaded the room; their gases and sweat, and the odour of their wounds. Blood half-filled a porringer, its surface forming a thick crimson skin that wrinkled whenever the table got jolted, and the water in the washstand sat cloudy and peppered with hairs and scurf. Mr Cotgreave, the surgeon on duty, examined the man's head.

'Anthony Wells,' said Mrs Seward to Dr Tylston. 'Anthony Wells is responsible. It is well-nigh a murder.'

'Good God,' said the doctor. 'What could have provoked him to that?'

'Gin is involved.'

'Ah.'

Mary could have sliced the matron's eyeballs with a lancet. The stifled glee in them brought sickness to her throat. 'He wasn't drunk,' she said.

'The doctor did not ask for your opinion,' Mrs Seward replied. 'Sir, what she means by her boldness is that Anthony Wells has a whim to throw off gin – admirable enough in intention, I own, but sadly laughable in its futility.'

Dr Tylston slowly shook his head. 'I've heard the governors comment on his drinking, but I'd no idea it was bad enough to have this effect.'

'Well, sir, I have no doubt it is very bad indeed, and the only question in my mind is which of gin and the gallows will claim him first.'

'It wasn't his fault,' said Mary. When her fingers curled into fists, she felt fragments of skin lingering under their nails. 'This feller and the others tarred him on.'

Mrs Seward's nostrils widened. 'Nurse Helsall . . .'

'And he only ever drank at all to block out how much you hate him.'

Dr Tylston cleared his throat and handed her a piece of paper. 'Go along and fetch this from Mr Crane, dear,' he said, and though his tone was kind, it was not one to argue against. Outside the room she forced in a few deep breaths. Mrs Seward still gloated within, but the patient spoke too, his voice strong. Would the matron have preferred him to die? Would it have been a source of joy to her, to see Anthony a murderer? The notion was too real and frightening; it made her think of gin.

From Dr Tylston's small, obscure writing she could not make out the patient's name, and had no recollection of him saying it. But underneath, in the brown hospital ink, the line was clear: *1 phl 1 oz. Tinctura Thebaica.*

The paper flickered in her hand.

Catarrhal sounds rumbled behind the partition, and liquid trickled as if from a great height. Outside, the patients' chatter had become more subdued. Mr Crane's quill fluttered in its holder. The ink bottle beside it caught light from the window, and in it a distorted reflection of the Northgate.

Would Selwyn do this for her?

The stopper came out easily. Mary rubbed her shoe over the blot that patted to the floor. Mr Crane mumbled a curse to himself and sniffed again, and the pour of liquid continued. She kept her breath shallow and steadied the paper on the counter. The fronds of the pen brushed her hand. Hesitation made the ink dry on it; it left no more than a grainy scratch. Mary breathed in the dung-scented air from the main entrance, and dipped the pen again.

2.

A very upright 2. But she knew better than to try harder to correct it. She replaced the pen and ink and stepped aside from the counter.

No, he would not have done this for her. Mary blew on the ink and tried to hold the paper still. He would have visited her, no doubt, in gaol, and been angry at the filth and the shackles, but she was the only one to whom he would have made his anger known. He would have waited for her to fight her own way out.

She rapped her knuckles on the counter. The apothecary held out his bony fingers for the note. 'Two phials at once?' He lifted the paper to the light, and Mary gauged the clear path to the door.

'There's a man terrible bad in there,' she said. 'That ragglement before – he got hurt, and the surgeon said his skull might be all shivered inside, like an egg.' The apothecary lowered his tufts of eyebrows and assessed her with distaste before he turned back to his shelves. Mary rubbed her fingertips across her sweaty palms.

Mingling scents of the medicines gave her something to concentrate on; metallic, floral, sweet, spicy, herbal. On the other side of the wall behind her, the patients' coughs and complaints merged with sounds of the street.

Mr Crane's pen eked agonisingly over the page of his ledger. At last he passed the phials to Mary. Cold and smooth, the feel of them made her hands shake.

In the doorway of the treatment room, where neither Mr Crane nor the doctor could see her, she separated the phials and slid one into her pocket.

Mrs Seward asked someone from the line to go and engage a sedan chair, which Dr Tylston paid for from his own money, and the man with the broken head went on his way, cursing too much to be in danger.

Anthony sat on the floor with his back to the bedstead and his legs drawn up. The commotion and delay had made some of the patients give up and go home, and by one o'clock the infirmary was quiet. Anthony's shirt bagged crookedly around him, his jacket and waistcoat sprawled on the floor. He pulled himself up on to the bed.

'D'you mean to hold me prisoner, and force me to keep my promise?'

Mary pushed the door to. 'I was feared you'd be hurt. I'm sorry.'

'You didn't trust me?' She pressed the key into his hand. He examined it closely, its grubby metal dark in his unsteady fingers. 'Mary, help me.' The taste of salt on his cheek shrank her lips. 'If it weren't for my heart . . . It rattles. It's like a fist at a prison bar. If it would only stop I could take the rest. I need to make it stop or it'll shatter me.' He took her hand, and brought it to his chest.

A clatter from the kitchen made her start, but no one came out. Someone laughed.

About her. About her and Anthony; it must be. She pressed her hand against the dampness of his shirt. His arm was hot around her. Sweat glistened in the grey caverns of his eyes. 'Press harder,' he said. 'It does some good.'

'When did this start?'

The skin under the opening of his shirt was as smooth and cold and wet as a frog's. 'I don't know . . . Last night. I woke up – I don't know what time. I didn't know there was owt wrong at first, and then I rubbed my eye, and there was sweat on my face.' He wiped his palm across his forehead. 'I was soaked, like this, and it an't stopped.' Anger infected his eyes. 'Gin dun't look so harmful now, does it, eh? It would stop this, and yet you . . .' He pinched the bridge of his nose, and when he opened his eyes again they were sunken and darkened in terror.

'You look afeard,' she whispered. His fingertips hurt her arm.

'I am. There's some stuff . . . blood, in my throat. Ebbing and pushing. It scares me. What if I die? I in't ready for it.' Mary stroked his sodden hair. He recoiled. 'Get off me!'

Mary fought to keep herself from lashing back. She ran her hand over the bed-sheet. How different it would have been had he not stumbled. 'What can I do?' she said. 'I want to help you, but there seems to be nowt . . .'

'You know damn well what would help. Last night I couldn't move – could scarce even breathe. Some choice you've left me – to fail or die.'

Mrs Seward's voice grated at the kitchen door. Mary tried to stand up. 'I have to go. She'll see us. She said we must keep it quiet. Please.'

He pulled her back to him. Distraction displaced anger in his face. 'One cup, Mary, that's all it'd take. It in't so dreadful, is it? To drink one cup of gin? To stop my heart from bolting – to stop my veins being stripped out through my fingertips.'

'I must go.'

'Don't leave me,' he whispered. She snatched her hands away and he flinched at the violence.

'I can't keep promises for you,' she said. 'You're not my prisoner. Do as you choose.' She shut the door hard behind her.

All Mary could think of was the bottle in the cupboard. There was still some in it. Not much, but perhaps it would be enough. Enough to stop the feeling of frogs jumping inside her. Enough to make them drowsy, so she could think. She had promised nothing to Anthony. A draught curled round her ankles and she sensed the oppression of someone's gaze. Mrs Seward observed her stonily from outside the kitchen.

'And how does he do, Mary?' she asked. Mary stood up straight and lifted her chin.

'Badly. I think we should ask Dr Tylston to look at him.'

'Dr Tylston is very busy,' said the matron. 'Wells will survive. He just needs a good long sleep, though God knows he does little else at the best of times.'

Mary did not argue. She would ask the doctor herself.

'He has really left off gin, hasn't he?' the matron said quietly, and Mary nodded. Mrs Seward's lips pressed into a tight 'O', a myriad of tiny lines branching through the wispy hairs on her skin. 'For your sake?' A red vein formed a crooked angle in the white of her left eye.

'Yes,' Mary said.

'For ever? Or does he say he will stop for a time and then take it up again?'

'He said two weeks.'

Mrs Seward laughed and pushed her spectacles higher on her nose. They distorted her green eyes.

'Oh, they always say such things,' she said. 'Half the time they don't manage it, and even when they do it proves nothing. Two weeks and an hour, and they are lying insensible on the floor, if not in a ditch.' The matron smiled ruefully and the dimmest hint of sympathy skulked across her face. 'Mary, it's not worth it. Find yourself someone sober and industrious. There are plenty of young men who would work hard and look after you. I promise you, he will never come to any good. I can see why you might find him charming; I've seen the smiles and

looks he gives you. But no number of smiles will ever make up for it.'
Her expression hardened again. 'Nothing will.'

CHAPTER 11

White patches showed through the stubble on Hartingshall's head. He did not see her approach, but hunched as if carrying a sack, and scraped his foot on the walkway. A harsh breeze whipped tresses of hair in front of Mary's eyes. She tucked them back under her hat and they broke free, lashing before her as they had the night of the wreck. She remembered the picket gate, solid and rough in her hand, the clouds rushing over the moon, the storm pushing its fingers through her hair.

Hartingshall scratched the back of his head and inspected his fingernails for the spoils. His face was weary. Weary with pain, weary with grief. The smooth glass phial nestled in Mary's palm.

A couple passed and he spoke to them. Begging? They directed their eyes to the path and hurried on. Indignation made Mary press her lips together. The man acknowledged her. Acceptable enough, was she? Not bereaved and diseased. Hartingshall watched her, his face emotionless.

'I've brought it,' she said, and the silent breeze chilled her cheeks and drained the sound from her words. The gusts carried the scent of infection, dull and cloying. 'I've brought a bandage an' all. I could put it on your arm if it still ails you.' Hartingshall shrugged and took the phial. 'I didn't steal it. Only changed the doctor's note.' He tugged out the stopper and took a sip. 'You're not meant to gulf it away so. You must measure it properly.' Hartingshall only shrugged again. On the bank far below all manner of detritus rested on top of the brambles. Bits of paper, potato peelings, an old bucket, a dead cat. One bottle of physick for a life. It could not be enough. 'Will you speak to him now?'

'P'raps,' he said. 'If I sees him.'

'When's that like to be?'

'Don't know. Ain't been back to Chester since he brought me here. Back in that shite-festering pit of a village, I reckon, duping the country puts out of their gains.'

Country puts! It had been a better living than this miserable Londonish beggar had ever made. Would he have had the guts to row out to Hilbre in the pitch of night, or to ride decoy along dark cliffs?

Amusement joined the dejection in Hartingshall's eyes when she turned on him. 'He doesn't dupe anyone but the Customer,' she said, and Hartingshall chuckled. 'We worked for him and he paid us wages, fair and square.'

'Ah.' A glassy lustre overwashed Hartingshall's eyes. 'You mean he kept the goods in his own house, eh? Took all the risk, like a true gemman?'

Mary frowned. 'No.'

'What? Don't tell me he made you all keep it in your own hovels 'til he felt like sending a flunkey to collect it?'

'It weren't like that. That was just the way the scheme worked.'

'His scheme.'

'Ours too.'

Hartingshall took another lengthy sip of laudanum, the phial delicate in his graceless hand. 'Believe that if you like,' he said.

'D'you want this bandage on or not?'

Hartingshall coaxed his arm out of his jacket. Thin yellow liquid smeared across it, forming a flaky crust. 'Here, watch this.' He pressed his thumb into the inflamed skin and a thicker bead of pus exuded from the cut, retreating like a wary maggot when he let go. He observed her, but she took out her pocket-handkerchief and wiped the wound clean. It was only pus, for God's sake. Did he expect her to faint dead away?

99

'Forgot,' he said. 'Don't do for a murderer's mort to be squeamish.'

Mary clapped the dressing on to the wound and Hartingshall swore. 'He in't a murderer,' she said.

Hartingshall's eyelids drooped and his laugh was slow and unnatural. Mary bandaged his arm and could not help but admire her work. It was neat – every turn overlapping the previous one by half, the ends tied in an even knot. Perhaps she would make a good nurse after all. Hartingshall hauled up phlegm from deep within his lungs and yocked an oyster over the wall.

'Thanks,' he muttered. 'Don't hurt so much now.' His brown irises had darkened to near-black islands in the pinkish hue surrounding them.

'Then you'll ask Bryce to drop the case?'

Hartingshall grinned. 'Oh, "Bryce" is it? Very friendly. Mind you, from what I hear, you've been very friendly with him indeed.'

Betsy Roberts and Liza Mobbett – may the Devil himself take their chitlins for sausage-skins. They had even found a way to get their rumours to Hartingshall. Had they sent a legion of incubi over the whole country to tell everyone and his dog what they thought of her? Mary thumped her fist on the wall and the graze of the sandstone stung.

'When did you meet that pair of witches? They'll say anything against me. They're jealous he's never paid the slightest heed to their wizened old faces, and that's why they want to make me out a whore when I'm not. Whatever they've told you, it in't true. Ask Bryce.' She rubbed her grazed hand. 'Mr Warbreck.'

Hartingshall struggled to get his arm back in his coat. 'Ain't never seen them,' he said. 'Rather, seen them, but never met them.' He smiled distantly and took a languorous breath. 'Not long 'til spring, eh?' Was he mad? The wind made Mary's ears itch. 'You know, if Jones was hanged, you could find yourself a decent husband.' Mary banished the guilty stab from her chest.

'He won't be hanged, if you speak to Bryce.'

'Oh, I don't know,' he said, rubbing his eyes and letting them rest closed for a moment. 'It's an 'ard thing for the justices to let go, once there's promise of a scragging. But still, I'll have a think. Same time a week hence?'

'What?'

Hartingshall patted the pocket where he had put the laudanum. 'Well, this ain't like to last long.' His smirk made her want to throw him over the wall.

'I can't get you any more,' she said. 'Go to a gallipot's shop and steal it for yourself.' Hartingshall pointed down at the brambles. 'Look, there's a dead cat down there,' he said. At first, when Mary followed his gaze, she saw only the cat, the rusty bucket, the rotten peelings. But then her eyes became accustomed to discerning individual things, and it seemed death lay everywhere. Bones, half-obscured by the bramble-wires, protruded from the soil. Shrunken creatures dissolved into the ground, the sheen of their viscera blackening in decay. There was something that looked like a tail, and something else that looked like tiny white fingers, splayed and alone on the lightless bank. Mary looked up hurriedly and Hartingshall laughed. 'Dead, dead, dead. And the Lord have mercy upon its soul, eh? P'raps tomorrow'd be better.'

He held the laudanum up to the light, his hand giving a leisurely wobble, and laughed to himself. Slowly, and watching her closely, he removed the stopper and drained the rest of the liquid. Then he pressed the empty phial into her palm.

'You'll be the dead one if you go on like that,' she said. Hartingshall put his elbows on the wall and bowed his head to his hands, chuckling.

'Off for a kip,' he said. 'In my palatial habitation. I shall see you tomorrow, shan't I?' He felt his way along the wall, staggering.

'You've took too much,' she said, catching up with him. 'It'll do you a mischief.'

'I'm used to it. Don't do a mischief, this. Not like gin. Makes your heart grow. Like bread with too much yeast in. Makes you know what to say. Makes you see things how you would see them – how you should see them, if it weren't for life.'

'You can hardly stand.' Mary took his arm. 'Where are you living?'

'Watergate Street,' he said. 'Beg off people. Say I was shipwrecked.'

He tried to laugh, but the look in his eyes matched the bleakness of the sky. 'Don't hurt now. Off for a kip. Bring more tomorrow.'

'No. Sunday,' Mary said. He rolled his eyes, and held his bad arm as he strolled down the walkway. He balanced himself with broad steps as though he crossed the deck of a boat.

Mangham rested on his broom handle, and his eyes narrowed at the rush of light from the gaol door.

'I know you, don't I?' he said, scratching his neck with long, yellowing fingernails. 'Ah. 'Course. Mrs Jones.' The turnkey glanced towards the gaoler's room and showed his palm. Mary handed him tuppence and he led her up the dank stairway. She had no vinegar-soaked rag this time. She felt for her handkerchief, but her fingers touched the pus and she resolved instead to breathe through her mouth.

Selwyn's companions let out a ragged murmur of approval that echoed down the room, and hands stretched through the grille.

'Brought me owt?' Selwyn said.

'No. I didn't know if I'd have the chance to come here.'

'Then why'd you bother?'

Shadows mottled his face; his beard was thicker now, and filthy, and his eyes were sunken, as if a thumb had tamped them into his head. His broken tooth formed a sharp triangle behind the cracked, pale lines of his lips.

'I do wonder,' she said, and paused. 'I came because it's my duty to get you freed. Because I've seen Hartingshall and bethought me you might have a mind to know what he said. But I'll leave, if my lack of food makes me unwelcome.'

Selwyn hauled himself up, his chains bashing the grille. 'Don't start,' he said, his teeth clenched. 'What's he say?'

'Was his brother. The man you killed.'

Selwyn nodded, keeping resignation one step before panic. 'What does he want?'

'To see you hanged.' Selwyn's knuckles paled on the bars. 'But there might be a chance. He said if I got him physick from the infirmary he'd speak to Bryce.' She lowered the lantern from her reddening face.

'Get it, then, for God's sake!'

'I did, and he went back-bargains on it. I'm to get more. Happen next time he'll do it.'

Selwyn's eyes changed. Hope darted about their corners. 'You're a good wife to me.'

Mary shifted uncomfortably when he took her hand. The stink of excrement drifted up from the floor, scalding her throat and making her eyes smart. 'You never used to think that.' She struggled not to retch at his breath.

'Aye, well. When I get out we'll forget all this. Go somewhere new. Forget all that's happened before. Forget Warbreck.' He touched her cheek; she recoiled, and the gentleness deserted him. 'Don't smay from me, Mary. You're my wife and you never would have been his, dream all you like.'

Mary smeared the grime from her face. 'We could stay in Chester. I could keep working at the infirmary—'

'I'll not live apart from my own wife.' His expression blackened – the familiar cowardly anger that made her roll her eyes, the way she always used to. 'We'll go to London.' Decisiveness hung oddly about him. 'You mun save up your addlins ready.' The harshness in his face softened and he gave a grim smile. 'It'll be a new life. A new chance. We might have a child.' His words struck Mary so hard she wanted to run. Wanted to flee a thousand miles, wanted to jump in a river, wanted to drink a gallon of gin. What stupidity, what cruelty, did gaol put into a man?

'You know that can't happen,' she said. 'It's been two years. It would have happened—'

'It's still possible.'

Everything stifled her: the stench, the dark, the hurt, until she could scarce breathe. Silently she handed him sixpence, and looked down the room for Mangham.

Lantern-flickers illuminated faces – the bony, the rough, the sad, the impassive. And bowed heads, grimy arms half-covered by ragged sleeves, teeth interrupted by gaps and framed by sores. Eyes shrinking back into skulls covered with tight skin, hair twined into ropes of grease. Flints chinked and sparks leapt into the thick air, and then a thread of yellow flame joined the rays of the lamp. Two faces looked up from behind it, their eyes cold under lowered eyebrows. It had never occurred to her she would see women here. One of them nudged the other.

'Miss Princums there's waiting for you to do a trick.' Laughter followed Mary through the gate. She ran her fingers over the shape of the phial under the layers of petticoat and pocket.

'What are those women here for?'

'Theft, I 'spect,' said Mangham. A coating of damp descended on Mary's face. She kept an anxious silence until he halted at the top of the cellar steps.

'Any gin this time?' he asked.

'No. The man I work with – he's given it up.'

Mangham laughed, the scrawny skin under his chin flapping like a turkey's dewlap. 'Still be here when he wants it.'

He grinned as he opened the door to Northgate Street. Brightness dashed in, but the light dispersed and neutralised to grey, and revealed the patina of algae on the walls and the wisps of Mangham's breath condensing and falling. He stepped out with her and took a lengthy taste of the air.

'I 'spect you don't mind a drop either, do you?' He gulped the breeze, closing his eyes.

'What? Why do you say that?'

'Well. Working in an 'ospital. Liverpool infirmary's nurses always had more gin in them than blood, from what I remember, so I can't see it being any different here.'

Mary looked up at his rabbit-mouth and quizzical eyes. Scratchy grey hairs pierced through the wrinkled skin on his neck. He was grubby, in the light. 'How do you know I work at the infirmary?'

Mangham grinned. 'My wife had green eyes just like yours. I used to say they were like a cat's. So was she – bone idle and apt to lash out. Dead now, o' course – that's why I came here.'

'I'm sorry,' said Mary. 'But how do you know where I work?'

'Don't stay in there all the time. Not like that filthy lot. Saw you yesterday, breaking up a fight. That gangly lad – he the one who's left off gin?' He regarded her with sly amusement. 'Not a bad-lookin' feller, eh?'

Her face flamed. 'I s'pose not.'

Mangham laughed. 'Well, as I say, Mother Gin's here when he's ready for her.' He squinted as he pulled the gaol door shut behind him.

Mrs Seward's face formed a solid mould of repressed fury. Mrs Stout had gone home; Mary lacked any support. The matron motioned at her to sit down. She took off her hat and placed it, without urgency, on the kitchen table.

'I've a mind to stand,' she said, and the matron's nostrils flared.

Fresh bread sat cooling on the sideboard, its warm scent out of keeping with Mrs Seward's glare. Coals collapsed in the grate, sending cinders up the chimney. Their heat made Mary catch wafts of the stench of the gaol.

'I have given you a chance, Mary,' the matron said, her turned-down mouth as jowly as a dog's. 'I have tolerated levels of hysteria that no mistress ought to be obliged to accept of a servant, but I cannot countenance liberties of time. Even Wells would have delivered those messages within the space of half an hour. Look at the state of you!' Mary looked down at her topcoat, its hem smeared with dirt, and at her muddy boots, and at her hands, begrimed by Selwyn's. 'You've clearly been gadding about at the Lord only knows what, and I am not prepared to accept it.'

Mary lifted her chin. Not prepared? Well, the matron was quite prepared to let Mary stop yesterday's fight, prepared to let her see off a man the size of a cart-ox, prepared to let her take charge of Anthony.

And what had Mrs Seward done? Screamed, that was what, and shouted at people who knew they needn't listen.

'Well, then,' Mary said, staring straight at Mrs Seward's bespectacled eyes. 'You had like to tell Mr Barnston all about me. If he sees fit to turn me out on the street, then I will go.'

The matron's downy cheeks coloured. Mary held her gaze until it turned away to the dying fire. 'Mr Barnston . . .' Mrs Seward's haughtiness faltered. 'Mr Barnston insisted on employing you against my judgement and I know not why. What is it? If it were any of the other gentlemen – any of them – I would think you must have been a servant to him, and fallen foul of the peculiar enthusiasms to which some men of his station are so inclined. But not Mr Barnston.'

'I've been a servant to no one. Mr Barnston has been kind to me, that's all, and if he bids me leave, I won't disobey him.' Mary snatched up her hat.

Up in her room, its wide brim sank slowly to the bed through a feeble streak of sunlight and the air puffed out from under it. Across the corridor Agnes sang a mournful song of ghost-loves and given hearts, her tune pure and melodious in the echo of the empty ward.

Thurstaston, Night, 27 December 1755

Stairs. Up and down, they lead sometimes to rooms and sometimes to more stairs. Rooms with children's toys strewn across the floor; an ark with spilled animals untouched on stone tiles. More stairs, narrowing. Doors get smaller, harder to open, resisting. Bare floorboards in a room with rafters, a cradle with something in it she dares not look at. Narrower still, the walls close in; the ceiling lowers to meet the steps. Something behind her. The space tiny now. Walls press in from every side. A roar like that of the sea. An opening at the end of the space beckons her to push through, taunting her to find out if it will close round her mouth. Something reaches out and scrapes at her ankles. A vision of a tiny, bloated hand.

Feet land in puddles; a fist hammers on the door. Mary gasps aloud, waking herself, and puts her hand to her mouth, staring at the bed-canopy. Selwyn props himself up on his elbow.

'Wreck!' The splash of feet moves away, and the picket-gate bashes into its latch. More shouts ring into the night. Selwyn is up and pulling on his breeches; Mary lies there, heavy-eyed, unsure whether or not she is awake.

'What is it?' she mumbles, and the words are slurred.

'Get up,' he says. 'There's a wreck.'

'But the ark is on the floor.' That's not right; it's not what she thought she was saying, but the blankets are so warm. She gasps again when Selwyn grabs her shoulders and wrenches her from the bed.

'What are you on about now?' His voice is in the room, somewhere, but she's not sure it comes from him. 'Get up and help me.'

107

Blearily, she pulls a petticoat over her shift. Then he's tugging hard at the strings of her stays – so hard that she swears, and her hand meets the bed-post.

If only he would undo them, sometimes, like that.

'We'll take the cart.' He reaches down the hatchet he keeps above the door. Rain smatters Mary's face. She is awake now, just about, and yet the notion of the path, the gate, the stable, the surprised snort of the pony, the feel of the familiar harness-buckles, are all somewhere else, because there is no light to make them real.

Jakey chucks his head up, wary to back into the shafts while the wind lashes under his tail. Selwyn's teeth are gritted in the orange light of the lantern. There's a dark shadow across his jaw, and he lifts his fist.

'Don't you hit him!' The scream catches away from her, and her husband's hand closes around her raised wrist.

'Get him in the bloody traces, then.' For all his anger his shout whips harmlessly away on the suddenness of the air. In the end Jakey submits, and they lead him the half mile to the cliff-top.

They need not have rushed.

Lanterns strike triangles of light over the sand. People stand about, their cheeks casting shadows into their eye-sockets. Nothing has come ashore yet.

Seagulls cry on the gusts. The thought darts across the back of Mary's head that there should be no seagulls – not at this time of night. The cries are distant and human. Selwyn has disappeared, so she stands in the dark, outside the circle that surrounds the lanterns. Backs form a phalanx against her. She walks a short distance away and hugs her arms beneath her cape. Laughter rises behind her. Turning, she sees smirking eyes.

Many weeks have passed since she has talked to another woman. It's always Selwyn whose ears meet, and block out, the ordinary utterances she makes.

Not thoroughly true; she spoke to a woman less than a week ago – Liza Mobbett – to tell her she or her family would suffer a horrible disease if she didn't stop her canting.

Liza stands there on the shore, along with Betsy Roberts and that prim cow Susan Merry and old Mrs Wickes, and the rest.

It was two and a half years ago – two and a half years, for heaven's sake! – that she came home in Bryce Warbreck's carriage, after he'd kissed her. And every one of them had been spitting bile in envy and feasting on the rumour that he'd given her more than a kiss and, God, had they been disappointed when no child came along.

Not that it would have done, anyway.

Where the hell is Selwyn, leaving her alone like this?

Out of the reach of the lantern-light she stands in the dark, her breath catching in the battering air, and there's a curious sense of belonging, as if the night is hers. Not really – it's more that she's the night's – like last night, when it had rushed through her and she would have gone with it, if it had asked.

They never do ask, though, nights or men.

CHAPTER 12

Mr Crane had guts of iron. The laudanum phial, filled with gin, lay in Mary's pocket for two days, and not once did the apothecary leave his shop in order to visit the privy. At half past eleven each day he locked both halves of the door and left for the Golden Talbot, whence he returned at a quarter to one smelling of gravy and woodsmoke, ready for an afternoon of mixing, chopping and coughing behind his partition of shelves. The chance did not come until Saturday.

The click of the latch in the lower door reached Mary through the scratch of her scrubbing brush on the step. Mr Crane walked towards her, his pall-bearer's expression unchanged by the light reflecting from the snow-burdened clouds behind the Northgate. Mary flicked the water from her fingers and dried them on her apron, their skin smarting with cold. The north wind eddied round the courtyard, doubling back on itself and icing her neck. Blood stuttered back into her hands and they burned red. Mr Crane trampled the clean step, crossed the cobbles and disappeared under the arch to the back of the building. Her knees throbbed as she rose.

Mrs Stout sang to herself in the kitchen, Agnes's broom clunked the floorboards overhead, and Mrs Seward had been in her parlour all morning, sewing sheets.

The catch on the door loosened easily. Papery fragments of dried herb-petals strewed the floor, crisp under Mary's feet. She flitted in and stretched on tiptoes to exchange the old phial for a new. She was back at the step before Mr Crane crossed it again. He trailed wet footprints down the corridor, and if he noticed the way her hands shook on the brush, perhaps he thought she was shivering at the first gobbets of snow that flopped on to the cobbles.

Anthony's face wore a pallor as blank as the clouds. Exhausted, with tremors still agitating his hands, he crawled back into bed after the chapel service on Sunday and took a swig of the physick Dr Tylston had prescribed.

'I've an errand to run,' Mary said. She straightened the blankets around him and smoothed his wild hair. 'I won't be long, but if you want owt you must call Mrs Seward.'

'I'd be as like to call the Devil himself,' he said. He was already asleep when she kissed his forehead and crept out of the room.

Drab blobs of snow dissolved on the paved promenade of the city wall as Mary hurried to her appointed meeting with William Hartingshall. Her eyes watered in the snatches of wind that struck the unsheltered walkway east of the Northgate. Thank God she would get rid of the phial today. It had sat in her pocket in the cupboard all night, while she lay awake picturing the hour when Mr Crane discovered the switch, and it had lain against her leg all through chapel, less than a foot away from Mrs Seward. She would not do this again. Needs must: she would save her two shillings a week and let Hartingshall buy medicine with that.

Annoyance – that he was not there – made her sigh. Crystal-speckles settled on her cloak and she turned her back to the flow of air from the north. The cold left her cheeks raw and her lips sore, and when she wriggled her toes in her boots she could scarce feel them.

Above half an hour she stood there, shivering and looking along the walls, lowering her gaze to the stones each time a man walked by and tried to catch her eye. Well, this stuff must not be so important to Hartingshall after all. The blue glass phial sat, pretty and innocent, in her palm. She was damned if she was going to take it back to the infirmary now. If Hartingshall didn't want it she would find someone who did, and make a few pence while she was about it.

She stood there for so long that some of the men passed a second time, having made a circuit of the walls. She moved further down the walkway. Smells of pomade and musky cologne circled in the air. Gazes bored into her neck; she imagined spirals of sawdust falling out as from a worm-raddled beam. Hands dipped into pockets, lips curled into leers, a shilling flashed in a sweaty palm.

Is it true? Is it true, sweeting, what they say about nurses?

She went back towards the Northgate, keeping the brim of her hat tipped forward over her face.

Down at the foot of the wall, the dead cat still lay atop the brambles. Guts protruded from its belly.

Then the thought stabbed her. William Hartingshall: *dead.*

Dead of cold, dead of pain, dead of grief for his murdered brother. Dead from downing a whole ounce of laudanum, or from toppling over the wall in a daze. Pity moved her, and when she descended the Northgate steps she turned not towards the stinking passageway but south, in the direction of Watergate Street.

The flakes of snow became bigger, falling in powdery silence into the hoof-hollows outside the Pied Bull, gathering on the jutting cheeks of the cathedral's gargoyles, making people huddle under the arches of the Exchange. Relentless white processions slid down in front of her, made distant and theatre-like by the sheltering brim of her hat. At the Cross dirty cobbles showed through the layer of white, and the freshness muted the scent of slops and rotting food from the gutter-channels.

'D'you know someone named William Hartingshall?' she asked a benign-faced old man who hunched under Fleshmongers' Row. He smiled and said no, so she described him. Well, no one could forget a big, strolling, stubble-headed, itch-infested cull with a bad arm, could they?

'Ah, I've seid 'im,' said the man. 'Couldn't say where he lives though. Ax Dog-Breath Annie.' He motioned along the snow-obscured street.

'Sounds like the sort despert enough to get vittles off her. Believe me, m'dear, you have to be.'

A smile was all the payment she could make, but he seemed happy enough with that.

Dog-Breath Annie's, more properly known as Anne Abbiss, Victualler, crouched under a chandler's shop on the south side of Watergate Street, offering hot bread and meat to those too poor to afford fuel. The queue at the top of its steps was as uninviting as the aroma of putrid flesh that wheeled through the snow and saturated the flakes, till it seemed drips of lard plummeted from the sky. People blinked like moles from the stairway, clutching nameless cuts of gristle wrapped in pages of *Adams's Weekly Courant*. Hunched-up dogs cringed around their feet, putting on their best faces. Mary joined the end of the queue, feigned a glower and kept her eyes down.

Dog-Breath Annie was a big, blonde, double-chinned woman with a wart as big as an acorn on her left cheek, and she wore a short-sleeved shift in spite of the snow because her shop boiled as hot as the deepest pit of hell. A vast fireplace spewed out fragments of scraggy meat, black without and pink within, to the populace of Lower Watergate Street. Mary's shivering turned to sweating as the queue progressed down the steps. Nothing illuminated the cellar but the fire and the grey light from the entrance. The man in front of her picked his nose and wiped it on the wall. Then he did it again. Glutinous green beads punctuated the brickwork. Mary looked back, and the street seemed miles away. Below, in a room no bigger than her own cellar at home, grubby pennies chinked into the hands of thick-armed girls, who scowled from behind greasy curtains of hair. Steam and heat moistened Mary's eyelashes.

'I've no money to buy owt.' She had to shout over the hubbub at the front of the queue. Dog-Breath Annie looked down at her with disdain, her lips shrinking back over brown snaggled pegs. 'But a man out there said you might know where I can find William Hartingshall.' Annie wiped the sweat from her brow and returned her fists to her hips. 'Great hulking fellow, 'flicted with the scrat. Has a game arm.'

'Ah. The sailor?' said Dog-Breath Annie. 'Warbreck's warehouse, round the back. Go up in the Row over-way, and down a gennell. Door in a white wall.' She blew out with the heat. Mary recoiled.

Warbreck's warehouse. The movement of the white flakes put her in a dream. Bereft of carriages in the worsening weather, the street had given itself up to silence. Whiffs of fat lingered around the cellar entrance, and the people in the queue hucked into their ragged clothes and looked dejectedly at the tides of moisture soaking up into their shoes.

Warbreck's warehouse. Mary made herself still, like a brim-full gin cup set to spill at the faintest nudge. Someone had said his name. Ordinary people knew it – people like Dog-Breath Annie. Jealousy twinged her heart at the thought of a stranger's lips forming the word.

Mary hugged her arms and watched the last dark lumps of ground drown under the whiteness. She could not even remember what Dog-Breath Annie had said.

'Mind there!' A carriage came up behind her and she stepped aside in a daze. Grumpy horses passed her, the hair on their necks curled by the wet, and fine wheel-spokes jolted over the snow. A white wall, she remembered. An alleyway.

The Row was deserted, its beams and boards ugly and filthy after the purity of the white-coated street. Sawdust oppressed the air, its prickly scent rising from the walkway, where wet feet had left it gathered in clumps. Here was the house where a man had ogled her and, next to it, the whitewashed warehouse. Trust Bryce to have it smart, even in a place like this.

Round the back, Dog-Breath Annie had said. A narrow alley led between the buildings, one wall white, the other stained and crumbling. A distant rectangle of brightness showed nothing but the descent of snow. Mary fiddled with a thread on her cloak.

Bryce Warbreck's place. He had been here. Behind the padlocked doors must be the Manx beer, the soap, the silks – the rosemary-flower blue. If he would only be here now. She stepped into the alleyway and all her courage crumbled. She gaped at the curtain of falling flakes, imagined the light disappearing and the end of the alley shrinking together like a closing mouth, and could not go on.

'Excuse me, my dear.' Sharp fingers dug into Mary's elbow so hard that she swallowed a scream. 'Oh, I never meant to frighten you, dear.' The feeble voice was not unkind, but Mary tugged her arm away and her accoster staggered. And then she felt like a lummocking bully – a looming giant – because the woman who stood before her was the smallest person she had ever seen.

Wisps of powder issued from the woman's claggy hair like puffs of cold breath, and her eyes narrowed to a short-sighted peer. Her tiny, gnarled hands ended in nails as delicate and slender as a squirrel's claws.

'Wouldst help me read a receipt for jam, dear?' Her accent had a foreign turn to it, like Hartingshall's, but held a trace of friendliness too, and she gave a genial smile. 'Mine eyes are so weak these days, and my family are all gone out to church.' A sticky mixture of gin and perfume hung about her, blending with the sawdust and the fresh smell of snow. 'My kitchen is but the other side of this wall, and if you come back when it's set you shall have a pot for your kindness.'

'Jam?' Mary inched back and the woman glanced behind her. Wrinkles cracked through her heavy maquillage and the red paint on her lips had bled to the edges, leaving the centres pale. Mary looked over the cloud of hair to the window of the house.

'You might ask that man to read it,' she said. Thick-set and expressionless, the man left the window and disappeared into the gloom beyond.

'Ah, well,' said the woman, 'poor dear Ned ain't good with words.' The slender fingers closed around Mary's arm. The sturdy man appeared in the alley opening.

'What d'you make jam from in February?' Mary asked, her voice rising. 'Cabbages? Or d'you fly on a besom to fetch strawberries from the Devil?'

The woman's beaky nose flared. 'I beg your pardon!' Phlegm rattled in her throat. 'That ain't no way to answer an old person needing help.

You want to learn yourself some manners, girl!' Now her eyes were open and clear. Hard as jewels, and as cold. She wheeled round and jerked her head at the man. Mary lashed at the hand on her arm and dragged her nails down the papery skin.

'Ow! You little—' The grasp sprang loose and the thin lips curled back like a dog's. 'Still.' The woman lunged forward again. 'Some of my gemmen have a yen for a challenge. Ned, where—'

Mary ran, the sound of her feet echoing from floor to ceiling to wall. Then, icy air rushed under her cloak. Snow swirled on to her cheeks and fell on every side of her, shrouding all ways forward. The alleyway magnified the voices behind her.

'Shift yerself quicker, you fat turd.'

'Ah, forget it, Sarey. Can't say I'm arsed to go running after them in this weather. Wait 'til she comes back.'

Mary took a few steps more across the snow and halted. Around her, buildings stretched up, their roofs invisible behind the floating flakes. Not homes, but more warehouses, with doors shut and mute. Piles of tar-lagged barrels gathered a coat of white. Silent and enclosing, the courtyard felt no bigger than the infirmary's empty ward. Mary breathed hard, cold air shocking into her lungs. Cobwebbed windows with cracked panes blanked her. The warehouses seemed to draw closer, the silence to become more menacing, the alley to gape, jaw-like, behind her.

For a moment she covered her face with her hands and let tears scald her numb fingers. Think. It would be better to think. She pressed her palm to her stays and breathed out, faking calmness.

That spiky, spindly bitch she could fight off with no trouble, but Ned would take more than fingernails and anger. She snatched up a stick from beside the barrels. Rotten and light, it crumbled, leaving fragments of wet wood on her palm. She smelled decay, and the musty urine of rats, and the slime of standing water.

No one stood in the alley. But they would wait, behind the square dusty panes of that window, watching. She nibbled pieces of skin from her lips. All heat had deserted her; even the sweat of fear under her stays had gone cold, and her petticoats flapped, crunchy with hems of ice, against her legs.

A cough barked from behind the door at the back of Bryce Warbreck's warehouse. Relief melted through her like a hit of gin. Hartingshall. No one would hurt her with him around. The thump of her fist rang through the silence and a single swear word made the relief spread.

'Who is it?'

'Mary Helsall,' she said. 'Mary Jones.'

The sense of shelter proved fleeting. Snowflakes hurried past her feet and shrank on the floorboards, but the gust of fresh air made no dent in the stench of stale bedding and an unemptied pot. Hartingshall lay on a mattress, his arm trailing out across the floor.

'How'd you know where I was?' His head hung back against the floor, his eyes dull. 'What day is it?' Mary knelt beside him and fumbled at the phial stopper. He shook his head. 'No more. Made me think I was dead. Thirsty.' He pointed at an old desk pushed to the side of the room. Behind it was another door, secured with a padlock, and on it were a cup and a plate smeared with grease and a speckling of soot. Mary swished snow until it melted, and held the cup to Hartingshall's lips.

'Let me take this bandage off,' she said. She undid the tie and peeled the linen away, and Hartingshall put his hand over his eyes.

Watery ooze covered his arm. The wound was bigger, its edges livid and irregular, as if they had been nibbled by a mouse. The chill from the open door whipped up the odour and thickened the air.

Confusion and panic evaporated. Mary flooded the wound with snow water, talking all the time about the infirmary beds and how there would be a fire and warm blankets, and a pound of meat every day. The water dripped down his skin, putting the hairs on his arm into line.

'Does Bryce know you're here?' she asked. He looked at her with bloodshot eyes.

''Course. It's his place.'

'I know,' Mary said. Hartingshall propped himself up on his good elbow, with a woozy sigh. 'He didn't see fit to pay for you to stay in an inn, then?'

'Not from the wreck 'til arter the trial.'

Mary's hands paused, her wet handkerchief poised over Hartingshall's arm.

Dog-Breath Annie: 'The sailor?'

The ice at her fingers spread slowly up her arms and sank to her stomach. 'The wreck?' Shivering now as she had shivered then, she tried to remember. Darkness, screams, faces in the lamplight, familiar and full of hatred. Blood draining away into the sand. Hartingshall shivered too, and pulled his stiff brown blanket closer over him. 'Thought the thug was chopping driftwood, first off. Then I saw a girl covering her face with her hands, and I knew.'

The snow had slowed and the light dimmed in the deserted warehouse yard. Everything glowed blue. The tops of the buildings loomed far above, black against a half-lit sky. Mary's fingers and toes burned. Drips of melting snow fell from the gutters, a tiny echo surrounding each one. Should she be angry? Should she have screamed at Hartingshall and demanded to know why he hadn't told her? Why had he let her lie to him? Why had he let her think she had a chance? Perhaps she could still persuade him. Everyone had compassion somewhere, didn't they? Even if they knew the truth.

He told her about the narrow door in the gates on the other side of the yard. There – he cared enough not to make her go back past that old bawd's house. She slipped through and made her way back to familiar places, the snow crunching under her feet.

She could pass the cathedral and keep walking down Northgate Street. She could get back to the infirmary, peel the snow-soaked stockings from her legs and doze in front of the kitchen fire, and let Hartingshall rot. Let him be discovered by the weasel-faced bawd when the stench started to drive off her cullies. Giving evidence would be tricky for him, dead.

But when she hurried under the arch by the cathedral into the genteel, modern calmness of Abbey Court it was because – whatever he had seen – she wanted him to live.

CHAPTER 13

'For the love of God, John, why can you not take patients with money?'

Dr Tylston shut the dining room door on the purposeful chinking of cutlery. High sconces lit the entrance hall of the doctor's house, the flames reflecting in a looking glass bigger than any Mary had ever seen. Water dripped from her hem on to the polished floor.

'She sees medicine as a business, not a calling,' said Dr Tylston as they retrod Mary's footprints across Abbey Court. Scaffold-poles, stacks of bricks and piles of sand lay capped with snow around the unfinished buildings nearby. 'You'd have thought this house would have quietened her, eh?' His lanternlight wobbled over the glittering ground. Cold weighed heavy on Northgate Street. Under the arches of the Exchange the lantern made blue-lipped beggars blink. Dr Tylston fumbled in the pocket of his greatcoat and held the light down, but he could not conceal the soft scrape of coins.

Rats scuffled from the warehouse yard gates, and shadows took refuge at the feet of the buildings and behind the barrels, and in the alley that led to Watergate Row.

'Were you here alone?' Dr Tylston looked over his spectacles, which were clouded with cold.

'Yes, sir,' Mary said. 'A woman knew me from the infirmary and said there was a man desperate bad.'

The ends of Dr Tylston's wig brushed the topmost of the capes on the shoulders of his coat as he shook his head. 'Now, don't you be going off with folk on account of their every sorry tale about a sick person,' he said. 'If it happens again, you must send for me or one of the other physicians, d'you hear?'

'Yes, sir.'

'I know some lasses these days like to put on bravery, but don't you go a-dangering yourself, now. I'm sure you went about the dark lanes without a thought at home, but this isn't the country. People have different ideas, here – some of them not so savoury.'

The dim light caught the glassy sheen of Hartingshall's eyes. 'No bloody doctor,' he mumbled. 'It don't hurt so bad now.' Dr Tylston did not baulk at the smell of damp and infection. He hummed to himself while he searched in his bag.

'The best medicine of all,' he said, and handed Hartingshall a penny-loaf wrapped in newspaper. 'You'll need a bandage on that arm of yours, Mr Hartingshall, or it'll suffer agitation from the poisons in the air. You had one, I see.' He indicated the dirty linen strip that snaked across the floor. Hartingshall sniffed and drifted a vague look towards Mary. The phial of laudanum lay on the floor beside him. Crumbs puffled down his front.

'She took it off.'

'Aye, well, then, she can put on another.' Dr Tylston smiled. 'I warrant women work neater, though you won't catch the surgeons crediting it.' Mary nudged the laudanum under Hartingshall's mattress. 'At least the itch is clearing, eh? Good old flowers of sulphur – always does the trick.'

Only just above the plane of sleep, Hartingshall nodded at Dr Tylston's instructions on how to take the medicine he would leave. The physician turned to Mary.

'Well, well. Perhaps we shall arrange with Mrs Seward for you to attend this fellow every day and help him with the dose.'

'Oh . . .' The cracked window showed nothing but darkness. She had no memory, now, of what Ned looked like. Only remembered his lumbering shape at the end of the alleyway, his head stuck straight on to his body without a neck in between.

'You mustn't come on your own, of course,' said the doctor. 'Anthony Wells – is he up and about yet?'

'Recovering inchmeal, sir. He came to chapel today, though he was right tired, after.'

'Well, I suggest he accompanies you while you care for our friend here.' Dr Tylston gave Hartingshall a genial tap on his raised knee and he started awake. 'You're a lucky man to have a good lass like this willing to look after you.' The doctor placed the packet of medicine on the desk and put next to it a blue glass phial. 'Laudanum for the pain,' he said. 'No more than twenty drops at a time, though, d'you hear?'

Hartingshall caught Mary's gaze, and he nodded wearily.

The covering of snow lent Northgate Street a still and muted light. Dr Tylston's lantern had gone out and Hartingshall lay in the dark. Mary listened to the crunch of the doctor's feet and the whisper of her own breath hitting the crisp air.

'How do you like working at the infirmary?' Dr Tylston asked; but he sounded subdued and preoccupied, his cheeriness artificial.

'It's not what I expected, sir. I didn't realise how little some folk'd think of nurses.' A howl echoed through the Northgate passageway, its strains prolonged and eerie. The doctor engaged a link-boy to light them through, and the lad's torch flickered on the face of a madman who licked the moisture from the stones, his chin dripping with green slime. His soiled breeches made the passageway stink as though someone had been at shite in a stagnant pond.

'Poor creature,' said the doctor. The gate of the Blue Coat School whined and an answering wail came from the passageway. 'I hope one day to raise a subscription for an asylum. I've enough of a job for the time being trying to persuade the Board to admit . . .' He paused. 'Ah, perhaps I speak too freely. I mean, to admit certain patients. Venereal patients. I see a great many of them – I suppose I'm getting a reputation for discretion in such matters. I don't deny their immorality but I seem the only daft fellow who doesn't think they deserve to suffer for it.'

'I 'spect the women can't help it, if their husbands give it them.'

'No, I warrant that's very true.' Dr Tylston cleared his throat. 'Mary, is that poor wretch Hartingshall a friend of yours?'

'No, sir. I've only ever seen him when he came to the infirmary with the scrat. He's naught to me, else.'

'I suggest we ask a surgeon to go with you and take a look at his arm. It'll need a poultice or some such. I think, for now, the poisons are confined to the wound, but . . .' The doctor tailed off, and the silence was only broken by a distant filthy curse from the madman.

The shelter of the north wing's porch made Mary even more aware of the sag of her wet petticoats against her legs. 'May I ask . . .' Smears of light daubed the darkness behind her companion, so faint as to be scarce more than fadings of the black. Rushlights in the Northgate. 'May I ask, sir, for it not to be Mr Racketta?'

'Oh, no – not him,' said the physician. 'Much as he might have a talent for swift cuts and neat sutures, I'd not let him spend a moment alone with you or any other girl.' Dr Tylston coughed awkwardly again. 'Well, I feel a mite sorry for the poor fellow, but still. I shall ask Mr Cotgreave.'

Mrs Seward's eyes displayed a tragedy of disappointment when Dr Tylston entered the infirmary ahead of Mary. She smiled blue murder at every aspect of the doctor's plan for Mary to care for Hartingshall. She listened, with her lips pursed, for the clang of the gate before she let out a tirade about the damage to the infirmary's reputation if its nurses were always trallocking about the streets after dark.

Mary thought only of Hartingshall, alone and cold in the warehouse room. Did Mrs Seward prefer that he should die? She folded her arms and concentrated on the matron's pinched-up face, and it reminded her of an unbought chicken left a week on a poulterer's stall.

By eight o'clock the next morning runny footprints pathered the tiles, and the open doors sucked in air saturated with the vapour of melting snow. Shouts echoed in the corridor. Lengths of timber made dents in the store-room door each time the carpenters manoeuvred them on to the staircase.

Mary took a crust of bread to their dejected horse, and the walk over the courtyard spattered another pair of stockings, her old quilted petticoat getting daggled at the hem.

Fore-Northgate Street lay buried under dirt-rippled slush. Drips fell from every corner of the Blue Coat School and a haze involved the ramparts of the gaol.

She and Agnes kept to the warmth of the kitchen, where Mary's clothes were still drying from the day before. The smell of damp wool undermined the aroma of Mrs Stout's bread.

Mary allowed herself a smile at the cosiness of the room. Hemming nightgowns was no hardship; she could almost sleep while she did it, if it were not for Mrs Stout chattering about her son.

'Just-a-meet your age now,' she said. 'But I wouldn't let him visit here – not with you two around, eh?' Agnes tutted at the sharp nudge to her shoulder.

'I swear he's safe from me, if he's as much of a two-faced lump of rat-shit as all the other men in the world.'

Mrs Stout's blubber wobbled. 'Oh, give it a week or so. Some other lad'll come along and you'll be thanking every star Anthony's jilted you.'

Furious tugs snarled the thread and Agnes sniffed. She worsened the knot with a series of needle-stabs. 'I see this trull of his – this supposed love of his life – hasn't been to see him while he's been ill. Too busy, I expect. Can't find the time even to think about him, what with all the other men to be stolen. Bitch.' The thread snapped and Agnes swore.

Mary studied her own neat stitches. 'They can't be stolen if they don't want to be.'

'Well, well,' Mrs Stout flung her a sharp look. 'Mayhappen you should take the carpenters some ale, and tell them there'll be dinner for them in the board room at half past eleven. I 'spect that surgeon feller'll dine at the Golden Talbot.'

'What surgeon?'

'You know. Old Mundungus.' The cook tapped Mary's arm. 'He were axing after you this morn. Now he's after telling the carpenters what to do.' A purposeful shudder wobbled Mrs Stout's chest.

The rasp of saws filled the ward. Fluffy spiral shavings carpeted the floorboards. Mr Racketta inspected a finished piece of wood and one of the men shot him a weary look. 'Thank God, the beer's here,' the man said. Mr Racketta turned and his lips spread like a slug.

'Ah, it's our little Mary,' he said. 'I thought you were hiding from me, my dear.'

The sawing stopped and the carpenters and labourers crowded round for their ale.

'I were.'

'Wish we could,' said one of the men. ''As he ever towd ye? He can saw off a leg in four minutes dead. We've heared that an' better heared it this morning.'

The surgeon winked at Mary. She closed the ward door behind her to afford a few seconds, retrieved the key from the inside of her bedroom lock and secured it. The thought of him fingering her last pair of stockings – the good ones – made her feel queasy. She grimaced at the creak of his feet on the floorboards.

'So this is your bedroom, hmm?'

Mary slid the key deep into her pocket. 'No, it's Mrs Seward's.'

Fusty air stuttered from the surgeon's mouth when he laughed. 'Mrs Seward has her parlour over there,' he said, pointing his thumb down the landing. 'This is yours, isn't it? Right handy for the ward, eh? That is, should some one or other of the patients want you in the night.' The greasy odour of pomade competed with the tobacco. 'You and the other girl share a bed, hmm?'

'There's nowt odd in that.'

'Do the pair of you press together for warmth?' Saliva glistened at the corners of his mouth.

'We've a fair power of blankets, thank you.'

The surgeon leant his shirt-sleeved elbow against the wall. Yellow tidemarks encircled his armpit, like cat-piss on a bed. 'Would you not rather share it with a man?'

Mary ducked away. 'No.' She got as far as the stairs before Mr Racketta's hands slid round her shoulders. The stale warmth of his breath fell on her ear.

'Mary, my dear, I've no patience for wheedlery and colloglement. Lie with me, and I'll give you a shilling.' A trace of amusement edged his voice. Mary struggled her shoulders free.

'Stick your damned shilling up your backside and enjoy it.'

There were a few seconds of silence, and then his laughter followed her down the stairs.

'Oh, keep still! You're making the place untidy.' Mrs Seward huffed past and slammed the kitchen door. The smile did not leave Anthony's lips.

'She doesn't know what day it is today.'

Mary smiled at the straightness of his shoulders, the way his clean hair curled behind his ears, the smartness of his jacket with the buttons she had sewn back on. 'Two weeks,' she said.

Brightness animated his eyes. 'The *first* two weeks. Will you come out with me tonight, to celebrate?'

'Where?'

'We could walk down to the river. We could say we're visiting Hartingshall, and go there instead.'

Mary supposed William Hartingshall could wait.

Frost-solid points of mud pressed into the soles of Mary's boots. Each time she stumbled Anthony's arm tightened around her, and she laughed and stumbled again. Ahead, distant and invisible, the river rumbled away from the city, its surge subdued but constant, under-pinning the silence of the night. How soon would that same water meet the salt of the sea, and swirl into it, and hiss on to the blood-stained sand of Thurstaston shore?

They walked at first in the shadowed half of West Dee Lane, its hedge cloaking them from the moonlight. Leafless brambles stretched over the pockets of ice on the track, as sharp as snares. Beyond the hedge the city walls loomed in front of the stars. Anthony pulled her into their shelter.

'Well?' he said, his voice so soft as to seem no more than a progression of the silence. 'How d'you like me, sober?'

'I like you fearful well,' she said. She stood on tiptoes to kiss him, and liked the way she could dispel the chill from his lips. But two weeks, he had said. And now two weeks had passed. Footsteps on the wall high above tapped like the ticking of a clock. 'Anthony,' she whispered. 'Are you to go back to it?'

'No,' he said, 'I'll not give this up.' They walked on until they reached the slope that had once been the riverbank. Now, the water glinted some distance away. Tufty marsh-grasses thrived on the silt, their fronds plated by frost. Sandstone blocks littered the bank, the remains of some ruined riverside building. 'What I like best is waking up feared and then remembering I don't have to be. And going to bed tired – proper tired, but clear enough to imagine you by me.' Mary hid her face in the shadow of her hat. 'Everything seems so warm. I can see the ice all around, and yet it smells like spring.' He brushed the frost from one of the stones and sat down. Mary smiled. For her, the stark cleanliness of the air muted every scent but that of winter, with its darkness and its bite. A heron stood, motionless, on the salt marsh, its wings silvery. Anthony drew her on to his knee. 'D'you believe it now, that I love you?' The belief made her uneasy. Had he imposed on her a gift, and with it an obligation? Nothing she did could ever match it.

'Yes, I do.'

'And that I'm not like him?'

Blood rushed to Mary's face. 'What? Not like who?'

Moonlight whitened Anthony's face and cast the spidery shadows of his eyelashes on to his cheeks. 'I heard Agnes and Mrs Stout talking. They said you must be pondering after some fellow who'd broken your heart.'

'Did they now? Well, the pair of them have a fine nerve, to blabber so. What have they been saying about me?'

'That they think he was a rich man, and you loved him more than he loved you.'

'Well, then. What's so odd about that?' They'd been laughing at her, no doubt. *No wonder, a little plain crink like that. These daft country lasses get fancy ideas, but who'd look twice at her?*

'Did he kiss you?'

Mind, you know what some men are like. It's not a girl's face they're after.

'Yes,' she said. 'And then married someone else not a threeweek later, and that was the end of it. Must have been near three year ago. Not worth harking back to now.' She wrapped her cloak around him and cocooned them both in its warmth. His hand strayed to her ankle.

'Desperate cruel, that,' he said. 'But I in't the same. I'll kiss you today and I'll kiss you in a threeweek and every day in between, if you'll let me.'

She smiled. 'I will.'

A moving red spark, like an ember, progressed up the lane.

'There's someone there,' Mary whispered. Ice cracked under the tread of feet. Anthony's eyes were not grey in the light of the moon, but glitter-edged dark. He pulled off his hat and shielded their faces with it as he lowered her to the bank. The brim of her own hat crumpled and the heat of his body pressed her against the ground. She laughed, and the footsteps crunched away up the lane. Anthony put aside his hat.

'You look so beautiful in this light,' he said. She rolled her eyes.

'I shouldn't wonder, it being dark.'

Heat and ice overtook her at once. Her petticoats brushed up her legs and frosty air wound round her stockings. She breathed hard and looked up at the pulsing stars. Not yet an adulteress. Not yet. Anthony's hand pushed higher, cold on her bare thigh. Frost crackled behind her ears. The listless river growled on its journey to the sea. His cold-burned skin tasted sweet to her lips.

Then he righted her and smoothed her petticoats down to her ankles.

'I'm sorry,' he said. 'I promised myself I'd behave perfect tonight.'

Mary closed her eyes and tried to imagine the near-frozen river water in her veins, fizzing out the fire.

'This rich man,' said Anthony. Mary brushed flecks of frost from her skirts. 'Did he—'

'You never told me what happened after you left the Blue Coat School.'

His tread fell unevenly on the rough ground. He walked aside of her in silence, looking across at the heron on the salt-grasses. Then he kicked a frozen lump of mud and put his hands in his pockets, dipping his shoulders like a crow about to fly.

'Signed indentures with a watchmaker at Namptwich.' Mary linked her arm with his. She craved his warmth. Perhaps, when they got home, there would be no one to hear them sneak into his room. She had to ask before he would go on. 'Wanted well enough to learn the trade. Often wonder what it would be like if I had my own shop now. Some rum watches there were. Have you ever seen inside one? Some of them – the movements are that small, the tools to fix them are scarce more than a pin. That's the sort I would have liked to fix. If I had a shop of my own I'd fix watches all day, and it wouldn't be as work.' Another lump of mud bumped over the hard ground.

'I 'spect it would, after a few weeks.'

Anthony looked down at her with a smile. 'Perhaps. Still, I often wonder.' He rubbed her cold hand gently between his palms. 'Then I'd be able to buy you some gloves.'

'Why didn't you finish your apprenticeship?'

'Weren't to be. I went there at fourteen. By sixteen I'd learnt nowt but how to sweep a floor and how to carry messages from the watchmaker's wife to a fat butcher, who delivered his meat to her every time the master were out. I didn't get near a watch all that time, so I took one – trust me to pick the most expensive. I don't mean I stole it, only wanted to take it apart.'

The thought of him poring over the inner workings of a watch, his eyes bright and his tongue sticking out of the corner of his mouth, made her smile. 'Then you couldn't put it back together?'

Anthony grinned. 'The Master looked like God's revenge against murder and vowed he would thrash me. Well, that weren't to my liking, so I scarpered. Whether they looked for me I don't know – perhaps they were fain to be rid of me – but I lay low in Crewe for a while, then walked back to Chester. And that was the end of that.'

'Couldn't you start again, somehow, with another watchmaker?'

'Not here.' His tone held finality. As if he had plans. The nervous knot writhed below her ribs and she longed for gin to quiet it. 'Come with me,' he said. 'To London. We won't warn Mrs Seward; we'll just go. There'd be a chance for me there – if not watches, some other way of making summat of myself. There's a stage from the Pied Bull on Friday—'

'I can't.' Mary's words rang loud. So incongruous in the silent air that she thought they echoed. 'I can't.'

Everything was still. The heron's wings glowed silver.

Anthony's fingers brushed her face. 'Is it because of him?'

'No.'

'Then why?'

He would laugh at first, if she told him. Laughter would catch in his throat and the moonlight would be enough for her to see him grin and search her expression for the truth. Then he would believe her, and she would watch him hunch away up the lane, and if she ever saw him again his grey eyes would harden in hatred.

'I must stay in Chester a few months.' She sought his hand. 'Get a problem sorted out, and then—'

'You're not . . . forgive me. But you're not carrying this man's child?'

'No.' She breathed calmness into her. 'I can't tell you. But when it's over, then . . .' His face, close to hers, his hand warm on her fingers;

she would not give them up. Let Selwyn live, and that was all she owed him. 'Then I'll come with you. I'll go anywhere. Leave it 'til the summer, and I'll go anywhere.' Friday. She could go. Selwyn could live or die as God willed. She could be in a coach to London, to a new life.

But the stench and darkness of the gaol filled her thoughts, and she pictured him waiting for her and realising at last that she would not come. Let him be freed and then . . . 'I will run away with you, but you must let me tell you when. As soon as I say, then we'll go.' Anthony let go of her hand. They walked apart back to the hospital.

'You go in first,' he said. 'I'll come back later. Pretend I'm visiting my woman.'

Mary's heart shrivelled.

CHAPTER 14

'I see he made you walk back on your own.' Agnes, alone in the kitchen, fiddled over a hospital nightgown. Her shoulders sagged; she smiled at Mary, but her eyes were dull and red-rimmed.

'He didn't even attend the patient with me. He went off . . .'

'To visit the harlot?'

'Aye.' She kept back from the light of the candle and busied herself undoing the tie of her hat.

'And who've you been visiting?'

'What?'

Agnes brightened enough for her eyebrows to give an arch skip.

'Well, look at you – all dazed and dizzy, and your neck all red. What's he like? It's not this patient, is it?'

Mary flopped down and her limbs and head hung heavy. Agnes's cup of colourless tea, wrung from Mrs Seward's discarded leaves, wobbled. 'No, t'int him.' Damn – she should have said it was. If she had only thought for a moment. 'I'm not to tell anyone.' Something in the greasy fumes of the candle made her think of gin. 'His family – they don't approve.'

Agnes abandoned the nightgown. 'Oh, he's not a gentleman, is he? You could have a mansion – you could be mistress of hundreds of servants. What if he decides he loves you more than anything and marries you whatever they say? Oh, just think of that!'

'He's no gentleman, just a saddler. But me – a nurse. As far as his ma thinks, he might as good marry a whore.' Agnes's semblance of brightness dissolved. 'I didn't realise,' Mary continued. 'When I came here I didn't know what folk'd think of us.'

Agnes stared at the flame. 'I did.' Light flickered on her chestnut curls. She drew breath to speak again, but halted. At last her voice came quiet and sad. 'I suppose Anthony has told you about me?'

Apprehension crawled over Mary like a swarm of lice. Agnes rested her chin on her hands and blinked hard.

'I was thrown out of my last situation because I had got a child.'

Subtle currents of ice dripped down Mary's arms. She remained silent. Agnes's eyes searched for her reaction, and a tear flopped on to the table with a soft pat.

'It didn't survive. I tried to pretend I'd been poisoned by some bad meat, but I couldn't hide the blood. It'll be a year ago tomorrow.'

Mary passed over her pocket handkerchief and her throat tightened. 'The father?'

'He was a footman, where I lived. Josiah.' Agnes curled her lip and Mary's breath released. 'Wiry fellow, like a jockey. Not so very handsome, I suppose, but I was smitten enough with him at the time. He would never have married me. They said it was for the best.' Agnes picked up her needle and scratched dirt from a groove in the table. 'It would only have been a monster, they said. I shouldn't have wanted it. I escaped the greater shame, didn't I? They said I was lucky for that – but, still.' Her eyes were weary but calm when she looked up. 'But still, it would have been my monster, wouldn't it?' She folded the nightgown, pressed her fingers along the creases and lined it up to perfection. Then she took a gulp of watery tea and forced a smile.

Currents of air travelled under the door and over Mary and Agnes's bed. Mary listened to her breath, its whisper quickening. Crusts of frost stuck to her eyelashes. The strike of the clock shocked through her; she counted the twelve chimes. Feet splintered ice outside. Mary waited for the sound of the door, but the feet grew distant. She pressed her fist to her stomach.

Damn him.

A click. No, it was just something outside. Under the covers she breathed herself a warm cocoon until the air had gone. Just as she had done when she was a child, hiding from the huge black hounds. Their breath had echoed hers, quickening when it quickened, stopping when she listened. All they had to do was wait, crouching by the side of the bed and blinking their white saucers of eyes until she must lift the blankets for air. Was that them now, that scrabbling? It was overhead; just a rat in the roof. Still no sound of the door. The hounds would wait, their tongues streaked with blood. Any movement would bring them.

The doors crashed and she stifled a scream. Agnes did not stir. Bolts echoed. Mary hesitated before she put her feet down – afraid they would meet wiry hair – but she grabbed her shawl and shivered out to the top of the stairs. A key clanked in a lock; the sound went on and on. A stream of curses accompanied each new turn. At last – the thump of a door against a wall, a collision of bone and furniture, louder curses. And the door slamming, more chinks of the key, a jangle as it fell to the tiles. Then silence.

Mary waited in the darkness. Ice stiffened her feet.

Another crash. The ice turned to fire.

The cupboard door creaked; her hand shook between the folds of the bag. The gin scalded her throat, swig by swig. Head back, she drank until the bottle stood upright on her lips. She clutched it in her fist. She would put it back quietly and go to bed.

Then she thought of him kissing her. How clear his eyes had been, how full of his hope for the future, and how she had destroyed it. The bottle struck the back of the cupboard like a gunshot and rumbled over the floor. Agnes woke with a shriek.

'Mary!'

'Leave me alone.'

The gin hit as she dragged the covers over her. Darkness whirled on darkness but the anger stayed alive. Mrs Seward hammered on the door. Agnes's voice sounded high and ethereal.

She had a nightmare. She does regular. She's quiet now.

Still the anger did not die, but fed. She grasped her head to her knees and tried to shield herself, but it pulsed and stabbed.

Damn him. Damn him to hell.

'Believe me, Mrs Stout, there are only two uses for the likes of him. One is to keep the distillers from starving – the other is to serve as a living reminder to the rest of us how fortunate we are to be blessed with moral fortitude.' Mrs Seward moved from table to fire as though her shoes were made of air. The kettle hissed and the roar of the flames hurt Mary's head. 'I said so all along, did I not? Two weeks and an hour, and he would be drunk as a wheelbarrow. Look at him!' Anthony wrapped his shaking hands round the back of his head and breathed into the table. His breakfast congealed in front of him. The cook whisked a frying pan past Mary's ear and the odour of grease settled in her throat. 'They're always the same. Two weeks and an hour. I might have reckoned it upon a watch, mightn't I, Mary?' Mary kept her head bowed. The heat of the kitchen made gin boil in her stomach. 'Mightn't I, Mary?'

She met Anthony's eyes. Inflamed and vague, they regarded her from deep within his pallid face.

Mrs Stout's frying pan hissed into the dishwater and steam clouded the window. She wiped the sweat from her cheeks and patted Anthony's shoulder. 'Won't you eat summat, sweetheart? Dunna dwindle such good bacon.'

Anthony lowered his head back to the table.

'That's all very well, Mrs Stout, but if he cares nothing for letting his whole life dwindle away, then I'm sure your bacon is of even lighter consequence.' Mrs Seward's mouth contorted into a gloating smile. She prodded Anthony. 'Get up and accompany Mary to this wretched patient of hers.'

'I'll go by myself,' said Mary. The matron huffed so vehemently that Mary thought she saw steam come out of her nose.

'You will not,' she said. 'Oh, I've no doubt you would be safer on your own than subject to the sort of protection this crapulous idiot might afford you, but Dr Tylston has given strict instructions.'

When Mary stood, the scrape of her chair legs sawed through her head. She grabbed the table. Mrs Seward's gown and starched apron and silvery hair all dulled to flat grey. Even the cook's red face and the leaping flames lost their colour. The stuffiness in Mary's nose and throat tasted of gin; the ache behind her eyes shouted of it. Her heart beat out of time, hurting the more when she blamed Anthony, and more still when she blamed herself.

Crowds distanced the sound of Anthony shouting at her to wait. The crisp air cleared her head and settled the gin in her stomach, and the rhythm of her boots on the paving stones of the Exchange calmed her thoughts. She would forget all he had said last night. She would stop being angry. He wasn't worth it.

Stallholders jumped from one foot to the other and beat their ungloved hands on their arms. Their shouts sent curls of mist up to the feet of the rabbits and pheasants that hung, limp, above their heads.

No law against being disappointed. Men let you down all the time. Mary blinked away tears.

Beyond the Exchange's arches and their bustle of people, the temperature dropped and the smooth stone floor gave way to mud-coated cobbles. Mary picked her path over the peaks and hollows. He might go back to Agnes for all she cared. Let him drink to the death, if he had such a mind to.

'Why are you angry?' Anthony touched her shoulder and she shrugged him away. Cold had returned the colour to his face but his hands still trembled. Could he pretend not to know? 'Not alung o' me drinking?' He opened the door for her into the warehouse yard. 'Well, you drank an' all. The old bitch was telling Mrs Stout you were in a state last night, throwing things, so don't put on the 'ump over me having one dram. How else were I to quench my sorrows?'

'Don't you begin on me!' Mary shoved him in the chest and he staggered back. 'I looked after you – there were times I feared you were fit to die, and now you've wasted—'

'I only ever said two weeks.'

The look she gave him made Anthony avert his gaze.

Sheltered from frost, rat-trails criss-crossed the limits of the warehouse yard. Hartingshall's bucket stuck to the ground, and only came free with a violent tug.

'Go and fetch his water,' she said. Anthony folded his arms.

'What if I an't an inkling to?'

Mary stopped herself from flinging the bucket at his head. 'Then I'll fetch it, and you may swill out his pisspot and scrape the pus off his lame arm.'

'Off you go, then.'

The entrance to the alleyway stood in shadow, a smear of mud stretching into it like a tongue. Her anger faltered.

'Wait.' Anthony took the bucket from her. 'I won't let you go through there on your own.' A soft smile infected the corners of his lips. 'I'm sorry. How'm I to make you forgive me?' He kissed her hand, but she pulled it away.

'I don't know,' she said. 'But it'll want more than wheedling like a lost dog.' Anthony's cheeks flushed and the smile left him.

'Suit yourself.' The bucket-handle squeaked as he stalked off towards the Watergate Street well.

'Where's your friend today?' Hartingshall sat on his mattress, a bundle of blankets round his shoulders.

'Fetching water,' Mary said tersely.

'Sounds like he's in trouble.'

The stubbornness of the bandage knot made her fingernails hurt. Hartingshall shivered when the cold air struck his weeping wound.

'Why don't you look after your bandages? Look at it. How did it manage to shred itself to nowt, just sitting about your arm?'

Hartingshall chuckled, but she hardly noticed. On the table sat a fresh loaf of bread, half covered by a sheet of newspaper. The pleasant scent of the crust broke through the sour atmosphere of the makeshift sickroom.

'What's this?'

Hartingshall snorted. 'Bread,' he said. 'Don't you have it where you come from?'

'I mean, where did you get it? Are you well enough to go out?'

He sniffed, and winced as he flexed his hand. 'Walk round the yard sometimes,' he said. 'Need the air. But, nah – someone brung that for me. Was here this morning.'

'Who?'

Hartingshall grinned. 'Mr Warbreck.'

She had known before he said it, but the inward flinch struck no less sharply than when she had heard Dog-Breath Annie speak of him. It must be nothing more than a habit, to feel so shredded inside.

Mary turned from Hartingshall and waited for the tide of heat to ebb from her face. The newspaper over the bread wafted in the draught. She let her fingers slide over the table towards it.

'God's life!' Hartingshall said, and Mary snatched her hand away. 'To touch a bloody loaf of bread just because he's touched it? You sorry cow.'

'I only meant to break off a hunge for you.'

'Never said I was hungry.'

Neither would she be, it seemed, ever again. Urgency spun her insides. Urgency to see him before he spoke to anyone else in the city. Before anyone claimed his attention.

'Does he . . .' She swallowed. 'Does he stay in Chester?'

Footsteps echoed in the alleyway. Anthony looked puzzled by the way she looked at him when he clanked the bucket down. Hartingshall fished a pack of cards from his pocket and got Anthony to deal at penneach or somesuch game. She measured out the medicine and half-listened to their talk about London. How many times bigger than Chester was it? What were the names of the streets? Where did the watchmakers trade?

'Was the Thames where you learned to swim so strong?'

Medicine powder spilt over the table. Hartingshall laughed. 'Had an uncle in Kent,' he said. 'He learned us both to swim in the Channel. Me and my brother. We dreamed of getting all the way to France.'

Anthony's silence tightened the air with the discomfort of having stumbled too close to grief. Mary made Hartingshall come outside to have his arm washed.

'When did you tell him? How much does he know?'

Standing up had made colour abandon Hartingshall's face. 'When the surgeon was here saying my arm was good and strong, other than this. I said I wouldn't be here if it wasn't. He knows what happened to Jem, but he doesn't know about you.'

A bolt shot, then another, and the great gates swung open. Hoof-beats hollowed under the arch, dirty harness creaked and the growling breath of a horse with the heaves made steam rise into the thawing air. The driver puffed acrid smoke from a pipe in one corner of his mouth.

'You and Wells, eh?' Hartingshall sniffed a powerful breath. 'Ain't surprised, from what Warbreck says.' Mary's hand paused in the bucket, the washcloth catching a bag of air under it, like a jellyfish.

'*What*? What does he say?'

'He says modesty stops being your favourite virtue when you've a mind to take peculiar over a man.'

Mary slapped water on to Hartingshall's arm and made him flinch. 'Well, he—'

'And that he had you before you was married to Jones, and you went off something 'larming when he got sick of you.'

'Why did he say that?' Her voice cracked. 'It in't true. He kissed me once . . .' She tailed off, and Hartingshall's triumph crumpled. He rested his good hand gently on her shoulder.

'I'm sorry. Must have made it up, what he said.' He gave an awkward smile. 'Look, if Jones died you could marry that lad. Be happy. Let Jones swing, get yourself free, forget Warbreck, marry Wells. Simple.'

'It in't simple. I've known Selwyn since I was born. We were friends. We climbed Thor's Stone together. Threw mud at each other. We plotted to have a pirate ship. He married me because he thought he ought, and I've been ungrateful. I can't forget about him and let him die.'

Hartingshall's features blurred beyond the salt in her eyes. All she could feel was his clumsy hand on her arm. 'Poor Mary. Ain't your fault.' He paused. 'You know I can't go against him, don't you?' She nodded. 'If I don't stand up in court I'll be next. I'm thankful for you coming here, but I can't get your old man freed. If that's all you're after, best leave me to fend for myself.'

Mary smeared her eyes, supported Hartingshall's arm and dabbed at the wound. 'I'm after making you better,' she said; and he returned her smile with a grin.

Anthony woke at the prod of Hartingshall's foot.

'Idle bugger.'

But he did not lash back. Instead, he stood tall and stretched his arms, without the guilty wince that had accompanied his movements all morning. Then he smiled the kind of smile that hurt. Hartingshall made a strangulated noise and picked something up from the mattress.

'He's drank it.' His big hand cradled a medicine phial. 'There was enough in there to last the day. He's drank it.'

Anthony slipped his hand under Mary's cloak. 'She said you didn't want it, after it nigh-on did for you last time. But we'll get you more, friend,' he said. 'The doctor'll do anything if Mary asks – and who could blame him, for so would I.'

Mary squirmed away. 'Stand outside, then, and wait while I do his bandage.'

'I know what I'm to do,' he said, when she returned to him. 'I'm to get a watch, and work out how to take it apart and put it back together, and when we go to London at last I'll fix watches to look after us.' He closed his eyes and drew in a deep breath. 'It's all obvious.'

The men with the cart laughed when Mary wouldn't let him kiss her. 'Obvious? How? How will you get a watch? Steal one? How will you go into business without an apprenticeship?'

'I'll fix watches for fences. When they get a broken one brought in they'll bring it to me and I won't ask where it came from. You might be angry with me now, and have this secret of yours, but I've seen how it'll be. We have to be together and there's nowt either of us can do about it.'

'You're talking nonsense. For goodness' sake – drinking a sick man's medicine?' She glanced over at Hartingshall's door. 'As if the poor bugger didn't have—' But she broke off and stared at the entrance to the alley.

Bryce Warbreck halted too, and for a moment seemed to struggle to mask his surprise. Then he lifted his hat, gave a curt nod and walked back towards the Row, his footfalls hollow between the alley walls.

'Mary?' Anthony spoke softly. Sounds came back to her – the jokes of the warehousemen and the rumble of boxes of goods along the cart-bed. 'That was him, wasn't it? The man you told me about.' The hazy contentment in Anthony's eyes vanished, leaving something dark and more disturbing. He studied her face, his cheeks flushing. 'You said you didn't love him any more.'

'I know . . .'

'But you do. That's why you want to stay. You want to stay and try and make him take you back before you cut your losses and settle for me.'

'No.'

But Anthony walked away, his hands in the pockets of his shabby greatcoat and his gaze fixed on the ground.

Bryce Warbreck fiddled over the padlock on the warehouse door. Mary watched him from within an arm's length of the bawd's window. His neckcloth showed violent white over the collar of his coat, and his lips moved in a silent curse over the stubbornness of the lock. Six weeks had passed since she took the bolt of blue silk to his house. He looked tired, and thinner. She collected herself before calling out to him.

'Mr Warbreck.'

The corners of his eyes crinkled into the smile she remembered. Mary crumped her thumbs inside her fists and returned his bow with a dignified nod.

'Mrs Jones. How delightful—'

'I go by the name of Miss Helsall here.'

The sparkle dissolved. 'You are right to seek to forget your husband, madam.' Melting ice dripped from the overhanging building behind him. Cold beads gathered on Mary's lips.

'I've forgotten nowt,' she said. 'I haven't forgotten telling you he'd gone to Liverpool. Why didn't you believe me?'

Bryce gave an indulgent smile. 'You won't miss him, Mary,' he said. 'I will ensure you are never destitute.'

There was something unsettling about the smart coat, the confident bearing, the white neckcloth. Something that distanced him from her and inclined her to keep silent and modest and invisible, as she might before the infirmary Board. Did he mean to flick ha'pennies into the gutter and laugh to watch her scrabble?

'You would sell a man's life for a hundred pound reward, then give me money to live on? What if I were to last to a crone of sixty years, still dwindling your money away?'

Bryce looked up and down the Row. The scuffle of a rat in the beams sent chavins floating on to his hat. 'The hundred pounds will be most welcome, of course, but you are well aware of Jones's plans to complicate the scheme, and why I could not let them continue.'

What grumblings of resentment had Selwyn betrayed after a night at Kate's tavern? Had he boasted of the stash at Hilbre? Had the stupid lummock gone and trusted someone?

'He only said he was damned sick of you. He can't have been the only one to say that. He wouldn't have acted on it.' Her words became louder and less controlled. 'He complained a piece. Everyone does. It doesn't mean he would—'

'I sent Jack Joseph to Hilbre to collect the contraband. Five barrels of Manx beer. A modest first haul.'

Mary fixed him with a look she wished would scald his skin. 'They weren't his.'

'Perhaps you would care to step into the warehouse, madam.' Remnants of courtesy struggled into Bryce's voice. 'I fear the cold agitates you.'

'I would not care to.'

He undid another lock, the grind of it loud in the damp air. 'Then I will not keep you. Your mistress must wonder where you are.'

'No one is my mistress. There's only Mrs Seward, and I'm forever stopping out and she durstn't say a word about it.'

'Then you will step into the warehouse rather than regale Watergate Street with one of your scenes.'

She firmed her lips and followed him between the uneven beams of the doorway. Dust irritated her nose. In the dim light of the warehouse it was all she could sense, at first. Then she smelled woodsmoke, too, and a dampness, like leaf mould. Light fell from somewhere above, but not until Bryce opened one set of window-shutters could she see the surroundings. Crumbling white cornices adorned with grapes and cherubs encircled the ceiling, and kindling lay ready to be lit in a marble fireplace, dulled by disuse. Bryce ignored Mary's questioning look.

'My warehouse,' he said, with a brief smile.

But though stacks of crates filled part of the room, and a pair of beer-barrels sat aside of the door, the place was not really a warehouse at all. Plaster flaked from scars in the ceiling where inner walls must once have stood. Tarnished stair-rods stood propped in a corner. Shreds of damp wallpaper peeled over the staircase. Above her a plaster rose surrounded a rusty fixing, its pattern one of leaves, with veins and pointed tips. She tried to work out how it was done. Bryce left to get a coal to light the fire.

That door at the back, at the end of a passageway of crates, must lead to Hartingshall's room. She pressed her ear to it, thought she heard him snoring, and smiled.

143

The crates smelled of damp. Smelled of the cellar at home. Mary didn't let tears come to her eyes. What was the use of being sentimental about the cottage when all her times there had been filled with dullness and frustration?

She would never be able to go home now. Not with Betsy Roberts and Liza Mobbett there. Let them have the gorse and silver birches, and the lines of evening sun on the sea and the fleeting shadows on the distant hills of Wales. She would find something else.

She climbed the stairs, her hand skimming the mahogany banister, and tiptoed to look out of the window. Below, the warehouse yard formed a square of mud. The cart had gone and the gate was shut. The barrels looked tiny and unthreatening, and if rats darted at the feet of the walls she could not see them.

Cobwebs and grime clouded the windowpanes, but in line with one of the bands of lead was a word, scratched in the glass. Mary dabbed her finger to her tongue and cleared away the dirt.

Laetitia.

More stairs doubled back up towards white doors. Mary stilled herself and looked away. That dream, the night of the wreck; she had not thought of it again until now. The strewn toy animals, the shrouded cradle with something in it. Something dreadful, and yet could it have been so horrible, that she could not have loved it, if it were hers?

Dust rucked under her hand on the banister. From the stairs the first thing she could see was an old sofa, facing the fireplace. What if she were sitting there when Bryce returned? What if he sat next to her and slid his arm around her and pressed her against the dusty burgundy damask? What if that was what he planned?

Hinges creaked. She fingered the dust on a crate as Bryce hissed the coal into the kindling. 'I hear you've taken work as an infirmary nurse,' he said.

'Aye. What of it? I'll not starve on the street, much as you'd like me to.'

'Do they treat you well?'

'Not especially. Mr Barnston does, I suppose. And Dr Tylston.'

'Tylston? He has a good reputation, I believe.'

Mary shrugged. 'Most of the patients don't come back, so I 'spect they must be cured.'

Bryce stood up from the grate, rubbing his back like an old man, but he did not turn towards her. 'Where does he live?'

'Abbey Court.'

He nodded once and rested a moment with his hand on the mantelpiece. There was a faded square on the wall, where a glass must have been – a huge one that must have doubled every flame of the chandelier hanging from that rusty fixing. If she lived here she would have a glass opposite too. She turned and selected the spot for it. Then the glasses and flames would reflect one another into world after world.

'Who lived here before?' she asked.

'Some gentleman. I believe his wife died and he no longer had a care for the place.'

'He might have let it as a house.'

'The story has it that he wished not to see another man so happy here.'

Perhaps that gentleman loved his wife. She must have died before he realised what a wife was all about.

'Did you fetch the coal from the other side of the alley?'

'I did,' Bryce said.

'That woman who lives there's a reddled old bawd.'

He smiled grimly. 'Your short time in the city has made you very worldly.'

She inched closer to the sofa. 'I only know because she and her bully tried to bundle me into their house.'

Bryce's smile vanished. '*What?*' Measured and authoritative, his voice encircled her, gathering her up like an arm. Mary held her thumbs tighter. 'Tell me what happened.'

'A tiny woman, 'kin to a bird . . .'

'Sarah Hodder.'

'She asked me to cipher a receipt for her. She grabbed my arm – her nails were yellow as cheese-rind. Then she went cross and said . . .' Heat blistered her face. 'Said her gentlemen would like me, because I would fight.'

Bryce's eyes widened for a fraction of a moment. 'I will tell her to leave you alone.' He was close enough for her to catch the delicate scent of the powder on his peruke, and to taste hints of bergamot in his cologne. Close enough to see the smoothness of his lips, and watch them part, and almost feel their softness. 'What business have you in such a place, in any case?'

'I must come here every day to look after William Hartingshall.'

He stepped back; it was like a fist ripping at her chest. 'Hartingshall?' Bryce's gaze shot to the rough door. The line of his jaw was taut, the contours of his throat clean-shaven. 'What the hell do you want with Hartingshall?'

'He's ill,' she said. 'His arm was cut and it's gone to an ulcer.' Bryce seemed about to speak, but halted. 'I know who he is. I know everything. I know what disgusting lies you've told him about me.'

Spirals of dust rose from the back of the sofa when Bryce sat down. 'I sought to reassure him that Jones's wife would not stand by him at the trial. That's all.' He smiled apologetically and rested his arm along the back.

'I suppose you flamed the cant at home, an' all?'

Bryce did not answer at once. Mary remembered the turned backs, the sideways glances, the sudden-ceasing whispers. She thought the women had jumped to conclusions. Perhaps, after all, they had been pushed. 'Well, it would have been true, had it been up to you.' She could make no reply. 'What's your intention? To cosset him into refusing to stand as witness, or to feed him the sort of medicine that will prevent him standing as anything?' Bryce went to the window and rubbed a circle in the dirt. Then he paced to Hartingshall's door and listened a moment.

'No. I want him to get better.'

Bryce laughed. 'You've never cared about anyone in your life but yourself.'

'I have . . .'

'You mean you think you cared about me? Cared enough to make an idiot of yourself, perhaps, hammering on the door, begging me to run away with you.' His eyes hardened. 'Cared enough to distress Mrs Warbreck when she was with child.'

'I didn't know . . .'

'It was five months after our marriage. It might have occurred to you.'

Coldness smarted in the corners of Mary's eyes. Thumping sickness welled up in her throat. 'It doesn't always happen,' she said quietly.

He was close behind her when she stepped out on to the Row. The scent of the air changed from dust and smoke to vapours of mist and slops wafting up from the street. She blinked ahead at the black-beamed buildings on the opposite side, their windows dark behind curtains of damp.

'Mary, who was that young lad you were talking to earlier?'

As if that was any of his business.

'Porter at the infirmary.' Suspicion deepened the blue of his eyes. Then he gave a sudden, uncertain smile.

'Most women at least wait until their husband is dead.'

She lowered her gaze to the sawdust-strewn boards, and when he shot the bolt of the warehouse door behind him she clamped her hand over her mouth and fought back a sob.

Thurstaston, early hours, 28 December 1755

Betsy Roberts's voice creaks in the dark, like a cart-axle straining over ruts.

'It's scarce a wonder, to me.'

Will Mrs Roberts choose an old story or invent a new? Dull windows, or rumours far from dull? Last night's storm, and Mary's hair thrashing loose? Mary shelters her ears and listens hard.

'Two years married, and no child? Well, where's the surprise in that, says I, when she makes him sleep in the chair every night? How can that be good for a man?'

Wind flutters the brim of Mary's hat.

'Aye, they need their sleep, true enough.' *Liza's voice is younger and shriller, with a whine to it that keeps it poised between indignation and disgust.* 'And other things.'

'And that great gollumpus gets neither!'

Perhaps they do not realise, in such darkness, how close she stands, and how easy it would be to conceal their gossiping behind the thunder of the sea if they chose. But then, perhaps they do.

'He ought not to stand for it.'

'Well, that's what I say. He ought to take her in hand. Can you imagine my Adam abiding that?'

'John neither,' *says Liza.* 'Shall we tell the both of 'em tomorrow night, eh? "Chair for you, lad, while I dream of Mr Warbreck lyin' by me."'

Washboard-rattles of laughter whip up into the wind. The women move away, their gossip unbodied and ungrounded, catching directions so that now it seems to come from the sea, now the cliffs.

. . . hair flying everywhere . . .

. . . his own fault . . .

. . . put her in her place . . .

. . . if he were my husband . . .

Wet sand pulls around Mary's feet.

'Liza!' *A lull in the wind amplifies her shout.* 'Liza Mobbett! Betsy Roberts!'

'There.'

'I said, did I not?'

'And where's her husband, I ask, to stop her insulting us?'

'Durst not bring such a temper on himself, the big cradant.'

Their bodies, both taller and broader than hers, are now close enough to change the temperature of the air, but she sees only glimpses of light on their clothing.

'Why won't the both of you shut your reeking potato-traps and ask God to send you summat more important to worry about?'

There is a sucking-in of breath. 'A fine thing, indeed – to speak to your elders in such a fashion.'

Unable to see Betsy's face, she has to make her own image: scrawny, furrowed, weather-flayed skin. Yellow eyes cutting sideways, mouth straight and thin as a razor-shell.

'Elders? Being old doesn't make you any less of a nasty, lying bitch.'

'Good Lord! Oh, good Lord!' *Betsy works up a shriek.*

'I've never made him sleep in the chair. Are you so idle that you have time to invent such things?'

Liza's cry is seagull-like, a mockery of the ship's crew clinging to their breaking vessel. 'Us, idle? Is it our homes that look like dug-out middens? If I looked after my husband the way you look after yours he'd be as like to thrash me, and I'd have no right to blame him.'

Weariness descends through Mary's limbs. The wind's sting carries fatigue in it, and pours it over her until fighting feels more of a defeat than walking away. 'Bitches.' *She means it as a whisper, but it rings out clear.*

'You're no better.' Liza's crow-caw makes her shrug and hug her cape around her. 'Don't suppose yourself better than us, Mary Jones, just because you've been tupped by a rich man.'

Betsy laughs, but her sodden hat is the first thing Mary's fist meets, and a spray of water bursts from it like mud from a shaking dog. 'Good Lord!'

'It's not true!' The scream hurts Mary's throat and makes her cough, but the words are unheeded. The two women grab her by the elbows, and she must take great strides to avoid falling on to her knees. 'Ask him, and he'll tell you it in't true.' But every word makes the fingers clamp tighter on her arms, and Liza and Betsy are silent. 'Selwyn!'

That breaks their silence; their laughter rings in her head. Sea-spray shocks full in her face and lantern-specks flit ahead of her, on the far shore of Wales. Water hisses around her ankles.

'Here's a lesson for you, girl.' Betsy sounds far away. 'Learn it.' One last struggle – her heel hits a shin – and then the hands propel her forward, water rises, cold rips the breath out of her and her fingers splay deep into sand.

One note of laughter breaks the growl of the waves, and then nothing. A second is a long time in which to think, and she sees Betsy and Liza rock-faced, in a cart, hempen necklaces setting off the wrinkles of one and the bug-eyes of the other. Pure cold floods through her. The weight of her cloak makes her elbows too weak to lift her, and sand hurries away from her hands. Salt rasps the back of her throat and her lungs seem ready to crumple, but another second passes and she is not frightened. It is too quiet to be frightened, and too dark.

Hands again on her shoulders, then arms around her, and the quietness turns to a blast of shouts, rain and sea. Water rushes from her nose and mouth. Her legs don't support her when she is set down on the sand, but there are arms to help her and she cannot let go of them, at first.

'Why won't they leave me alone?' Speaking makes her cough, and she clings tighter. 'They must know it isn't true.'

'Get yourself home, lass.' The speaker is old and gruff, and Mary starts at his harshness. 'And stop raising trouble.'

Adam Roberts leaves her, and she shivers so hard she fears she will shuffle herself a grave in the sand. Through swollen eyelids she sees lamplight. In it, the sight of Betsy's snide eyes.

'Don't you start on my husband, you selfish witch.'

Whether Adam has struck his wife, Mary cannot see through the new veil of water that has covered her eyes, but Betsy cries out and the lamp's glow moves erratically away.

'Where's the sense in killing the wench, you spiteful owd cat?' he says. Betsy's reply is shrill and lost. 'D'ye think turning murderer is like to make Warbreck fancy your wrinkles?'

Mary pulls herself to her feet and finds she is not drowned, only heavy with water. She discards her cape and it seems all her bones jangle.

'You hurt?'

Here he is, then, at last.

'No.'

Selwyn holds up a lamp. His eyes are deep and wary. 'Why won't you ignore them?'

Mary tries to speak, but salt has shrivelled her throat and she coughs until her face burns with tears.

'Why must you fly at them so?'

'You didn't hear the things they said.'

Selwyn lowers the lamp away from his face.

'I did,' he says. Mary's shivering pauses. 'And I heard what you said back.'

Unsteadily at first she walks up the shore, then with stronger steps, and he follows. 'Why didn't you stop me, then? Why didn't you stop them throwing me in the sea? Why did you let an old man half your size pull me out?'

Selwyn's eyes are weary. He sets the lamp down, places his own coat round her shoulders and turns away. 'Because I'm sick of it, Mary. Damned sick of it.' Waves snatch his words and rein his anger out to the timbers creaking somewhere on the sandbanks of the Dee.

151

CHAPTER 15

'You mun drink all of it, my poor love.' Mrs Stout clasped Anthony's head to her blubber and held a cup of hot water to his lips. 'Or your innards'll be no more than icicles and fit to shiver to pieces.' She knelt beside him at the kitchen hearth, her fat arm red and speckly around his shoulders. The sparkles of frost had melted, darkening the coppery sheen of his hair to dull brown.

'Oh, my poor lad.' Mrs Stout planted a kiss on his head. 'Why didn't you come in? You been well-nigh froze to death, out there on the door-sill all night.'

Anthony swallowed the water painfully.

'Didn't know . . . Didn't know I was there.'

'And you'd have known less than that if someone anner left this old blanket on you. Oh, love, why must you do this? You split my heart as near as if you were my own lad.'

Not much more than a mess of hair and a pair of long legs, he lay inert on the ash-coated hearth tiles. Did he feel better now to be back drunk? Did this quell his sorrows and make him think the world bearable? Was he glad, eh? To have left off being sober, with all the hurt and anguish of it?

'That Mary,' he said. The cook looked up at her with an uncomfortable smile. 'Mary Helsall. She's all hell to me.'

Mrs Stout stroked his head. 'She's here, my sweetheart. She's feart for you, going on like this.'

Anthony pulled away from Mrs Stout and fell back on the floor. The firelight painted a glow on to his ashen cheek. 'She's feart for no one but herself,' he said. 'And so she should be, the false bitch.'

Mrs Stout said later he didn't get out of her way until near ten o'clock, when he struggled from the floor to a chair and slumped good as dead with his head on the table until half past eleven, when Mrs Seward, sporting a gleeful smirk, escorted him to the board room.

'Y'do pick your times, you lasses,' said the cook. 'Breaking the poor boy's heart when there's inpatients on the tad of arriving. Some other feller's took your fancy, I suppose?'

Mary avoided Mrs Stout's searching gaze. 'It's naught like that,' she said. 'I'm only cross at him for swilling gin.'

Mr Hesketh's ponderous voice seemed to wobble the board room door. *Constant drunkenness . . . habitual idleness . . . lewd behaviour with regard to the nurses . . . violence to the patients . . .*

Mary pressed her ear to the keyhole and kept her broom ready to be put into action. Mrs Seward came out first, the lines on her forehead deep with fury. Her petticoats whooshed along the wall up the stairs and her parlour door shook the floorboards when it slammed.

The smell of gin and frost-seared wool followed Anthony out, overcoming even the governors' cloud of tobacco. He supported himself by sliding his shoulder along the wall.

'Well, then,' Mary said. 'Are you thrown out?' He crashed into his room. 'Anthony? What did they say?'

Anthony lay back on the unmade bedclothes and pressed the heels of his hands into his eyes. 'I stay for now. Noble of 'em, eh? Condescend to let me stay.'

'Was it Mr Barnston who persuaded them?'

Anthony's knees poked up, square and bony. 'Aye. Said I mun leave off gin or I'm out in April.' He hauled himself on to one elbow and trembled a cup of water to his lips. God only knew how long that had been sitting there by his bed.

'Sounds fair, to me.'

'Fair?' The cup thumped on the night-table. 'There was half a dozen in there today. Where are the rest, eh? At home abed, wambling over a hair o' dog brought them by their servants, that's where. When was the last time you heard of any on 'em told to leave off brandy?'

Mary let her broom handle rap against the wall. 'Well, when was the last time you saw any of them dragged home three-parts dead at pitch of night and lumped on the doorstep like a sack of sharp-flour?'

Anthony's cheeks coloured, deepening the grey around his eyes. 'That's a fine thing from you. You're fond of gin as I am. I'd wage you were drinking it that whole fortnight I hadn't ever a drop, and laughing with your fancy-man that I was daft enough to do it all on your account.'

Mary snatched his cup and tipped the contents over his face. He gasped, open-mouthed.

'You want me as fuddled as you, do you?' The cup struck his cheek and clattered to the floor. 'Would you feel better to know you weren't the only drunken idiot in the world? Then I'll soon make you feel better.'

Let Mrs Seward sack her. Waves of anger cleared a path for her through the mist. Near-ice air made spirit-forms swirl before the Northgate turrets. Figures materialised from the passageway like the phantoms of sailors they said haunted the Dee. Hoofbeats echoed and wheels rattled on the ruts. They bethought her of the stories of ghost coaches with skeletal horses and headless coachmen.

Well, gin would soon see off such childish visions. And Mrs Seward would do nothing about it, for all her talk. She might shout and complain, but she was no more a proper matron than was Mary. Always out at market with no idea what happened in the hospital, or sitting upstairs drinking tea and leaving her staff to do as they liked. Shouting was no substitute for authority. Who was to say she didn't keep her own supply of gin in the poky room she insisted on calling her parlour?

Mangham seemed different. His smile had a curve in it. Stench surged down the stairs of the gaol. The turnkey winked at her, not unkindly, took her bottle and descended to the cellar. When he returned he held out his hand.

'Nurses, eh?' The stubbly hairs on his chin pointed forward as he grinned. Bony fingers contracted around the tuppence she gave him. 'Not surprised you haven't asked to see him. Leave him there, eh? That's what I says you're right to do.' His rabbit-teeth showed when he laughed. 'I thought you were such a modest little mite when you first came here. Such a sweet, hard-done-by little thing.'

Skin wobbled on his neck, his lanternlight making shadows in the folds. Mary seized the bottle. 'If someone's told you stories, well, they in't true. Has someone been here, visiting Selwyn? If he has—'

'Good luck to you, lovely, that's what I say. Go with every man you fancy and enjoy it. They'll all of 'em be better 'an Jones.' Mangham's voice resounded from the dripping walls.

'Did he look like a gentleman? Fair, with blue eyes? He'll say anything. Whatever he says, it's not true.'

But she couldn't believe Bryce had been there. Not with the chill emitted by the stones, and the water collecting in the hollows and the wails and smell. He wouldn't risk begriming his white neckcloth or getting lice in his peruke. Mary stepped out into Fore-Northgate Street uneasy. If she imagined Bryce in there she imagined him scared.

Soft laughter followed her. She stopped a moment, just able to make out the cathedral tower through the billows of mist.

Damn Mangham. Let him believe what he liked. She swigged from the bottle, right there in the street, and fired back the disgusted looks from the passers-by.

Anthony had not moved. Drops of water still beaded his hair and the beginnings of a bruise reddened his cheek.

'Sit up.' Mary grabbed his jacket. His foot hit the tin cup and sent it rattling across the floor. 'Here's how much better you'll feel, to see me in the same state.'

She gulped down the gin like water on a hot day. The spirit stripped the feeling from her tongue. *Gin.* The word, to her, sounded grey and black – the colours of the funereal window it made on the world. It made her splutter and scrunch up her eyes, and the smell of it dirtied her skin. Points of light dotted the brown glass when she held it up to the window. Just a few inches more. She paused, nauseous and uncertain, then raised it again to her lips.

'Mary.' Anthony dragged himself to his feet and reached for the bottle. 'I'm sorry. Don't hurt yourself because of me.' She wrested it from him and took more. 'Mary, for God's sake – it might kill you.'

'You don't care if it kills you. Why should you care if it kills me?' Her words broke into a cough.

'I'm sorry. Don't drink any more. I'm sorry.'

But she had to now. 'You want me to be drunk as you.' Anthony's bed and its rumpled blankets moved before her eyes. 'You'll feel better to know it in't just you.' The neck of the bottle shook so violently that the liquid spilled into her clothes.

Anthony's eyes changed. She hesitated before she tipped the bottle again, and then a blow numbed her hand and the brown glass shattered on the floor.

'I *said* I was sorry.'

A starfish of gin spread across the tiles. In silence, Mary rubbed the red mark on the back of her hand. It was strangely painless. Unfeeling. She let Anthony's cold fingers stroke it.

'You know why I'm angry,' he said. 'You went into the warehouse with him, didn't you? I waited outside the yard: I thought you'd follow me. Then I went back, afeard the bawd would be looking out for you, and you'd gone.' Mary lowered her eyes. 'You've always sworn you weren't like that.'

'Nothing happened, other than he spoke cruel, as always.'

'You mean nothing happened because he didn't want you?'

Mary's stomach quivered with gin. 'If you hadn't got drunk . . .' she said.

'I wouldn't have done if you hadn't refused to come away with me.'

'I told you I would, in the summer.' An odd sensation prickled Mary's skin. She breathed faster and the room's contents swayed.

'What, once your swell's convinced you he doesn't love you? Once you could bring yourself to stoop to the likes of me?' Anthony slumped on to his bed, his shoulders dipping within his ill-fitting jacket. 'Why d'you have this idea you could ride in a carriage every day and have servants to bring your supper, eh? You're no better than I am, and you'll end up an old maid if you don't admit it.' A crack in the plaster wormed upwards, repeatedly. Her vision separated and she saw Anthony twice, the sandy waves of his hair doubled against one another. 'I say a maid, but you in't, are you?' She shook her head. 'Was it him?'

'No,' she said. 'But it's not as bad as . . .'

Anthony's elbows folded like hairpins and he dropped his chin to his hands. 'I thought that if you were that struck over him he might have taken advantage, and it weren't your fault, but now there's someone else an' all.' He pushed his fingers through his hair. 'When I came here, folk joked the nurses'd be whores without the shilling, but I didn't think it of you.'

Speckles gathered at the limits of Mary's vision. 'Well, it sounds to me you only want me in your bed so you can boast to your gin-drenched friends. So I've lain with a man. Hate me all you like for it, but you wouldn't have been half so 'raged if it had been you.'

Anthony guided her to the door. 'I think . . .' He steadied her gently when she reached out for the wall. 'I think we'd be best to act civil in front of the others.'

Mary tried to return the forced harshness in his eyes. 'Very well,' she said, and she stood for a minute outside his closed bedroom door, and heard the tin cup clattering across the floor.

Mary staggered up the stairs and tumbled on to her bed.

Drink some water. It'll wash the drink away.

On the other side of the room the wash-jug floated far out of reach. Cracks on the ceiling rotated clockwise, clockwise, clockwise. She shut her eyes and the blackness careered into a spin. She scrabbled under the bed for her pot and vomited clear swathes of gin. The rotation of the cracks slowed. Mary smeared the sweat from her forehead and breathed heavily until she blacked out.

The strike of the clock woke her with a stab. One. She must have slept half an hour. Unless . . . No, it was still light and gulls cried outside the window, their calls resonant in the mist.

Sour fumes of gin surrounded her; everything still doubled in front of her eyes. There was no headache. Hangovers required some element of sobriety.

The image in the glass above the washstand made her look away. She rinsed her mouth and spat into her pot, just keeping from being sick again, then emptied it from the window. Sticky dribbles of half-digested gin stuck to the bricks. Mary neatened her kerchief and flinched down the stairs to meet the first inpatients.

No day could have been worse for drinking near a whole bottle of gin. The wall hit Mary's arm and she swore. She set her face to stoniness when she passed Anthony's room. *Damn him.*

'Mary, what's wrong?' Agnes looked pretty as an apple; pretty, and healthy, and sober. Mary pretended to smile, aware of her own hated freckles standing stark in the deathliness of her face.

'Nowt,' she said. She pictured her eye-sockets turning black. Gin sloshed in her stomach and she teetered against the wall.

'Good God!' Agnes caught her before she could slither to the floor.

'Only . . .' She focused on the latch of the store room door opposite. 'Only tired, is all. Looking after Hartingshall, and that.' The main doors opened.

Agnes gave a rueful smile. Then she hugged her, like a friend. 'Don't lie, Mary. It isn't just that, is it?' Unease flooded more sweat from Mary's skin. 'I'm not stupid. I've seen—'

Agnes's whisper flailed into a shriek and Mary started back. In her confusion she smelled tobacco and unwashed linen, and felt fingers slide down her back and seize her buttock so hard she was nearly sick.

'How's my best pair o' wenches?' Wool scraped her cheek and the hand moved to her side, and when she looked down it was sliding up to her breast.

Then, abruptly, Mr Racketta loosened his grip and patted her backside. Agnes's face clouded with indignation.

'Mary is feeling unwell,' she said. 'And I wasn't, but I am now.'

The surgeon slobbed a kiss on to Mary's cheek, scraping her with stubble; then he winked at her and strolled away.

'He just grabbed my behind!' Agnes glared after him, pulling her kerchief together at the front. 'Filthy bugger. No wonder his wife left him, though why she married a filthy bugger like that in the first place I don't know.'

'Wife?' Mary heard her slurring voice as if it were someone else who spoke. Some old crone, sitting on a pile of straw in Cow Lane, ranting about kill-grief. 'It never struck me he'd be married.' Tobacco and stale food and port-wine polluted her skin.

'My God. You don't hear about much in Wirral, do you? I know they say it's all shooting customs officers and burning longboats, but I never thought you wouldn't have heard about *that*.' Agnes's eyes shone. 'You don't know about Mrs Racketta?' Agnes's curls swam in front of Mary's eyes. 'She was getting bulled by a hundred different men – everyone knew that for years – but then she ran off with an ostler from Clarke's Livery. He was only twenty, and she must've been nigh-on thirty, for she was pretty faded.' Agnes smiled slyly. 'Not the ugliest fellow I've ever seen. No one has heard of them since. That must've been about three years ago, or more even.' Agnes's eyes were as round as an owl's. 'Some people say she married him. I don't know how they know, but would you believe it?'

Mary peered through heavy eyelids. 'What? She couldn't. Not with Mr Racketta still alive.'

'Well, you'd think not.' Agnes seemed to be examining her. Studying a museum curiosity; a relic of innocence. 'But people do. They take a different name, and go somewhere no one knows them. So now she has two husbands, if what they say is true.'

Gin poisoned every breath, and Mary's head churned.

The ward was full by four o'clock – all the new patients washed and attired in hospital nightshirts and lying in bed, eyeing one another with suspicion. Mrs Seward read out the rules to them: no swearing, no cards or any other variety of gaming, no candles, no smoking, no spirituous liquors, no food or drink brought from outside, no improper behaviour of any description. There were but twelve beds, she told them, and at least fifty more unfortunates in need of them.

That first evening the patients behaved themselves.

Mary and Agnes went to bed exhausted but afraid to sleep. They listened for sounds from the ward, uncertain what to do if they heard anything. In the warmth of the blankets Agnes joked about each patient's looks and manners, but her giggles seemed false.

Mary's sleep bore her like a raft on waves. She rose and fell, between imaginary sounds and dreams of stairs, always waking from one nightmare into a worse and sleeping to a worse nightmare still.

Then there were words, clear and close by her ear.

I'm not stupid. I've seen.

Mary put her hands against her heart. Why couldn't she have left him to sleep and gone about her work and told herself he wasn't worth getting in a state over? Dry headaches queued behind her forehead. She pictured herself an oil portrait with turpentine splashed in its eyes.

I'm not stupid. I've seen.

Agnes stirred just as the clock struck six. Mary started from a doze and tasted a sickening sourness in her mouth. 'What did you mean?' She could not hear whether the words had come out right. 'You said you'd seen me. Before Mr Racketta grabbed us. What did you mean?' She dreamed Agnes told her she knew everything. That she wished them well, and that she could not be angry – for it was right for Anthony and Mary to be together. Although, of course, they weren't together at all.

Agnes paused a while, then squeezed Mary's hand. 'We've all seen,' she said. 'Me and Mrs Stout and Mrs Seward. We've seen how much gin you've been drinking. We could hardly have missed it. Mrs Stout says Mrs Seward ought not to stand for it.' Mary felt herself crumple. 'It's worse since Anthony started drinking again, isn't it? He seems to have taken right against you. Did something happen, when you were looking after him, to make him cross with you?' Mary noticed how cold her own hand was. To Agnes it must seem like a dead person's hand.

'No. It's just I shouted at him when he drank.'

'I'm not surprised. After you being lumbered with caring for him, and then for him to let you down like that. I think his trull might have jilted him – the state he's been in. Has he said anything about it to you?'

'No. Mayhappen she has. I don't care.'

The first fragments of daylight grew in the window.

'Gin'll kill him.' Agnes stroked Mary's hair. 'I don't want it to kill you.'

Mary closed her eyes, the pain in her head half-soothed by Agnes's hand. 'I'll not drink it any more,' she said.

After they had cleaned the ward and emptied all the pots and served the patients their breakfasts, she took one of the empty wine bottles from the store room and went to the gaol.

CHAPTER 16

Selwyn was thin.

Mary had never known him so. The ragged remains of his shirt hung off him. She reached through the bars with the bundle of food scraps collected from the patients' breakfast, and he took them with subdued thanks and shoved them into his mouth.

Mary's headache worsened in the stink. She clamped her vinegar-cloth to her face and waited in silence while Selwyn palmed back escaped bits of food. Sounds rasped at her fragile nerves. Fire, crackling at the far end of the room; the whistle of air through the window-crosses; the clank of fetters; the whispers and random shouts and inhuman cries.

'I'm to be tried on the 21st of April,' Selwyn said, his eyes vacant. He spoke deliberately, as Hartingshall did when he had taken laudanum. The stench of excrement rushed under Mary's cloth.

'You mean they're to make you stop in here for another two months? That's—'

'No.' Selwyn wrapped his grubby fingers round the bars. 'No. I'm not to stay here. You must get me out.' An unnerving kind of control filled his words. 'You must tell Warbreck I'm innocent.'

She smiled sadly. 'Don't you think I would, if there were a way? He'll not heed me. I've seen him.' Selwyn studied her. 'It's not just the reward. He knows about the beer. He sent Jack Joseph over to Hilbre to fetch it back.'

162

'That was mine.' He brought his face close to the bars. 'That was mine. What's he done with it?'

'I don't know. It might have been in the warehouse. There were some barrels—'

'You've been to his warehouse? Alone with him?'

'Yes.' Mary inched away. 'But—' He lunged forward and grabbed her arm. More pains raced through her head.

'And did you beg him to abandon his wife for you once I'm dead?' The remnants of gin inside her exaggerated his shout. 'You're as eager as he is, in't you, to see me hang?'

''Ere we go.' Someone mumbled, disembodied, in the dimness behind him. Selwyn yanked her hand through the bars and she stumbled forward.

'You'll damn well get me out.' The bones in her wrist slid over one another with the strength of his grip. 'You'll do as I say, Mary. It's your fault I'm here.'

'You're hurting my arm.' Hasty and quiet, her words were buried in his shouts.

'If you won't get me out I'll make them bring you in here with me, and see how you like it.'

'Selwyn—' Her shoulder hit the bars and she cried out. Drips of sweat forged pale channels in the dirt on Selwyn's forehead.

'That's enough, friend,' someone said. 'Don't frighten the lass so.'

Selwyn darted a wild glance behind him and tugged her harder. She remembered the gurgle of air in Jem Hartingshall's throat, and the chill of salt water on the backs of her hands.

'Where's that old get? Mangham!' Fetters clanged near her ear; he grasped the back of her neck. A tuneless whistle progressed down the passageway. 'Open the gate. My wife stays with me.'

It was only Selwyn. Cold iron pressed against the fluttering vein in her throat. Only Selwyn, and he would never harm her.

'You know I can't stay.' Gin pounded behind her eyes. 'I can't do you any good in here.'

163

'You're not doing me any damned good wherever you are.'

Mangham's lantern sent darts of light over Selwyn's shirt. The ragged linen flapped a few inches from her face, the hairs on his chest congealed with sweat and filth. She could feel nothing but the cold bars and the strength of his hand on her neck. The whistling ceased when Mangham thrust his stick through the grille and stabbed Selwyn in the stomach.

'Get your fucking hands off her,' he said, but there was something weary about the fierceness in his tone. Selwyn let go with a grunt and Mangham held the lamp up to Mary's face. 'Sorry, love. It's the only sort of talk this lot understand.' He guided Mary away.

Selwyn tried to shake the bars. 'Open the gate,' he shouted. 'She must stay with me.'

Mary held Mangham's elbow and he glanced awkwardly at the other prisoners. But she would not let go. If she could only have a sip of gin it would stop the tremors and the nerves, but until then she would hang on to Mangham's arm. The empty wine bottle hung heavy in her pocket and her mind felt like a shrunken apple in need of liquid – in need of gin – to fatten it.

'Mary!' Selwyn's shout bowled down the room. 'Mary, stay. Stay with me.'

Mangham yawned. 'They all get like that now and then. 'Specially the ones as'll hang.'

The women at the other end of the ward laughed at her when she followed him down the stairs.

Both she and Mangham hesitated in anticipation once the iron gate whined shut. The bottle wobbled in Mary's hand. But this time there was an excuse, and the indignity seemed less acute. No one whose legs trembled as much as hers could begrudge it. Not even the worthiest paragon of temperance could pass up a sip if she'd just been in the hands of a murderer.

'Might I have this filled?' she asked. Mangham scratched his head and laughed within himself.

'Swilled through the last lot quick, didn't ye?'

'The patients stole it.'

Mangham guffawed. 'Patients stole it.' He wiped away an imaginary tear. 'Patients stole it!' With his back hunched he shambled down to the cellar. The hollow sound of his feet continued after darkness swallowed him and his lamp. Condensation dripped, and distant howls and shouts came from above. Mary's fingertips touched walls as cold as snails. They were far enough away, for now.

Mangham's shoulders jiggled with suppressed laughter when he handed over the bottle.

'Is it still tuppence?' Mary said. 'I know it's bigger than the other one, but that one got shivered and I didn't have owt else.'

Mangham's face gathered into a smile. The light of his lamp defined flaws in the sandstone. 'Here's a rum deal for you, love.' He pushed out his lower lip in a pout of contemplation. 'Make it a shilling, and I won't tell 'im.'

'What?' Mary touched the greasy coins in her pocket.

'I said gi' me a shilling, love, and I won't tell your husband you're carrying on with another man.'

'Has Bryce been here, spreading his lies? Because—'

'I saw it.' Mangham's jacket brushed the wall, the cloth sucking up algae like a sponge. 'I like to walk down to the marshes sometimes. Have a smoke. Need to get away from this place when I can. I saw you take a tumble with that long 'n' lither lad o' yours.' Shame prickled her face. 'Oh, I don't blame you, lovely. Can't blame you for wanting a decent feller. Only I need to make the odd shilling here and there in this job.'

Mangham's eyes hardened. So did Mary's. 'I've nowt but sixpence.' She sought out the crooked coin among the others in her pocket and smiled. He relented. She held the bottle tight to her and stepped from the gloomy passageway.

'Pretty knees,' he said, and she looked back at him, dismayed. 'Gave me a bit of a stir.' He laughed to himself with a wheeze.

The mist of the previous day had lifted, and a miserable sludge coated Fore-Northgate Street. Mary squelched the few yards to the terrace of the Blue Coat School. As soon as she stepped inside she smelled the sour fog of the ward. Anthony met her at the foot of the stairs.

'Where've you been?' he said. 'Mrs Seward's in the boughs over you sneaking off again.' Whenever he spoke to her now, his tone was flat. Mary pushed past him, ashamed of the way it made her feel so sad.

'Damn her.'

She thought she heard him say her name as she went up the stairs, but the sound melted into the patients' coughs and groans.

While the mornings were still so dark Mary and Agnes had until eight o'clock to clean the ward and use the stiff brush to scratch dried herbs into the floor to combat the smell. Once a week, Mrs Seward ordered, they had to mop the floors with soap. She didn't seem to care if it made the patients' lungs damp.

Mary scarce had time, now, to slink back to her room for a sip of gin. From eight she was occupied with fetching the patients their breakfasts and answering back the grumbles of those last to be served, and those who did not like Mrs Stout's cooking. She told them they might go back to their mansions and ask their own cooks to make their breakfasts, and she didn't tell Mrs Stout what ingrates they were.

Then she had to change foul dressings on people who complained that it was not proper to do it so often. 'Have you done that right?' they would ask uneasily, and she wanted to tell them no, she did it wrong on purpose so they would die. If the doctor was there they kept quiet, and he always said what a good job she had done.

Then they were sick all the time, so she had to clear up after them, and they were always trying to light a pipe or play cards. The only time they stayed neat and kept their language proper was when the house visitors were due to inspect them. In the first week one of them was Mr Barnston; he looked around the ward and nodded with satisfaction, and gave Mary and Agnes a sixpence gratuity that they decided must be from his own pocket, not the Board's.

And then there were the pots. Turds of all consistencies and colours, forming stinking islands in oceans of vomit. Mary became good at holding her breath; she could have competed with the half-fish natives in newspapers who dived for pearls.

During the week after the visit to the gaol she continued to tend Hartingshall, relishing the time away from the demands of the patients and their meaty cloud of farts. Anthony often came with her part of the way, then diverted to the gin shop while she measured Hartingshall's dose and set his room fair. Sometimes he met her on the way back, walking in silence beside her, taking a sharp breath now and then as if to speak. He stood back to let her walk first into the hospital, and sometimes she sensed him looking at her.

And then one of the men took bad with a fever and had to be thrown out in case it was the smallpox. When three of the others said they would not stay in a fever-ridden house, on a sudden there were four beds empty, and Dr Tylston recommended that Hartingshall should have one of them. He even told the Board it was because of Mary that Hartingshall stood a chance.

Mrs Seward sent Anthony with a note to the warehouse room, and Hartingshall lumbered into the infirmary with a wild look in the whites of his eyes. 'What will they do?' he said, holding his arm guardfully in front of him. 'They ain't going to cut out the bad bit, are they?'

His walk had tired him; his face looked grey, reflecting the light from the whitewashed corridor wall.

'I don't know,' Mary said. 'But if it were to make it better, in the end . . .' Fear threaded Hartingshall's eyes. 'No, it's the food and the warmth that do it. It's no wonder it still hurts, getting cold every night. The food and the fire and the proper bed'll set you right.'

Another of Mrs Seward's petty rules decreed that every patient must be washed on arrival, and a bath was set up in a small room next to the kitchen for the purpose. Hartingshall eyed the tepid water suspiciously.

'I'm meant to wash you,' Mary said. 'But I've more of a mind to make you wash yourself.' Mrs Seward had said to her and Agnes on the first day, *Oh, for goodness' sake – when you've seen one, you've seen them all*, and she said any pretence to virtue had been negated the moment the gentlemen considered them fit to be recommended as nurses. Agnes had cried over it in bed.

Hartingshall grabbed the flannel and waited for her to leave the room. 'Mind you,' he said with a grin, 'you might send that other girl in. Got a decent bit of flesh on 'er, eh? Devilish comely. I might like this infirmary lark, after all.' Mary could not help smiling at him, and he smiled back, shaking his head. 'Devilish comely. Volumptious.'

She remembered the first time she had seen him – the rain on her eyelids and the nervous knot heavy in her stomach. She remembered how frightened she had been. And now he was no monster at all. No hulking, snarling beggar. Now worry laced his eyes, his hair had grown and his countenance seemed softer. Even when he sneered the curve of his lips was kinder.

But while he might have changed, she was not so different. Still silly little Mary, thinking more of men than they thought of her.

She waited outside, wishing she could sleep standing up. Voices murmured, somewhere down the corridor – hardly more than whispers. Anthony strolled past her and she saw Agnes disappear up the stairs.

'What—' She managed to stifle her words.

Anthony's footsteps slowed. 'Hmm?'

The way he lifted his chin made her hold her breath. A butterfly of red smattered his cheeks; his forehead was pallid and his eyes fiery with drink. A button on his waistcoat had lately been sewn back on: the thread was the wrong colour. It wasn't the way she would have done it.

'What were you talking to her about?'

Anthony raised his eyebrows. 'Nowt. Why should I not speak to her?'

Mary shrugged. 'No reason. You might speak to anyone you like.'

He looked at her in silence for a moment. 'Well, thank you for that permission.'

He stalked off to the kitchen, his hands in his pockets.

Hartingshall at last appeared at the door, dressed in his hospital nightshirt and grimacing with embarrassment. The shirt was so white and tidy, and his hair flattened so neatly to one side that Mary laughed.

'What? What's so bloody funny?'

The skin of his wide feet was peppered with scars, and his hairy white calves disappeared up into the shirt.

'You look different, clean.'

'What good does it do my arm?'

Mary went in to fold his clothes. There was not much left to them; the wool stood stiff with dirt and the linen grey with sweat. They were beyond smelling. She could not see the bottom of the tub. A pair of lice country-danced on the surface and then sank so sedately they might have been immersed in laudanum.

'I hope no other new patients come in today,' she said. 'Else they'll be dirtier after their bath than before.'

Hartingshall's scrubby eyebrows lowered.

'If it's in there, it's off me,' he said. 'That's what you wanted, ain't it? You're never bloody happy, you morts.' He hitched the sleeve of his new nightshirt above his bandage and the linen glowed bright against the grubby folds of the dressing. 'What's the other girl's name?' he asked as he followed her up the stairs. 'Just so's I know.'

'Agnes.' Mary paused. 'You're meant to call her Nurse Hewett. We're meant to be nurses, though it still feels daft to me.'

The ward, once so bleak and dusty, was now full and warm. Rhythmic snoring filled the far end and chattering filled the nearer as the three remaining women sat on one bed, giggling. On the bed nearest the fire two men dealt cards.

''Ere, do you let us play for money?' Hartingshall's eyes widened in tentative glee.

'It's nowt to me what you play for,' Mary said. 'The old bag doesn't like it, but when she's not here you might play for what you like, far as I'm concerned.' Mary turned back the blankets of a bed. She always felt a frisson of pride when she touched the clean sheets. It gave her a taste of what it might have been like to have a neat house. The scent of the soap broke through the curdled atmosphere and calmed her. Sometimes she imagined she could have been a proper wife, keeping her cottage nice. Sometimes it seemed all she wanted.

'This is Mr Hartingshall,' she said to Agnes, and stole a smile at the way he avoided Agnes's gaze. 'He has had a badness in his arm since Mr Racketta cut it.'

Agnes did a sympathetic pout. 'Well, I think anything Mr Racketta does goes bad.' She laid her hand on Hartingshall's good arm, and the tiniest of spasms went through his muscles. 'It must be a fearful fright for you, coming to such a place as this, but I swear we make everyone feel better. Don't we, Mary?' Hartingshall's face went pink. Agnes tucked the bedclothes around him. 'There, I swear that must be the most comfortable bed you've ever been in,' she said. With a faint nod Hartingshall went straight to sleep.

'Oh, look.' Agnes's lips widened into a giggling smile, and she took Mary's arm. 'He's the nearest handsome we've had so far, don't you say?'

Mary looked aside at her. 'No. Are you mad? He's scabby as a cur. How ugly must a man be to escape you ogling him?' Agnes rested her cheek against Mary's shoulder, and Mary shrunk within herself.

'His eyes are kind,' Agnes said. 'They're like chocolate.'

By the next evening, before it was full dark, she was sitting on a bed with Hartingshall and two other patients, holding a hand of cards for him while he used his good arm to play them, and he shared with her the sixpence he won when Mrs Seward was not looking.

A day later Mr Racketta examined his arm. The other patients were silent, watching Hartingshall flinch and grimace with every prod of the surgeon's fingers. Mr Racketta wiped away the worst of the ooze and handed the cloth to Mary. She folded it in on itself, hiding the pinkish smears. She had taken such care of him and yet she must have done something wrong, for the wound had grown, the skin at its edges dark and flaky.

'Flex the arm,' the surgeon said. Hartingshall tried to straighten it, but pain contorted his face and he gripped the blankets tightly with his other hand. 'Hmm. Difficulty with the joint, I see.' The surgeon indicated to Mary to go to his case. 'There's a roll of probes at the bottom. No, the other end.' As she rummaged in the bag she heard him speak to Hartingshall in a low voice. 'I'd fetch them myself, but we get a more pleasant view this way, eh?' She straightened up and flung the roll of instruments on to the bed.

Mr Racketta extracted a delicate steel rod with a wooden handle. 'Keep still, now, while I have a look.' He held Hartingshall's forearm and used the probe to part the edges of the wound. Hartingshall clenched his fists; a purple vein swelled in his temple. Two of the other patients came closer to see. The surgeon put the probe in deeper and Hartingshall swore.

A bubble of blood welled up into the wound, turning the pus into a globule of pink slime. Mr Racketta moved the probe in circles, as if he were churning butter, and the colour of Hartingshall's face lowered from puce to ash.

'That's enough,' Hartingshall said through gritted teeth. 'Leave it alone.'

'It's as I thought,' Mr Racketta said. He pushed the instrument further into the wound. Hartingshall gave a short, belching groan and put his good hand to his mouth. Mary reached for his pot but it was too late; vomit spurted between his fingers and spattered the bed linen. Acid briefly overcame the odour of the wound.

Mr Racketta wiped the probe on the blankets, replaced it in its pocket and tied up the jute roll.

'The bone is rotten,' he said. 'That accounts for the cadaverous smell. In fact, it may well have been rotten for some time, and only now has my incision allowed the poisons to break free. It was lucky I bled you for some other reason, else you might never have known of this until your whole arm decayed from the inside.'

'There was nothing wrong with my arm,' Hartingshall said. 'Never hurt, nothing, 'til you cut it.' He stared with a mixture of fear and indignation at the wound.

'Such is the way of things sometimes,' the surgeon said, abruptly clipping his case shut. 'The nurse will bandage it up again, won't you, sweeting? There, you can't complain: many a fellow would pay good money to have a girl like this at his service.' He patted Mary's arm and then left, turning back to smile at her as he reached the door.

'Get that bloody bandage back on before I puke over you again,' Hartingshall groaned. Mary bundled up his bedclothes and took them outside to scrape the vomit off. A pair of stray dogs came in from the street to gobble it up.

The next outpatients' day Agnes volunteered to stay in the ward and let Mary do the ferrying about downstairs. Two o'clock struck before the last patient left.

Mary permitted herself pride in the neat way she left the treatment room. She breathed in the scent of the thyme she had rubbed into the floor. She did not notice, at first, someone behind her.

'Nurse Helsall, might I have a word?'

It still made her feel odd, to be called that. Like an impostor. Not much of a nurse, and no longer properly a Helsall, either, except in blood. Mr Barnston pressed his fingertips together and smiled.

'The Board would like you to prepare this room for use,' he said. He indicated the store room where they kept buckets and mops, and empty wine bottles and beer-flagons, and flour-sacks waiting to go back to the baker, and the sicked-on linen ready for the laundry-maid's weekly visit. 'Dispel the dust and ask Wells to remove the contents, if you would.' He had no idea where they should go. The mildewed odour of the mops made Mr Barnston twitch his nose, betraying an uncomfortable recognition of their existence.

'Very well, sir,' she said.

And then Mr Barnston's phlegmatic calmness dissolved and he glanced furtively towards the main door. 'I hear you looked after him before he was brought in.'

'You mean Hartingshall, sir?'

'Hartingshall. Indeed. You do know . . .'

'Yes.' How odd it would be to look after Hartingshall without ever realising who he was. 'I know everything.'

Mr Barnston's expression chilled for the tenth part of a second. Then he smiled.

'You have seen . . . You have seen Mr Warbreck, perhaps?'

'I have, sir.'

'And . . .' Mr Barnston paused as the matron passed behind him. 'What did he say?'

'He were hufted about Selwyn buying a few barrels of beer, that's all. They were only a few barrels. Selwyn meant to sell them, and we'd move further up the coast and make a better life for ourselves. He never meant to compete. He only wanted a better life for us.' Mr Barnston's clean-shaven jaw tightened.

She remembered him, brandy in hand, looking with concern out towards the door. He had swilled the liquor in the great round glass, and his eyebrows had dipped in sympathy.

'He was angry with me,' she said. 'The sailor – he was in my place. Sir, he would never do such a thing again. It were my fault, and I wouldn't be so ungrateful again. Why won't you tell Bryce to drop the case?'

Mr Barnston glanced down the corridor. 'Mary, be silent.'

'He'd have to listen to you. You must've been one of his best customers. Why won't you help us?' Confidence flooded her. 'If we were on the wrong side of the law so were you.'

Mr Barnston's composure returned. 'Ah, poor Mary. I know it's not your fault.' He adjusted his cuffs, taking an age to make the lace into an even border of white around the sleeves of his jacket. 'But your husband is guilty. Whatever has gone before, he has killed a man. You would not deny that, would you?'

She could only shake her head.

'I might have purchased smuggled goods from Mr Warbreck, but that is in no way akin to murder. It is not morally wrong to eschew taxes that are only levied to line the pockets of those in power – those who seek purely to subsidise their own extravagances. The free trade helps people like you and those from your village who would otherwise eke out a difficult existence. Murder is something quite different – something that goes against the whole foundation of society and, worse, the laws of God.' His smile was like a parenthesis, closing his argument, and he turned away.

Boldness darted through Mary and she made fists. 'Well, sir,' she said, 'if you don't forsake God why do you forsake mercy?'

He paused, then continued to the board room and closed the door quietly behind him.

Over the next few days Mr Racketta attended the hospital to observe Mary and Agnes clearing out the store room, and when they had finished he and Mr Cotgreave placed a sturdy chair in the centre of it and remarked on the quality of the light.

Thurstaston, early hours, 28 December 1755

Mary is alone on the shore. Where is he, her husband? Husband! The one who is supposed to protect her, and is too much of a coward to see off a couple of old bitches who wish it had been them in the carriage with Bryce Warbreck, in the copse of silver birches, in the early-evening sun.

She is half-drowned already and cannot be any colder for the loss of her topcoat, so she discards it next to her cape on the sand.

She has more or less decided to climb back up the cliff path and wait with Jakey, or do as Adam Roberts said and go home, when something catches her eyes. Walking so close to the waves that they purl round her feet, she strains her vision out across the water. It seems there is nothing there, but when she looks away a darker shape teases the limits of her gaze. Something rises and falls with the waves.

Fifty yards away or more the others still wait. Their lamps move and the wind catches grabs of laughter and fragmented words.

'Selwyn!'

But she can only feel, not hear, her own shout. The shape comes closer; it is ten feet, perhaps, from the shore and only dips and rises, as if wary to land. The gallop of a cloud past the moon ends in a shimmer of light on the water. Thousands of silver sparkles flash once, the shape appears defined, and the darkness returns. Mary ties her remaining petticoat in a knot at her thigh and wades into the sea.

Lack of light aids her. There is no dizzy movement of the sand if she looks down, and no overwhelming mass of water ahead of her – only the shifting under her feet and the cold numbing her legs.

The wooden chest that meets her hands is bulky; she tries to pull it towards her. Not so very heavy, but cumbersome, it is reluctant to

175

submit. So, with her petticoat dragging at her waist and her hair half-loose and plastered to her face, she gets behind it and pushes it until it grinds a corner into the sand. Exhausted, she tries to recover her breath.

A lamp darts a few feet away, then settles on the shore, and Selwyn grasps the box.

'Get the other side. Have you a whim to drown tonight? Why did you not shout for me?'

'You didn't listen.' Together they move the chest up the shore.

'I said, why did you not shout, Mary? I'm sorry for what I said before. You might have been swept away.'

'I said—' She jumps at the crack of Selwyn's hatchet on the clasp. He holds up the lantern, and the light shows the sheen of water on his skin and his hair forming sodden stalactites on his forehead.

All they seem at first to be are blankets. Neat rolls positioned side by side, and another flung in a haphazard way on the top.

Mary unravels one of them and the light enflames a bright glint of blue. Another spark leaps – this time into Selwyn's eyes – and he looks at her with the first twitchings of a smile. 'G'won, gal. Let's see it.'

Mary unwraps the blanket further, her cold hands fumbling.

Then, there it is: a roll of silk so beautiful it seems woven from strings of tiny gems. Selwyn laughs, with a harsh glee that discomfits her, and slams the lid down. 'Guard it. This is one thing o' mine Warbreck has no claim to.' He watches her as he hands her a pistol – the heavy one she takes when she patrols the cliffs – but she takes care not to react to his words. Then he is gone, and she shivers in her wet clothing and points the gun at the waves.

Why can't she be a witch and transport herself into her bed? The sheets, not clean, she admits, not having done much washing lately, but at least dry, and the blankets, three of them, warm and heavy over her. Her eyelids droop and the cold bites less. Don't go to sleep. The cold tells you to sleep and it only wants to take you. Sometimes people get lost in the snow and think it's warm, and take their clothes off, and then their bodies are found, solemn and blue, a few yards from their own barn.

But now it really is warm. Mary huddles in Selwyn's coat, the pistol angled at the sea. Her fingers burn.

'So you've barleyed first spoils, Mary Jones?' There's a lantern and, in its light, yellowish eyes. 'Did you bargain with the Devil for you to have first chance?'

The warmth is like the warmth of brandy. It makes her think nothing of raising the pistol barrel to Betsy Roberts's wrinkled face. 'If I did, I could bargain with him for you to be swept out to sea.'

Betsy moves aside hastily. 'If you shot me, girl, you'd hang.'

'It might be worth it.'

Betsy gasps, but her gasp is weak and contrived. 'Adam! She's like to kill me!'

She could fire it now. The trigger, under a film of salt water, begs to be pressed. Blood, screaming, gaol, gallows. She looks away and points the pistol down at the sand. 'Leave me be, Betsy, while you can.'

Betsy smiles, such as her wizened lips are able. 'I'm just keen to know what you've found, so the rest of us might know what to look forward to.'

'Silk.' Then it is Mary who smiles. Though her teeth are not very straight, she knows her smile has something about it – that it makes strangers smile back. Men, anyway. Whereas Betsy has only three teeth at the top and two at the bottom, and those as brown as the cargo chest.

Betsy is talking again. Why can't she just shut up? But Mary doesn't hear what she says, because she is distracted. Something else lies at the line between sea and shore – a sack-like shape, a pile of rags. Betsy follows her gaze and holds up the lantern.

A man lies on the sand, as wet and angular as a newborn calf.

Should she leave the silk and help him? Mary condemns herself for even wondering, but as she starts towards him her husband arrives, and here's one time when he might be some use.

177

'Selwyn, look! I think he's still alive. Pull him out.'

'Do as your wife says, Jones. Be obedient, now, afore you're henpecked to your death.'

'Shut up, Betsy.' Selwyn's eyes take on a new darkness; a glint of black that makes Mary grip the gun tighter. Hatchet in one hand, he grabs the sailor's shirt and pulls him up on to the sand.

'A well-looking lad,' says Betsy. Mary puts the pistol down, barrel in the sand, distrustful of her hand, knowing what's coming next. 'Not as handsome as Mr Warbreck, though, is he, Mrs Jones?'

The sailor's face is bleary and salted. Water streams from his hair, snot pours from his nose and his eyelids are swollen and red. She meets Selwyn's gaze.

'It's no time to gabble about what he looks like,' she says. 'We might look to our hearts' content when his life's saved.'

A bubbly cough spews from the man's nose. Selwyn takes him by the collar, raises his head and rams it down into the sand.

'Selwyn, no!' She tries to scrape the sand from the man's mouth. 'Help me carry him to the cart.'

'Hark at her, I say. He's half-drownded and she's already got her hands on him.'

'Get back and guard the cargo,' Selwyn says.

'Forget the cargo. We must help him.'

'I said guard it. He in't going to take that from me.' Betsy's arms are folded and her lip cocked in a sneer. 'I said guard it, damn you. Guard it! You'll do as I say!' Selwyn's voice is louder than the gale. A vein pulses in his temple, blue under his rain-chilled skin. Don't be stupid, Selwyn. She thinks it calmly but something stops her from speaking it. 'You'll damn well do as I say!'

The hatchet lifts high above Selwyn's head. He wouldn't. Not to her, his own wife.

She flinches away and covers her face with her hands, and then she hears a thud and a rattle of air, and Betsy screaming. When she looks up the anger has gone from Selwyn's eyes, and they are filled with fear.

CHAPTER 17

The cook's singing seemed to grate more than usual on Mrs Seward. The dirt was gone from the ward floor and the herbs were scratched into the boards. The patients were left to finish their breakfasts in the healthful flow of air from the open windows. The fifth day of March had brought with it a touch of springtime that cheered the curdled atmosphere around the beds.

But Mary, Agnes and Anthony sat in an awkward triangle at the kitchen table, avoiding one another's gazes, their plates squeezed in amongst the clutter of Mrs Stout's cookery. The heat of the fire battered Mary's petticoats. She ran her fingers under her kerchief; Anthony looked quickly away.

Mrs Seward prodded the coals. Each jab of the poker crackled tension into the room. Porridge congealed in front of Mary, its grey folds petrifying on the spoon. She sighed, and the hush of air came out louder than she meant. The matron fired her an evil look. Magnified by her spectacles, Mrs Seward's eyelids were puffy.

'If this fire were to be kept hot,' she said, her face turned away, 'the tea would not taste as though it were drawn out of a ditch. I warrant Mr Bagnall does not donate tea to the infirmary only for it to be wasted by the use of improperly heated water.' She fired more coal from the scuttle and Agnes jumped. The flames shrank, engulfed; the heat on Mary's skirts subsided; and Mrs Stout eyed the matron's back

179

with an insolent wag of her head. Agnes paused between each mouthful of breakfast as if about to speak, but studied her plate whenever the shuffles of coal threatened to drown her out. At last she raised her eyes.

'Happy birthday,' she said. Anthony's shoulders hunched into a cringe.

'Thank you,' he mumbled. He fidgeted with his knife, and mined curlicues of dirt from the grain of the table. Mrs Seward became still, resting her hand on the mantelpiece. Mary pushed her plate away, her insides all knotted. She imagined a trace of triumph on Agnes's mouth.

'Oh, I didn't know it were your birthday, my love.' Dishwatery fingermarks smeared Anthony's forehead as Mrs Stout clasped his head to her bosom and plunged a kiss into his uncombed hair. 'My lovely boy – I'll make you a special pudden later, shall I? Wi' currants.' She released him and patted his cheeks. 'Oh, bless your heart – you're near as handsome as my own dear lad.' Anthony rolled his eyes, but the corner of his mouth crept upwards in a grin.

'And how old might you be, Wells?' Mrs Seward's tone damped the cook's enthusiasm.

Anthony rested his forehead on his fists. 'Five-and-twenty.' Even Mary, across the table, could only just hear him.

'Speak up.'

'I said five-and-twenty.'

Mrs Seward no longer hid her face. A wash of purple spread through her bloodhound cheeks. 'Five-and-twenty!' Spittle launched like venom from her mouth. 'Old enough to have made something of yourself. Old enough to have established yourself in a gainful business and taken a respectable wife, and to have earned the esteem of your peers.' Redness flushed Anthony's cheeks and his eyes darkened. 'Old enough to have stopped drowning yourself in gin every night and wasting every day in bed. A quarter of a century!' Mrs Seward grabbed a handful of Anthony's hair, her knuckles bulging. Agnes gasped. 'Do you think drinking your guts to rottenness and whoring your way into disease won't kill you before you're thirty?'

Mary's chair screeched back across the tiles. '*Let him go! Let him go!*'

Her hand flashed to the nearest object, but Agnes whipped it aside. The matron shoved Anthony's head away. His chair clattered to the floor and he slammed the door so hard that one of Mrs Stout's pots fell off the dresser and hummed on the tiles.

'And you're no better, girl.' Mrs Seward's face was as contorted as a witch's. 'Hiding gin in your cupboard. Taking gulps of hospital wine whenever the doctors turn their backs. And how many times did Mr Hartingshall even see you when you claimed to be looking after him? I'm sure there were finer gentlemen than him getting a shilling ready for your attention.' Mary widened her eyes. 'How long before you start bringing men back here? I know the type you are, girl – you even make eyes at the governors. And there's . . .' Mrs Seward's throat stopped. The cook and Agnes watched in silence.

'Nothing you can do about it?' Mary's head felt light and hollow. Sparks raced up behind the matron. 'Why? Because Mr Barnston won't let you sack me?'

The purple glow of Mrs Seward's cheeks intensified. 'Only you,' she said, 'could have chosen such a day to behave like this, you selfish little witch.'

Two searching gazes followed the matron from the room and then swivelled back to Mary. She sank into her chair. 'I'm sorry.'

Agnes observed her steadily for a long moment, and then looked away.

Iron drew the heat from Mary's cheeks as she leant her face on the railings. Spring had made a hesitant expedition into Fore-Northgate Street and sucked warmth from the mud, its scent fungal and moist. At the foundations of the bridewell opposite, turgid green shoots yearned away from the shade.

Daffodils. Just like the ones in the grass outside her cottage, at home. Seagulls cried on the turrets of the Northgate.

Who might live there now? What must they have thought when they went there, and saw the state of the herb garden, and the dust on the bedstead legs?

Now there would be bread standing every day to cool by a clean window, and children making hand shadows in the spots of sunlight on the floor. Whoever lived there now would be a proper wife, looking after her own home. Not a servant scraping up sick for a pair of shillings a week. Not a skivvy made to stand being called a whore by a poisonous old woman not content to hate people for their true faults.

Perhaps Mary was becoming inured to hatred. She must be, because Mrs Seward's behaviour towards her seemed more a curiosity than a source of anguish. How strange – how close to the cliff-top of madness – for a woman of the matron's age to derive her only self-worth from grinding people into the ground. What a side-show she was; what a macabre fascination she excited. Mary forced a quiet laugh. Observing Mrs Seward was like hedging around a street corner booth, sixpence in hand, gleeful with fright at what might be inside.

Except, that was, when she turned on Anthony.

Mary rested her forehead on the bars and thought about gin. Perhaps it would soften the anger that streaked through her every time she pictured the matron ripping at Anthony's hair, and the time after time she heard her words.

Old enough to have made something of yourself.

Drinking your guts to rottenness and whoring your way into disease.

Mary's fingers tightened round the railings, and she wanted to tear them up and fling them like spears through Mrs Seward's rotting raisin of a heart.

She hadn't realised, at the time, that it was her knife she reached for. Perhaps it would have bounced off Mrs Seward's stays, or perhaps it would have caught her in her pinched-up face. But now it seemed Mary was the gashed one; the one opened up and raw. She would have killed Mrs Seward for treating Anthony like that. She could kill anyone who tried to hurt him. Easily. The breath wouldn't flow into her lungs; she gripped the railings harder. It was too late to pretend it was all for the best that he had guided her from his room and said, in such a cold way, that they must be civil. Too late to keep telling herself she rightfully belonged to Selwyn. What could be right about it? What was belonging? Was it only being taken pity on? Because Selwyn had been good enough to take her on when he knew he could never love her as a wife, must that mean he owned the lips Anthony had kissed and the heart and mind that had fallen in love of their own accord?

The spring breeze licked the back of her neck. She looked up at the wall east of the Northgate and remembered the first time Anthony brushed his fingers down her skin. Why could she not be like the bolt of blue silk, adrift and ownerless, free to float or sink according to its own powers, and to wash up on any shore?

An awkward cough made her turn. Anthony stood with his hands in his pockets, his eyes weary and his waistcoat done up wrong. 'I thought I'd best tell you,' he said. 'I'm to leave for London. The Pied Bull runs a coach a week on Monday. I'll go as far as a shilling takes me and walk the rest. I won't tell Mrs Seward – I'll just go. But I thought I'd best tell you.' Mary dug her nails into her palms. He hunched his angular shoulders as if to lessen himself to nothing. 'I'm twenty-five today. That's nigh-on thirty, and thirty's nigh-on forty, and I've done nowt to be proud of – not one thing. I'll not stay and be treated like she treated me this morning. I have to go and make summat of myself, and London's the only place I have a chance.'

A loose stone bounced across the cobbles as he slouched back to the building. Blacker than ever, the Northgate overshadowed half of the courtyard, keeping the cobbles imprisoned in the damp of winter. Mary slumped sideways against the railings and let tears slide hot between her cheek and the iron.

'Mary! Wait there.' Mrs Stout waggled a pudgy hand at her. 'You may take this chocolate to the board room for the surgeons. They sent poor young Mr Hughs down to say they will want it at half past ten. Bless him – with his leg an' all, sending him down the stairs like that. They might have senten you, if you weren't so catched up in your love-affairs.'

Mary snatched up the tray and the chocolate splashed out of its spout. She turned away before the cook could remark on the blotchiness of her face or the way she bit hard on her lip.

The surgeons arrived at the bottom of the stairs just as she left the board room: Mr Cotgreave, Mr Racketta, and another stocky man whose leathery skin hung off his face like a sheet draped on a hedge to dry.

'Ah.' Mr Racketta slid his gaze over her. 'Mr Venables, this is our Nurse Helsall. The one I was telling you about.' He pointed the end of his clay pipe at her. 'Is she not right pretty, eh, for a nurse?' The leather-faced surgeon did not answer him.

'Mr Hartingshall's arm,' he said to Mary, 'requires replacement of its bandage, if you would be so good.'

Mr Racketta winked and blew out a stream of rank smoke. 'Make it nice and tight, my dear,' he said. 'The flesh is right swollen.'

Hartingshall focused on the ceiling, his face so grey that the pillow beside it seemed yellow as curdled cream. His arm rested outside the blankets and the odour of the wound overcame the fragrance of thyme from the floorboards. Vomit congealed in his pot. The patients in the beds either side of his lay with their backs turned to him.

'Did they say anything?'

'The surgeons? No, only that I must put this back on.' She rolled up the bandage and put a fresh linen pad on the wound – gently, she thought, but Hartingshall jerked in pain and it flew on to the floor. His arm trembled, as Anthony's sometimes did in the mornings.

'They want to cut it off,' he said. Mary's hand stilled, reaching for the pad. She wiped her first thought from her mind. The thought that said, *He can't stand up in court, dead.* For a time she just concentrated on the weave of the linen, and picked from it strands of thyme and grains of dust.

'When?'

Hartingshall shrugged his good shoulder. 'Didn't say. Didn't say a word to me. Just ummed and muttered between theirselves, and went off to plan it.'

'But they said they wanted to cut it off?'

He gave a weary shake of his head. 'But that's what they want. You could see it in that fat bugger's piggy eyes.'

Mary tried to smile. Then a natural lull in the sniffs and snores exposed a whisper: *Sixpence says they do it*, and she coughed, but Hartingshall heard, and closed his eyes.

'They mightn't have a mind to do that at all,' Mary said. If anything, the swelling had gone down. Flaccid and pale – from the light not getting to it, she supposed, like grass under a pot – the skin had lost some of its redness and gone crinkled. 'Mayhappen they'll cut away the grey bits, is all, and stitch the sides back together. It'll hurt a bit – but then, it does anyway.' Hartingshall's face twisted until she had finished the bandage. His fingers were cold as seaweed. 'Well,' she said. 'They can't cut it off if you don't let them.'

Hartingshall blew out a dejected whoosh of air. 'Look at it,' he said. 'How can this get better? It ain't mine any more. I don't know. It's a worry that the worse it gets the more I think it might be best off gone.'

There had never been a death in the hospital. Would Mrs Seward panic? Would they have to keep the body somewhere until it was buried? Would the ghost ever be able to get out of the place, or would it come into her room every night and stand by the bed, a faceless shape against the window?

'Where's Nurse Hewett?' Hartingshall asked.

Mary smiled. 'Cleaning our room. It's her turn. It won't take long.'

'Makes me sad, you know, to see her,' he said. Mary's smile dropped. 'Knowing there's someone like her in the world, and me like this. Knowing that when she's kind to me it's only because she's kind to the rest of them too. Why didn't I just let my boots fill, and take a lungful of brine?'

And then, on a sudden, she wanted to confide in him. To ask him, did it feel like a pair of fists wringing out his heart? Did he have to fight not to beg Agnes to love him? Did he have moments when something distracted him and he didn't think of her, and then the thoughts came back, hard enough to steal his breath? Or didn't men feel like that?

'Some folks,' she said, 'have a talent for keeping alive. Happen you're one of them.'

In the evening Agnes brought his supper. When she turned away his fingers brushed her petticoat, and Mary thought of Anthony standing in the springtime air by the railings, telling her he was leaving her.

Safe fire, cold kettle, the shape of a leaf bobbing in shadow on the table. The greasy glow of her candle pushed the moonlight back through the kitchen window. Tendrils of smoke needled her nose. All was quiet and in order. Mrs Seward would have no true reason to berate her, though she would no doubt come up with a false one.

Anthony's dented tin cup sat empty on the table, a crescent of candlelight brightening its rim. She imagined sheltering in the shadow of the Northgate, unseen as she watched him scramble on to a coach outside the Pied Bull. The image knotted her insides. She ran her finger along the cup's rim, where his lips had been.

Well, it was all for the best. She must pretend it didn't hurt so much in her heart, because the heart, after all, wasn't hers to hurt with.

'I forgot my cup.'

She spun round, blocking the light of the candle, dimming Anthony's solemn face. When he took it from her, his hand touched hers. He seemed to wait for her to speak, the blunt tips of his fingers white. Then he looked towards the embers, hesitated and turned away.

'Anthony, I hope everything turns out perfect for you, in London. I hope you get to fix watches all day and it never seems like work.'

Mary held her thumbs tight in her fists. He studied the inside of the cup. 'I don't want to go. Without you.'

Relief made her hands tremble. 'I don't love anyone else. I don't love Bryce Warbreck. I thought I did once, but I didn't. Because it wasn't like this.'

'Then you'll come with me? To London?'

Light sheened on the candle-holder. Any movement, or look, he would take as an answer. Any hesitation now and the flood of happiness would fade to nothing, and he would embark on the coach to London alone.

'The end of April,' she said, and as soon as she heard herself speak she knew it was not good enough. 'I must bide in Chester 'til after the Great Sessions.'

Until then wary, his expression became quizzical, half-amused. 'You an't killed someone?'

'No!' Her voice was too hasty and sharp. 'Don't joke about such things.'

'Then tell me,' he said, gripping her shoulders with deliberate calm. 'Sit here with me and tell me.' He dragged out a chair and pulled her on to his knee. 'Tell me what's happened. You have to. It's beyond keeping secret now.' He blew out the candle, leaving a tiny red ember that pulsed and faded until he dabbed his fingers to his tongue and fizzed it away. Candle gas wound through the darkness and Anthony's arms encircled her while he waited in silence for her to speak.

'Hartingshall's told you,' she whispered. 'Hasn't he? About the wreck?' He squeezed her closer to him and she sensed him taking deeper, wary breaths. 'His brother was killed and I was there.'

She kept whispering close to his ear, her words sparse and full of pauses. She stroked his cheek, prickles of day-old stubble rasping her palm. Eight o'clock struck. She waited for the chimes to finish, and then she kept whispering, telling him most of the truth. Behind him the last spots of red winked in the ashes of the kitchen fire.

'Selwyn Jones?' Excitement threaded Anthony's whisper; all the excitement of a boy catching a glimpse of a renowned highwayman. 'You know Selwyn Jones, the murderer?' Thank God he couldn't see her close her eyes.

'We grew up together. I never had a brother. I suppose he was like one. That's why I must wait 'til the Sessions. I have to stand witness for him. His other friends are that feared of Bryce they'll say what he tells them.'

'But you're not feared?'
'No.'

She felt him smile as he kissed her. 'My own brave Mary. Why didn't you tell me? I thought you loved someone else. A murder's not much to that.'

'You might not've believed I didn't help him kill. And some folks'd be shocked at a woman riding decoy for the walks. The ghost walks, I mean. The smuggling trips.'

His lips moved against her neck. 'My own Mary, fighting off the law with a pistol.' She did not think it funny enough to warrant such humour in his voice. 'You would trounce a thousand officers before you ever surrendered.'

She remembered her pale hand quivering on the gun, the way she held it towards the heather and the way her stomach spun at every sound.

'Selwyn Jones, eh?' He cupped her chin and held her face near to his. 'Sel-wyn Jones. Like a brother to you.'

'He was.' She could not tell whether the embers cast any glow into her eyes. Her cheek burned under the light stroke of his thumb.

'April, then,' he said. 'Springtime, and we'll go to London. The roads'll be drying up. If we both save, we can save enough for a coach all the way and it'll take no more than a week and then we'll never have to be apart. Here's a choice for you: would you rather marry here, or in London?'

Mary made herself laugh. 'It depends whether anyone asks me.'

He told her to stand, and the chair scraped back. For the second time within three years she listened to a man ask her to marry him, and this time she smiled as he did it, and ran her hand through his wild hair, and pretended she was a normal, innocent girl with her first sweetheart, and fought the guilt down to a fragment. A shred; a dry piece of kindling in a dark corner.

The first proposal had been in a proper setting. It was evening, and an emberous sun ignited rows of clouds as straight as the ripples of a full-bottomed wig. A streak of red pierced the gentle waves, and the fields of Wales retained remnants of the light that had abandoned the side of the estuary where she and Selwyn walked.

Her mother was soon to die. It would take another two months, though she did not know that then. But she did know it would be soon, and she knew her own sewing skills would not be in demand from a village that did not accept her. Like a rock pool isolated from the sea, she must let them flood her with scorn when they chose, but had no waves of her own to repel their united surge. Neither could she earn enough to support herself, and Selwyn knew that.

'We must marry, I suppose,' he had said.

'I suppose so,' she had replied. She let him kiss her; his lips were still and cold, and his smile failed to infect his eyes.

That sun had nothing to commend it but colour; it granted no heat, only drooped in the sky and sank into the sea without even a hiss.

A good, solid young man, her mother had said in relief when she told her. *He will keep you steady.*

But now, in the dark, the candle and the fire dead, her whole body flamed harder than a thousand of those suns. 'Yes,' she whispered. 'Yes.'

Well, Mr Racketta's wife had managed it, somehow.

Watches would make their fortune, he said, and they talked of her taking in sewing, and they imagined simple, tidy lodgings in a modest but respectable street.

'And if we have a son I'll put him as apprentice to a real watch-maker, and make sure he's taught proper, like I never was.'

Mary picked at the rough skin around her fingernails and stilled her insides against the pang.

It was getting late.

'Is London by the sea?' she said.

'Not far.'

She dreamt of a short walk to a long, deserted shore.

When at last they rose from the chair, Mary's nerves sprang. She followed him, her hand in his, to his bedroom door. Distant sounds murmured down the stairs – coughs and creaks of bedsteads and a snort in someone's sleep. Anthony kissed her, and then stepped back.

'I know you won't want to come in with me, and I understand.'

'What?' Disproportionate hurt shocked her. He might just as well have turned her out into the mud.

'Mary, it's because of what you said, that time. About me wanting to boast. I don't want you to think that. I don't want you to think I'm tricking you.'

'You mean you want it to be my fault?' The terseness of her voice sounded loud. 'You mean you *don't mind* whether or not I come into your bed?' She turned away from his hand on her face.

'No. Mary, for God's sake, I don't mean anything like that.'

It was too late not to ruin everything. Too late to be a forward enough trollop to insist he let her in.

'I know,' she said quietly, and tried a smile. 'I'm sorry. Happen we'd best say goodnight.'

A few stairs up she stopped and listened, but she only heard him swear softly and then open and close his door. She hesitated, about to go back to him, but then she ran her hand up the smooth banister and held up her petticoats to stop them swishing on the stairs.

Her own room was locked; she tapped on the door.

'Agnes!' Mary put her mouth close to the keyhole. 'Agnes!' Nothing. She coughed; still nothing. 'It's me. I fell asleep, in the kitchen.' The latch rose to its limit but the door remained fast. Then a low voice muttered a few words. Mary pressed her ear hard to the door. 'Agnes, have you a feller in there?' Two whispers competed, then the man murmured; she could not hear what he said. She lowered her mouth to the keyhole again. 'Disgusting.'

Mary walked up and down the ward, and felt for each patient's feet. She stopped at Hartingshall's bed. His bulk filled it. She touched his shoulder and he half-awakened.

'What?'

'It's nowt. Go to sleep.'

Hartingshall sniffed and gave a pained groan. 'Wake me up to tell me to go to sleep? Bloody women.'

Some grubby ostler, then, she supposed. Some footman who'd promised a ribbon. Poor Hartingshall; she wouldn't tell him. Mary pulled a chair close to the fire, but the coals glowed feebly under a flaky grey mantle of ash. Half-formed thoughts swirled in her head. *Mary, will you marry me? . . . London . . . If we have a son . . . You're not sure . . .*

Someone down at the farther end dragged in a piggish snore, and the hollow, sulphury pall of a silent fart suspended itself in the air.

If she could only get into her room she might have a sip of gin. Make sense of things. Quench the embarrassment that had taken hold the moment she had stepped on to the stairs. She walked along the ward again, chafing her arms.

'Nurse Helsall, I've a job to sleep.'

'Stay awake then.'

'I can't.'

Mary smiled. Young Tommy Hughs was after laudanum again, for his sore leg. There was none in the ward to give him – Mr Crane would bring it tomorrow – but she reached down Hughs's bottle of hospital wine from the shelf and let him take a swig. He had not seen anyone with Agnes, he said.

'I'll move aside, and you might sleep here. I'd not try owt.'

'Thank you, but I'd best not.' She paused. 'I must have a sup of this wine, to keep warm, but you won't tell the matron, will you?'

''Course not.'

Sweet as a cordial, the wine fell, smooth and succulent, down her throat. She drank half of what was left in Hughs's bottle, then felt along the shelf for another. This one was fuller. She took it back to her chair. If any of the patients woke they would not see.

Tumbles of hair fell around her shoulders as she removed the pins and rubbed her tired scalp. She stretched her feet to the remains of the fire. The wine stroked through her limbs and made her eyelids droop. She reached behind and touched the tips of her long hair.

He would have furrowed his fingers through it, if she hadn't been so stupid. He'd lift it high and let it flutter, tress by tress, against her back. Would he brand his lips to her neck first? Would he push her kerchief aside and bring his mouth to her breast? She let her knees fall slightly apart. Would his slim fingers pull the pins from her jacket, or would they reach first for her petticoats, gathering up the folds?

He had not meant to turn her away. He'd only meant to do what was right, but it wasn't what he wanted. He wanted her.

Mary emptied the bottle and licked the bitter, gritty residue from her teeth. She listened at her own bedroom door, and heard nothing. She did not try the latch again, lest it opened.

The windows that faced the Northgate allowed only a greyish slick of light to fall on Anthony's door. When he answered she could just make out his hair, wild about his head, and the shape of his white shirt.

'Hmm?' Sleep slowed his voice.

'She's locked me out of our room,' Mary whispered. Anthony drew a sharp breath.

'My God.' He touched her shoulders, his long fingers gentle. 'Mary.' Beneath the coarse linen shirt his body was slender and warm. He took handfuls of her hair. Its whispering sounds melted into the hush of his breath, quickening.

'If you don't want me here—'

'I do.' His skin smelled of soap. 'I do want you here. I want you anywhere. How did I upset you? I don't understand.'

'It's nothing. You just made me think of something. It weren't your fault.'

He drew her into the room. Catches of gin hung in its air. The quiet crunch of the key in the lock made her heart turn over.

'Does she know?' Anthony whispered. 'She's seen us?'

The base of a bottle scraped along the night-table and, well-practised she supposed, he poured out a cupful in spite of the dark. It always surprised her, the sweetness of the Cow Lane gin. Sugar hung in it like seaweed in waves.

'There's a man in there.'

Was there some way of telling when a bolt of jealousy shot through someone? Whenever it happened to her she thought it visible. A flame or a hiss of lightning. But Anthony did not flinch. His arms tightened around her and a smile threaded his voice.

'Not Hartingshall, the state he's in?'

'He's still abed. In the ward. I thought to sleep there, in the chair, but—'

'But you'll stay here,' he said. 'Won't you? With me.'

'Do you want me to?'

He laughed quietly.

Tiny, soft sounds inhabited the darkness. The rustle of the feathers in the bed-tick; the whisper of her kerchief across her skin. She listened, at first, for the tread of feet on the stairs. But then her heart beat faster, and she heard nothing but that, and the smoothing of Anthony's hand round her waist, and the brush of her stay-laces, coiled around his finger and worked undone.

CHAPTER 18

The strings purred with each confident tug, higher and higher. Air slaked into her lungs like the first breath after quenching a thirst. Anthony pushed the stays over her head; they smelled of her body, warm and familiar. She smiled at the heat of his hands through her linen, and the swiftness of the tug at her petticoat-laces.

Bryce. For a moment it was him touching her, him guiding her to stand before him, so close that his breath chilled the sweat at the gaping neck of her shift. But the thought faded, unreal and unnecessary.

Her petticoats fell to the floor, one after the other, in a billowing ring. Her hair fell against his face when she bent to kiss him.

The bed-tick crinkled, cold and yielding, under their bodies. A distant sound made her listen a moment, but she dismissed it – one of the patients coughing, or an irregularity in the clock. She heard only the speed of her own breath increasing and her soft sighs grow louder as his fingers worked between her legs, defining tiny circles in time to the movement of her hips. Then they plunged, deep and fleeting, inside her and worked up her craving for him until her body felt ready to shatter, like a delicate glass to a piercing note. When at last he moved over her she held her breath, fighting the fear that he would turn away and leave her, burning and frustrated, in the cold and dark. But fear and conscience dissolved under the crush of his lips on her neck; his grip, almost strong enough to leave bruises, on her thigh.

'I didn't know,' she whispered, and liked the boldness of her voice in the darkness, 'I didn't know it should be like this.'

The rattle of the door-latch broke the air. She cried out and clamped her hand to her mouth. Anthony's body tensed. Mary listened, uncertain of anything but the uneven, sweaty flicker of his heart against hers.

What if it were Agnes? Perhaps the whispers she had heard were nothing; perhaps she had been mistaken.

Anthony stroked her hair distractedly. His breath hushed in bursts past her ear.

Minutes passed. No sound came from outside. He kissed her again, and the urge of his hips continued, slow and just-controlled, but still he listened.

Then quiet footsteps retreated; a long stride. Bolts slid, and the main doors opened and closed. Anthony breathed more deeply and the muscles in his back relaxed.

'Must be her lover-boy. Trying the doors to see what's worth pinching.'

Whoever he was he would tell Agnes. He would say, 'The porter had a girl in his room, an' all,' and then Agnes would know.

'What if he lets in a gang of thieves?' Darkness gathered in on her. The only heat came from Anthony's body, weighting her to the bed. All the life seemed to come from him; all the warmth.

'I'll check the doors,' he whispered. He linked his fingers with hers and pressed her hands against the bed. 'Afterwards.'

Some time later unfamiliar blankets scratched Mary's shoulder. She sought the shape of the window, but it wasn't there. Nothing took its place, only darkness. Her hair clung to her face and icy air flooded under the covers. Gin had left a sour taste at the back of her throat.

'Anthony?' Mary stretched her hand over the creases in the sheet and found her shift, its linen stiff with cold. She slipped it over her head. Now, in the wall above her, she could make out the window and the blinking of stars. They seemed unfair. Why must they break the darkness? Why must they remind her of a reality beyond the night? She huddled under the blankets and stretched out her arm again, in case she was mistaken and Anthony was beside her.

Bolts clunked and then he returned, chattering his teeth and saying he hadn't found anyone: whoever it was had left the main door unlocked but hadn't stolen the key. Perhaps he'd rattled the latch by mistake, trying to find his way out in the dark.

Anthony's cold hands made her giggle.

'You're so warm,' he said. 'So lovely, and warm.' The clock upstairs cranked into life and struck one. Mary waited for another chime, and when she heard nothing she smiled. So much night-time left. So much darkness.

She loved everything around her. Draughts from the window, tingling her skin. The soft bed-tick rustling behind her head. She loved the way Anthony exaggerated his shivering at first, and the way he hitched up her shift without ceremony, almost cruelly, using her to heat his flesh. She loved the way he held her so close to him that their skin might melt and part a path for their ghosts to fuse.

'It'll be best, won't it,' he said, 'for us to go in April?' Mary thought of the stars again, and how they would expand into a skyful of light. 'It'll all work out perfect. We'll have time to save up.' His hand firmed along her side. 'It seems obvious now. I'll save enough to buy a watch before we go, and I'll have time to learn how to fix it. I wouldn't have had that if I'd gone next Monday.'

Cloud obscured the stars. April. It seemed a long time away.

'I used to dream of being a watchmaker,' he said. 'I used to dream of making something of myself. I've wanted to be able to hear people laugh, and not think it was me they were laughing at.'

'They don't—'

'But I don't want to dream any more, Mary.' His lips brushed her ear, confidential and assured. 'Dreams are for folks without certainty. We'll have things we'll make happen, and things which aren't that important.'

He moved lower; the circling of his tongue round her nipple

made her curve her back. She stretched her arms above her head, letting the chill of night-time breathe on her wrists, and forgot the stars.

With her stays bagging about her and her stockings loose around her ankles, Mary kissed Anthony goodbye and stole up the stairs. The door was unlocked now, and she hurried into bed, pantomiming a grimace at the feel of the waxy sheets. Their grubbiness made her legs twitch. But she could blink up at the ceiling with a silent laugh. Complications seemed distant, problems conquerable. Even Agnes. Perhaps they could stop keeping secrets from her now.

His ma saw me off at last. He weren't worth it, for that. Imagine marrying a saddler and then getting saddled with a ma like her . . .

Perhaps Agnes was staring upwards in the same way, smiling, reliving each touch. Perhaps, in the morning, she would tell Mary all about him. How much she loved him. And Mary would be able to say that, just lately, she had become close to someone too.

You won't think harsh on me, will you, if I tell you that . . . ?

The circumstances would piece together without a visible seam.

I haven't slept, some nights, feared I were betraying you. But just lately . . .

Yet she wished that, just for tonight, the first twines of anxiety would refrain from sidling back to her.

Four o'clock chimed and Mary pulled the blankets up to her chin. Euphoria ebbed and the air seemed lifeless and heavy. A low, sere headache wheedled through the side of her skull. Stars enlivened the window, but they were distant and caged by the leaden lattice. There was something not right about the air. The uneasy way in which it suspended the darkness; the way darkness and air pulled from each other and tautened their link. Mary curled on to her side and hugged her pillow. Grease touched her cheek.

'What . . . oh God!' She started up, smearing it away. The oily fragrance of pomade rose from the pillow. 'I'm going to be sick.' She whispered it loud enough for Agnes to hear, but there was no movement from the other side of the bed.

She flipped the pillow over and tried to settle again, but now the heaviness of the air had dispersed itself into odours that congested her head. Sweat, grease, breath, cologne. Musky, stale and insidious, permeating the air, imprisoned by the glass and unreachable by the impassive stars. Then a trace of tobacco. Mary swallowed a cry.

'Agnes?'

Panic burst through her. She leapt up and backed towards the door. The darkness clotted into grey sparks.

'Agnes!'

There was a stifled sob.

Mary let her breath out, but her legs shook and she stayed by the door, the floorboards rough on her feet. She was just being silly. Thousands of men wore pomade and smoked tobacco. It didn't mean . . .

At last she climbed back under the rumpled blankets. 'Agnes, what's happened? I don't understand.'

'I'm sorry.' Agnes's breath convulsed into her. 'I shouldn't have let him in.'

Mary reached for her hand, and found it cold and smeared with tears. 'Mr Racketta?'

'He must have been on the school landing all evening. He was waiting for you.' Agnes's anger dissolved into more sobs. 'But he must have decided I would have to do.'

If she hadn't gone to check the kitchen. If she had stopped at her room for a sip of gin . . .

'You could have called for help when I came to the door.' She would have screeched and lashed at his eyes. She would have run into the ward – that would have been the best thing, with seven of the patients men who could have seen him off. Even if he had been violent there must have been time for a shout.

Agnes's head rustled her pillow. 'He wanted to open it but I said no. I knew you would scream, and Mrs Seward would find out.'

'Well, she could have got the patients and Anthony to throw him out. She could have told the Board never to let him back.'

'No.' Vehemence filled Agnes's words. 'I let him in. I'd be the one thrown out. I let him in. It was my fault.'

'It can't be – he must have pushed the door open.'

'Mary! Stop defending me. I was the one who let him in here. I said yes. I wanted . . .' Hopes of an end to secrecy buckled in on themselves and died. 'I wanted Anthony to find out.' Agnes's sobs split the darkness. 'Maybe he will find out. Maybe he'll realise, on a sudden, that he's jealous.' Mary covered her face with her hands. 'I don't know what to do, Mary. It's seeing him every day. I try. I know a girl's meant to pretend she doesn't care, but it's having to see him every day.'

Tobacco and pomade poisoned Mary's lungs and she bit so hard on her lip that it tasted of blood.

Springlike but melancholy morning light revealed a sixpence on Agnes's table. Mary heard the scrape of it across the wood, and the weighty silence of the next few seconds. Then Agnes screamed, and flung it so hard that one of the window's diamond-shaped panes crunched into an instantaneous spray of spines.

'My sakes alive!' Mrs Stout's chest wobbled at the vigour with which she stirred the porridge pan. Anthony and Mary whisked their hands away from each other, but the cook's shoulders shook with laughter. 'It's either all honey or all turd with you pair.' She flumped a spoonful of porridge into a bowl. 'One minute you're throwing gin-bottles. The next . . .' She chuckled, open-mouthed and wheezing. 'Well!' She flapped Mary's arm with the back of her hand. 'Where's Agnes today, then? She'll go without if she dunna get sat down prompt.'

'She in't well this morning, that's all,' Mary said.

Anthony laughed. 'Love-sick, is she?'

Mary gave a tiny shake of her head.

'What a waste,' the cook said. 'One of you'll eat it up, won't you?'

Mary scraped some porridge from the side of her bowl. How could she ever eat again? When Anthony looked at her, her stomach shrank with urgency. Food, work – everything that wasn't him – seemed worthless.

'Give it here,' he said, and the cook ruffled his hair. The porridge disappeared even before Mrs Stout finished laughing.

'Need to keep your strength up, do you?' She winked at Mary and fanned her chest. 'It's a wonder you stay such an ottomy, the amount you pack away.' She patted his shoulders, and then she became serious and gave Mary a meaningful look. 'Will you fetch me another bucketful of water, my love?' she said to Anthony. 'I want to have a word with Mary afore she gets back to the patients.'

Anthony pressed his foot up the inside of Mary's leg, under her petticoats, and watched her face. She tried to keep it impassive. The cook raised her eyebrows as she turned back to the fire.

'Anything for you, Mrs Stout,' Anthony said.

Mary fought off a stupid longing for him not to go. It was only the well, for God's sake! But the well handle would have his fingers on it, and the spring air would caress his hair, and there might be girls walking on the wall who would see him and watch him draw the water, imagining the working of his muscles under his clothes. Imagining him doing to them what he'd done to her. She studied her nails.

'Off with you!' Mrs Stout flapped her apron at Anthony and swung the door shut behind him. She stood a moment with her hands on her hips, and then she raised a finger, its flesh moist with sweat.

'Now, just you be careful,' she said, moving her face close enough that Mary smelled the fat on her hair. Faint yellow tides of grease spread through her cap. 'I can see what you pair have been up to.'

Why couldn't Mrs Stout just concentrate on her damned frying pan? Did nothing escape her notice? 'What do you mean?'

'You know what I mean, young madam. I'd see it in your face even if he hadn't sat here grinning like the cat's uncle. I know I'm a fine one to talk – but that's just why I don't want you getting into any trouble.' Mary rolled her eyes. Perhaps it seemed insolent. Mrs Stout, after all, couldn't know. She must think Mary an innocent lass – come to the nasty city and fallen foul of men's natural wickedness. 'He's a lovely lad, but he's a random-shot, and I know well enough what it's like to be swooning over a mischievous smile one minute and weeping over a lumping pinnyful the next.'

A flash of bitterness unsettled Mary. Bitterness at girls such as Mrs Stout must have been. Whores drinking flagons of gin and scalding themselves stupid with baths. Murderesses, some of them. How many tiny skeletons curled at the bottom of privies while passed-down cribs gathered cobwebs in attics, and cottages were filled with nothing but quiet, grey, winter light?

'Thank you, Mrs Stout,' she said, and pushed her chair back.

'You inna set to heed a word, are you?' the cook said. 'Some warning I am, I know – my chance-child proved the only one I'd ever have, when Mr Stout couldn't give me any more, and he's such a fine lad now that I wouldn't be without him. But it weren't like that at the time, my love. I had to leave home – slept the first night back of the White Lion in Maxfield, with rats scurrying over me. Then I ended up here in Chester, trallocking from parish to parish as my time got nearer.'

The cook's kind face was in shadow. Beyond and above her the window framed a surge of white clouds. A trickle of ice water collected in Mary's stomach. 'What?'

'The parishes, sweetheart,' said Mrs Stout, tilting her head as if to soften harsh knowledge. 'They don't want another bastard on their books. They move you on.'

'No.' Mary's fingers tightened round her thumbs. 'I mean, what did you say about Mr Stout?'

The cook regarded the fire for a moment, puzzled. Heat buffeted Mary's petticoats and made her feel faint.

'Ah, bless him; such a kind soul. Saved my life. But he never could get me with child.' Mrs Stout gave a sad smile. 'Some fellers'd have took against Joe, but he treated him all the more like his own son, he were that good. I think even if he'd known I weren't really a widow he'd have been the same.' She wiped her eyes and laughed. 'You've got me filling up thinking on him, you little rap-a-tag.'

Mary smeared the glow from her forehead. Currents of air from under the main doors made the step from the kitchen to the corridor a relief. She stood gazing at the imperfections in the whitewashed wall, unsure what was true and what wasn't. Then a heavy, wet flop met her shoulder and a dishclout splatted at her feet. Mrs Stout threw her head back in a laugh.

'Don't worry, lass – I won't ask if it's as long as the rest of him!'

'Come here to me,' Anthony whispered. He captured her at the door to his room, his hands slipping round her back. 'She's warned you off me, an't she? She's jealous, and wants me all to herself.'

Mary met his kiss tensely. 'She thought I needed a lesson in the facts of life.'

Anthony laughed. 'You might have all the lessons you want, from me.'

She tutted. This sickness she had started feeling – just anxiety? Or something else? Anthony pulled her into his room and closed the door. 'What's wrong?'

The room smelled of gin and tangled sheets. It was warm and salty, the air full of last night. The bottle still sat on the night-table. Perhaps it didn't matter. Perhaps she was being silly. 'What if there are consequences? Of what we've done?'

Sporadic fumes of liquor increased her nausea. Interwoven in Anthony's clothes, the scent churned her head. He grinned. 'What's Mrs Stout been saying?'

Mary hesitated; he would laugh. 'She had a child afore she was married.'

The scenario overtook her – how soon she would first suspect. Would she know at once, with some instinctive warmth, or would she fret and wonder for months? Would some wizened old woman in the street be able to tell from a tired smile, or would she be able to keep it hidden like the girls in newspapers who ended on the gallows? Would she feel as much shame as she ought, or would she secretly be glad?

'You needn't worry about such things. We'll be wed anyway in the summer − sooner if you'd agree to it. We could have the first banns read this Sunday in the chapel—'

'No!'

'Well then, you'll have to trust me.' Steeliness edged his voice; her own reduced to a whisper.

'You won't leave me?'

'What is this? Have you been reading penny-ballads about milkmaids? It doesn't always happen like that.'

'It happened to Agnes.'

He shrugged. 'She and Jos Cleeves were at it like confounded mice. It in't surprising. She got away with it, any end.'

Mary said nothing; her instinct told her to say he was heartless. But then there was that slight setting of his jaw and hollowing of his cheeks, and the darkening of his eyes.

'You never worried about this when you came to my room.'

'There was more drink and less daylight then.' She smiled, but his gaze was not on her; it had slunk towards the bottle. 'I'm sorry. I do trust you. I'm just being daft, listening to Mrs Stout.'

Relief struck her when he softened and took her in his arms again. 'Don't worry,' he said, and the dark look was gone, his smile warm, his eyes gentle, every facet of his attention at once devoted to nothing but her. 'I won't leave you. I promise.'

'Agnes,' she whispered, when the clamour of the ward had subsided, the fires were made safe and she had stretched her bare legs between the fresh sheets. 'Is it true some men can't get a woman with child?'

Agnes hissed a rancorous breath out through her nose. 'Of course it is. You're such a bumpkin sometimes.' She plumped her pillow. 'I swear if it were up to me I'd make sure it was a damn sight more of the filthy swines.'

Best just to go to sleep. She oughtn't to pry. 'Hartingshall looked feared for you this morning. You looked that ill.'

'What makes it his business?'

'He likes you. He's always saying how pretty you are.'

The hush of air came from Agnes's nose again. The atmosphere constricted and the room's volume of night-time crushed down on them. 'That's all I need. Some Cockney sailor with a gammy arm. Fall in love with him, shall I, and break my heart when the surgeons kill him?'

Mary twisted a thread on her pillow, winding and unwinding it round her finger. 'They might not need to cut it off—'

'You didn't see it this evening, Mary. It's worse. His hand's gone funny. Mrs Seward had to send for Mr Racketta. While you were out getting your gin.'

The thread sliced into her flesh like a cheese-wire. The visit to Mangham had been so quick. She had not even seen Selwyn. She couldn't, after last night. Sixpence to have the wine-bottle two-thirds filled, and then out. She'd stood for a while enjoying the fresh air, reluctant to go back, but it had only been two minutes. Maybe five. Time outside the hospital went faster than time inside. But no one could have unravelled such discretion unless they had followed her; been a miserable sneak.

'I was running an errand . . .'

'That's it – cover for yourself first, think about him after.'

Mary hugged her knees to her chest. 'What did Mr Racketta say?'

Agnes took a deep, angry breath. 'They do it tomorrow,' she said.

CHAPTER 19

A pyramid of water-gruel wobbled on Hartingshall's spoon. Clanks of cutlery were the only sound from within the ward. The open windows brought in shouts, with the splash of hooves and wheels in the mud. The smell of Fore-Northgate Street's gutter was strong on the temperate March air. Hartingshall lowered the spoon.

'Can't eat any more.' Every gaze in the ward flitted towards him. His blackened fingers opened and contracted like the legs of a dying spider. He grunted a laugh of sorts. 'At least it's only my arm, eh? And not my head.'

Mary sensed the other patients observing her. Was it only that they daren't look at him? Or did they know what he meant? Had he told them, over a game of cards, that in Nurse Helsall's cupboard you could hardly find the stash of gin for skeletons?

Tommy Hughs smiled across, his eyes pained and dishwater-dull. 'Chin up, friend,' he said. The chink of cutlery halted. Hughs's neighbour snorted and threw a piece of bread at him. Hartingshall glared.

'See if it ain't your bloody leg next.'

'Leave him be,' Mary said. 'He means no harm.' Hughs blushed and the man next to him laughed; a loud, incongruous chortle that died to an echo in the rafters. The clock whirred and chimed eight. Hartingshall wiped a gleam of sweat from his brow.

'Mary.' He spoke so quietly that she had to bend close to him. The sour smell of the bedsheets made her hold her breath. 'Will you get me some gin?'

Mary hesitated. Her bottle was still more than three-quarters full. She wouldn't have had to go back to the gaol for a few days. The prospect of losing it made a strange kind of panic well up inside her.

'I don't know,' she said. 'Where would I get it from?' Hartingshall looked at the ceiling and sighed.

'Wherever you stow it.'

'I don't. I an't drunk any for ages.'

Hartingshall watched her, his face grey. All the life in him seemed to recede into his arm; to be siphoned off and freed, bit by bit, from his wound.

Mary's nerves pulsed with each image that came to her; the minutes on the clock, the chair in the old storeroom, the surgeons at their breakfast in the Talbot; the bed that evening, empty and stripped of blankets. She took Hartingshall's good hand. 'Of course I'll get gin for you. But you don't have to go ahead. You could still say no.'

He gripped her fingers and nodded towards his shaking left arm. 'Look at it, Mary. It chills me to my very guts to see it. It strikes me I'm seeing a corpse's hand, and that's what it will be if I don't take this chance.'

At ten o'clock she brought the bottle from the cupboard and shared her gin with Hartingshall, right there in front of the other patients. They heard the surgeons arrive; a shock went through her at the sound of the doors. Feet echoed in the corridor; and discussions, muted and serious, reached them in snatches up the stairs.

Punctually at eleven o'clock the surgeons sent Anthony to collect Hartingshall. He pulled on his breeches and staggered barefoot down to the old storeroom, cursing each time he hit his shoulder on the wall.

Dr Tylston grasped a pocket handkerchief down by his side, as if to subdue its instinct to dab his beading forehead. The main doors allowed a breeze to move the ripples of his peruke. Behind him the doorway to the makeshift operating theatre framed a fug of smoke. Shirtsleeves moved in the haze; murmurs were distorted by the buzzing in Mary's ears.

Anthony gave Hartingshall a solemn pat on the shoulder and retreated to his chair at the entrance. His shape dark against the calm sunlight beyond, he rested his chin on his hands and studied the floor.

Hartingshall's fingers tightened around Mary's arm. 'Are they ready for us yet?' he asked.

Dr Tylston peered into the room. 'Aye.' He must have caught a whiff of gin; he raised his spectacles. 'I thought I said you've to wait until afterwards. I know some folk say it helps, but I'm more of the mind that you need possession of your faculties.'

Hartingshall's grip strengthened. Mary pictured a row of blue, round bruises on her flesh. Within the room someone pulled the chair half into her view. Unease intensified the fuzziness in her head. Anthony seemed a long, long way away.

'She'll be my faculties,' Hartingshall said. Mary looked up at him with a start.

'I in't going in with you!' She tried to catch Anthony's attention but he was looking out at the courtyard, pensively scratching his head. The doctor cleared his throat.

'Come on, now,' he said. 'You don't want a little lass like this fainting away. The surgeons need their concentration.'

'She ain't squeamish.' Mary met Hartingshall's eyes. 'She ain't the type to cover her face and scream. Are you, Mary?'

Dr Tylston allowed the handkerchief to pat his forehead. Strange energy filled Mary. She held Hartingshall's gaze. There was no mockery in his eyes. Only terror undimmed by gin.

'She'll be here for you when you come out, and she'll look after you then, won't you, dear?'

Panic scurried across Hartingshall's face. All colour had left him and his forehead glistened. He breathed hard. He had to let go of her to support himself on the wall.

'I won't faint, sir,' she said.

''Scuse me, sirs.' A lad as thick-set as a fighting dog and with a mouth as red and wide moved past them with a basin of water. Dr Tylston formed an unconvincing smile.

'Ah, you're a brave girl, Mary, but it's not a thing for a lass to witness.'

Mary strode into the room and blinked in the rank ghosts of smoke. Mr Cotgreave, Mr Racketta, Mr Venables and his apprentice blinked back. Mary held her thumbs. The light from the high window made her see squares before her eyes. Mr Racketta's lips twitched around the end of his clay pipe. He had his sleeves rolled up into flat bands above his elbows. Black hairs covered his arms.

'You're doing it, ain't you?' Hartingshall spoke to Mr Cotgreave, whose face was as white as the wall. 'Sir.'

'Indeed,' Mr Cotgreave said. He raised the lid of a case on the table. Hartingshall took to the chair and glowered at Mr Racketta. The apprentice, whistling, stood ready to close the door.

'Thank you, Nurse Helsall,' Mr Racketta said. Hartingshall's chair groaned as he turned.

'She stays.'

The off-pitch notes of the apprentice's tune quietened. Mr Racketta jerked his head towards the door. 'Off you go, sweeting.'

Mary folded her arms. 'He said he wants me to stay, and I will.'

'Anyone'd want you, my dear, but the distraction's too much during an operation. Out.'

Mary looked for Dr Tylston; he had disappeared. The surgeon guided her towards the door until she wrenched her elbow away. The apprentice smiled widely.

'There'll be a devilish lot of blood, madam – a devilish lot. The last one I saw was a leg, and if I'd have been a butcher I might have made black pudding for every table in Chester.'

'Stow it, Beeks,' Mr Racketta said.

Hartingshall loomed close by, clenching his good fist. 'I said she stays.' Gin had made his eyes wild. 'Or we both go.'

Mr Racketta fired a whoosh of smoke from his nose. 'Well, if you faint,' he muttered, 'expect to be kicked aside.'

Pieces of linen sat on the washstand. Were they meant to be put in the water? Would she do the wrong thing and make the surgeons laugh? She took up one of the rags.

'I'll not faint.' But the room was beginning to become warm, and the stale sweat of the surgeon's clothes made her feel sick. He sneaked a hand under the back of her jacket and she wrinkled her nose.

'Happen you should loosen your stays, to be certain.'

She stepped aside. 'Get off me.'

'If I'd've let you in the other night I'd've soon taught you not to be so wilful.'

The other surgeons looked away when Mary wheeled round. 'Why didn't you, then? I'd have killed you, and no one would have had any right to blame me for it.'

Mr Racketta brought his mouth close to her ear. 'I were in a position to be persuaded otherwise.'

She drenched the linen in the basin and wrung it out, ignoring him when his hand brushed her back. When she turned she saw the apprentice twining rope round Hartingshall's shoulders. 'I can . . .' Hartingshall's voice disappeared, and he hacked it out with a cough. 'I can sit here myself. I won't move.' He tried to stand, and couldn't. Nausea welled in Mary's stomach.

'Don't panic, friend,' said the apprentice. His mouth was so wide that, if he were to laugh, there would scarce be enough of a hinge to keep the top of his head on. 'It's only so's you don't fall off while we're cutting, and break the bones halfway through. You don't want to end up with a desperate great splinter, do you? Mighty tricky when that happens.'

The chair legs clattered against the floor, flimsy as kindling under Hartingshall's weight. Mary's skin washed cold. She passed her fingers round the collar of her shift; Mr Racketta drew the end of his pipe across his tongue.

'You're set on distracting me, aren't you, Mary?' His hot breath made her neck crawl.

There was a second's thick silence, and then Hartingshall drew breath and bellowed.

'Good God,' Mr Racketta said. His hand skimmed her buttock. 'We haven't even done anything yet.' Hartingshall's roar commuted into curses, the like of which Mary heard every day in the ward. But the apprentice looked at her apologetically, Mr Venables tightened his leathery face and Mr Cotgreave's hand paused over the table.

'I suggest the nurse leaves,' said Mr Cotgreave. Sweat made a grey patina on his face and his hands moved jerkily, his movements dramatic. 'It is quite . . . quite inappropriate to . . .' He scanned the floor as though the words scuttled away from him like cockroaches. 'To . . .' His upper lip shimmered; he wiped it and frowned. Mr Racketta went to speak to him quietly and Hartingshall emitted an agonised sigh.

'I've heard worse before,' Mary said, emboldened, and sensing that her cheerfulness was exaggerated by gin. 'People think because I'm small I must be modest, but I in't really.'

Beeks smiled. 'I'm certain what we hear is devilish false, madam,' he said with a bow. Then he met her gaze and his cheeks reddened. He looked away.

'We have agreed,' said Mr Racketta, 'that I will perform the operation. Mr Cotgreave is inconvenienced by the kippers we 'took of this morning.'

'No.' Hartingshall was emphatic. 'Either he does it or I'm leaving. You've near as killed me by stabbing my bloody arm in the first place. You ain't finishing me off. At least he don't look like he's drooling for the blood.'

'Mr Cotgreave has not completed one half the number of amputations I have performed.'

'You mean you've killed more people than what he has?'

Mr Racketta huffed an affronted laugh. 'I think you'll find I've had several successes.'

'I could have a go, sir,' said Mr Beeks. 'I'd be fearful quick about it. I've sawn a marrow in under a second.' Mr Racketta's nostrils flared, and he unloaded instruments from a cracked leather bag.

'Wait,' said Hartingshall. 'What'll happen to it?'

'Your arm?' Mr Racketta exchanged a glance with Mr Venables. 'It's to be interred. I've arranged it with the sexton at St Mary's. He'll bury it.' Hartingshall contemplated the floor.

'And I'll be buried with it?'

'Perhaps not immediately, eh? You might live. Some patients deign to trust me.'

Grey, dark creases delineated Hartingshall's knuckles; he uncurled the fingers and winced. 'But, just suppose,' he said, 'just suppose I do live. I'd go home. To London. And suppose I died there – well, I'd have no arm, would I?'

A noxious puff of tobacco stung Mary's eyes.

'I expect you'd make do without it in that instance,' said Mr Racketta, winking at Mary. Lagging remnants of smoke snaked from his mouth as he laughed.

'I don't mean in the bloody grave,' said Hartingshall. 'I mean later. I mean—' He swore softly, lowering his head to his good hand. 'I mean Judgement Day, don't I?'

Mr Beeks gave a philosophical nod, Mr Venables uttered a lugubrious 'Hmm' and Mr Cotgreave considered his reflection in the washstand water.

'I mean, if we're to rise up and I'm in London, do I have to come back to this shite-heap of a town to fetch my arm, or what?'

Mr Racketta laughed silently, and drew in another suck of smoke.

'I expect they'd make you a fresh one,' said Mary gently. Heat made her head light. Her scalp itched with sweat and her cap hung heavy against her hair.

'There,' said Mr Racketta. 'A theologian as well as a nurse, and quite the prettiest I've seen of either.'

Mr Cotgreave had his jacket on and had begun to fit the instruments back into his case.

'Right,' Hartingshall said, pointing at him. 'I've decided. He does it.' The surgeon dragged a handkerchief across his face and took the instruments out again.

Mr Cotgreave looped a tourniquet around Hartingshall's arm, fumbling the pad into the right position. Mr Venables's face betrayed unease as he watched his colleague unsteadily tighten the screw. Hartingshall looked up at the ceiling and expelled two hard breaths. The bones of his good hand tensed; he hung on to the seat of the chair until Mr Beeks suggested it would be a sight safer if he hung on to him instead. Hartingshall snatched his arm from Beeks's grasp, and Beeks grinned.

'There, see – you've nothing to fear from a short fellow like me, have you?' But when he took up Hartingshall's arm again his own thick muscles bulged and he seemed to bed his feet into the floor, as sturdy as a tree. Mr Cotgreave twisted the tourniquet until the strap dug into Hartingshall's skin and it bulged out, red and mapped by veins.

Mr Venables held the bad arm and Mr Beeks the good. Hartingshall laid his head back against Mary; her heart pounded under the pressure. His shoulders knotted as tight as fists.

With two sudden strokes of the knife Mr Cotgreave sliced the skin up and then downwards, and the red circle was complete even before Hartingshall started to scream.

Mary damped his face and talked without knowing what she said, and stepped aside when Mr Racketta's bulk shoved into her. He ignored her now, pulling back the skin and exposing the meat for Mr Cotgreave to slice. Blood streamed from the stump, its consistencies winding into one another. Thick black gore and watery red liquid twined into a thread that pattered the sawdust-box. Then the sound changed; the thread splashed the floor, and someone kicked the box until the persistent, purring sound returned, joined by the grating of a saw. Gin the thickness of egg-white flooded down Hartingshall's bare chest.

It was when she was blindly wiping the sick away, her head resounding with the volume of the screams, that Mary felt something become wrong. Mr Racketta's pipe fell to the tiles and cracked; he spoke with urgency; Beeks struggled with Hartingshall's strong arm and shouted, 'There he goes!'

The saw left Mr Cotgreave's hand, swung upside down round the arm, bounced off the sawdust-box and droned on the floor. Mr Cotgreave lurched to the door and vomited down it. Hartingshall's body shuddered and Mary held his head close to her. His sweat slid under her fingers, and her own soaked the inside of her shift and trickled into her stockings.

'Mary, hold this. Quick.' Her hands disappeared under Mr Racketta's and he pressed her fingers into the flesh around the bone. 'Pull it back hard, like this.' Everything below her wrists was lost in blood. 'Good girl. Keep it like that.' He grabbed up the saw and made three harsh rasps; the screaming ceased and Hartingshall's head sank to his chest.

'Still alive, sir,' said Beeks, grasping Hartingshall's pulse. 'Good and strong, considering.'

Mr Venables whisked the arm away as though there were a dancing-partner on the end of it. A drizzle of red speckled the wall, and a deep, coarse retch brought Hartingshall's gruel into his lap.

'Good fellow!' Beeks bobbed up and down. 'Good fellow!'

'Here,' said Mr Racketta, moving Mary's hands higher up the remains of the arm. 'Pull the skin. Don't let it slip.' The surgeon loosened the tourniquet for a moment, and lowered his eyebrows in concentration as he took a curved needle from Mr Venables. The hairs on his arms were stuck to his skin and his rolled-up sleeves glistened red above his elbows.

Mary's fingers hurt. The skin slipped forwards under them and she pressed harder. Mr Racketta kept his eyes on the stump. The needle flitted up, down, round and up again, until Mr Venables's poised scissors cut the thread. Again and again Mr Racketta loosened and tightened the tourniquet, seeking out the gaping arteries. Beads of blood smattered his eyebrows.

Every trace of gin left Mary's head. The sharp scent of the blood cleared it; the heat of the room and the fumes of the broken pipe were nothing. Capability infected her. Calmness took a hold and she pictured herself doing such things every day. Stitching the blood vessels as Mr Racketta stitched them. Drawing the thread through the meat as though it were linen. Half-enjoying the flood of life her thudding heart sent round her body.

Mr Racketta lifted Mary's wrists away, his fingers hot and slippery. 'Good girl. Look to the patient.'

Hartingshall's head lolled forward. Mary held her red fingers over him, motionless. It seemed wrong – disrespectful – to move.

'Put them in the bowl, I'd say.' Beeks spoke close behind her shoulder, as a conscience might. Clouds of scarlet billowed through the water. Silence thickened the air; Hartingshall's screams remained only inside her head. Speckles crowded her eyes.

'I'd say you've done mighty well, Nurse Helsall,' Beeks said. 'You'd make a surgeon, if you were a man, I'd say.' He gave a broad, awkward grin. 'But no one'd think the less of you if you went out for a spot of air now.' He offered her his arm. She looked back at Hartingshall and her vision cleared.

'Thank you, but I'd best stay.'

Hartingshall would not wake up when she patted his cheeks, nor when she smoothed his forehead with the cloth. Pinkened drips of water rolled down his face. Beeks said it was best if he stayed out of it for now. A bandage, neat and perfect, hid the stump. Mr Racketta let out a restrained sigh and picked up the shattered pipe from the floor.

'Fetch the porter,' he said. 'He and this young fellow may carry him up to the ward.' His eyes were free of any lewdness. He examined the ragged end of the clay and turned away.

Feet hurried from the door and a welcome draught rushed against her. Anthony, Mrs Stout, Agnes and Mrs Seward halted halfway down the corridor and looked back, forming an irregular silhouette that made Mary suddenly want to laugh. Agnes shrieked and clutched the cook's arm.

'Anthony.' Could the others sense the waver when she said his name? 'They want you to carry him.'

The matron's papery neck shook in a swallow. They all seemed far away and shrinking. Even when Anthony stepped towards her he seemed no more than a shadow before the light from the far door.

'They've done it. Mr Cotgreave—'

'He left. He didn't say owt.'

'Mr Racketta took it over. I think Hartingshall's still alive. I don't know.'

Anger ran through his eyes. 'Mary—'

'Don't be cross,' she whispered. 'There's no harm to me.'

'You shouldn't have let them take you in there. You should have shouted for me.'

'Shhh – Agnes watches. I stayed for Hartinghall's sake. I didn't let them do anything. Do you think me so weak—?'

'You take the head end, friend, and don't spill him.' Beeks hoiked up the chair legs with a cheerful grunt, and Anthony's face grew whiter as he backed up the stairs.

'You must have a bath,' said Mrs Stout, quite collected and firm. 'Your petticoats must be soaked, and your shift – well, I 'spect it'll come up tolerable.' The cook's arm rested tentatively around her shoulders. 'Come on, dear.' Mary let Mrs Stout guide her into the patients' washing room, and stood examining her hands. Flaky blood described the creases in her palms. Transfixed by the intricate pattern of the lines, she hardly heard the talking around her, or felt the ties of her apron and stays undoing.

Agnes sobbed. 'Oh, Mary, they oughtn't to have made you stay. They oughtn't.'

A stain the size of a soup-plate reddened the front of her topcoat. Flecks of blood peppered her arms and crimson splashes spoiled her stockings.

Even Mrs Seward carried water. Mary sat in nothing but her shift, its sleeves stiffening, until the tub was full enough, and then they left her to sink into the bath and watch red threads snake away from her body. The feel of the water was strange but not unpleasant. It lapped at her thighs and, gradually, she sank deeper and watched it inch over her stomach. It collected into beads on her knees.

No sound came from outside. Was he already dead? The quality of not knowing became something precious. She had not had a good look at the arm, but she imagined it, inhuman and isolated, lying on the table, its days over.

Mary closed her eyes and heard seagulls cry. The movement of the needle was all she could see. What would it be like, to sew flesh? She splashed the water over her legs, as if that would cool her racing mind. What if, next time, the surgeons handed the needle to her? They must have noticed how well she had sewn those endless sheets and nightgowns. Blood was only blood. It was not frightening at all. What if she could save lives – even one life?

Mary held her hand out in front of her, her fingers splayed. It was as steady as the statue of Queen Anne on the front of the Exchange. Her head felt as clear as the north breezes that swept over St Martin's Fields. Her pulse beat as strong as the surges of the Dee around the legs of the bridge.

Agnes brought in her gown – the one she didn't often wear – and her quilted petticoat and another pair of stockings.

'Does he live?'

Agnes nodded, her eyes brimming. 'He's back in bed. The lad with the funny mouth said his pulse is still going.'

'Mr Racketta sewed, just like ordinary sewing. Don't you think we should be doing that?' Her words sounded loud and strange. Agnes widened her eyes.

'Mary, are you all right?'

'If we had lots of patients as needed bits cutting off, we could help the surgeons. We could invent a special apron that'd keep the blood off our clothes.'

Agnes bit her lip. 'Shall I fetch Mrs Stout?'

'Why?'

Agnes left the things on the chair and shut the door hard behind her.

When she dressed and stepped out into the corridor, Mary found the air tainted by smoke. A new pipe drooped from Mr Racketta's lips and Anthony stood facing him, his arms folded and his face no more coloured than the wall.

'You're the bloody porter,' said Mr Racketta from the corner of his mouth. 'Port something for a change.' He pointed the end of the pipe at Mary. 'There – our little Mary thinks naught of being in the midst of an operation, and you daren't even carry a dead arm a mile and hand it to a sexton. What? Are you scared it'll come to life and steal your gin bottle?'

Anthony pushed past him and reappeared even paler with a long, well-wrapped bundle, which he carried out into the band of sunlight that had daubed itself over the north part of the courtyard.

Thurstaston, early morning, 28 December 1755

At first sight the silk is pale and powdery, pretty and delicate; suitable for a gentlewoman to wear at tea.

But Mary can't look away. She needs something to concentrate on; something that will stamp out panic.

As she studies it, it reveals a greater depth; a capacity to suck in light and spit it out again. A vibrancy that borders on life. It seems made from layers of brush-strokes, each a different dimension of iridescent blue and lilac. Candlelight changes and coaxes it, calling out darknesses and lightnesses of hue. Spread on the table, its creases smoothed out, it holds an intensity of blue so profound it seems to rest under flowing, crystal water.

'I could make this into a gown,' Mary says, and at once condemns herself for such a stupid thought. Selwyn grasps hard at his hair, his fists pulling his head towards the table and his head pulling just as violently back. His eyes are terrified.

'Is some damned gown all you can worry about?' He steps out of the cottage, then steps back in and paces in front of the fire and Mary's drying clothes. He breathes fast; now puts his hands behind his head, now presses them over his eyes. A stream of rhythmic swearing flows from his lips like rote-learned prayers.

Mary folds up the silk and tries to think.

Perhaps it will look as though the man was injured and drowned before he washed ashore. No, too many people saw.

Perhaps they could bury the body and, if it should ever be found, say the neighbours hate them and are accusing them falsely. After a few brandies this begins to seem like the best option and, after a lot

218

more thickening of the air and striding about, Selwyn agrees that this is what they will do: they will go to the shore before it gets light, and together they will bury the body very deep in the sand.

Then he goes outside and vomits into Mary's unkempt herb garden.

Neither going to bed nor sitting up proves any use, so Mary and Selwyn hurry back to the sea. From the top of the scrub-clad low cliff they see the motion of lanterns and hear men shouting. They have to go home again and spend the night awake under rumpled blankets, Mary almost smothered by Selwyn clinging to her. When they return to the shore, early the next morning, more bodies gurn in their lantern-light. None of them have their heads cut half off, and the place where they thought they had left the corpse is empty. There are two possibilities. Either it didn't happen, and they know each other so well they can share nightmares, or someone has taken the body away and is obtaining a warrant to arrest its killer.

Back in the cottage Selwyn makes himself sit very still in his chair by the grate. He drinks several more cups of brandy – so does Mary – and his hands become less taut. Finally they decide he will go away until it becomes clearer whether it's considered a murder or not.

'I'll take the silks to Chester and sell them,' he says. 'Then, once I've got the money, I'll move on and send word to you where I am.'

'You know Mr Warbreck will expect us to sell the silks to him.'

Even before the words are out she can tell, from Selwyn's expression, that they were a bad idea.

'Mr Warbreck? Can't you get that bastard out of your mind for a single second?'

'It's nowt to do with that,' she says, with the sense that she's the one who will have to take over here. 'I mean he'll want every one of his workers to offer the goods to him first. I don't think we'd gain owt from upsetting him.'

Selwyn considers this, and takes on a mantle of decisiveness that doesn't suit his big, wary self. 'I'll go today. You take one of the silks to Warbreck to keep him sweet, and pretend that's all we salvaged. I'll get a message to you somehow within two weeks.'

Mary's gaze rests on the bolt of blue silk. 'I'll take that one,' she whispers, and for all that she has fumed and tutted against him and wished he were someone else, it's strange to think he won't be there.

He loads the silks on to the cart. It is still only six o'clock in the morning, still dark, and the after-storm rain is now a drizzle that rises from the puddles as much as it descends from the sky. Mary strokes Jakey, guilty to make him an accomplice, and then Selwyn pulls her close to him and kisses her, his hands unmoving on her back; no impatient fumbling. It's how she always wanted him to kiss her. And then he drives away to Chester and she sits alone in the grubby cottage, cobwebs hanging over the door and dust ensconced in the carvings of the rented bedstead.

The cottage silent, she spreads out the blue silk again and imagines the gown she would have made.

She'll take it to him, later.

Chapter 20

Whenever Hartingshall groaned in his sleep the other patients paled and regarded him with wary eyes.

Silence filled the ward. Beds lay empty, vacated the moment Beeks and Anthony delivered Hartingshall back. The clean scent of dew and mud freshened the sourness of the sheets but, a day after the operation, open windows could not dispel the mood of suppressed fear.

Anthony had come back in his altitudes after taking the arm to be buried, his pallor gone and his eyes bright. 'The sexton looked busy, so I gave him a hand.' Mrs Stout cuffed him round the head and wheezed with laughter. 'What d'you do that for? I mean no 'arm.'

The cook had nudged Mary. 'You're set for a lifetime of this, my love.'

'What are you smiling about?' Agnes took one end of a bed-tick and, between them, she and Mary beat the bug-nests out of it. The creatures, drowsy with daylight, tumbled on to the floor and, recovering themselves, scurried away.

'Nowt.'

'Seems a funny thing, to smile so, after yesterday.' Suspicion laced Agnes's tone. She caught a fat bug and crushed it between her finger and thumb. Innards and blood popped out. 'You looked like a murderer.'

Mary looked up quickly. Dark lines underscored Hartingshall's cheekbones and sweat covered his forehead. His breath was shallow and noisy. Crusts of blood still clung around Mary's nails.

'My ma read me a play, once, about a woman as could never wash the blood off her hands.' She smiled, but Agnes's serious look made her uneasy.

'They oughtn't to have made you go in there. It's not right.'

'They didn't,' Mary said. 'I insisted on staying.'

'Why?'

'For Hartingshall's sake.'

Agnes's harsh look lifted. 'Then you and Hartingshall . . . ?'

'Oh, no!' Mary laughed. So it was nothing more sinister than jealousy. 'He talked about you nigh-on constant.' Tears came to Agnes's eyes. 'We got to be friends while I was looking after him in the warehouse, but I'm not in love with him, nor him with me. I couldn't love him if he had a thousand pounds and were as handsome as—'

'Anthony?'

Mary avoided Agnes's gaze. Outside, shouts bandied across the street, cheerful and oblivious. The last of the morning sun made tiny shadows of the pieces of herbs on the floorboards.

'I . . .' Her voice faded. 'I 'spect some girls'd think Anthony handsome, but—'

'You were near fit to kill Mrs Seward the other day, for his sake.'

'It angers me to see anyone treated so.'

'And he looks at you. I swear there's never a moment you're in the same room when he isn't looking at you.'

Mary smoothed the new sheets, the linen cold and crisp under her fingers. 'He might look at whatever's in front of his eyes. I can't stop him. D'you think it's my dull black hair he wants to gawp at? Or my freckles, or my eyes? He might as good look at algae in a ditch if he likes such a colour.' Her cheeks smarted.

'Perhaps.' Agnes did a tight-lipped smile and her shoes sounded hollow on the floorboards.

Patchy stubble obscured the whiteness of Hartingshall's face and his eyes lay deep in their sockets as if drawn back, about to be fired. For a week Mary squeezed water from a rag into his mouth and kept his face clean of sweat. The bandage reddened and then browned; she covered it with another to hide the blood, and whenever Hartingshall awakened she gave him laudanum or wine to quieten his cries. Other patients filled the empty beds, but none stayed more than a night once they heard him.

Mrs Seward had no advice to impart. She kept up her routine of registers and readings and cursory inspections, but her spectacles did not hide the trepidation in her eyes every time she neared Harting-shall's bed. She still became angry, still insisted Mary ought to have respect for her, and was still more vicious towards Anthony, but Mary felt only a calm, powerful invulnerability whenever Mrs Seward shouted. When had the matron ever attended an operation? When had she helped save anyone's life? When had she ever shown herself worthy of respect? That word made Mary smile. *Respect your elders, you bobberous tike.* She never believed it, even as a child, and now it seemed she had been right. They had made it up to disguise the real-isation that years were all they had to commend them.

And where was Mrs Seward when Mr Racketta, Mr Venables and Mr Beeks came to take off the bandage for the first time?

The skin had formed a congealed line, the folds pressed together like angry lips. Hartingshall hung on to Mary's hand and kept his face turned away from the stump.

'Excellent,' said Mr Racketta, and a new bandage flew round the arm. 'You're a strong fellow; brave an' all.'

A spark of hatred enlivened Hartingshall's eyes. 'I ain't brave,' he said. 'Just bleeding unlucky.'

He caught her eye before his head sank back on the pillow, and she smiled.

A day later she got him to take a few spoonfuls of plum-gruel for his breakfast. He threw it up into his pot and lay back flat in his bed, shak-ing, but it was a start.

And that, she remembered afterwards, was the day when everything changed.

She had just left the patients' dirty luncheon-plates in the kitchen, and stood by the fire until Mrs Stout told her to get out of the way, when she found Anthony blocking her path along the corridor. She tried to duck under his outstretched arms, but he caught her up and kissed her, laughing at the way she glanced aside at the stairs.

'Anthony! For God's sake! We must be guardful, after what Agnes said.' But he did not appear to listen. His whole aspect seemed blurred, as if it was she who had been drinking. 'Why do you grin so? What have you done?'

Anthony spread out his palms as if in surrender, and smiled even more. 'Ah, Mary, just look, won't you? Look. You might see at once what I've done, if you look.' He shoved his fingers through his hair, creating a wild halo. 'You're set to drive me mad. How can you not notice?'

'Notice?'

He rolled his eyes. 'Summat different about me.'

The brown jacket still hung shapelessly from his shoulders, his thread-bare neckcloth still formed a bandage-like knot at his throat, his shirt-cuffs still peeked from sleeves too short for his arms. The excitement in his eyes caught fragments of daylight and spun them into a glassy lustre.

'I mind I'm to rule out sobriety,' said Mary. The lustre brittled.

'I an't drunk anything.' Anthony's expression tensed. 'Look—' He rummaged in his pocket and retrieved a bottle. 'I bought this. I'm not pretending I didn't. But it's still full.' He held it up to the light and the liquid-line settled near the top. 'All I had were a couple of sips, to make certain they hadn't filled it with water. It's just to have in. You know I don't get much time for drinking now there's always errands to run for the surgeons, and patients to lug about.'

'But you had to make sure it was empty, to get it that full.'

Anthony's fingers tightened on the bottle and he spoke through his teeth. 'Mary, don't harp on it. I bought some gin, is all. Don't spoil everything.'

She took his hand. 'Tell me then, what do I fail to see? You've got me keen to know.'

At once his smile returned. She followed him outside and watched his stride subsume lengths of the cobbles, until he stepped out of the shade, turned in the light and held his arms wide like an actor solilo-quising the close of a tragedy. 'Mary!'

No one was behind her in the corridor; the Northgate door was deserted too, but a coachman looked down into the courtyard and a young woman, waiting by the daffodils, observed them from under a hat tied with a red ribbon.

'People are looking at us,' she said.

'Mary, you're the one who must look. I've found our future. Look!'

Sunlight caught it; a spark of metal, a flick of brightness on the chain that curved across his waistcoat. She grabbed the watch from him, and he laughed and said what a desperate poor pickpocket she would make, near pulling him over like that.

'Where did you get it?' The watch filled the centre of her palm, its case engraved with swirls, obscured in part by the tarnish. He cupped her hand and pressed the remains of his bitten thumbnail into a groove in the rim.

'Bought it,' he said, easing the watch open. 'From a pawnbroker.'

Whether the watch was a poor one or a good one Mary could not say, but she liked its smallness and the intricacy of the swirls, and the way its metal warmed on her skin. 'It's so delicate,' she said. Fine black numerals lay, slender as cornflies, on a white face. 'Look at the hands.' She examined them closely, fascinated by their fragility. 'The ends are like spiders' feet.' But she sensed he did not look at the watch's face so much as at hers, and the delight in his laugh made her smile and let him kiss her again.

'It dun't work,' he said.

'Oh.' Mary scrutinised the hands. Perhaps, if she willed it hard enough, they would move.

'But it will, once I've fixed it. That's why it was cheap.' That was it, then. One tiny squirm of anxiety left her. 'And . . .' Anthony searched the sagging pocket with the bottle, and then the other, and the first again. 'That's how I could afford these, too, for you.'

Mary pictured rows of eyes blinking in the ward windows, the female patients nudging one another and cackling. She imagined gossip, amused and loud. 'Ooh, would you look at that! I fear you've missed your chance, for he's down there in the yard, giving a pair of gloves to the plain nurse, and smowching her, welly in the street an' aw!'

The gloves were of fine, creamy kid-leather, so soft that even Mary's rough fingertips did not catch on it. She moved into the shadow of the building. 'What do you mean? To buy me these?' The words sounded ungrateful.

'Do you like them? I saw them, and they were so pretty and so small, I couldn't help but think of you. I thought how I'd told you that when I had some money I'd buy you a pair of gloves.'

Carefully she drew them on to her hands, and admired her fingers. They were not her own. The redness and the chapped skin were gone, and the fingers were slim and long, as dainty as a proper lady's. She put her hand to her face, and laughed at the softness of the leather on her cheek. Just for that second it did not matter if the ward windows were filled with eyes; she walked into the light, and held her hands before her. Sunshine deepened the somnolent cream colour, its richness like a pool that she might sink into. Was it mercenary, to feel so swelled with love for someone just for a pair of gloves?

'You mustn't think I love you more because you've spent money on me,' she said. 'You know I don't care about such things. It's more—' His lips moved to her hands, and she did not care whether anyone was watching. 'Did you really think of me? Even though I wasn't there? It seems strange, that someone might think about . . . I didn't know people thought . . .'

She imagined him in the pawnbroker's shop, amid the piles of goods, seeking a watch to practise on for her sake, and seeing the gloves and impulsively deciding she would like them. And she thought of Selwyn in the same situation, and how he would not buy them, in case she didn't want them, but would come home and ask her whether she did, and mull over for a few days whether he ought to spend money on them, and go grumbling back to the shop to find that someone else – someone like Anthony – had taken them away.

'You make it sound as though there are times I don't think about you,' he said.

'No, it's just I didn't . . . I thought I was always the one, thinking about people. About you.' His fingers, touching her face, were clumsy with gin. 'They must have cost a fair penny.'

'I had a bit of luck.'

'What, gaming?'

He held her gaze again and smiled. 'Aye, that's it.'

'When will I ever wear them? Am I to go about the ward, empty-ing pots, with these on?'

'You might wear them on Sunday – you've got the afternoon off, haven't you? We'll go walking round the walls.' He fiddled with the knot of her kerchief. 'And you might wear them whenever you're in my room. You might wear them for a while now.'

She laughed. 'I'm supposed to be—'

'No one will know.'

The time to come, when people would know, seemed distant.

Anthony fumbled every pocket before he found his key. A laugh floated down from the ward; a fixed laugh, of someone who meant to stay there. Mrs Stout sang tunelessly in the kitchen. At the other end of the corridor Mr Crane's mortar and pestle grated and the scent of brimstone drifted from his shop. The door shut behind her, closing away the laugh and the creak of bedsteads and the smell.

It did not matter if there were patients waiting for her. He pulled her on to him, the feathers in the bed-tick swishing like the sea.

Selwyn: *what do you want me do?*

Anthony was silent, lifting her petticoats until they bulged over his arms and spread across his chest. Mary giggled nervously, and he touched one fingertip to her lips.

Selwyn again: *I suppose you want to . . . ?*

Voices moved down the corridor, muffled and transient. Doors closed with latch-clicks, feet scuffed the floor, and they were nothing.

People might listen at the keyhole, they might fume with disgust or jealousy or grief, but they were nothing.

Sunlight warmed Mary's bare leg. She gazed up at the specks of dust in its beam. Were they everywhere, unseen, or did the light attract them and make them leap to revel in it? The clock droned out two, and Anthony looked at his watch. It read twenty past twelve.

'It'll be right twice in a day,' he said, 'which is more than I ever am. We must get back. She will've missed us.'

'How can I work now?' Mary's lips moved so close to his ear that it felt wrong to speak louder than a whisper. 'You've used up every scrap of me. I feel like a bowl of gruel guzzled clean away.'

He squeezed her thigh. 'You're a choicer morsel than that. As choice as ever any man might hope to get his teeth into.'

Mary laughed. 'His teeth?'

Then the sound of feet halted outside. An emphatic rap on the door made Anthony swear, more resigned than startled.

'Wells!'

Mary leapt up and squirmed back into her jacket, and collected up her stockings and shoes.

'I'll get rid of her,' Anthony said.

Mary held her breath, watching the movements of Mrs Seward's skirts through the crack of the door. The matron suspected she was either out buying gin and consorting with unsuitable types or . . .

'It would be of little surprise to me if she were hiding behind the door.' She paused. 'If not still in your bed, like the common trollop she is.'

'Don't talk about her like that,' Anthony said.

'Look at the state of you. You're scarce dressed. You're drunk again, aren't you?'

'Not very.'

Mrs Seward's voice lowered. 'If you only knew what a waste was the spark that ever enlivened you.' All Mary saw of Anthony was his fingers gripping the door. Their tips pressed hard into the wood, his chewed nails turning white. 'If you would only think how many better young men than you have died innocent, while you stay living through all your efforts to destroy yourself.'

The wall behind Mary trembled at the slam, and Mrs Seward's rant became high and muted. Anthony ripped the key from the lock and flung it at the height where her head must be. It hit the door with a crack and tinkled to the floor. He took a swig of gin and sat on the bed, his face scarlet. 'She can't speak about you like that.'

'I don't care if she does.'

'Well, I do. What right has she to insult a man's wife to his face?'

'I in't your wife.'

'But you will be.'

He held out the bottle to her and when she sat beside him his anger ebbed, and the sound of the matron's futile shouts became funny.

'Imagine her, out there,' Mary said, 'with steam coming from her nose, like the beasts in Cow Lane. What are we to do now?'

'Well,' he said. He brushed her hair away from her face and smiled. 'I must occupy you 'til she's gone.'

Mrs Seward stopped shouting, and her thumps became adamantly regular, alternating with the creaks of the bed. At last she conceded defeat; the sound of her pattens retreated down the corridor, and Mary and Anthony laughed until seriousness overtook their glee.

Anthony pulled a blanket over them, and the lack of sound outside seemed a licence to remain, waiting, for time to start again.

'When I'm your wife,' Mary said, 'we'll lie like this every day, in our own home, and there'll be no one to hate us.' She slipped her hand into the opening of his shirt and felt the beat of his heart through her glove.

But at last he dragged himself from the bed and dressed, peering into the looking glass as he fastened his neckcloth, with a serious expression that made Mary smile. Stockingless and capless, she lay with her hair ranging over his pillow, and watched him rub his eyes and smooth his own hair ineffectually against his scalp.

'I'll tell you when there's no one looking,' he said, but when he closed the door behind him she could not be sure she still wanted to hide.

Alone in his room she gazed at the ceiling for many drowsy minutes, then drank from the bottle on the night-table and felt under his mattress for love letters. Then she drank some more, and put on her shoes, and splashed her face at the washstand. The scales of a dead moth shimmered on the water.

Mary folded her gloves, touched them to her face again and tucked them into her stays just as Anthony returned, his eyes impish as he beckoned to her. Out in the corridor the smell of sulphur from Mr Crane's laboratory made her eyes smart.

'Mary!' Anthony whispered.

'Shhh.'

'One more kiss. Just one.'

There could be nothing to worry about, not with the warmth of gin enveloping her. She laughed softly and stretched her arms round Anthony's neck. 'You do like to test your luck.'

'And what luck it is, eh?'

She stood on tiptoes to kiss him, delaying the ebbing of the heat from her flushed face. Then his smile disappeared.

She spun round.

It was the longest look she had ever given or received. Agnes seemed far away, her plump figure become small and fragile. She stood with her hands clasped in front of her, her curls as pretty as ever about her face and her eyebrows half-lowered, as if puzzled.

There might still be time to make a joke of it. But Mary set her jaw firm, some insolent stubbornness inside her forbidding her from contrition. Agnes put her hand to her mouth and her shoulders sank. She ran up the stairs and there was a sound; a stifled scream, and a door slamming.

'There's no reason any more for her not to know.' Anthony's hands warmed Mary's arms. 'We don't have to hide now.' She let him pull her back against him, and felt his lips touch her neck.

'They were right,' she said. Faces came back to her now; bug-eyes and brown-toothed sneers. 'Weren't they?' Anthony only held her tighter. 'The women at home. They were right about me.'

Mary lay awake on one of the empty ward beds until one o'clock, when she could no longer stand Hartingshall's groans. Why should she stay out of her own room? Was she so scared of Agnes that she would spend every night with the stench and noise of the patients? On the landing the cold mist of her breath condensed around her face.

Pulses of blood throbbed in her ears – her ears, this time, she thought ruefully – but she undressed and slunk between the covers, and listened for the soft sound of Agnes's breath. The sound was not there. She cringed into the blankets. Lattice-shapes fell across the bed, shadowed by the full moon, and Agnes's face was silvery-white, her eyes open and staring. Mary listened to the clock outside, timing her breath to each tick of its pendulum.

'Bitch.' It was more a breath than a whisper, as though the silver light itself had condensed into a half-formed word. 'You venomous, lying, deceitful bitch.'

'I'm not. It wasn't like that . . .'

Agnes's voice slowed and chilled. 'When did it start?' Mary sat up, silent and cold. 'I said *when*? Last week? Today? A month ago?'

Lies of different sorts caught in her throat. *Today? Oh yes, today; he just caught me as I walked along, and it was such a shock! I feel sorry for him, for I had to tell him I'm promised to someone else.*

'January.'

The word sounded loud and stupid without light to temper it. For less than a second the hush struck her, then a fist thudded between her shoulderblades and rammed a cry into her throat.

Whatever Agnes screamed was jumbled behind her; her own sobs were all she could hear. Not sobs of regret – she knew that even then.

This grief, this shrivelling feeling that scrawns your heart to nothing, is not for what you've done, but for what you've been caught doing.

'*I said*,' Agnes screamed through the darkness, 'I swore she was some bedraggled, drunken whore.' The heel of her hand shoved Mary's head against the wall. 'And it didn't strike me how very close to the truth I was.'

The door-key would not turn. Mary shrank back, but Agnes's fingers ripped at her hair and she struggled to beat them away. 'You're a fine one to call me that. It weren't me as let Mr Racketta wap her for sixpence.'

Pain tore across her scalp. She thrashed out and felt Agnes's skin catch under her nails, and heard a scream that turned to words. 'You pretended to be my friend.' The back of her head thumped twice on the wall. 'That's the worst of it. That's the worst. That you were telling me to forget him. All those times you were shirking and I was doing your work I felt sorry for you. I cried sometimes, that you were so in thrall to drink, and yet you were down there, in his bed, laughing at me.'

The next jolt made Mary's neck crunch. Speckles squirmed before her eyes and she fought to stop her back from sliding down the wall.

CHAPTER 21

'I've known, once, for a girl like this to be taken into a kind home and put to gainful work, with a benevolent but strict master who would not suffer her to gad about in search of gin and improper liaisons.'

A crack split the ceiling. One person spoke, and yet Mary sensed someone else breathing near her. Her eyes hurt. 'I always knew she would be trouble. Mr Barnston – oh, he is such a good man, but that, if you ask me, is his failing. He would take in any waif that contrived to show a doleful eye on his doorstep, and with this one – well! I knew she had a streak the first day she came here.'

A cough croaked above her. Mary gasped at the pain that thudded through the back of her head.

'Mrs Seward, I beg to opine that you're a little unfair.' At first, Mary's recognition of the voice was only to accept it as someone kind. 'It's not she who's knocked someone clean unconscious. She's a bright lass, and a tough one. How many girls do you know who would help amputate an arm without so much as quivering?'

Watery shadows of candlelight formed themselves on either side.

'That only confirms it, Doctor.' Bitterness embroidered the matron's tone. 'Young people today have no concern for those in need. She was hardened enough to help with such things because her mind was absent – on the sort of matters of which you and I would never dream.'

A silence, and the clearing of a throat. Mary's eyes rolled back, beyond her control, and she struggled to focus on the crack in the ceiling. 'Is he dead?' That was her own voice. Loud and eerie, its sound made her forget what she meant.

Bustle started up around her. The shadows rose and the violent odour of sal volatile made her splutter. 'Well, she lives. I had no doubt her skull would prove stronger than her virtue.'

'No one's dead, Mary.' A hand touched her hair.

'Hartingshall . . .'

'He lives still. Don't you worry about him. It's you we've been fretting after. You were out cold for a good five minutes, and not much clearer since.' A pair of spectacles rounded into view.

'I didn't mean to faint. I in't frightened of blood. I must have . . .'

Cold water slapped on her face.

'There's no blood.' Mrs Seward pressed the flannel hard on to her forehead. 'Now don't you think I'm looking after you out of sympathy. We all know where you were when you disappeared yesterday morning, though I hardly dare mention it in front of a Christian gentleman.' The matron's face appeared, wishy-washy, above her, her cap a starched, square box.

'Nothing shocks me, madam,' Dr Tylston said, 'but for man's willingness to delight in the imperfections of others.' His round, kind face appeared between Mary and the ceiling. 'Take this.' Drops landed on her tongue.

'Is that the stuff . . . ?'

Mrs Seward moved about the room, a wavery figure that changed the quality of the light too much for Mary's eyes. And then gradually the thud in the back of her head faded into a friendlier sort of ache and the taste of the medicine spread through her consciousness, soothing and summery.

'Has Anthony come back yet? He was taking the arm . . .'

A shrieking huff.

Dr Tylston replaced the cloth on her forehead. 'He waits outside the door, to hear if you're living.'

'I am.'

'Good lass.'

Mary dreamed of waves and cliffs. People moved in and out of the room. Cracked and rough, the ceiling firmed better into view, and she recognised the softness of bedding around her.

'Will they let me do the sewing next time?'

'Shh. Still now.'

'Still?' She sat up in one wrench. The room whirled. She retched; a pot appeared in front of her and she vomited. Hands guided her back to the bed. 'Can I have some more of that stuff?' The medicine dropped into her mouth, and she breathed it into her veins and smiled at the way it encouraged her and made her feel there was nothing so very bad. And then a clear plan came to her. They would go to London, she and Anthony, and while he fixed watches for fences she would find work in a hospital and become a surgeon's assistant. The simplicity of this plan was so startling that she had a sense of having known it for a long time. Perhaps she had thought of it before and dismissed it as impossible, but now it seemed obvious. She breathed deep and her heart rose, and every pore in her body stretched itself into a tiny smile.

She spread her arm out, and the bed felt cleaner than she expected, and smooth.

'You're in Mrs Seward's room.'

She laughed. 'You won't let her get in bed with me—'

'Quiet, now.'

'But I've got an idea. When the hospital's built – the proper one – you should have a ward for folks with the smallpox, then you wouldn't have to throw them out like that fellow the other day.'

Mrs Seward snorted. 'Good Lord! She wants doctors, nurses and all dropping dead on the floor. Patients would arrive with a sore foot and leave in a coffin.'

'Put them in their own ward and don't let anyone go in and out, and only people as have had it before could look after them.'

'Shh, Mary,' said Dr Tylston. 'Don't excite yourself.'

'They should have their own plates.' She yawned, and the yawn was a rush of life-giving air that made her want to get up and dance. She dozed for a second, and then her own voice woke her. 'Their own spoons and plates.' Then she dreamed of the sun rising out of a glittering sea.

For some time – she could not say how much – she lay in the comfortable, fresh bed, gazing at a vase of daffodils on the table, as it grew light and then dark. Her head cleared and anxiety overtook her. Curtains blocked out the moon and stars, and she dreamed of the hot breath of ghostly dogs. When the morning arrived, she felt she had not slept.

'You'll have to get up today,' the matron said. 'I shan't pass another night in your room. We can't manage the outpatients as well as that lot.' Mrs Seward wore rosewater. Its scent was too sweet for her.

Mary waited for the spinning to stop before she reached for her petticoats. They lay on the back of a chair and she was unsteady walking towards it.

'Mary, sit down.'

She flumped on to the bed at once. Mrs Seward put a cold, raspy hand on her arm. 'You're wasting yourself as much as he is.' The ache had spread to her shoulders, dividing them like a lathe. 'I can't pretend to like you, but I can see how sharp you are, and you can do better than him.' Mrs Seward's square nose came into focus, her spectacle-shielded eyes appalled. 'I would not have condoned my boy ever taking a girl like you, but . . . well.'

Then Mrs Seward was gone, and the hour passed white and cracked, until Mary got up and dressed herself, staring about at the plain bedroom. The fireplace stood empty, a patterned rug before it. And a frame sat on the bedside table, with a few pencil strokes in it, delineating a young lad with big eyes, and hair curling over his temples.

Her first steps on to the landing were tentative. Laughs, sobs and whines echoed in her head. When she went into the ward the sounds ceased. Eyes turned towards and away from her, and her courage melted.

Only Hartingshall did not look away.

'You've heard what happened?' Mary expected sympathy, but when she neared his bed he wore the leaden expression she remembered from the first time she saw him begging. She fought the same twist of apprehension she had fought then. 'You heard, didn't you? Dr Tylston said . . . I can't remember, but he said she—'

'I never knew until yesterday that you stole Wells off her.'

'I didn't—'

'Snakeish, that.'

'It wasn't—'

Hartingshall jabbed his finger at her. His face greyed with the effort. 'Just what anyone ought to expect of a wrecker.' The other patients' silence deepened. 'You clawed her in the eye! What, were you so jealous of her pretty face you had to try and spoil it? Do you know what it does to me, to see her hurt?' His face faded from grey to white and his eyes blanked. The side of his bed might have been the side of a boat, the way he vomited clear of it.

The smell of the ward, like its sounds, had been normal – sour and sharp, so familiar as to be almost unnoticeable. Now, as Hartingshall struggled back to his pillow, it spiralled up around her, sickening her and amplifying the hostile mutters that scuttled like insects from the other beds. She did not look at anyone as she left the room.

Mary spent the next few days going about her tasks in silence, sleeping in one of the empty beds, with all the sounds and odours of the patients intruding into her dreams. She left the care of Hartingshall to Agnes, who would not bide in the same room as her. Red marks peppered Agnes's left cheek, a stain of blue subsiding, as the days passed, to yellow around them. Impressive how that bruise diverted every stream of sympathy towards it. Mary's own forehead smarted with scratches and her head always ached, but that did not soften the disapproval of the patients. Her unconsciousness, brief though it was, had allowed time for Agnes's story to get about first.

Back to that again, then – the raised eyebrows and sudden-ceasing conversations, the laughter and the glances.

It was not jealousy that made Mary feel scrunched each time Agnes helped Hartingshall eat his breakfast. Not that sort of jealousy anyway; only a faint regret that Hartingshall seemed to have been her friend and now looked to her enemy for care.

Perhaps not so very much an enemy. Only circumstances made her so. She might just as easily have been a friend, too. At least, as much as a woman can ever be. Ah well; no use being sentimental about friendship, Mary thought each night as she lay in the bug-ridden bed. Friends drift here and there; they might one day be strong – if they want something – the next weak, if they don't. They are like a pretty ribbon or a flower in a hat: a pleasure to have, but of little necessity and wont to fray or wither.

The Board had taken no action over Agnes attacking Mary. They had met the day Mary still lay in Mrs Seward's bed, and there had been no mention since of the incident or its consequences. The gentlemen, by all accounts, had left their meeting glad to get to their next appointments with coffee or liquor, and had not decreed any dismissals. One of them, Anthony said, had patted him on the back as he left, given him an encouraging wink and said 'Fill your boots, lad.'

Anthony said that if she ever got in a fight again she must call for him, and she said she would make sure to win it next time, and not need him.

'And it wasn't a fight. She attacked me. You know that.'

'What, and fell over and trod on her own eye while she were about it?'

He smiled, rueful and sympathetic. But Mary's last thread of composure fled and the smile became unsteady before her. 'Side with her, then, damn you.' Hurt crossed his face. 'Why don't you go up there and join in with that stinking lot? You could tell them a few tasty stories to work their jaws on.'

She was too exhausted to sob at first, but let tears hang heavy in her eyes until he gently pulled her towards him. 'I'd never do that,' he said. 'I in't like *him*, I promise.' He did not let go until feet sounded on the stairs; then she parted from him, sick of the corrosion of salt on her face.

Later they talked for a long time about London, and it cheered Mary to think of a new place where people would not know her, and where there would be so many of them that she could be invisible in their crowds and invulnerable to their friendship.

They decided it would be best not to go walking that Sunday. It fell to Mary, along with Mrs Seward, to accompany the more mobile patients to the chapel, and she sat throughout with her head bowed.

'I trust that has given you something to reflect soberly upon,' said the matron on their return across the yard. Two of the women sniggered.

Mary declined dinner, too knotted to eat, and went to the gaol, to see people guiltier than her.

Selwyn, this time, was not so wild, but skinny and stinking, his back hunched against the glow of the rushlights as he pored over a hand of cards. One of his companions looked up through wiry eyebrows.

'Abandoned you, you reckon? Here she is, looking juicy as a plum and guilty as a dog in a pantry.'

Selwyn stretched through the bars and clasped her towards him, making more tears come into her eyes. 'What happened to your face?'

She had hoped the three raised lines on her forehead would not show in such dim light. 'A patient did it. I couldn't blame him – his arm was being cut off and I'd have fought the same, if it had been me.'

She spent about half an hour with Selwyn, telling him about the operation – though not who the patient was. The story flowed easily from her, for even the ache of anxiety that she'd had since the fight did not quite diminish the pride she had in not fainting and in not being sick, even though Mr Cotgreave – a proper surgeon and all! – had yocked his whole breakfast down the door.

'What the hell sort of place are you working in?' Selwyn's anger was so impotent as to be near comical. Safe enough to be angry with people when there's no chance of you ever having to meet them. 'They shouldn't make you do such things.'

'No one made me. I wanted to.' The air from the window-crosses made her shudder. It was the more horrifying for the waft of spring-time in it. Its scent withered in the foulness and sank to give breath to the colonies of lice on the floor. 'I've a mind to run away to London and become a surgeon's apprentice.'

Selwyn tried to laugh, but it came out unpractised. 'Happen you should, then, and see how many patients'll let their limbs be sawn by a woman.' He put his fingers round the top of her arm and their tips almost met, for all that she was proud of her strength; and she could say nothing, because the idea of her sawing through bones was every bit as absurd as he said. 'You do come out with some rubbish some-times.'

And though she was used to letting such things offend her, the vague plan she had, to find work in a London hospital helping the surgeons, was, after all, rubbish. She had let herself think about it – how inter-esting it would be to stitch wounds and think of new ways of doing things and see if they would work. But it was stupid. The idea swivelled from possible to ridiculous.

'I must go.'

Selwyn's fingers tightened on her arm. 'No.'

'I can't stay. Selwyn, please don't—'

'It's only three weeks away.'

Quiet and scarce-controlled, the words ripped through her.

His clasp undid and she made an uncertain smile, hurrying back to where Mangham had waited at the top of the steps. He was not there, and the gate was locked. The bars that separated her from the pris-oners glistened in the glow of her lamp and the rushlights reflected in impassive eyes, so it was not for a moment clear who was looking in and who out. She allowed herself one panicked rattle of the gate, and then looked behind her at the inmates and tried to cloak herself in a layer of nonchalance.

Mangham would come back. No one could expect him to wait for every visitor. He would have to return sometime. She started back to Selwyn but halted, weary. She did not want the dirt of his hands on her clothes again, or the guilt that gnawed at her when she met his black eyes. Her topcoat brushed the hair of someone resting their shoulders on the grille, and she scrunched her nose in disgust.

Like a sheep's greasy wool, the cloud of hair pressed through the bars, powder clagging on its collapsed curls. Real hair, perhaps once dressed like a wig. Mary wanted to prod it and see if it would crumble in her fingers, but some of the other prisoners watched her and she returned to the gate. When she looked back from the gloom she frowned. She saw wrinkles delineated by shadows and a nose, like a beak, stark against the glow.

Mangham's feet scuffed on the lower steps, but Mary looked harder. And a swell of triumph brought boldness to her step when she crossed the passageway and jabbed a finger into the fleece.

'Mrs Hodder?'

The woman turned, scowling, her face sallow. Grime had replaced its white maquillage. She drew herself up, her eyes level with Mary's neck, and squinted through the bars. A heart-shaped patch clung, upside down, to her cheek. Traces of perfume wheedled through the smell of excrement.

'Well, Sarey Hodder,' Mary said. 'I hope Ned minds your jam, else it might boil over, mightn't it?' The woman's chin tipped and she pressed her face through the bars. 'Did you pick on some girl as had a brother bigger than Ned?'

Mrs Hodder sucked in a whistle of air and stood on tiptoes, enlarging herself like a cornered cat. 'Who in all fuck are you to speak to me like that?"

'Or did one of your gentlemen complain to a Justice that he didn't get enough of a challenge?'

Mary raised her lamp and Mrs Hodder blinked in recognition. Mangham jangled coins in his pocket as he waited by the gate.

'On'y here a week,' he said when Mary returned to him. 'Then she'll stand in the pillory. Everyone knew what sort of an 'ouse that was, but she riled her neighbour and he shopped her to the beak. Spiky old bitch. Throws food at me like it was common as shite.'

'What neighbour?'

Mangham did not seem to have heard. 'Bet she won't be doing it by tomorrow, once she gets hungry.'

'You said her neighbour—' Mangham shrugged and said he was never in the Justice's house, and did not know even half of what his prisoners were about; he was just there to keep them from escaping.

'I must go back and ask her something.' Mary looked down at Sarah Hodder's bony face, framed by bars. 'Why did you end up in here?'

Mrs Hodder crooked her lip over her mottled teeth. 'You ought to know. You're his convenient, ain't you?'

'His what? Who?'

'He was happy enough with my establishment for years, and then sudden-like he sides himself with the law, because of you.'

Heavy weights pulled Mary's heart into her guts. 'Do you mean Mr—'

'Mr Warbreck. I ain't stupid. He said I tried to make a friend of his come into my house. A friend! And the rest. I says who? And he says you was a slight girl, with black hair and wont to be fiery, and so I knew who he meant – you was there one day it was snowing, wasn't you?' Mrs Hodder's eyes slitted. 'You want to choose your friends more careful-like, girl. He's a crook. So much for his fine clothes and that bleeding wig – they're bought off a gemman on hard times. I know what he's about – I've known it since I came to this tin-pot town. He has a whole herd of bumpkins at his command, and fleeces them out of smuggled goods they might keep for themselves.'

'It's not—'

'He's got a wife, you know. You know that?'

'Yes, I know damn well! And he's faithful to her.'

Mrs Hodder squawked – it might have been a laugh, or it might have been pain, or anything. The sound was high and prolonged. 'Faithful? So's mine arse. You looked newer than ever any snow that fell that day, and yet there was muggins, trying to waylay a confirmed whore, who'd been on her back on his couch only a minute before. I get it wrong sometimes, eh? Never saw you as a sly enough bitch to ruin an honest business out of spite.'

Mary smiled unpleasantly at Mrs Hodder. Rotten cobbets of fruit would balance on her thicket of hair. They couldn't even forge a path to her scalp through that lot. Mary would have to aim for her face.

'Are you staying, love?' Mangham's coins chinked louder in his pocket. 'On'y I've got things to get on with.'

'I'd better be gone,' said Mary to Mrs Hodder. 'I must start gathering dead rats for the next time I see you.'

She kept up the confident demeanour until she was halfway down the stairs.

'Did she upset you, lovely?' How Mangham knew, in the dark, that she was brushing away tears she could not tell.

'No.'

'Foul-mouthed old hag. I've heard it all in here, but a frigging sailor'd blush to hear some of the words she comes out with.'

Mary sniffed. 'I don't care about that.'

The understanding between them was silent. He took the bottle from her and she waited, staring at the flame of her lamp.

Sudden-like, he sides himself with the law.

She slipped the money into Mangham's hand and the bottle slipped back into hers.

Because of you. Because of you.

Mary blinked, as always, in the light outside the gaol, but it was a weary light and even the paling mud of spring held no promise. She trudged up on to the walls and round to the Watergate, the breeze fresh on her cheeks. She could not see as far as Bryce's warehouse from there. The cork hurt her finger and thumb – Mangham always put it back in so hard – but she managed it at last, and numbed her lips with the drink.

There must have been some money in it. That was the thought she kept repeating: there must have been some money in it. It was not revenge on Mrs Hodder for accosting her; it was not done out of love, or even regard. There must have been some money in it.

The gin did nothing but make her stomach cramp.

'I hate you,' she said. The breeze touched her lips and caught the whisper away from her up the bleak incline of Watergate Street. 'I love someone else now, and I'll go to London with him and it'll be too far for you to make me think of you again.' She put on her gloves, feeling the delicate leather, brushing it against her lips. When would Bryce Warbreck ever have thought of her like that? There could not have been a time when he had even wasted the energy to look at her, but when she happened to place herself in the line of his eyes. If she were a surgeon she would invent a kind of saw to amputate rotten loves and send them to be buried so deep that even the worms would be crushed trying to reach them. He had always wanted rid of her, until she wanted to go.

She walked on, sat on the bench in the remaining half of the Goblin Tower and gazed out over the Hey towards St Martin's Fields. Except to raise the bottle to her lips she did not move until the late-afternoon sun dimmed to an eerie yellow that goldened the silver birches in the shelter of the walls. She closed her eyes to block out the sight of their flaking bark.

'I hate you,' she whispered. 'I hate you, Bryce.' A thread of dirt spiralled round her heart.

Thurstaston, afternoon, 28 December 1755

Jessica Warbreck's drawing room is a calm space where everything is spotless. Not even a cobweb on the ceiling. No dust; not one woodlouse. The carved table legs offer thousands of niches for grime to settle into, but there is none. Mary decides she will clean her own house when she gets home.

She sips tea from a bowl so delicate she can't hold it without burning her fingers and awkwardly admires Mrs Warbreck's little boy, while a servant goes to fetch Bryce from the stables.

Mrs Warbreck knows all the village stories about her, and appears not to care. Mary can see, from the perfect shiny curls, the radiant smile, the skin still rosy and flawless – at eight-and-twenty, for God's sake! – that she is not likely to see some little, silly, snaggle-toothed, black-haired girl as much of a threat.

Footsteps approach the house and Mary's tea-bowl rattles on its saucer.

Bryce Warbreck regards her with coldness. Wary of trouble from her, no doubt. She won't let herself look at his lips, and glances only briefly at his eyes. The unnatural blue strikes her as hard, and not quite how she has been remembering it. Nothing like when he turned to her in the carriage that time. She holds the bolt of silk to her chest like a shield. It works, somehow; she smiles and keeps her heart still.

'Mrs Jones has brought something for us,' says Mrs Warbreck. 'From the wreck.'

His expression relaxes. Mary does her best to look businesslike.

'Come through to the office, Mrs Jones,' he says, and his words have none of the clipped harshness she has expected, but are cheerful and

ordinary and almost kind. That is worse, in a way. She can't watch him kiss his wife, but looks aside and makes a face. The servant puts the tea things on a tray and carries them through.

'You'd rather something other than tea, wouldn't you?' Bryce speaks even as he closes the door. 'This was brought in yesterday.'

He picks up a bottle from the sideboard. Mary has to cut her losses and blush, telling herself she has done pretty well to last this far.

'That's kind of you, but tea is more proper at this time of day,'

He pours some brandy into a sparkling cut glass. Well, pour as he might she will not drink it. She could not pick up a glass like that anyway; it would be shattered within seconds.

'I hope your husband is well,' says Bryce, holding her gaze for longer than he ought. 'It's an unusual event, for him to send you.' A non-existent event, before now, because she has not been to Bryce Warbreck's house since her marriage. Not so much that Selwyn forbids her – more that she has not had the energy to spend a night in tears afterwards.

'He's well enough, thank you.'

Bryce's smile is strange. The rim of the glass rests on Mary's lip. She holds it delicately by the stem, just as she supposes a lady would. Might as well drink it, then – drink back some of the profit he will make from the silk.

'Well, then,' he says. 'What have you brought?'

She opens the silk out across the table. Ripples flaw its surface. Indignation rises in her against them.

'Ah,' he says, and she grasps the sound to her as though it falls against her ear. 'Beautiful.' Slim and neat, his fingers stroke the shimmering blue. She examines her own chapped hands. 'A miracle,' he says, 'that it survived the sea.'

She refuses to meet his eyes, attending instead to the different effects of light on the silk; the way a tilt of her head can bring to it whiteness, another tilt lilac, another rosemary-flower blue. Bryce's fingers stretch within the range of her gaze. She bows her head *further. Then he fills the glass again and she is confused, because last time she looked it wasn't empty.*

'Not often we get a wreck around here, is it?' he says, and she shakes her head. 'It's the Hoylake lot that get the best of it. Wallasey is tolerable, too. Too sheltered here, in my opinion.'

'Yes,' she says. 'We could do with more storms.'

'I'm surprised you didn't keep this for a gown.' She looks up at last, and the corners of his eyes crinkle further into a smile. 'You like blue, don't you?'

She waits a moment, pummelling her feelings into some sort of containment before she dares speak. 'I wanted to. But Selwyn . . . Mr Jones . . . wouldn't let me. He said it was no use, as I'd never have need to wear it, and that's true enough.'

'What a terrible pity. It would look beautiful on you.'

That's the point when all the substance goes out of her heart, and leaves it a shell of thin glass, waiting for the tap of a hammer to touch it in just the wrong way.

'Do you think so?' she says. He nods – so sincerely that she must dig her nails into her palms. 'Well, the money's more important than some silly gown.' The glass walls thicken, thank God. 'I can't just swan around in silk all day like some idle lady, can I?'

Ha! She gets the courage to smile, because Mrs Warbreck, with her fair curls, is in the other room, in a gown of primrose silk, her petticoat sprigged with flowers of precisely the same yellow. Now she can look at him directly. But he smiles back, and the glass in her hand trembles.

'A most unusual colour,' he says, as he examines the silk for damage. 'It reminds me of rosemary flowers.'

She bites her lip.

He wraps it back into its protective blanket and, with her last glimpse of the very corner, Mary tries to imprint the colour into her memory. After he pushes it aside he goes to another room and she can hear the sounds of locks turning, and him whistling under his breath. When he returns he has a small purse, but there has been enough time for her hand to sneak to the brandy bottle and refill her glass, and for her to gulp it down so the level looks the same as before.

'This seems fair, I think,' he says, but all she can absorb is the glimmer of laughter that invades his eyes. 'I trust it will be acceptable to you.'

She tries to open the strings of the purse but the brandy has befuddled her. When at last she looks into it she is not sure whether she ought to take out some of the money, or what. Shillings and battered sixpences and grubby tuppences nestle together in the dark cloth.

'I'm sorry,' she says. 'I don't know much about this side of the business, and I don't know . . . well, what I mean is – how much do you mean to give me?'

'A pound,' he says. 'I thought it would be convenient for you to have it in small change.'

Mary examines the contents of the purse again. 'A pound? It can't be worth that much, can it?'

Bryce laughs; he sits back in his chair, looking at the ceiling. The contours of his close-shaved throat stretch above the white of his shirt; a thin scratch shows red on his skin. 'You're supposed to look disappointed and try to wheedle more out of me.' He smiles.

'Oh . . . well, thank you.'

'You're welcome. Now, where are the rest?'

CHAPTER 22

Mary hadn't eaten since breakfast. Her hands shook on the cork. Gin scalded her tongue and, sip by sip, turned her hunger to heaviness. The sun moved behind the Goblin Tower and the silver birches dulled; the daffodils at their feet hung their heads. The bruise on the back of Mary's head sent tendrils of pain through her scalp. Was gin not supposed to stop this? Had it not, at times, removed the ache and the knot in her stomach? She stood and reached for the sandstone at the tower's opening. Far along the walkway a few figures moved, their shapes drawn upwards and elongated. The stones and figures blurred together. The breeze touched cold sweat under Mary's eyes.

There must have been some money in it.

They should have gone to London. They should just have gone.

Panic scurried through her and she sat down heavily. Perhaps one of those figures would help her. She hung on to the bench and watched a seagull on the railing opposite repeat itself, left to right and left to right again. Mary rested her head back; tears slipped down her temples and gathered, cold, in her ears. The image of the seagull still repeated in front of her closed eyes.

'Mary, are you ill?'

She jumped, and moved the bottle closer to her side. Mr Racketta's bulk dimmed the light within the tower. She saw him double; his plain brown hat, his workmanlike coat and his cracked leather case all moving before her, left to right. Out on the wall behind him a couple passed by. Mary tried to catch their eyes; they found sudden interest in the daffodils.

'No,' she said. 'There's nowt wrong. I must get home.'

But when she stood, the walkway outside tilted like a ship's deck. Mr Racketta guided her back to the bench.

'I'll walk you back,' he said. 'You'll not be safe.'

'I will. Someone's to meet me here, in a minute.'

Mr Racketta sat down beside her. Hints of coffee and port threaded through his aura of ash. 'Then I've a minute to talk to you, in private,' he said. 'I've meant to, but with all that's happened at the infirmary these past few days . . .' He knew as well, then, about the fight. Everyone in the whole city must know. 'I mean to thank you, for helping me with Hartingshall.' Mr Racketta's expression approached sincerity. 'I'd not be exaggerating were I to say that, should he live, he'll owe his life to you as well as to me.' He studied her face. A skip of pride made her look back.

'Mr Beeks might have done it just as well,' she said. She sounded clear and sober, to herself. Behind her the sandstone gave off a chill that soaked through her clothes.

'Aye, if there were time to chat about it. But I had to think fast, and you were nearest.' Perhaps he meant it. His eyes did not seem to hold mockery.

'Do you think . . .' This time she had to pause so as not to stumble or slur. 'That, if I were a man, I could be a surgeon's apprentice?' It was a sensible enough question. Why must his shoulders shake in that silent laughter? She edged away.

'Aye, m'dear.' Mr Racketta pressed closer to her and the gin turned over in her stomach. 'You'd be a sight more versatile than the likes of Beeks.' His arm slipped round her shoulder and she shrank into herself. More herring gulls landed on the railing opposite, their vicious beaks parting in cries. The souls of the drowned stared out from their yellow eyes. 'But, as I said, Mary, I mean to thank you.' Mr Racketta swallowed, and the creases deepened at the corners of his mouth.

'How would you like some new clothes? A gown perhaps. Something pretty. I'd buy it for you. You'd like that, wouldn't you, hmm?'

Blue silk. Oh, the light would play on it and its hues would shimmer like a stream.

'No, I wouldn't.'

''Course you would.' He fingered a loose thread at the front of her jacket. 'This becomes you right well, of course, but all girls like something new and pretty once in a while.'

'Not me.'

'Like these, for instance.' His fingers on her gloves. Not disgust, just pure panic. She snatched her hands away. 'You must have saved your wages for weeks, eh?'

'They were given to me,' she said. 'By a man. And he won't be pleased to know you're after giving me things an' all.' She peeled off the gloves and folded them into her pocket so he might not begrime them with his gaze.

And then her hands were back, undisguised; her fingers red against her topcoat and doubled by gin. Rough hands that had pretended to elegance. A whiff of the ward smell caught away in the twilit breeze.

'Ah,' Mr Racketta said, 'I wondered what he would have spent it on.'

The sort of hands you'd find on the sort of girl who might be sitting unprotected in a urine-smattered alcove, too drunk to stop a fat old man breathing on her. She tried to stand. The tightening of his arm made a cold weight sink to her stomach. 'I said, I wondered what he would have spent it on.'

'Why do you care what he does with his own winnings?'

'He told you he won it, then? Well, it was a gamble, right enough.'

'What was?'

Mr Racketta waited while someone walked past. Mary hid under the brim of her hat. 'The arm, of course.'

Over the slope of the Hey, clumps of winter-paled grass bowed eastwards away from the river, as colourless as the silver birches in the dimming of twilight.

'The——?'

'Hartingshall's arm. Wells sold it.'

This new wave of nausea was not icy, but hot. It was making her misunderstand. Anything she said now must be stupid, must make him laugh, and say that was not what he meant. 'He couldn't have done.'

'It was never buried. The bundle he delivered to the sexton contained an old blanket. Mr Venables and I saw it for ourselves.'

The sun on the tips of the trees vanished, like a candle flame blown out.

'Who the hell would buy a dead arm?'

Mr Racketta unpinned the top of her jacket and slid his hand in. She kept still and outwardly calm, as if concealing fear from a wasp. 'An anatomist,' he said. 'I haven't told the Board, Mary. Do you think I should?'

'I don't think he'd care if he's thrown out. He has a mind to leave, any end.'

'It's not a case of being thrown out. Stealing an arm is a very serious matter.'

'He didn't steal it. You gave it to him: I saw you.' The hand slithered further under her clothes. Without suddenness or violence, Mary buried her nails in his skin. 'Why did you and Mr Venables see it? Because you went to collect it for yourselves?' Her teeth clenched with the pressure she dug into his hand. He breathed faster; his breeches bulged. The clamminess of his fingers, retreating, left a trail of grime on her chest.

'A young man in London was hanged last month for selling an arm.' Mary's breath stopped. Inside the tower the light had almost gone, but it glinted on a bead of saliva at the corner of Mr Racketta's mouth. 'Now, it's too cold to stay here. We shall repair to my house.' He angled his watch to the light. 'It's a quarter to six,' he said. 'I'll have you back to the infirmary by eight.'

She staggered at his strength as he pulled her from the bench. 'I in't going anywhere with you. I'll scream, and those people . . .' She waved her gin bottle at the blurred group down the walkway. 'Those people will hear me, and the men will throw you into the ditch.'

'Do you think they've never seen a fellow pick up a drunken harlot before? For God's sake, Mary, just give in.' Mary twisted her hand, but his clutch remained tight. 'I know where you were that night I was with Agnes. I heard you. If his gin-sodden cock made you cry out so, how much could a real man pleasure you?'

The bottle struck him on the side of his head. Fragments of glass sprinkled on to the walkway. Mr Racketta put his fingertips to his temple and swore.

Mary freed her hand. The scent of gin sidled up around her. She did not want it anyway. That was it now. She would not get any more, not if it was going to make her feel like this. She stumbled back, rubbing her fingers. Her pocket felt too light; it put her off balance and she supported herself on the wall.

Yellow smudges were all she could see of the daffodils, now the Hey lay in twilight. The silver birches merged against the grass, their leafless branches silent. Glass crunched under Mary's feet. Too unsteady to run, she took long steps away from Mr Racketta. A groan made her look back, but he did not follow. He rested his elbows on the wall and rubbed his hurt head.

'Mary,' he said. 'Why must you give yourself to some feckless young lad and not to me?'

Her voice rang loud and mocking against the stones. 'Is that what you said to your wife?'

Mr Racketta looked up slowly. 'Who . . .' He frowned. 'Who told you about Jane?'

'Everyone knows.'

He bowed his head, hunching his shoulders like a cat at its meat. She left him staring down from the wall at the blurs of the daffodils.

Anthony was not in the infirmary. No candles illuminated the kitchen, but the window still formed a pale arch in the wall and the remains of the fire blunted the darkness. The patients had eaten and Mrs Stout was folding her apron, about to go home.

'My sakes!' she said. 'Look at Dolly Maukin here, with her hair all over the place. I daren't ask what you've been up to.'

Fancy herself as one to judge, did she? Mary slammed her hat down on the table. 'Mr Racketta tried to drag me back to his house, and I threw a bottle at him and put a stop to it. Is that enough for you to gossip about?'

In the absence of any other conspirator Mrs Stout looked sideways at the fire. 'And what got you into that pickle, I ask? Gin, that's what.'

Mary slumped into a chair. 'It wasn't. I was only sitting there, thinking.'

Precise and violent pains drilled between her eyes. The table acquired an orange sheen; Mrs Stout had lit a candle and tied her apron back on. The bread she cut was not that day's and the butter was on the turn, but Mary imagined it soaking up the gin and stilling the churn of her stomach. Mrs Stout built the fire back up and put some water on for tea when she saw the way Mary looked at the jug of strong.

'Thank you,' Mary said, and the thought that someone was being kind to her made her cry. Mrs Stout clasped her shoulder and handed her a dishclout for a handkerchief.

'Dear, dear, have you fallen out with soft lad again?' Mary shook her head. 'Nowt's happened, has it? Like I warned you about?'

'No,' Mary said. 'But you would drink gin if everyone hated you as much as they hate me.'

'Oh, Mary, when will you start being what you wish people thought you were?'

'I don't wish for them to think anything. I don't care.'

'Ha! Wouldn't that be nice?'

The dishclout smelled musty, as though it had been scrunched up damp for weeks. In the candlelight tiny veins showed on Mrs Stout's cheeks, forming a web like the cracks in parched soil.

Mary told her about Bryce Warbreck – not everything, just how she had made a fool of herself and how he had stoked up the gossip.

'Well! He dunna sound much worth crying over,' said Mrs Stout. 'Those rich fellows are never after love, Mary, and we all have to learn that sometime or another. Just be thankful you've a pretty enough face to have made him kiss you once, and be glad you've found someone else who'll appreciate it afore you get fat and your teeth go.' The cook paused, her eyes again conspiring with the flames. 'Anthony will marry you, won't he? Has he asked you?'

'He has. You won't tell anyone . . . ?'

Mrs Stout hugged her and promised never to tell, and it was all the more reason to forget the other fellow.

'Oh, I don't love Bryce Warbreck any more,' said Mary. 'I know it sounds that way, but I don't love him. It's just he's like a splinter that hurts to leave in, and hurts even more to dig out.'

Mrs Stout shook her head sadly. 'Look at you,' she said. 'You want your hair brushing. Tell you what, I'll put it up nice for you, and you can find a clean shift and put on that pretty grey gown you wore the other day. I always say if you look respectable, it's easier to feel respectable, and if you feel respectable, it's easier to make other people think you are.' It took Mrs Stout almost a quarter of an hour to coax the tangles out of Mary's hair. Then she pinned it neatly, arranged Mary's cap, and fetched her other clothes down from Agnes's room. 'There! Doesn't that feel better?' The cook patted her cheek. 'Now, you know what you must do next, don't you?' Apologise to Agnes? To Mrs Seward? Go and repent properly, in church? 'Stop drinking gin.' Mary sighed. 'Now. Have you brought any home with you?'

'No.'

'Good. It won't be as bad as you think. You mustn't let anyone offer you a sip, mustn't buy any, and mustn't go anywhere where they sell it. Let Anthony drink as much as he pleases, but he can't make you put a bottle to your lips. And don't heed Mrs Seward if she mocks you for stopping. She mocks folk for everything. Just stop.'

Griping pains plaited Mary's guts and her eyes burned. 'I was going to anyway,' she said.

Very early the next morning Mary put her feet to the floor and waited for her dizziness to settle. Cautiously she dressed, and though her movements were slow and unsteady her head did not hurt as much as she dreaded. Her teeth ached and her eyes felt stiff and her insides dry, but that was all. She had got away with it; been rewarded for her decision to leave off gin for good. Draughts from the ward windowsill freshened her face and made her feel clearer. Mist hung over the track below – the track where she had walked with Anthony, after he had gone two weeks without gin – ready to flit away with the first rays of the sun. Mary imagined the last fumes of gin dispersing from her in the same way. She smiled a bit. Enough to pretend everything would soon sort itself out.

Then she turned and saw Hartingshall, and the smile left her.

Still asleep, Hartingshall sprawled on the bed, his three limbs hanging over the sides. Around the ward sniffs and snores broke the dawn light. Mr Racketta's words came back to her confused, as though she had strained to overhear them through a keyhole. She must have heard wrong. Been too drunk to understand.

Soft and smooth, her hair had been brushed, so that must have happened. And if that had happened, then the memory of telling Mrs Stout about Mr Racketta must also be true; and if that was true then Mr Racketta must really have put his hand in her clothes, and must have told her about someone being hanged for stealing an arm.

Mary shivered. He had tried to take her back to his house, but she had not gone. Had she? No, she wouldn't have done. He had promised her a gown, and that image was quite clear – the silk she would have chosen. And she remembered thinking how easy it would be to make him promise a petticoat to go with it. But she had not. Mrs Stout had still been there when she got home, and Mrs Stout usually left at about six o'clock, so there would not have been time.

Mary's hand drifted to her weightless pocket.

That was it. Splinters of glass had chimed to the walkway, and Mr Racketta had stared down at the flowers.

Echoes rose from her footsteps on the stairs. She flinched with each sound. Anthony did not answer his door. He missed breakfast, and when he at last staggered out Mrs Seward sent him to take the week's meat and grocery orders.

The evening was the first opportunity to talk to him, when the matron had retired early and Agnes was reading to Hartingshall. Mary let him kiss her once, and then held her candle up to his face.

'Will you tell me the truth – about this?'

She grabbed the watch from his pocket, and the bar popped out from the buttonhole of his waistcoat.

'Careful!' Annoyance coloured his tone and the candle-shadows on his cheeks deepened. 'That cost me an—' Anthony met her gaze and flushed. 'Your hands shake,' he muttered. He was right; however much she tried to still them, they trembled. But that was just because of the gin and the hunger yesterday, and that was the last time it would happen because she was not going to drink gin any more. She almost told him that.

'Is it true?'

'What?'

'Mr Racketta said you sold Hartingshall's arm. But I'll believe you if you say it was the sexton. Or the surgeons. They might have hid it here and given you the bundle for show.'

Anthony held out his palm for the watch. He fiddled with it, inspected the chain for damage, shrugged, and arranged it again in his waistcoat.

'Anthony?'

'It was me. What of it?'

Mary ushered him into the kitchen. Warmth lingered in the room, but the smell of meat and potatoes had turned cold and sour.

'What were you thinking of?'

'There are certain folk as pay good money for arms and such, 'specially off a strong bugger like Hartingshall. I didn't plan it – that's the truth – but I had to take the chance, for this.' He touched the watch chain gently; a caress.

'Where did you sell it?'

Anthony drummed his fingertips on the table. 'A place in Boughton. An anatomy feller called Mr Skedd. He paid a guinea for it.'

A guinea, for an arm?

'Why couldn't you just take it to the sexton like anyone else?'

He unhooked the watch from his waistcoat and ran his thumb over the case. Then he held it up before her. The candlelight burnished the metal, matching the determination that burned in Anthony's eyes. 'This in't a joke, Mary. It in't a toy. This is the start of our future. This is how we're going to feed our children. This is how we're going to prove we're worth something. There's no time to be sentimental. It was no use to Hartingshall any more.'

'Mr Racketta said someone was hanged in London for the same thing. For stealing an arm and selling it.'

The tapping of Anthony's fingers ceased. 'It in't stealing.' Mary did not answer. 'It didn't belong to anyone.' He nibbled the skin of his thumb. The haze above the candle shimmered in front of his face. He changed thumbs and picked at globs of wax, squashing them flat on the table. 'I'll say the blanket was already in there when I took it. How would Mr Racketta even have known, unless he'd asked the sexton to keep it for him?' The candle, its last pool of wax doddering in the holder, guttered and revived. 'Did he tell you he'd not shop me, so long as you let him get his dirty hands up your skirts?'

'Yes.'

'Well, then. He's lying. I've nowt to be frightened of.'

Anthony's hand jolted; he knocked the candlestick and the flame drowned in the wax.

Chair legs scraped on the floor and his footsteps moved back and forth. Mary's eyes attuned to the dark and she saw the shape of his hair against the window, and heard the meeting of his teeth on his thumbnail. He told her to wait a minute, he would be back soon; and Mary listened to his room door opening, her nerves building.

She could not remember very clearly what Mrs Stout had said. It seemed a little exaggerated now to have cried so much and to say she would give up gin. Hunger, after all, was what had made her feel so ill, and Mr Racketta would make the soberest of people sick.

Well, it could not be so very difficult, to say no.

No thank you.

Not for me.

The sound of it purled less than a foot away from her; a single glint of light flashed once on the bottle. The sight of it, the twist of the liquid and its splash into the cup she must picture for herself. Only the sound was real at first. Then, afterwards, the scent. Familiarity was its greatest merit: the way the vapour took charge and promised that, for a while, it would think and talk, and spare you the effort. She could not say she truly wanted the cut of the spirit in her throat, or its numbing of her tongue. But if it did not do that to her tongue, then how could it numb her nerves, or mellow the knot of snakes that thrived in her stomach?

The base of the cup grated over the table and the knot tightened. *Pretend to drink, and hand the cup back. He won't see. Just put it to your lips.* Vapours sidled into her mouth, as though they cleared the way for the gin.

'I don't want any.'

Where those words had come from she did not know. They formed as quick as a thought and were free of the jittery feeling that still made her nerves dart. She pushed the cup away.

'Fair enough,' said Anthony, and the gin glugged. Fair enough? Was that it, then? 'I don't blame you. I love being sober of an evening. It's just the morning after as gets me.'

Silence wrapped them, intruded upon only by distant sounds of the street, and then Anthony reached out to her across the table. His fingers were cold. 'If they try anything, if they try and bring me to the court, promise me you'll tell the truth and say you had nowt to do with it.' Mary hesitated a moment, listening. A metallic groan, like the sound of the courtyard gate. But she did not hear it swing shut, at once.

'I'd rather come to gaol with you.'

'It won't come to that. But if it does I won't let you in with me.'

The gate whined again, and shut softly. Anthony took a decisive swig of gin. The orange light became more persistent on the glass.

The locks on the main doors rattled and Mary leapt up. An insistent thump resounded down the corridor. Mrs Seward's pattens clopped on the landing and Mary thought of her waiting, hopeful that Anthony would neglect to answer the door.

He stayed in the kitchen. Mary undid the bolts and squinted out at the light of a lantern shining from above. It illuminated the puny man who held it on a tall, crook-like pole, and its glow flung swathes of light and shadow over Mr Venables, Mr Racketta and Mr Barnston.

CHAPTER 23

'Don't be alarmed.' Mr Barnston spoke with quiet assurance. 'We wish to speak with Anthony Wells. Perhaps you would be so good as to tell him we are here.' Mary peered into the light. Mr Venables's face was grave, Mr Racketta's expressionless. Behind them lamps moved in the street and the crosses in the Northgate walls glowed.

'I don't know where he is, sir,' she said. 'I thought that might be him.' Mr Barnston regarded her with an expression of disappointment – at her lies, she knew, not at Anthony's absence.

'Perhaps, then,' he said, 'we may speak with Mrs Seward?'

'Yes, sir. May I fetch a light and show you to the board room?' He accepted, and Mary hurried back to the kitchen. 'They're after talking to you. I said you weren't here. When I take them to the board room you'll have a chance to slip out.' She stirred the ashes and found enough fire to light a candle. Anthony kissed her.

'It's no use running away. I've done nowt wrong.'

'Please. Go while you've got the chance.'

Moonlight fled from the board room table, displaced by the flame. Mr Barnston and Mr Venables took off their hats and the dim light put shadows on to the sheen of powder on their perukes. At the other end of the corridor the lanternlight still spread a triangle of orange on to the floor.

'Mr Racketta and the constable will remain at the door, Mary.'

Mr Barnston's words misted away under the pulse of blood in Mary's ears. She heard Mr Venables saying it was in case she was mistaken and Anthony Wells had returned without her knowledge, and might leave again before they had a chance to question him.

'What's happened?'

Mr Barnston raised his eyebrows at her boldness. 'There is nothing for you to worry about,' he said. 'Fetch Mrs Seward, please.'

Pattens clomped on the stairs and questions followed them. Mrs Seward's presence took over from Mary's, and Mary became as redundant and unimportant as the moisture on the walls. The board room door clicked shut.

'What's all this about?' Mary said.

The constable shrugged.

'It's about the matter we discussed yesterday, Mary.' Mr Racketta tried the store-cupboard door and then Anthony's room: both locked. 'The matter with which you declined to assist me. An unseemly trade in body parts, the profits of which Wells used to furnish his whore with fripperies. Do you remember now, Mary?'

'No, I don't, because it isn't true.'

'Look,' said the constable, 'is he here or not? I an't had a morsel since breakfast.'

'He's not here.'

All Mary remembered after Mrs Seward's exit from the board room was a clamour of voices. Patients called down, Agnes came to see what was happening, and screamed and slumped to the stairs in tears when she found out. Mr Barnston fiddled with his shirt cuffs.

'Mary,' he said, 'if you know where Wells is, you must tell us.' Agnes ran back up the stairs.

'He might have gone to the gin shop aside of Dog-Breath Annie's in Watergate Street,' Mary said. 'I think he might have said that was where he was going.'

Mr Racketta shook his head. 'There's no gin shop there. Where is he? Or must we arrest his accomplice first?' The surgeon put his hand on her shoulder and she hit it away.

'Let go of me.'

The kitchen door scraped its arc on the tiles.

'Get off her. I'm here.'

Anthony's tall frame was hazy in the limits of the lamplight. Mr Venables led him towards the board room, and he did not fight. He reached to take Mary's hand.

'I'm coming in with him,' she said.

Mr Barnston shook his head once. Mary could not push through the door; Anthony's fingers slipped from hers and it shut. Muted impressions of speech were all she could hear. The shrill exclamations of Mrs Seward, the nasal whine of Mr Venables, Mr Racketta's mutter and the soft tones of Mr Barnston. She did not hear Anthony at all.

She returned to the kitchen and downed the rest of the bottle of gin.

'This institution can only fare better without him. I shall engage someone industrious and sober, who won't shirk his duties or entice the nurses into lewd behaviour. Then at least some good will come of this, though I have no doubt he will at last end on the gallows.'

Mary's head slipped from her hand and she started up. Darkness filled the corridor and a draught flooded in from the main doors, bringing with it distant drunken shouts and the clang of a stick along the railings.

'Aye, Mrs Seward.' Mr Racketta's voice made her shrink back into the kitchen. 'It's but a short step from this sort of thing to body-snatching, and from body-snatching, as we all know, to murder.' Mr Venables murmured agreement.

'And what poor innocent victim awaits such a fate now?' the matron asked. 'And that girl has something to do with it. No one can persuade me they didn't plan this between them, to get money for gin. I warrant it was her idea, for she's as wily as he is dull.'

A door opened and the surgeons at once took their leave. Mr Barnston exchanged a few words with the matron, who curtsied when she showed him out. Anthony held the candle ahead of him, and it made his eyes sparkle when he looked towards the kitchen, though he did not seem to see her. Mary smiled. She loved the way he shielded the flame with his hand. Its light showed a grin gathering at the corners of his mouth.

'Give me that candle,' said Mrs Seward, 'before it helps the Devil himself find you.' She snatched it away; the flame went out and she stormed up the stairs.

'I'm to go.' Anthony fumbled and dropped his room key and gave a strange kind of laugh. 'I'll go to Mother Starling's – the gin shop in Cow Lane. Will you meet me there, Wednesday night?'

'Yes, but—'

'They wanted him to send me to gaol and have me brought to trial, but he said no. Here.' Coins chinked and he brought Mary's fingers to their cold, greasy surfaces. 'He gave me two weeks' wages and ten shilling extra, and said he'll tell the governors I was discharged for drunkenness.'

The way he clung to Mary made her feel unstable. 'What if they take you to a Justice?'

'Mr Barnston is a Justice. If they took me to another one he couldn't say owt different.'

Half an hour later, when he had packed up his possessions, Mary said goodbye to him at the gate. 'You will be there, won't you? On Wednesday?'

The night breeze fluttered her hair across her face and Anthony brushed it away. 'Of course.'

'Or if you're not, you'll get word to me where you are?'

'I've enough money in my pocket that Mother Starling'll let me stay,' he said with a smile.

She waited until she could just make out the white shape of his hand waving as he went into the Northgate passageway, and then she retired to the cold ward bed. Encrusted spit soiled the pillow. She flung it away and sat with her chin on her knees.

Thank God for Mr Barnston. The thought of Anthony in the gaol made her go cold. What if they had brought another Justice? What if

Mr Barnston had seen the sale of an arm as a crime against society, or against God, or against whatever it was he valued?

And if he could be merciful towards Anthony, why not towards Selwyn?

She lay awake, staring up into the dark. The patients' snuffles were like the breath of black hounds, and the rustle of the bed-ticks like the skitter of claws on the floor. When the clock marked half past ten she slunk down to Anthony's room, and hugged his pillow until the dawn chorus woke her.

It fell to her to answer the door when Mrs Stout arrived, and to go and fetch the water for cleaning the ward. The morning was bright and fresh and there was no one else at the well. Springtime stirred in the scent of the air, and with it the promise of a new life. Over the roof of the school the top of the Northgate was surrounded by blue.

'Come along. You're even slower at this than he was, and that's saying summat.' Mrs Stout flapped her apron at Mary as she might at a goose. Images of the Northgate's three gables swam in Mary's eyes.

'Did it never eat at you,' she said, 'lying to Mr Stout all those years?'

The cook's rosy face paled a shade. She compressed her lips in a puzzled smile. 'You're a strange mite, you. The things you come out with.' She silently lifted one of the buckets and left Mary to follow.

Mary did not know exactly how the reason for Anthony's departure introduced itself to the ward. It was not there when she cleaned her half of the floor and woke the patients with the clank of her bucket. There was no change in their chatter while they ate their breakfasts, and the complaints about the draught were the same as ever. No one's condition had worsened for a night's sleep, and no one's improved. Hartingshall slept on, his face contorted and grey.

The news must have reached them while Mary was downstairs, picking at her own breakfast. Even as she approached the ward she sensed a change in the atmosphere; a winding and tightening, an oppressive hush. The voices stayed her hand on the door.

'To buy her a pair of gloves.'

'No!' Elongated and gleeful, the word hissed out of the ward and filled Mary's lungs like a noxious gas. She listened, unable to walk away.

'Such a wicked thing. And for a funny little creature like her.'

'Oh, she's comely enough for some fellows, I dare say – and she's the sort, that once they get their claws in . . .'

Mary coughed. There was a silence of confederation, and then the same person spoke again, louder.

'That once they get their claws into a man, he'd do a murder just to please them. Even an innocent-looking boy like Mr Wells. They ought to throw her out on the street.'

'Ha! Not likely!' Everyone on the ward must be able to hear now, for all other noise had ceased. 'Those gentlemen aren't hasty to give up the convenience, are they? "Just off to a *hospital meeting*, my dearest, just doing some *charitable work*."'

Mary walked in. The gossipers went quiet, but they looked at each other the same way Betsy Roberts and Liza Mobbett and the others had looked at one another, back home. A type of glance at once concealed and meant to be seen.

'I hope . . .' Mary swallowed. 'I hope your breakfast was to your liking.'

A piece of bread skirred over her shoulder, releasing a shower of crumbs on to her neck. She gasped, and the crumbs scurried into her stays. The two women looked down the ward.

'Poor shot,' Mary said, with a faint smile. A cobbet of milk-gruel hit her arm and fell away, tearing from her sleeve in web-like strands. 'Glad to see someone's rich enough to waste their vittles.' Then another parcel of gruel hit her cheek, a holler rose from the beds, and she recoiled under a bombardment of food and noise.

'Body-snatching whore!'

She dropped the dishes but the clatter did not shock them into silence. 'Body-snatching?' She pointed at Hartingshall. 'Does he look dead to you?' Hartingshall lay in his bed unmoving, his breakfast uneaten, his eyes full of hate. A bowl hit her chest and bounced to the floor, and she fled.

'Mary!' Mrs Seward's thumb gouged a piece of gruel off Mary's cheek. Outrage glinted in her spectacles.

'It weren't my fault. I did nowt!'

Mary found herself shoved into the matron's parlour. She brushed the crumbs from her clothes, fuming. Gruel stuck to her hair; she flung it away in disgust and wiped her fingers on her apron. Shouts came from outside, and the noise lulled.

'What happened?' Mrs Seward's nostrils were wide. Mary's mind raced in search of a story, and then she realised there was no need to invent one. It was a relief, just to tell the truth. 'They won't do it again,' the matron said.

'Thank you.'

Mrs Seward flinched as though the thanks were a curse. 'I think you would be well advised to have nothing more to do with Anthony Wells. He might have escaped punishment, but at least his departure is a blessing. Mrs Stout tells me you have forged some ridiculous plan to marry.'

That was the first time she even remembered telling Mrs Stout. It came back to her – sobbing, and saying something stupid about Bryce Warbreck. Shame smarted her skin, and then anger. So much for Mrs Stout's discretion.

'It in't ridiculous,' Mary said.

'You think you will live comfortably on stealing severed arms from hospitals?'

'We've plans of how we're to live, and it's—'

'What, in drunken penury and heartache?'

'He would leave off gin if I asked him to. He did before. You don't understand how much he loves me.' She glared at Mrs Seward's yellow teeth, uncovered in a sneer. How could she understand? How could she ever have known love, with her heart encased in its pickle-jar of bile?

The matron spun a chair away from the table and pushed Mary into it. Her fingertips dug into Mary's shoulders. 'My husband was just such a one. The smile, the handsome face – the promises. Do you think smiles are enough recompense for having chairs thrown at your head? For breaking your back hauling his dead weight over the doorstep while the neighbours watch? For lying awake every night for a week and dreading seeing a newspaper lest it tells of a body pulled from the river?'

Mary concealed a shiver. 'I'm sorry he was like that, but—'

'He must have blundered into a candle, or thrown it in a rage – I don't know and never will – but he burnt the house down and killed himself and my boy. Sam was but fifteen. That's what I'm warning you about, girl. Ten years ago it was, on the 5th of March, and if you think that's a long time just wait until it happens to you. No amount of time and no amount of gin will ever make it hurt any less.' Mary looked down at her hands. 'I don't want to see any tears. I've known enough. If you must always think of yourself, then think of your future. If you knew what he was going to put you through, you would do everything you could never to set eyes on him again.'

Setting eyes on him again was all that occupied her thoughts through the next day. Agitation made every task agonising. Hostility fumed through the patients' skin and spoiled every bandage. Every pisspot was fouler, every sore and ulcer gleeful in its suppuration, every bed and shirt filthier.

People made themselves vomit, so they could laugh at her attempts not to gag as she cleared it. Farts gathered in a weighty cloud above the beds. A luncheon-plate appeared in the middle of the floorboards, a turd as big as a cowcumber reclining on its surface.

When at last five o'clock, and the start of Mary's evening off, arrived, the agitation intensified. She pictured knocking on a grim door and finding she had gone to the wrong house – one where a gang of murderers lived – or to the right one, and finding that Anthony had left with a girl for London, or had never been there at all. She hurried through Abbey Court, past Dr Tylston's house, through the Kelyards Gate, through the orchard and into Cow Lane.

It was easy to recognise the gin shop, from the new bundles of straw. The rotten black spikes of the old straw sent up a sharp, twitchy scent from the mud under Mary's boots. Otherwise, the shop was just a normal house, held up by those either side. Its upper floor jutted out over the street, supported by worm-riddled pillars, and a layer of dirt besmeared the brickwork up to the height of Mary's waist. A cat jumped from the straw and rowled, shaking its ears and flexing its fingers on the door frame. Its tail quivered as Mary's hand skimmed the bumps of its arched spine.

He left for London this morning.

He left to flee some lass as'd wheedled a promise of a ring out of him!

Mary tiptoed to peer through the gap between the low door and its lintel. A blast of laughter made her clench her fists. What had they heard to make them hate her? Then she knocked, and the laughter hushed.

A woman – rather an old one, though not as ancient as the crone she had once seen sitting outside – opened the door, and the cat sidled in at her feet. Mary smiled, and suspicion warmed away from the woman's plump face.

'Is Anthony Wells here?' Mary asked, winding her fingers together.

The woman's gappy mouth widened into an attitude that might have been either a smile or a sneer, but her brown eyes sparkled and she gave a cheery laugh. 'And what might your name be?' She turned her left ear closer to Mary, and half-shut her right eye.

'Mary Helsall.'

At once a wall of heat hit her face and the woman welcomed her in. 'Oh, I was only making certain, sweetheart, but I knew it was you the very inst I opened the door, for you're the very image of how he says. Oh, look at you! The very image, if not even prettier.'

The noise built up again until the chatter and laughter were ten times as boisterous as they had sounded from outside. A huge fireplace flooded warmth into every corner of the room, subsuming the draught that sucked under the sacking at the windows. Decaying plaster flaked on to a miscellany of furniture: chairs, settles, tables, rugs, and a dresser with its pots, plates, spoons, knives and papers all held on by a skin of dust.

Twenty people – no, thirty, at least – were crammed into the room, playing dice, laughing, sleeping, sprawling before the fire. Woodsmoke and tobacco involved them all in a cloud, and when the firelight rebounded from their faces it showed their eyes cloudy too, and the sockets shimmering moist and grey.

'Who do you think this is, then?' Mother Starling had to shout, and reached up to tap someone's shoulder. 'Who do you think?'

A circle of people parted and looked at her, then one of them laughed and said 'Wells's Mary!' and the others laughed too. Mother Starling patted her on the back and said everyone knew, because it was all they could do to get him to stop talking about her.

A cup arrived in her hand, and its fumes joined the smell of sweat and smoke, and steam from a kettle on the fire. It was all very well, to resolve not to drink gin any more – apart from Monday night, which couldn't have been helped – but imagine the rudeness, the haughtiness, the embarrassment of handing it back. She drank it gladly and someone topped it up.

'Is it true, then, that you know Selwyn Jones, the famous murderer?' Mary swallowed her gin hard. The man who spoke staggered when Mother Starling jabbed him with her elbow.

'You know the rules,' she said. 'You don't ask questions here, about what people know and don't know.' Mary could not see Anthony. 'She's not here to listen to you lot. Follow me, dear.'

Everything about the house creaked. The narrow staircase pushed Mary's petticoats in and made them dust the skirtings. Fragments of plaster shuffled under her feet.

'A very lot of 'em in tonight,' said Mrs Starling, stopping to puff. Mary looked up at the dark space beyond, and imagined the stairs ending in a drop to a pit where Mother Starling fermented her victims into gin. Laughter rebounded round the downstairs room.

'Aren't you feared of getting caught, with all the noise?' Then she blushed because, for all she knew, Mrs Starling might have a proper

270

licence and be as reputable as heaven-knows-what, and might be insulted. But Mrs Starling winked.

'Ah, I don't sell gin. Some folks call this a gin shop, but it's no shop when I don't sell owt, is it? A friendly-house I call it, for folks to sit and talk to one another, or have somewhere warm to meet their sweethearts, and if they like to bring a spot o' gin with them, well – I've not the heart to stop them.'

The cat skipped ahead of them, a creamy-white worm gently waxing and waning on its anal fur. The floorboards sloped away towards a gloomy dead-end, but Mrs Starling knocked on the first door they came to, and it lurched open.

'Here she is at last, dear. Now, you two budge yourselves and let them have a bit of peace.'

Two drunken young men grumbled out of the room, each keeping a hand of cards turned away from the other. The door swung shut, and the feel of Anthony's arms around her struck her like the first effects of gin.

'I was feared you wouldn't be here.'

'Where else would I be?'

'I was feared you'd have gone to London.'

His expression darkened. Had she spoiled everything already? 'Do you still think I'd leave you?'

She smiled. 'No, I'm just being silly.'

If there had really been anger there it fled at once.

She told him what had happened since he left the infirmary, and about Mrs Seward's son, which made him solemn for a moment. The heat from downstairs rose through the floorboards, and the room was cosy in spite of its shabby bedstead and the two filthy straw ticks on the floor.

'Well,' said Mary, 'it might not be grand, but no one could say it in't warm. And you might lie in bed all day as you please. It's perfect for you.'

Anthony laughed and said she did him a disservice, because he had been more industrious since leaving the infirmary than he ever was while he was there. 'Look.' He beckoned her to a table by the window and showed her the watch, all undone and anatomised. Pretty pieces of metal, like tiny flowers, scattered the desk, their shiny surfaces reflecting the daylight. She brushed her fingertip over them, and he firmly moved her hand away. 'Don't touch them. They're all in the right place.'

Mary tutted. 'Well, I'll go away and leave you with them, then, shall I?'

He pulled her on to his knee, and explained what each part of the watch was called, and what it did. And unless he invented the names, and gave false explanations in order to impress her, his apprenticeship must have taught him more than he liked to pretend.

Delicate watch-making instruments littered the table. He said there was a rule, in Mrs Starling's house, not to ask where anything came from. 'I didn't steal them, though,' he said, and that was all she ever found out about them.

Small as the room was, its casement filled almost the whole wall above the desk. Through it Mary could see the billows of blossom on the pear trees in the Kelyards, and the massive cathedral, austere against the sky. Behind the white blossoms she could just make out the stones at the foot of the walls; the ones where they had sat, that time when she brought him home drunk and he had kissed her. He followed her gaze, and smiled.

'I think I know what's wrong with it. When I put it back together again it'll work. Then one of the lads who sometimes comes in here says he has a watch that runs slow, so I'll fix that too, and he'll pay me.'

'Then other folk might hear of you.'

'Exactly. What a piece of luck, eh, getting thrown out of the hospital? I can sit here all day, working on this. No errands, no fetching and carrying, no whining idiots. I can get food here. And drink. And you can visit me, with no old hag hammering on the door.'

He went downstairs to get them some gin, and laughed when she told him Mrs Starling said she didn't sell it. It was the first he had drunk all day, he said. He didn't know where the time had gone.

Gaps at least an inch wide separated the floorboards, and between them Mary saw the movements of the people below, and the watery glint of eyes.

'They're looking up my skirts!' She jumped on to one of the ticks.

'You'd best lie on the bed, then, hadn't you?' The blankets were rumpled. Mary took off her hat and lay down. A huge patch of damp covered half the ceiling. She inched her petticoats up towards her knee, and smiled at the way his eyes absorbed the sight of her stocking.

'I suppose now you'll want to lie on it by me,' she said.

'If I must.'

'Even with the cathedral watching?'

He reached up and let a piece of sackcloth fall across the window. Then he lay down beside her and worked the pins from her hair.

'I wish I could always live somewhere so warm.' Mary pushed back the blankets and fanned her shift against her neck. She stretched one bare leg up, admiring the white shape of it, and giggled at the touch of Anthony's fingers down the inside of her thigh. 'Would Mrs Starling let me stay?'

'Aye, but you'd have to bundle in with the girls, and you wouldn't like them.'

A twinge in Mary's chest banished all sleepiness and warmth. The noises downstairs became sharper; the rustle of the straw mattress more immediate; the moonlight harsh. 'There are girls living here?'

Anthony laughed softly. 'You sound ready to scratch their eyes out.'

'Are they pretty?'

'They might seem so, if they stood by Mrs Seward.'

She sighed. Would they be pretty after a few drams of gin? Would they be prettier still when she was out of sight across the city, alone in her cold bed? He was silent for a while and she heard him sigh too, but differently. As if he wanted to speak, and dared not.

'I know we're not wed yet.' There was something serious. Had he changed his mind? 'And I can't make you obey me.' Mary raised her eyebrows and he must have felt them move against his skin. 'Well, not that I could, if we were, but as we're betrothed I think it's only right you should listen to my opinion.'

She reached her lips up to his. 'I'll listen. It doesn't mean . . .'

'I don't want you to stand as witness in Jones's trial.'

Mary's heartbeat accelerated to a whirr. She sat up and pulled her shift around her shoulder. Anthony's face was smooth and silvery and perfect, the contours of his cheeks in shadow and his eyes trapping the glitters of moonlight that slunk under the sackcloth. 'I have to.'

'No you don't.'

Mary tried to think.

'It's only a fortnight, and then it'll be over and we can leave.'

'The time doesn't matter. I'm just scared you'll fall foul of the courts. It's this business about the arm. It's so easy to be wrong. So easy to make a mistake that leaves you dead at the hands of folk as've done worse and have the money to get away with it.'

'I have to.'

'Why?'

Mary hugged her knees. 'He's my friend.'

'You don't perjure yourself just for a *friend*. Has he no missus to do that for him?' Mary damned herself for the tears that spiked into her eyes. She edged along the bed, away from the moonlight. 'I don't mean it in't admirable, being loyal to someone you grew up with, but you've no duty to him and I won't let you lie to the court when it's obvious to every man and his scabby dog he's guilty.' Anthony reached out to conclude the matter with an embrace. Mary leapt up.

'It's not your place to let me do or not do anything,' she said. He groaned softly. 'I do have a duty to him.'

'Come off it. You're not his wife.'

Silence severed the room. The noise below distanced and died. All Mary heard was her own breath, quick and shaky. Moonbeams smoothed over the parts of the watch on the table.

'I am. I am his wife.' Relief stripped the strength from her, and her legs shook. 'I never wanted to marry him.' An icy silence washed over

Anthony. 'He didn't want to marry me. He did it out of kindness, because I had no money.' Anthony got up and she instinctively stepped back from him. 'I only didn't tell you because I love you. I didn't want you to—'

'Leave me alone.' Her petticoat flopped against her and fell to the floor.

'No. I can't leave you. I don't love him. We can still go to London.'

'And have a murderer after me for fucking his wife?'

'Don't call it that!' Eyes glistened up through the cracks in the floorboards. 'Just listen, and I'll—'

'I can't listen to anything now. Leave me alone.'

She struggled into her clothes and, her stays loose, staggered on to the landing. 'Don't hate me, Anthony.'

'I don't.' He spoke in a murmur; he guided her before him down the stairs.

She remembered afterwards the silence of the people as they looked at her: Mother Starling with her hands to her mouth; the cat, tail up, its back arched, on the back of an armchair, observing her with round green eyes. And then a last glimpse of Anthony's face, his cheeks flaming and his eyes flooded. And then the shock from heat to cold, and the splash of mud on her legs. Glints of moonlight sparked from the moisture on the ground. Water rippled in a trough, ribbons of silver worming on its surface. The breeze chilled Mary's tears. She sobbed and turned back to the door. It opened.

'Are you all right, dear?' Mrs Starling's brown eyes gleamed with concern.

'Yes,' Mary whispered.

'I'm sorry, dear. We all could've sworn he'd found the right one this time. Have this. On the house.' She pushed a cup into Mary's hand, and shut the door.

THURSTASTON, AFTERNOON, 28 DECEMBER 1755

Mary buries the panicky feeling and studies the table. She spreads out her white fingers against the oak, and sees how they are not white in a refined way, such as Mrs Warbreck's might be, but are a dead, yellowish white, and numb.

'The rest of what?' she says.

'The silks. The ones from the cargo chest. When will you bring them to me?'

Bryce touches her hand. Funny, how he can so easily forget his disdain for her, when money is involved.

'They're at home.' His eyes betray surprise when she draws her hand away. 'I could only carry one by myself. I'll bring them as and when I've a mind to.'

'Jones refused to help you?'

'He goes to his uncle at Wallasey. He often does so after Christmas.' She narrows her eyes. 'What is it to you?'

Bryce shifts in his chair and she holds his gaze. For a moment he looks uncomfortable, and she casts him a smug smile. But she wishes she had not had so much brandy, because it has made her face blotchy; she can tell from the prickling like day-old sunburn on her cheeks and chin. Three glasses, it must have been, perhaps even four. She won't accept any more. Bryce crosses his legs and rests his chin on his hand.

'Keeping out of the way for a while, is he? Sensible. But also very shabby, to leave you on your own with such valuable goods in the house. I'll send one of the lads to fetch them tomorrow and take them straight to the warehouse, so you won't have to worry about them being stolen.'

'No.' Mary reaches unsteadily for the glass again, afraid to misjudge and knock it over. 'They're safe, in the cellar. I'll bring them one at a time. I don't want all the money at once; Selwyn'd only spend it in the tavern. It's best to keep them back. Any end, I've a pistol, and I'll keep it loaded all night, and if a robber comes in I'll shoot him dead.' Bryce smiles.

'I'm sure,' he says, moistening his lips, 'you wouldn't be squeamish, but still, I don't think a damp cellar is quite the place for them. They will be damaged by mould. Rats might shred them. It would be most regrettable if, having survived a storm at sea, they reached the land only to be destroyed. Don't you agree?'

Headaches cluster between Mary's eyes. She takes up the purse in readiness to leave, and reaches for the table as the objects of the room make lulling movements. 'But he still might let me keep one of them for a gown. There's a green one – emerald green . . .' When next Bryce speaks his tone is flat and quick.

'You would have chosen this one. Sit down. He's taken them, hasn't he? He intends to sell them himself.'

Perhaps she could have thought of something, but the brandy has seized the capacity for new flights of imagination and left her overcrowded with the old, familiar ones – the ones that mostly involve him kissing her.

'Where is he?' His voice is soft again and the vision it brings is of the sea-breeze in the tips of the silver birches, the time when he halted the horses at the foot of Irby Heath. 'Don't frighten yourself I mean him harm, because that's not the case. To be frank with you, what I want is the pleasure of dealing in these silks. If they are all like this they are worth a lot of money. I can give him a good price for them – more than he would get from the merchants, who don't know him and will be suspicious about their origin. I can sell them to my contacts for more, and we are all content. Does that not sound like the best arrangement, Mary?'

'I suppose so.'

'Then tell me, and I will send someone to make an offer for the goods. I won't hold it against either of you that you sought to trade

elsewhere. If it were anyone else I admit I might be angry. I might feel
inclined to tell my friend the Customs Officer about the beer hidden
on Hilbre. But not you.'

Not her.

The third glass of brandy wraps its flannel round her brain,
although she has already finished the fourth. Or perhaps it's the
fourth wrapping, and the fifth . . . She closes her eyes and sees silver
birches and evening sun dropping behind the sandstone outcrops,
bouncing a high-up hectic yellow on to the clouds. High enough yet
to fall warm on her straw hat and lend a glow to his face as he looks
at her, the dimming rays sparking back at her from his blue eyes.

But that was years ago, and now he gets up and walks about the
room, pausing a moment to look out of the window before he paces
behind her. Mary keeps herself very still, fighting off the memory of
sun-warmth under her palm on the carriage seat; his hand sliding
round the small of her back; her body bending towards him like one
of the silver-flaked saplings yielding, uncomplaining, to the vigour of
the breeze.

If he touches her now – she struggles to arrange a proper thought
in the brandy-cloud. If he places his hand on her shoulder . . . If he
strokes her hair – this headache is desperate for a soothing hand –
the exhausting stillness will shatter. He must know that. Shards of
fragile stillness will hiss through the air like a glass hurled at a
wall.

'You must think . . . Ah, this is awkward,' he says. But there's a
smirk. 'You must think I treated you very cruelly the last time you
were here.' If she were to plunge her face in the Dee now, the water
would boil the toes of someone paddling on the Welsh shore. 'You
must understand that I had to marry Jessie. You do understand,
don't you?' She makes no response. 'But I still have what you might
call a soft spot for you.' Mary curls her lip. A soft spot! 'And that
means I would never do anything that would contradict your best
interests. On this occasion I only want to make sure your husband
– a man whom I respect for treating you with far greater integrity

than I, to my shame, treated you – does not lose out by being over-hasty in selling the goods to an unscrupulous merchant, when I could give him a fair price.' He has moved closer to her; she senses his warmth behind her. The fourth glass of brandy announces its delayed arrival; the fifth hit still lags behind – something to look forward to. Her mind takes a genteel, unhurried turn about her skull.

Then the faintest trace of a touch tingles on the back of her neck. Icy.

'Where has he gone, Mary?'

It is difficult to bring that much strength together all at once, but she leaps up, shoving the chair back against him, and he winces, and whisks the brandy glass to safety.

'Liverpool, if you must know.' She snatches her hand away as he tries to catch it. Then they are both still.

'Thank you, Mrs Jones,' he says with a smile; and he shows her at once to the door. No carriage-ride home this time.

CHAPTER 24

Vomit missed the chamberpot and splashed on to the floorboards. Dark, polished floorboards that she did not recognise. Mary grasped the side of the mattress and gaped down at them; the knots and grooves, the sick oozing between them. A draught met her back, as cold as a sheet of glass. She was sweating. The shift she wore had unfamiliar cuffs, with a thin trim of lace.

Then the sweat seemed to suck all the heat out of her body, and she shook. The shift stuck to her. She gaped at her hand, its knuckles white on the white bed. Sickness wrung her guts again, and this time the pot resounded as it hit. She felt better, for a moment so short that a watch wouldn't mark it.

Then, like a watch, her heart stopped, and she screamed.

'Anthony!' The scream choked her. She could not have told him. She would go to Cow Lane and find him. She clutched her head to her knees and breathed fast, too frightened to move. Crusty wads of mud matted her hair.

Another wrench at her stomach made her lurch for the side of the bed. The pot moved in a slow circle at the end of a tunnel of filthy black hair.

When she looked up, slowly and painfully, her eyes met those of a terrified young woman. 'I'm sorry.' The words hurt her throat. 'I'm sorry.'

'Mrs Evans! Quick! Mrs Evans!' The girl ran out of the room.

Mary sobbed at the pain slicing every part of her body. The sweat froze and warmed and froze again on her skin. Plaster carvings radiated from the centre of the ceiling; a pattern so simple and calm that it soothed her. The walls held the bluish tint of a duck egg, and a wash-stand and looking glass stood opposite the bed. The window framed the tops of some red brick buildings, surrounded by a bright blue sky. Mary pulled the blankets up to her chin, and found them smooth and soft.

'Lara, take this.' A woman picked up the pot. Mary half-recognised the gentle accent and the greying blonde wisps of hair protruding from her cap. The woman wore a smart grey mantua, and an apron as clean as the sky.

'I'm sorry,' Mary said.

She tried to neaten her hair, but each time she let go of the blankets the bed rocked like a hammock. Mud melted into the sweat and drew smudges down her shift.

'It's such a relief to see you awake, Mary. Will you be ready for something to eat soon?'

Mary's throat turned to grease. 'Please – what house is this?'

The woman smiled. Her movements were efficient and quiet, with a fluidity and elegance to them that soothed the air around her and made it still. 'Mr Barnston's.'

Mary rested her head back on the pillow and closed her eyes. 'Thank God.'

Someone who had once been a patient at the infirmary had found her lying under a hedgerow near Handbridge quarry, and run to Mr Barn-ston's house. That was early on Thursday morning; it was about midday on Friday when she woke up. Exhaustion seeped through her whole body. In the evening she ate some soup, and the chambermaid built a fire.

There was nothing more Mrs Evans could tell her, except that she had been grey with cold at first, and then in danger of going into a fever. 'You don't think anyone has hurt you, do you?'

Mary touched the back of her head, where the old bruise smarted again. 'My head hurts. Everything does.'

'I mean . . . You don't remember speaking to any men?'

Mrs Evans's earnest face was too calm to betray shock or anger, whatever the answer, but she gently touched Mary's arm.

Mangham. She remembered his face in lamplight, and the shadow cast by his head on a slimy wall. 'I did speak to a man.' There had been a fight in Northgate Street; she remembered hearing the shouts when she left the gaol, unhurt. 'But he didn't harm me.'

'Thank goodness.'

Mary's shivers did not abate when Mrs Evans put more coal on the fire. Panic convulsed in her chest, and the night ticked by, second after terrifying second.

In the days that followed the terror became raw sadness. She learnt that her clothes were for the most part ruined – Lara, the chambermaid, blushed when she said the word – with the dirt of the road and the scratches of the hawthorn hedge. Her stays and under-petticoat had survived, and her shift was presentable when laundered. And she had not been robbed of her pockets: they still held sixpence, and a pair of gloves.

Lara lent her a gown and petticoats, all a sensible shade of grey. The glass showed that Mary's face matched them, but for a few scratches and the black hollows of her eyes. She put the gloves under her pillow and bit hard on her lip.

She could feel the chambermaid's lightless eyes on her when she gazed from the window at the parterre far below. How many other servants would be in the kitchen that evening, waiting for the details?

'Was he very handsome?' Lara asked. Mary tasted blood on her lip. Lara's cheeks coloured. 'I'm sorry. That was a daft thing to ask. I always say daft things. I'm known for it.'

'Lara!' She grasped the girl's arm. 'Is there anyone here who might take a message to him?'

Lara hesitated. 'There's a lad – Davy. He runs errands. But Mrs

Evans said if you ask me anything like that I have to tell her. Mr Barnston might not like it.'

And when the notion formed more fully, Mary did not in any case know what she would write.

Mr Barnston's household was at once quiet and cheerful, and it seemed to Mary as if the place had been built to let sunshine flow through all the windows at the same time. Her bedchamber was in the servants' quarters, and when Mrs Evans showed her some of the other rooms she gaped at marble fireplaces taller than herself, vast looking glasses, window-curtains swathing from ceiling to floor, and soft carpets almost as big as the floors themselves, their fringes all brushed perfectly straight. A chandelier for fifty candles hung in the entrance hall, which was at least twice as big as the infirmary's ward.

'The previous occupants were fond of dancing,' said the house-keeper, with a hint of regret. 'I think if poor Mrs Barnston had still been alive when we came here she would have kept up the tradition.'

A portrait of her hung in the dining room – a handsome, bright-eyed lady, with a powdered wig and slender white hands folded in her lap. Her smile was suppressed for the sake of elegance, but it lingered at the corners of her eyes, and her cheeks held a natural tint of pink. *Laetitia Barnston*, the inscription read.

Mary, however, saw little of the finery from day to day. Mrs Evans set her to mending, saying she could be of use without having to be on her feet, and so she sat and squinted over seams and buttons and listened to the tick of the clock, shifting to relieve the ache in her muscles, and trying to control the tremors in her hands.

'Folk always say of sewing,' she said to Lara, 'that you don't have to think. But the dovetail of it is, you have time to think too much.'

Whether it was the medicine sent by Dr Tylston or the passage of a week that made the ache in Mary's head diminish she did not know, but there was nothing to numb the emptiness that kept her staring at the ceiling every night. The time arrived when the thought of gin no longer made her feel sick. She awakened each day having dreamt she still lived at the hospital, and so did Anthony, and he had forgiven her. Daylight struck through her like a chisel.

'Fix your hair smartly, Mary,' said Mrs Evans one morning. 'Mr Barnston has asked to see you, and you must show him how neat and modest you can be.'

Morning sun filled the drawing room with serenity. Pale green walls bounced light on to every surface, shimmering the display of crystal on the sideboard and printing miniature duplications of the windows on the sheen of the mahogany tables.

She had not seen Mr Barnston since he left the infirmary on the night he refused to send Anthony to gaol. The shock on his face, though at once masked, did not escape her notice.

'Good morning,' he said softly. 'I trust your health begins to mend?'

'Yes, thank you, sir. I'm thankful for all you and Mrs Evans have done for me.' She meant it, but it did not come out sounding very sincere.

The armchair in which Mr Barnston asked her to sit was upholstered in cream brocade, with a printed pattern of birds and branches, and gold thread delineating the blossoms. She smoothed her petticoats and sat down carefully, keeping her chafed hands in her lap.

Mrs Evans sat down too, and Mary tried to catch Mr Barnston's eye.

'I have acquainted Mrs Evans with the rudiments of your history.' Well! Mary drew an indignant breath, but Mr Barnston silenced her with a glance. 'So you need have no fear of speaking frankly. What happened last Wednesday evening?' Mary kept silence for a long time. 'Mary. What happened?'

'I went to see Anthony Wells, and he found out Selwyn's my husband.'

Neither Mr Barnston nor his housekeeper showed any surprise or outrage. 'I suspected it was something of that nature. And how did you come to be lying under a hedge beyond the bridge?'

Heat rose into Mary's face. 'I don't know, sir.'

'You had consumed ardent spirits?'

She nodded.

'If you had run away with Wells,' Mr Barnston said, 'you would have endured greater torment than anything you imagine you experience now. You would have kept it from him, I suppose, that you were married?'

Mary slowly shook her head. 'I knew I'd have to tell him, else we couldn't have escaped.' She bit the insides of her cheeks and focused on the pain.

'Anthony Wells is best left in the past. You must consider your future. Do you wish to continue working at the hospital?'

'Selwyn'll be after setting up somewhere new.'

Mr Barnston shifted uneasily on his sofa. 'The possibility of an acquittal for your husband is very slim. Even if I thought there was justice in letting a murderer go free, I have no influence over the Sessions jury. They must return their verdict according to the evidence. The question remains – would you stay at the hospital?'

'I would if it weren't for Mrs Seward and Agnes. The diseases are interesting, though some of the patients aren't up to much.'

'Have you any other means of supporting yourself? Any brothers or uncles to whom you might appeal?' Mary pursed her lips. 'Have you any skills?'

'I can fire a gun and ride a horse,' she said. 'I could take to the roads.'

Mrs Evans emitted a small, hurt 'oh', and Mary lowered her eyes.

'I can sew quite neat, sir,' she said. Mrs Evans agreed, with a benign smile, and Mary saw herself engulfed in linen, her eyes aching in the glow of a single rushlight. 'There is another idea.' They listened, and she paused, her throat dry. 'In London there's a hospital – a big one, in its own building – called St George's. I heard Dr Tylston and Mr Cotgreave talking about it. It has huge wards and hundreds of patients, and they do operations all the time. What if I could work there, helping the surgeons? I'm good at bandaging, and I'm not feared of blood. If you wrote to them, sir, perhaps they'd let me be a nurse in the operating room. It'd be better than the wards – the patients wouldn't be in a state to ogle me, or complain about the food.' Mr Barnston and Mrs Evans looked at each another with wide eyes. Mary sat forward on her seat. 'Why shouldn't I stitch arteries as well as I can stitch shirts?'

Mrs Evans paled and put a handkerchief to her mouth; Mr Barnston fiddled with the plum silk-covered buttons around his jacket cuff. 'Mary, that's an absurd idea.' That was that, then. 'Do you not wish to return home, to your village? I'm sure we could assist you in setting up as a seamstress there.'

'I tried that before, when my mother got too ill to work, but people took their custom elsewhere. I wasn't well-liked. Not by the women, any end.'

Mrs Evans swallowed hard. Then Mary noticed, in the sparkling array of cut glass on the sideboard, a decanter half-full with amber liquid, and her heart beat strangely.

Mr Barnston apologised for tiring her, and said, to her relief, that she may stay in his house until after the trial.

That was a matter of days away. Sunshine made the servants' parlour the more confining, with its unlit fire, its plain furniture and its sense of order. Mary did her mending by the window. Far below, trimmed conifer hedges described four triangles, enclosing a crossways path. Mary traced them over and over, finding the beginnings of numbness in the repetition.

He threw the hatchet and it hit the man. He did not see him, your honour.

He threw the hatchet in anger. Because I . . . He dropped the hatchet. He broke the clasp on the cargo chest with the hatchet, and then he flung it away, and it hit the man.

It hit his neck and fell away, and the man was dead. He was already dead, your honour, when he reached the shore. He swam that far, and then he gave up the ghost. I saw it. The ghost, your honour. There are lots of ghosts on the Dee, but that one was very likely his. So he was dead, when the hatchet hit him.

Dead. And the Lord have mercy upon his soul.

Monday morning, the 19th of April, was dreary enough for Mary's spirits to be above the level of the weather. Rain made pleasing circles in the water of the ornamental pond on the parterre, and the stream from the fountain splashed out on to the paving stones. She watched the movements of the huge gold fishes – for a moment felt sorry for them, out there in the rain – and smiled sadly. Weariness made every stitch an effort. Mrs Evans had set her to making an apron, a project unnecessary for anything other than to keep her occupied. Mary yawned, set the apron down and walked around the room. The movement did nothing to relieve the heaviness of her limbs, and she welcomed the housekeeper's light tread on the stairs.

'Might I go out for a walk?' Mary asked. 'I could sew faster if my eyes had a rest.'

'Perhaps later,' said Mrs Evans, 'when Lara is free to accompany you.'

'I don't need to put her to any trouble. I can go by myself.'

'I do not think you are quite strong enough yet.' Mrs Evans straightened one of the chairs. 'But, in any case, I came to tell you there is someone here to see you, so your eyes will have some respite after all.'

Strength left Mary's legs and she sat down hard on the window seat. 'Is it . . . ?'

'It is not Anthony Wells.' Mrs Evans's smile conveyed sympathy.

But it must be Anthony. It must be him, coming to say he forgave her and still wanted her to go to London with him. No one else could want to see her.

'He might have said a false name. You've never seen him.'

'No, indeed, I haven't,' Mrs Evans replied. 'But I have seen Mr Warbreck before, and hence I know who wishes to speak with you. I believe he intends to offer you employment.'

'Mr Warbreck?' Mary blinked. It took her a moment to accept the notion of someone else saying the name. She felt a claim to it, just as she had at Dog-Breath Annie's that time. A precedence over anyone else who might speak it. 'Well, I don't wish to speak with him.'

'Whether you wish to or not is by the by. Mr Barnston has asked me to fetch you, and that is what I will do.' Mrs Evans's mouth did not change from its natural position of a smile. 'Wilfulness is not commonly entertained in this house.'

Mary could make no reply. She silently followed the housekeeper down the stairs, a renewed tremor entering her hands. So he was here. Only to be expected, with Mr Barnston one of his customers. Why should he not call to cultivate such a wealthy man? Well, she would be polite and cold. He would pretend to be concerned for her, then make some jibe about Selwyn, then lose his patience with her and say something unpleasant before he left, and she would ignore it and forget about him the moment he stepped out of the house. That was all.

'I shall send someone to chaperone you in a moment,' said Mrs Evans, directing Mary towards the drawing room.

'Oh, that won't be . . .' But there was no point in arguing, and the housekeeper hurried away.

When Bryce Warbreck took her hand and greeted her as Mrs Jones, it seemed he reached through water; she heard his words distantly and his clasp was cold.

'What do you want?' she said.

His answer halted at the grind of the door handle. Lara brought in a shirt and started to sew a button on it, concentrating hard on the stitches.

'I must speak privately to Miss Helsall,' Bryce said.

Lara upset her bag of buttons and they shingled over the carpet. 'But Mrs Evans told me I must stay.'

He handed her a shilling and motioned his head towards the door. She gawped at the coin as if it were a creature he had peeled from under a stone. The shirt billowed to the floor as she fled.

'You do get into some scrapes, don't you, Mrs Jones?' Bryce's blue eyes crimped at the corners. 'At least we've got you away from that drunken porter. From what Barnston tells me, his influence on you has not been for the best.'

'How do you know what's for the best?'

'Did the housekeeper tell you why I have asked to see you?'

'She said you might offer me work. You mean me to risk getting shot for you again.'

Bryce smiled to himself. 'No. You will listen to what I have to say?'

Mary supposed there was no harm in that. He indicated for her to sit beside him, and set forth his plan.

A pleasant cottage – not in the village, but somewhere more secluded, and a small allowance to enable her to live as comfortably as anyone in her station of life should require.

'Even that in't enough to make me go back to being decoy.'

'It is nothing so dangerous, Mary.' He hesitated. 'You would need to promise to be content and not to ask any more of me than I am prepared to give.' He did nothing but hold her gaze, until her breath became stifled and prickles of heat flooded over her chest; she looked away, ashamed. 'I would visit you from time to time.' The clock on the side-table spoke three delicate chimes, like icicles chattering to the ground. A moment later the resonance of a distant church clock echoed it. 'It would be an arrangement. A business arrangement that I think could be satisfactory to both of us. Do you understand?' He stroked her arm with one fingertip. The touch iced her skin.

'For the past two years and more,' she said, 'you've loathed the sight of me. What's different now?'

Bryce sat back into the corner of the sofa and rested his elbow on the arm. Bringing his fingertips together, he watched her. 'I have never loathed the sight of you.'

'You had me seen off your property and shoved out into the mud.'

'There was nothing else I could do. You were causing a scene in front of an important client.'

'Mr Barnston.'

'Indeed.' He got up and moved about, studying the china in a glass cabinet, touching the sculpted marble of the chimney-piece, sidling a glance into the looking glass above it. 'I will be frank and businesslike with you. I do not mean to imply that I no longer love my wife – my regard for her has not changed. But she was very ill after she bore our son, and is frightened to repeat the experience. My respect for her prevents me from insisting, hence I seek other arrangements. That, I think, is as blunt as I need to be.'

'And Mr Barnston – does he know what you offer me?'

'No. I told him simply that I can find some use for you at home. He rather hopes not to be put in the position of having to employ you here. He tends to choose his staff from the more wholesome end of the spectrum. His household decamps to Churton after the Sessions. If his charitable inclinations oblige him to take you, he fears he will never get rid of you.'

Mary went to the window. She passed the brandy decanter on the sideboard, and sensed a change in the way the air felt within its range. So subtle as to be scarce perceptible, a touch of its scent wound through her nose and quivered itself into a taste at the back of her throat. 'Everyone seems to forget I still have a husband.'

Bryce smiled. 'Indeed,' he said. 'Everyone.' He paused. 'We would arrange proper terms, of course. Your time would largely be your own; you might maintain or neglect your dwelling as you wished; there would be the usual supplies of Manx goods you have been accustomed to in the past. And French brandy, of course, if this war business doesn't come to anything. Who knows – perhaps Providence will send us another wreck with a cargo of silk, and you might have your blue gown.' Mary took a sudden breath. Bryce raised a hand, his smile persisting even when he spoke. 'I know you're apt to decide things on impulse, but I want you to consider this properly. I will ask you again in a week, when, perhaps, the reality of your situation might have become clearer.'

He took his leave with a formality of politeness that left her ill at ease.

'Wait a minute,' she said. Bryce turned, his hat paused halfway to his head. 'Aren't places like Mrs Hodder's enough any more?'

His smile fell and his fingers tightened on the hat. The curves of his throat moved above his necktie. He made his eyes return to levity first, forcing an approximation of a sparkle into them, then he waved the hat in a dismissive arc. 'She happened to operate her business next to my warehouse. I can understand why idle people might infer such things, but—'

'She told me herself.'

'When?' Strained gentleness controlled his words. 'You don't make a habit of conversing with people like her, do you?'

'I saw her at the gaol. She said you informed on her.'

He rotated his hat in his hands, each point of its triangle directed in turn towards the floor. 'That is true. Did she say why? She has never been known for honesty.' Mary's confidence left her. Perhaps Mrs Hodder had been lying. Perhaps she changed the story to fix the blame on whoever was in her presence. *There must have been some money in it.* 'Mary, what's she been saying?'

'That you were angry with her because . . .' Mary cringed inside. 'Because she tried to bully me into her house.'

The sofa creaked as Bryce sat down, and his laughter was not cruel but warm and expressive of tenderness. 'Well then, that is the first time I have ever heard a report of Sarah Hodder speaking the truth.'

'Is it true?'

'Yes.'

'But the last time we met you shut me out and left me to walk past her house by myself. You didn't care so much then.' He looked up at the ceiling. The action made him wince; he pressed his fingers to his temples and sat forward, his eyes tightly closed. 'What's the matter?'

'Nothing.' He took a deep breath and smiled, but his face had paled. 'It's nothing. You are quite right. I was rude to you, and I apologise. It's a difficult thing to admit, but I was disconcerted to see you had taken up with someone else. That's all.'

'Were you?'

He only nodded quickly. She pictured it – him arriving at her pretty cottage, while the sun was going down; him kissing her and telling her how difficult it was – how *hard* – to keep away from her. Would he expect her to undress and let her hair down, or would he bunch up her petticoats and back her to the wall so he could get home to his wife in time for supper?

'Anyway, I shall see you on Wednesday, I suppose?' Wednesday? Why would he come back on Wednesday? Repetitive days of sewing and staring out of the window had clouded her head; realisations came to her after battling through the fog. When this one arrived a cramp of guilt jerked her mind out of its stupor. 'You are frightened about having to lie to the court?'

'Of course.' She paused. 'Though I wouldn't be lying.'

'If you were to decide not to attend no one would think the less of you, and you would spare yourself some distressing questions.'

'I will attend.'

'Very well.'

She watched from the window as he walked away down the street, specks of rain beading and winking on his black felt hat. He stopped at the corner and leant on the rail of a fence, stooping forward and rubbing the back of his neck. Then, slowly, he continued until he was out of sight.

If she said no, would he find someone else? Would she even hear of it, back at the hospital, facing the diverging paths of lifelong drudgery and death from the poisons in the curdled ward air?

Her eyes fell on the decanter again, and she saw how full it was; how the liquid was level with a point in the engraved pattern of the crystal, and how unnoticeably it would lower if she were to take one sip. One sip would be all that was necessary to lift the pall of lassitude and confusion. It would be so much smoother and finer than gin; so much better for one's health than the dregs of a barrel in a gaol's cellar.

'I have reprimanded Lara for failing to stay with you.' It was not until Mrs Evans touched her shoulder that Mary made herself mumble something about it not being Lara's fault.

'You are shaking,' the housekeeper said. 'Oh, I could never forgive myself if something improper has happened.'

'He did nowt wrong,' Mary said. 'He offered me a situation, back home.'

Mrs Evans smiled, or rather increased the latent smile she always displayed. 'I understood as much. How very kind. You will be leaving us, then, soon? At least, when . . .'

'I've not decided.' The truth sat gingerly on her. 'I must consider it carefully and not blunder into anything rash.'

'Oh, I am so glad you are being sensible. I think this environment does you good, does it not?'

Mary glanced around at the stifling neutrality of the walls, the cleanliness of the skirtings, the straightness of the carpet fringes and the dismal colourlessness of her borrowed gown, and strove to breathe.

CHAPTER 25

That night was long, and the next longer still, and the day between them too muted, too ordered. Mary had not left Mr Barnston's house for a fortnight, and she craved air and noise, the sight of interesting, anonymous faces, and voices untempered by a quiet allegiance to politeness. A fortnight, and though she dared not think of Anthony outright, a part of her thought of him all the time. Had he searched for her? Or had he shrugged over a lucky escape and found someone he could trust? Three-parts full tonight, the moon spread criss-cross shadows over her bed.

She traced its progress from one windowpane into the next, closed one eye to centre its waning shape in the diamonds of glass, and felt she would never sleep again.

Stairs, descending this time, a grave-chill flooding from the walls. The narrow gap at the end stifles her, then opens into brightness and noise; daytime, on the back of a cart, with two coffins, and hemp chafing at her neck. Mary Jones, do you confess your sins and call upon the infinite mercy of the Lord?

The moon had skipped a pane. She jumped up away from the net of shadows.

One night's sleep, and she would be able to think – to make sense of the confusion that stopped her burning with insult at Bryce's plan. Just a single night's sleep, and her mind would be renewed enough to order the multitude of futures crowding her, and to work out whether there was any choice.

William Hartingshall, is this the man you saw murder your brother?

Don't know, your honour, I couldn't rightly say. It might not have been him. It might have been Warbreck, your honour – that smug gorger over there.

They would leave Chester, when Selwyn was free, and travel away together. High up on the top of a coach they would pass the cathedral and the Exchange, skirt the corner by the Pentice and rattle down Bridge Street and over the River Dee. They would smile at each other perhaps, or perhaps she would have to keep her face turned from him.

One day maybe she would tell him of Bryce's offer, and how she had refused, and by then it would be long enough ago for them to laugh at his effrontery.

But – and though there could be no one watching, she moved her face into shadow – the trouble was, she had not refused.

Mrs Jones, would you say the accused has been a good husband to you? He has not, perhaps, by his brutality, caused you to look with longing at other men?

No, your honour, not by his brutality.

Just a business arrangement, and one that promised some degree of independence. One that promised comfort and idleness, and pretty clothes, and brandy. And with brandy she would be able to sleep.

A door from the servants' staircase opened into a niche tucked round the corner from the drawing room. Only a few steps, a matter of seconds. Mary got back into bed to keep warm, but she lay wakefully, poised in readiness to move, when courage permitted it. She would not sleep now, without brandy.

And perhaps one taste of brandy would foster memories of home, and feelings linked with it; and whether they were good or bad, perhaps they would help her decide.

Mary wrapped her kerchief round her shoulders. There could be no harm in it. If someone saw her on the staircase she would say she was thirsty – that was true – and meant to go to the kitchen. All being quiet, she would sneak to the drawing room, take a careful few sips straight from the decanter – she must make sure the stopper did not roll off the sideboard – and return to the stairs while she waited for it to calm her. If she needed more she would go back. Then she would be able to sleep, and by the morning the tiredness and confusion would have dispersed, and she would face the trial with courage.

The floorboards did not creak under her stockinged feet, and the stairs, too, were silent. The window at the bottom of the flight admitted enough moonlight to show a solid floor; to prove the stairs did not descend forever into deeper darkness.

All the way from France to the Isle of Man, and from Man to Hilbre, and Hilbre to the mainland. Brandy that might once have been carried by Selwyn, and that she herself had helped hide. It was special, not like the low, tainted spirits touted by Mangham and Mother Starling. She would never drink gin again.

Stillness pervaded the landing, and the drawing room was not locked. Mary's fingers searched the sideboard, spidering between cut-glasses and ornaments. She could not remember now what was there the last time she had been in the room. There might have been nothing; the sideboard itself might have been a mirage, when all that occupied her attention was Bryce, and his words. At last her fingertips found the decanter.

The stopper resisted and weighed heavy, its myriad of flat surfaces pressing into her palm. She set it down at once, in case it compelled her to see how much damage it might do, and breathed deeply in. The scent wraithed into the darkness.

A sound froze her – the distant swivel of a door-handle. She moved into the corner, her feet disordering the fringes of the carpet, and waited.

It must have been nothing. Just the sort of natural noise that inhabits every house. The clouds reflected enough moonlight to make the crystal just visible, and this time she found it easily. The brandy smelled sweet and pure, so different from gin. But the knot in her stomach crunched tighter.

It was the smell of waiting.

Waiting to be caught. Of lying alone in a dark cottage, with contraband in the cellar and the customs man but half a mile away, in his shore-guarding white house. The smell of a hollow promise of sleep – a promise that would transmute into half-waking nightmares. Of a numbness that spoke of relief and yet only recruited the fear's strength, so it might strike with greater violence when the numbness fled.

They had drunk it after the murder, their hands tight and shaky round the cups. She had drunk it again at Bryce Warbreck's house, until it had made her lies as transparent as the glass from which she sipped.

She did not want it.

After all this anxiety and stealth. After getting here without being caught – and then not to drink it? Perhaps Anthony, at this moment, was raising a cup to his lips. Perhaps the warmth of the brandy in her veins would tell him, somehow, that she was drinking too, and thinking of him.

She would take one sip, and then decide. The crystal pressed, heavy, on her lip.

'You will be stealing, Mary, if you drink it.' Mary shrieked and the crystal knocked her teeth. She strained her eyes towards the door. 'I've noticed you looking at it. I expected you to have crept down before now, but perhaps you have learnt some degree of restraint.'

'I'm sorry.'

'Sorry I have caught you?'

'No.' Mary pushed the decanter away. 'I only meant to take one sip, to help me sleep. You couldn't begrudge me one sip, could you, with tomorrow an' all?'

The door hushed across the carpet. 'Do you mean to lie as poorly in court? The situation would be worse for your husband than if you did not attend at all.'

'I've a duty to him to try.'

Mr Barnston's soft laugh came as a shock to her. 'I believe your sense of duty to him is rather selective. Still, that is not the matter I wish to discuss.'

Defensiveness bubbled in her. Did he mean to tell her to return home and get out of his way? To take the employment with Bryce

Warbreck? What had Bryce said? That his wife needed a maid? Someone to take a slide rule and measure her curls in case they were uneven? Someone to keep the looking glasses clean so they might reflect her halo all the better?

'I have appreciated your discretion at the infirmary. I would be obliged if it were to continue here. None of my household is aware that I buy freely traded goods from Mr Warbreck. I hope I do not say this too late, but I have not been at liberty to speak with you in confidence since you arrived here, with Mrs Evans always in attendance.'

'I've said nowt, which is lucky for you. Why didn't you tell Mrs Evans to go away? She's only your housekeeper.'

'I could not in all propriety do that. Just as there is little propriety in the way you speak to me now.'

It was not arrogance, but the very lack of it – the assumption of superiority so absolute it needed no conceit – that made her shrink away from the sideboard, fighting to stop her arm from sweeping along it, smashing the crystal into shards. 'Propriety! I've a mind to drink every drop of this, and let you get some more from your proper friend. The one who is so proper he smuggles it, and fancies himself a thief-taker too – the one who would send a man to the gallows for a hundred pounds, and invite his widow to be his private whore.' She tipped the liquor to her lips. There was one touch of it, one rushing of the fumes, before he snatched away the decanter and its base thumped back on the sideboard.

'What do you mean?'

'What I mean, *sir*, is that Bryce Warbreck has offered to keep me and give me fine things in return for letting him . . .' She stopped short. 'You understand me, sir. And the worst of it is, I haven't even said no.'

Silence absorbed the words. Even the fabric of the house itself seemed to drink in disorder and hide it within the layers of paint and the intricacies of the cornices. How many harsh words were trapped in it? Quenched even in the moment of speaking, never to be acknowledged, like walled-up bones.

'Do you invent this to discredit Mr Warbreck?'

'It's true, and I don't care whether you believe me. You are not my master. No one is, and I shall make my own decision.'

There was a long pause. 'Go back to bed, Mary.'

'I might not have a mind to, sir.'

'Very well, then. You may freeze to spite me, if you wish, but you will have to do so on the staircase as I intend to lock this room. You will not indulge in drunkenness while you are part of my household.'

A hiss; an intake of breath – her own.

Indulge, sir? Indulgence? Try having this pain, sir, and see if you can go a single day without wanting to numb it. Try having this fear, and do nothing to ease it. Try living with your veins jangling like icicles and burning like pokers, and your heart clawed out, and do nothing to fill the cavern it leaves.

Perhaps he took her silence for shame and obedience; it seemed to mark the end of the matter for him. She followed him on to the landing and heard the turn of a key in the drawing room lock.

Indulgence, in a house of gold-threaded sofas and carpets so thick they almost buried your feet? Just the price of that decanter would give her space to make a choice.

'Mr Barnston?' She sensed he was still there, prepared to listen. 'You said you would be obliged if I didn't tell anyone you buy contraband.' Her heart hammered. But the tiniest part of a hundredth of what he owned could make her whole future.

'Yes, that is what I said. I see nothing wrong in the free trade, but not everyone is of the same mind, and my standing in this city—'

'How obliged, sir?'

'I beg your pardon.'

'I said, how obliged?'

Muffled through the door, the drawing room clock struck one icicle chime. Mr Barnston sighed through his nose, as if he had half expected this. 'I can furnish you with some money if you insist on stooping to the vulgarity of blackmail, but it will be a single payment, and you will receive it as and when you leave this house and I am satisfied you have not told anyone. Ten shillings.'

'I think a guinea would be more in order.' How quickly she had spent almost that much before, with nothing in her possession to say it had ever existed. Inn fees, gaol visits. Gin.

'Very well. A guinea.' He reached to shake her hand on it, his clasp so warm and firm that when he let go she remembered the cold, and shivered.

His footsteps hardly made a sound. At the top of the main staircase his shape appeared in moonlight, and then he was gone. Mary returned to bed, and traced the paths of the stars from one window-pane into the next.

In the morning she was so sick that she might as well have drained the decanter, for all the good abstinence had done. She ate nothing, only sat by the kitchen fire with her hand over her mouth, staring at the flames until her eyes ached. It was still only seven o'clock. Three hours to go. What was her terror compared with Selwyn's? But she could not even pin her own hair for shaking, and Lara had to do it for her. Lara knew she was to a be a witness in a trial, but that was all. She said Mary was very brave.

'I'm not brave,' said Mary, and speaking made her gag.

Just bleeding unlucky.

Hartingshall. She had not given him much of a thought for two weeks. Would he be there? Was he even still alive? Could the trial go ahead if he wasn't?

Somewhere just outside her concentration, Lara was apologising, distant and lisping and nervous, for leaving her alone with that gentleman the other day. Mrs Evans had told her off and made her cry, she said, and she knew it was silly, but she thought perhaps, because he was so handsome, he might be the gentleman who – you know – and he had come to ask Mary to marry him.

Mary might have laughed on another day. 'He didn't ruin me, and he in't a gentleman.' She went to the servants' parlour to press her forehead to the cold window and retch dryly into her hand.

'Davy will walk you there,' said Mrs Evans at nine o'clock, knitting her fingers in a way Mary had not seen before. Lines gathered on her face and she regarded first the floor, and then the window, and the fireplace.

'I couldn't presume to take anyone away from their duties,' said Mary, but the housekeeper sighed nervously.

'You must not go alone.'

'Doesn't Mr Barnston go too?'

Mrs Evans hesitated and took her handkerchief from her pocket, clinging to it tightly. 'Yes, he does. But you can't walk with him, Mary – you know that.' She wrung the handkerchief into a twist. 'Besides, he has already left. I believe he had some business to attend to first.' Without her smile the housekeeper looked drawn and plain, her eyes unremarkable without the radiant tranquillity that, by habit alone perhaps, they wore. It must be because of the breaking of the house-hold's routine. That must be it. For years Mrs Evans must have gone about her tasks in a bubble of peaceful cleanliness, with no reason not to smile. And yet, within the passing of a fortnight she had been obliged to acknowledge drunkenness, adultery and murder, and to meet every day the reminder of their existence. The handkerchief twisted and untwisted again, its white folds wound as tight as an unopened bindweed flower. Mrs Evans's face relaxed when Mary said she must go to her room to prepare herself.

'Oh, yes – you do that, Mary. You have plenty of time, and it is essential to make a good impression. You have borrowed a hat, haven't you?' Mrs Evans's smile returned, as though she had said something very clever. 'From one of the other girls? You will need it in this rain. And you will pin your kerchief modestly, won't you? You don't want the judge thinking . . .' The housekeeper's gaze flicked away, and the handkerchief formed a taut rope.

Tied with a green ribbon, the borrowed hat sat neatly over a demure white cap, and its brim cast enough of a shadow to imply it was that, and not weariness, smudging under Mary's eyes. Pins held her hair in a coil, better than she could have fixed herself, and her own ragged petticoats hid beneath the topcoat Lara had lent her; together they spread out pleasingly under the clean grey gown. Very respectable. Too respectable to be sent to gaol for perjury. Mary bit the hard skin on her lips and they reddened against her pale face.

He has always been a good man, your honour. He never raised a hand to me, and we had been married two years. Never touched me.

It would take no more than ten minutes to walk to the Great Hall by the Castle, but she would leave twenty. She closed her eyes and retched again. Would she see Bryce as soon as she arrived? Would someone tell the court she had once begged him to abandon his wife for her? Of course not. That would make her seem disloyal, and only a loyal wife would lie.

The way he flung the hatchet, your honour, it must have looked to some folk that it hit the man, but it fell away. He was already dead, sir. Dead.

And then – was it safe to think of it? Or would the thought, once loosed, be free to become reality? What if the judge showed no mercy, and what if she was buried in a surging crowd, glimpsing a watery image of a body on the end of a rope? Or what if, her lies exposed, she stood there beside him? She sat down suddenly on the bed, her eyes and ears clouding.

Have mercy, your honour, and don't let him die. Oh, I don't want him to die, only to live without me.

A clock, somewhere outside, marked half past nine. She would go now. Steal out before Mrs Evans sent the errand-boy to accompany her. In a decisive swirl she flung her cloak round her shoulders, and checked her reflection one more time.

Something might happen – the thought hit her hard – that meant she could not come back. She took her gloves from under her pillow. Pulling one of them on, she watched the transformation of her weathered fingers into the smooth, elegant fingers of a lady. Perhaps it would be right to wear them. No. She drew a deep breath and folded them into her pocket.

Then she listened for movement outside, heard nothing, and quietly lifted the latch.

The door would not open.

Too feeble, too hasty, too agitated. She must not have lifted it properly. She tried again. She raised the latch as high as it would go, and still the door would not open. A ferocious rattle did not move it.

'Mrs Evans!' She subdued the rise of panic. 'Mrs Evans! Are you there? I think the door is stuck.' Feet sounded on the floorboards outside. Mary hammered hard. 'Mrs Evans? Lara? The door is stuck! The door—' Her voice cut itself off in a swallow. She listened to sounds of people trying not to make a noise outside, and then all the air in her lungs clotted itself into a scream.

'*Mrs Evans!*' Her elbows and wrists met the wood, and pain buzzed through them. She battered her body against the door, blanking out the hurt. The frame shuddered; her fists became numb. She stepped back, breathing hard, and then sickness overcame her and she scrabbled for her pot. There was nothing much to vomit. She wiped her mouth and ripped off her hat, flinging it down.

That twisting of the handkerchief – she should have known.

Mary looked down at the courtyard below the window. Such a long way down, so distant, with its neat triangular hedges and its great gold fish. She was calm for a second, storing up anger, while she poured some of the water out of her wash-stand jug. Just enough to make it light enough. Then she screamed and hurled it at the door, and a shriek from outside mingled with its smash. The basin was heavier, shocking a crystal wave of water on to her face. She gasped, and the bowl droned on the floorboards.

'Mary, it's for your own good.' The door deadened the unsteady voice. 'He told me to do it. There's bread in the drawer for you. I couldn't say no.'

Ceramic pieces littered the floor. Water trickled into the grooves between the boards and dripped from her petticoats, pooling on the polished wood. Cold droplets scurried down her chest.

Mary loosened her stays, sat on the bed and sobbed. Whether with anger or sorrow or relief she did not know.

The rain dispersed into agonising sunlight towards noon, and not long after the distant clock struck three Mrs Evans pushed a note under the door, telling her the judge had not shown mercy.

CHAPTER 26

They must let her out sometime. When the door opened she would shove Mrs Evans so hard that her head would hit the wall and break like an egg, and then she would run down the stairs and out to the street, and she would never come back. But when the key at last turned she faced the housekeeper quietly, everything blank but for the crack of the pieces of wash-jug under her shoes. Mrs Evans looked in distress at the broken china and the bedclothes on the floor, but she said nothing.

Down in the drawing room Mr Barnston stood by the window, straightening the cuffs of his shirt. Selwyn had pleaded not guilty, he said, and claimed he had thrown the hatchet aside without being aware of James Hartingshall's presence. But William Hartingshall appeared in court, as hale as could be expected with his lank sleeve, and said he had seen what happened, and Bryce Warbreck produced the hatchet, with blood and hair still stuck to it and 'S.J.' carved in the handle, and others came forward too, to say Jones had argued with his wife and killed the man in anger. The names meant nothing to Mr Barnston – Adam Roberts, Elizabeth Roberts, Elizabeth Mobbett, Susan Merry. At last Selwyn had confessed and begged for mercy, begged to be transported to the colonies, and shook so much when the judge reached for the black cap that the people in the gallery said they felt the building quiver.

The judges had handed him over to the city sheriffs at the Glover's Stone, and they were to hang him at eight o'clock on Friday morning.

Mary closed her eyes and Mrs Evans's arm steadied her. Cold fingers pressed her forehead and pushed back her disordered hair. *Oh, Mr Barnston, see how pale she is!* The fingers patted her cheek. *May we not give her just a sip of port-wine to restore her?*

Mary nodded, but Mr Barnston said no, and then a punch of sal volatile burned her nose, and she coughed and the blood flowed back into her face.

'I'm sorry about the wash-jug,' she said, and her vision came back into focus on the pattern of the carpet. Mrs Evans clasped her in a one-armed hug and told her not to worry. 'I must go and see him. Where is he?'

'They have taken him back to the Northgate.' Mr Barnston spoke softly. 'He will be in the condemned cell. It would be most distressing for you if you were to go.'

'I will go,' she said, and her head clouded again as she rose to her feet. 'I will go, and if you lock me in again I'll smash the window and cut my throat with the glass.'

Mr Barnston sighed, and when the housekeeper led her from the room she heard him pour himself a brandy.

Air fluttered on her face, strange and unsettling. She stood still at first, like a new butterfly waiting for the breeze to dry it, on the morning of Thursday the 22nd of April. Davy, the lad who ran errands, was to walk her to the gaol, go and collect some cheese from Mr Griffiths's shop in Eastgate Street, and come back for her. The brink of summer filled the air. Warmth rose from the very ground. Along Bridge Street the mud had paled and hardened, and a scraggy pony by a market stall snatched a fly from its chest. They went up into the Row, where countrywomen with butter and eggs and the first fat stalks of spadger-grass cried *What'll ye buy?* And she skimmed her gaze over the faces, but she knew no one. Fragments of gossip met her ears.

. . . sailor was set to ravish his wife . . .

Eight o'clock tomorrow. I'll not go. It makes me to shiver, that sort o' thing.

Big bugger. He'll snap straight off – a shilling on it.

Two shillings says 'e'll choke.

That thief taker? I tell ye, he might take me any time!

Well, you know what they say about Jones's wife . . .

'You might go down to Eastgate Street, and I'll walk on by myself,' she said, but Davy frowned, his concave apeish face solemn.

'Mrs Evans says I munna leave you, lest you buy gin.'

At the junction of Bridge Street and Watergate Street she stopped and looked over the railings, searching the throngs of people round the stalls. Smells of the soily goodness of spinach, and poultry on the turn, and spring greens in barrows, rose from the street. But it was the people she looked at. A long-limbed man lifting a barrel. The way the sun fell, coppery, on a head of untidy hair.

'Do you seek someone?' Davy asked, and she shook her head.

The terrace of the Blue Coat School lay in shadow at this time of the morning, and the north wing showed no activity. It was not a day for outpatients. She turned her face from Davy, that he might not see tears come to her eyes. If only she had Mrs Stout to talk to; to ask about things. Someone to say that being ill, as she had been, was bound to stop a woman's courses, and not to worry – they would be along soon. Common sense told her that. It had even happened before in her old life. Twice. She had conjured a false glow of life inside her, felt the warmth that other women always said they felt, but it proved to be in her head, not her womb. The first time she had told Selwyn, and he wore a tentative smile for almost a day before her blood betrayed him. The bluebells he'd clumsily picked for her had lived longer than the dream.

It would be nice to have Mrs Stout to talk to.

'That was where I worked,' she told Davy.

'You were a nurse, weren't you?'

'Yes.'

He raised his thick eyebrows to himself before he left her at the gaol door and went about his business.

Bateman, the gaoler, answered, a fungal bloom of stubble colonising his chin and his peruke on as crooked as the way he looked at her.

'I need to see Selwyn Jones.' Mary fumbled in her pocket. 'I can only give you sixpence – it's all I have, but it's important.'

Bateman sneered. 'Sixpence? To see a convicted killer? I've had folks willing to give a sovereign, and I couldn't be bothered to take them down the steps for that.' He muttered something down the front of his jacket. 'I don't know why you girls bother. He's naught to look at. On your way, and save yourself a seat at Boughton if you're that eager to gawp at him.'

'No! I have to see him now.'

'I tell you, there's naught to see. He's no hero, you know. Just a big ugly coward who's cricked one neck and is set to crick another.'

'I know. I'm his wife. I've been here before. You must remember me.' Bateman lifted his peruke and scratched his head. 'Where's Mangham? He'll tell you who I am.'

A hollow cough signalled that Mangham was somewhere not far away, in the dank passageway. Bateman turned from her. 'There's some mort says she's Jones the Hatchet's wife. D'ye know her?'

When Mangham saw her he laughed silently, and after a brief conference they allowed her in, and said that as she was near enough a widow they would, out of the tenderness of their rough old hearts, let her keep her sixpence. Then Bateman trudged back into his room, revealing a dingy, bare stone floor lit more by firelight than by the sun.

More than ever the gaol's coldness sucked the heat out of Mary's body. With greater care for her clothes than she had ever had before she kept her cloak from the damp on the walls, and was careful where she placed her feet. Echoes flitted from her shoes and rebounded from wall to ceiling to close wall. In the passageway the smell was inhuman – a dripping algal iciness uninfected by the sulphurous heat of the inmates' quarters.

'You've prinked yourself up a bit since the last time I seen yer.'

'I've been staying with some kind people.'

'Lucky. You might've come to harm, in that state. The last fortnight, I've been thinking you was either dead in a ditch or you'd done what you said.' An unexpressed chuckle made his lamp shake. 'You kept saying you was going home. I thought you meant the hospital at first, but it was the way you kept saying it. You were on about the sea, and silver birches and suchlike. Ah, don't be embarrassed, lovely: with the stuff I see in here, a drunken girl's nothing for me to get squeamish over.'

No daylight, not even the most muted tempering of the darkness, reached the end of the passageway where Mangham sorted through his keys. The gate he opened was not the usual one to the stairs, but another that Mary did not recall having noticed before. He held up the lantern and inspected her face.

'If you don't want to go down there, just say.' There was nothing to see, only blackness. 'If it were up to me I'd never let a woman step through this gate. Even the ones set to hang.'

Mary took another glance at the gaping space and nodded once.

The lantern guttered over a flight of descending steps, steep and narrow. Depressions in their centres marked the passage of centuries of feet. The swing of the gate behind made her breath quicken. A tremor wobbled Mangham's hand when he locked it.

Was it an illusion fostered by fear, or did the walls narrow? Mangham's lanternlight descended with him and Mary raised her hands to keep the walls away. They met a soilish, underground dampness; the sort of chill that spoke of worms stretching and curling out and falling to the floor.

Light-headedness made her blink and freeze. Mangham's grizzled face melted into a hesitant kind of sympathy.

'Come on, lovely.' He spoke gently, with an awkward scratch of his head. 'We'll go back.'

'No,' she whispered. She collected the terror, folded it in on itself, and took the next step.

The stairway did not taper to the cramped point she feared. Instead it ended in a close-walled ingress with two solid wooden doors.

'You must go in quick and I have to lock you in,' Mangham said. 'If he escaped it might as well be me on the cart tomorrow.' His arm moved behind her, blocking the path back up the stairs. 'I'll go and get another light, then I'll come right back, and you just hammer hard when you want to go.' He pressed the lantern into her numb fingers, unlocked the door, and, as it dragged the air out of the darkness beyond, he placed his hand on her back and compelled her in. A harsh, choking smell razored the back of her throat. Selwyn's eyes glittered, cold and black as a rat's. He rose from his low bunk, hunching his shoulders to keep his head from the ceiling.

'You're still living, then.'

The light of the lantern quaked over a floor about eight foot square. The room was a box of rock; a cave hewn from the sandstone, its walls shiny with a glutinous layer of filth. Mary backed away.

'I can't stay. I can't stay in here.'

She thumped the door. Mangham had not yet returned. All the breath rushed from her and she went dizzy. Selwyn peered down at her, and his lips curved over his gappy teeth.

'Frights you, does it? Like you were frightened of the court?'

'I wasn't frightened. I was locked in my room. I promise you, I tried to get out. I tried to break the door down. They kept me in there 'til the trial was over. Mr Barnston didn't want me to lie for you, and I promised I would—'

'Mr Barnston?' Selwyn's tone was slow and tempered, chilled and controlled.

'Mr Trafford Barnston. The infirmary governor. I took bad and he took me into his house. He's a good man. He—' Words wheeled into a cry, shocked out of her by his grip.

'*A good man?*' There was no room for the shout to echo; her shoulder blades bashed hard on the door and her shrieks soaked into the walls.

'*Mr Barnston?* You've been staying in Mr Barnston's house?' Anger stabbed in Selwyn's eyes. 'What the hell is your part in this, Mary?' Pain jerked in her neck and blood tasted sharp on her tongue. 'What sort of plot have you against me?'

It was the wildness she had seen on Thurstaston shore; his expression the one that had flashed in the orange glow of a lamp, his hatchet raised above his head. The surge of darkness of a killer. And what frightened her was not its threat but its familiarity; the recognition that one might not be ruled by its presence or absence, but its distance from the surface. This time he had no hatchet to help him. He would have to use his bare hands. She went calm.

Anger mutated into horror; he let go and sat down, his hands sinewy on his grubby hair. 'I wouldn't have hurt you. You didn't think I would hurt you, did you?'

She breathed out with difficulty; there seemed no more room in the cell for breaths. 'No.'

'Barnston's the beak Warbreck and his lads brought me to. He's the one who sent me here.'

'But he would have said . . .'

'He said I had the horrible aspect of a murderer. I swear I saw him look at Warbreck and smile when they took me out.'

'Not him.'

The breath hissed from Selwyn's nostrils. 'You're a damn sight quicker to defend him than you were me! Couldn't you an' Warbreck just have run away together? Why have you plotted to send me to my grave?'

'I don't love Bryce Warbreck.'

He dragged in a gruesome sniff. 'Now's a fine time to decide that. Who is it you'll think of, then, while your next husband's fucking you?'

The question was too sudden and its wire of resentment too harsh. She bit the insides of her cheeks until the pain blocked out all other pain and she was able to force calmness into her answer. 'I don't think anyone would marry me.'

Selwyn's eyes narrowed. 'You credit men with a deal more sense than some of us have.' Hesitant, his hand pushed beneath her cloak and round her waist, and a sick, cold heaviness descended into her stomach. 'It's a sorry thing,' he said, and the pressure of his fingers cupping her chin increased beyond the limit of tenderness, 'a sorry thing for a man to have a wife who won't give herself to him. And I a coward, too timid to put you in your rightful place.'

'But it was you who smayed from me—' Her teeth met in a clack at the upward force of his hand.

Inwardly she shrank from him, but there was nothing she could do but let him press her against the bunk and fumble her petticoats up over her knees. The close ceiling glistened with algae; his foul mouth smeared across her face and down her neck. She shut her lips tight and pretended there was no crushing weight on her chest, that the floor didn't crawl with dusty black maggots, their movements rustling the straw. It was not a difficult thing, to turn her mind away, after two years of it.

'You were a bad wife, Mary, and I ought to have took you in hand.' She blanked out the pain of his bony hips grinding into her thighs, and his fingers gripping her hair, and the smell of his stiff shirt, its stale opening flapping above her face.

She let him rest his sweaty cheek beside hers, and then he sat up, and she wiped the fetid taste of his mouth away, and he tied up his breeches.

'Have you any money that I might buy gin for tomorrow?' Silently she threw the sixpence on the floor and returned the black flicker in his eyes. 'Will you be there?'

She nodded, compressing her lips.

A moment's pause. Then he clutched her hand and pressed it to his cheek when she tried to snatch it away. 'Mary, the time is so near.' He wiped his face with his sleeve, smearing snot and tears over the cloth. 'What will I do? What am I to do?' He looked up at the drips of water that ticked from the end of the airpipe. 'What will I do? If it's like this?'

She got up without speaking, and thumped on the door. Mangham was there at once.

'Mary, you don't know what they're going to do to me . . .'

When the turnkey clanked the door shut behind her she did not look back.

Reaching the top of the other staircase, the one that led to the gin cellar, Mangham eyed her expectantly.

'No money,' she said. 'I gave it to that . . .'

Mangham frowned, his mantle of concern sitting uneasily on him. 'Has he hurt you?'

Tears rose to her eyes. 'He only took what he thought was rightfully his.' She spat the words and he looked away, almost embarrassed. 'But it in't. It never was.'

Davy's eyes widened at the state of her when she blinked out into the light.

Five o'clock. She had kept the door off its catch, and tied a piece of string to the handle and to her wrist, so that if a tread sounded on the landing she could pull it open before it locked. Speckly light arrived long after she had woken. She slipped out of the servants' door and started the walk to Boughton.

People were congregating in Bridge Street and Eastgate Street. The growing light revealed lanky forms, fat forms, laughing mouths and pensive ones; some had tankards in hand, some shouted festive greetings. Their jokes rang loud and singular, like the rich, echoing warbles of birds in the early morning dusk.

Gallows Hill loomed high above the meandering Dee. The crowd would have to look up, up: everyone would have a view. And he would look down at the snake of water, brightened by then in the sun that promised to sneak above the horizon.

Already they were gathering on the slope, stretching arms hauled from rest and talking with fascinated solemnity. Lanterns in a tavern at the bottom of the hill spread friendly light from the open door. Mary stood on the damp grass and waited.

Selwyn's words about Mr Barnston troubled her. Mr Barnston, who had issued Bryce the warrant for the arrest; who had arranged for the authorities to offer the reward; who had then, of course, refused to try to get Selwyn freed. Mustn't go back on his word. Mustn't admit a wrong decision. What would people think?

People would think what they liked. They always did. Mr Barnston seemed rather too old not to know that.

313

Light filtered quickly – too quickly – into the air. With every blink it seemed stronger, the tavern lanterns extinguished and the fresh scent of dew lifting from the ground. The sky held a tinge of gold away from the city, beyond the scaffold. By six o'clock Gallows Hill was infested with people. The hours then passed slowly.

Now, perhaps, he would be walking up the sandstone steps from the condemned hold, now blinking from the gaol and crossing the strip of dusty ground to the chapel of Little St John, in the south wing of the Blue Coat School. At seven, or thereabouts, perhaps the cart would set off through the Northgate and creak past the cathedral, slower than walking pace.

The Strange and Terrifying Account of the Horrid Murder of Jem Hartingshall, shipwreck'd! The read of your life, Ladies an' Gemmen, the read of your life!

Down through Northgate Street, past the Exchange, past the Wool Hall and hard by the blank wall of St Peter's Church. Within yards of the pillory, and left into Eastgate Street, eyes in their hundreds looking down from the Rows.

Cheated the rage of the sea and succumbed to the rage of a vicious wrecker!

Creaking slowly, slowly, through the crumbling Eastgate and on to the Bear's Paw. Ale mingling with the rise of vomit in his throat, the tankard rattling against his teeth.

Smuggling, wrecking and murder – an astounding assortment for a penny, friends! The one true and faithful account!

Both near and distant, the church clocks knelled the half hour, and not long after that the first people saw the procession crawl along the straight road from the city, and shouted their discovery until all eyes turned that way. The cart seemed small and remote, surrounded by men who were armed after a fashion, using their pikes as walking-staffs.

The cart took a spiral path up the hill, but Mary caught only glimpses of it between the shoulders and hats. Two men stood with Selwyn – one in a clerical collar and the other a scrawny fellow who she thought at first must be another felon. Only when the cart backed under the beam could she see them better, and hear the black-clad man praying for Selwyn's soul. Sweat greyed Selwyn's face. His gaze flitted her way, but there was no change of expression, no glimmer of acknowledgement. He looked down at the end of the rope, and staggered as the cart halted.

True Dying Speech at noon prompt from Mrs Adams's press! Buy Adams's Weekly Courant, every Tuesday, Ladies an' Gemmen! Someone next to her took a broadsheet for a penny; she tiptoed to see what it said, but it whisked away. 'What are you, a *Peer* of the realm?'

A young lad scrambled, squirrel-like, up the beam and shinned along the top, sitting upright in the centre and swinging his legs. He grinned when he caught the rope, first time, that the scrawny man threw to him, and his arms tightened with the effort of securing it hard. He made a thumbs-up sign at the hangman, who adjusted the halter, and then, looking round at the eyes of the crowd, all fixed on him, the boy stood up on the beam and waved his arms. Laughter and a patter of applause rippled round the top of the hill.

When the laughter subsided the boy had already swung down from the beam, ducked the hangman's fist and gone to the head of the horse.

The mood hushed and the air tautened.

He's to speak.

What does he say?

Shut your own potato-ole and you might hear.

She could not make out the words at first; he faltered and swallowed, wiping his nose on his hands.

Speak up, sir!

Blank and glassy, Selwyn's eyes made an ineffective and indiscriminate glare.

You, your . . . The Ordinary started to write, and looked up when Selwyn paused. *You, your miserable selves, might die as game as you like when your time comes, but I'm a coward. I'm a coward, and I'll not stand stone-faced and stone-hearted just for a minute or two of esteem from the likes of you.* A contemptuous grumble swelled through the crowd. *The Lord's mercy means more to me now than your cheers . . .* The Ordinary's head bobbed in approval. *And if you see me quake, let yourselves quake with me and pray for your own filthy souls as much as mine.* The Ordinary scribbled hard.

And if the Lord has as little mercy as the judge, then at least my ghost shall have the pleasure of coming back to this scaffold and seeing Bryce Warbreck down to a deeper pit than mine!

The Ordinary did not seem as certain, but wrote it down anyway.

Murmurs of dissatisfaction sounded above and around Mary's head. Faces crumpled in disgust, lips curled in derision, noses were picked, heads and armpits scratched.

A pair of grey eyes, meeting her gaze and holding it.

Then Mary was swept back in the oniony stench of bodies, her head throbbing with shouts. She fought and elbowed and shouted.

Have a care, girl! A sweaty hand shoved her face away. A drunk man's arm draped round her and beery breath heated her cheek. She pushed him and he was lost in the surge.

Hats off in front! Hats off!

Selwyn's eyes were closed tight, his forehead pressed to his bound fists and his lips moving rapidly. The Ordinary patted him on the shoulder and stepped back, and Selwyn stumbled and righted himself as the cart started to move.

Dead silence, and the jostling ceased. Mouths hung part-open. Eyes gawped in the glee of horror. The clamour of blood in Mary's ears suspended itself, and her heart stopped. Then every one of his future breaths hushed at once into the thousand open mouths, and freed themselves in a great roar, rising like steam and dispersing, parting, infinitely upwards; up into the remote and silent mist of the weightless spring clouds.

He twitched only twice and then was still, his eyes bulging down at the glittering ribbon of the Dee.

Shutters rattle and Mary starts awake, her heart in her throat. Footsteps squelch under the window. Past the door. She has put the bar across; it bounces in its catches and cold sweat breaks out on her skin. All she can see are the last embers of the fire.

Get up and get dressed. Get ready to run. She can't.

Someone is back at the window now. Robber? Customs man? Or . . . ? He knows she's alone. Oh, what if . . . ?

Two pairs of feet. No, three. Murderers?

More of them?

The men have spent the day rowing out to the wreck, competing with the Welshmen for the timber and salvaging what they can of the tattered silks trapped on board. The silks now hang on hedges and gates, their colours subdued by salt. The women have had something of a merry day.

Scarpered like the cradantly rogue he is.

Straight to Mr Warbreck's house the moment he'd gone.

Mark my words, she'll have a visitor tonight.

Aye, if he can find a path to her bed through the dust.

Now there are more feet. A sniggering hiss. Mary's fingers tighten on her bed-tick; the straw inside crackles.

The howl starts uncertain, awkward even, and is garnished by stifled laughter.

'Ooooooh. I be the ghost of Cap'n Bloody Bones. Revenge I seek, and revenge I shall have. Arrrrr.' The sound sputters into giggles. Mary rushes from the bed and hauls open the door.

'And I'm the witch of the Dee, and I hope all your chitterlins fall

out of your nasty little backsides!' Small feet splash away, shrieks of delighted fright amplified by the darkness.

Two cups of brandy and a long night later, Mary has the fire going before dawn and, in a flurry of desperate occupation, bats down her cobwebs and sweeps the floor.

Where is he now? Still in Chester, in a grubby inn, or moving on with a horse and cart that aren't really his, and money in his pocket? How much might he have made? Five pounds? Five pounds, think of that!

Bryce's coins – her coins now – are tucked in the corner of the bed. When Selwyn sends for her . . .

The knock comes a few minutes after midday, when it has stopped raining and the wind has veered, bringing a mantle of iciness from the north.

He was in Bridge Street, Bryce's stable-lad stutters, pulled up outside a silk mercer's, when he was taken. He is in a gaol called the Northgate, and will be tried for murder at the Great Sessions.

The boy stands on her path with his hat in his hand, so worried-looking that a sudden movement might make him run.

'The Great Sessions?' Of course she has a hazy idea what they are, but just now it becomes hazier. Such a jolly name; so full of pomp. At Chester the judges try to contrive it so they can stay in town for the Races. But that can't be right, because the Races are always at the beginning of May.

'After Easter,' says the lad. He puts his hat back on urgently, as if it were a protective charm.

All her fault. If she hadn't made him so angry. If she'd somehow blocked his arm. If she'd fired the pistol to startle him. If she had done as he said. For hours she sits on her bed looking at the dirt floor, unable to move.

Four months. A pound suddenly doesn't seem such a fortune. Four months' rent, four months' food. Four months of living alone next door to Betsy Roberts, perhaps reduced to asking her for the occasional loaf of bread.

Inertia scurries from her and she throws some clothes into a bag. In the morning, her purse hanging heavy in her pocket, she shuts the picket gate behind her and sets off, unseen, for Chester.

Two miles from Thurstaston the road is pitted with water-filled hollows, tiny ripples wrinkling their surfaces. The sky is blind, the trees stark and black, the hedgerows bereft of birdsong. Silent, but for the north wind hurting her ears and the squelch of her boots between the cart-ruts. The bag gets heavy; Mary hugs it in front of her. Like a child. Behind her the track is deserted. It doesn't beckon.

Then she looks ahead and falters. The city, with its coaches and market stalls, its huge buildings and maze of streets. Its walls, its vast cathedral, its tame, winding river. Or staying at home, her money gone, begging the parish to take pity on the wife of a murderer. Looking out for Betsy and Liza every time she opens her door. Whispers in every house, in every hedge and tree.

The ice in the air pales her face to numbness: she should have brought some brandy. Well, it is too late now. Direction seizes her. Chester is where someone needs her, so that is where she must go.

CHAPTER 27

The quiet progress of the river calmed her. For perhaps half an hour Mary watched the sparkle of the sunlight on the water, and paid heed to the breeze that soothed the tiredness under her eyes. No tears collected in them. No knot of anxiety stifled her breath, no nausea flooded her stomach.

Feeling nothing. This was it, then.

'Miss Helsall!'

She turned, her movements slow. A thick-set young man with a wide mouth and a greatcoat too heavy for the season bowed inelegantly before her. The image in her mind, of blood soaking into sawdust and acidic cascades of gin, aroused no emotion. She ought to acknowledge him. He no doubt thought her rude.

'Nick Beeks, madam. The surgeon. Almost.' He smiled. 'I've had the pleasure of meeting you before, at the infirmary.'

Mary took a vague look back at the slope, where the crowd had begun to thin. 'I'm sorry. I didn't mean you to think I'd forgotten. I'm just . . .' Patches of footprint-crushed grass appeared between the people. Around the gallows, the guards leant on their pikes and yawned.

'I was mighty sorry when I heard you'd left on account of your health. It's good to see you looking so . . . on the mend.'

'Thank you.' She spoke too weakly; his eyebrows dipped in concern.

'But a spectacle like this is fearful tiring, isn't it? If we walk down to the bottom of the hill you may sit down.'

The breeze did not move Selwyn's bulk greatly; he hung still and limp as an old coat on the back of a door.

She had no notion of what to do. Claim the body and take it back to Mr Barnston's house? How? Borrow money with which to give it a burial? She ought to have asked someone. It seemed wrong to leave him, and yet she could be of no more good to him now than she had ever been. She and Beeks walked down to the road, where a rowdy throng of people mushroomed from each tavern door.

'I'd be exceeding glad to walk you home, if I were at liberty. But Mr Venables'd take the owl over it, and you'd not confuse him with a sunbeam when he's angry. I'm to fetch beer for him and Mr Racketta while they wait.' She did not envy him having to push his way into one of those heaving taverns. She sat down on a wall in front of a house.

'I saw Mr Hartingshall up there,' Beeks said, sitting next to her. 'Leaning on someone, but roaring with the best of them – as well he might, considering the connection. Devilish wicked business. Still, he'd be as dead as his brother if it weren't for you and me, eh?' His face opened into the broad smile again, like a tomato split by the rain. Perhaps he would know what she should do.

'Mr Beeks, may I ask for your help?'

He hopped up from the wall and bowed again. 'It would give me the greatest pleasure to be of service.'

'I'm the dead man's next of kin, and I don't know what I ought to do now.'

That confounded him. 'The dead man? But Mr Hartingshall . . .'

'No, sir, the hanged man. Selwyn Jones. I'm his wife, and I don't know how to get the body for burial, and I've no money to bury him besides.' She listened to that calm voice, the well-modulated tone that might have been commenting on the warmth of the sun or the prettiness of the river. But Beeks's expression did not match it for composure. He spent a silent moment staring at the ground.

'But, madam,' he said at last, 'he is promised to us.' With his mouth turned down in dismay he resembled one of the fishes in Mr Barnston's ornamental pond. 'The Judge allowed it as part of the sentence. He must hang for an hour, and then we are to take him, and Mr Venables and Mr Racketta will dissect him before such surgeons and physicians as wish to attend.'

Mary was still calm. 'They will not.'

Beeks looked away, his face flushing. 'I'm mighty sorry, Miss Helsall.' Confusion swept over him again. 'But there's a fearful lack of hangings in Chester and we mustn't miss this chance.'

'Where are Mr Venables and Mr Racketta?'

Beeks nodded up towards the gallows. 'In that carriage next the scaffold, but . . .'

It hadn't lasted long. Feeling nothing. The pounding of the ground under her feet shook every feeling in the world back into her.

'Mr Racketta!' She pulled open the carriage door and the dozing horses threw their heads up. A cloud of tobacco smoke stung her eyes.

Mary could not remember, afterwards, what she said. She remembered the javelin-men turning to the source of the shouts, remembered untidy locks of hair falling in front of her eyes, remembered Mr Racketta saying *You and your gin-drenched sweetheart have an eye on selling this one, have you?* Remembered a great earthquake of rage tearing through her, and not knowing whether it was the surgeons, or Selwyn, or Anthony, or Bryce, or herself who was the object of it. The stragglers must have been glad they stayed: a circle formed around the carriage, and the driver bellowed at her as one of the horses sidestepped.

Wife? Mr Racketta did not seem to understand her screamed explanation. Afterwards she remembered striking at him and hurting her knuckles on his coat button, and him putting his hand on her chest to shove her away.

The point of a pike, a few inches in front of her, silenced her. On the other end of it was a man who must once have pressed his face against a window just before the breeze changed.

'Is she causing trouble, sir?'

Mr Racketta pushed the pike away and moved his face close to hers, his lips retreating over tobacco-stained teeth. 'Some wife you must have been, to have it off with a drunkard while this poor bugger was languishing in gaol. If what you say is true you ought to be glad he's dead, so you don't have to relinquish your paramour.'

Selwyn's body hung dark against the bright sky. She remembered its weight, crushing her; the graze of his chin on her face, the way one flare of anger and resentment had condemned him to a place where it was teased out and fostered until death was the only way to control it.

Instinctive horror at the thought of the surgeons' knives had snapped her, not love for him. 'I wouldn't have given him up. We were to go to London.'

She wished she had not said it. Mr Racketta frowned, studying her closely and yet seeming to see through her. 'You mean you would have run away with Wells, even had your husband lived?'

'Yes.' The crease at each side of his mouth deepened and he looked at her without amusement, without lust, without anger or frustration – only with disgust.

'Then you're a hypocrite, Mary.' His voice was quiet. 'Believe me, no cut made by us could be as deep as the one you planned for him.'

The javelin-man took her by the arm and, with a last feeble wrench of anger, she shook him off. Mr Racketta's eyes were dull with hurt.

She ran most of the way back to the Eastgate, then stopped to regain her breath and went through the middle of the city, back to Mr Barnston's house. She sat at the window and watched the fish milling in the green water. Did they feel anything? Were they content, circling and drifting, or did they sometimes look up at the sky and wonder? The rage had left her now, and brought relief, like blood draining from the crook of an arm.

She borrowed pen, ink and paper from the head footman, Mr Pettipher, and hunched over the table in the servants' parlour. When she had finished her letter she pressed the handle of a spoon into the

sealing wax, and asked Davy to take it to Mr Warbreck at the Red
Lion in Lower Bridge Street.

When she told Mrs Evans she was leaving, and would like to return to
the infirmary to collect the things she had left there, the housekeeper
sent a note to Mrs Seward, and Mary and Lara walked there together
through the city, a week after the surgeons had released Selwyn for
burial in the grounds of the Castle.

One half of the infirmary's double door was open, allowing the
sleepy odours of Northgate Street into the corridor.

'Will I see the patients?' Lara whispered.

'You might take a look at them if you want.'

Lara shook her head.

'Mary!' Mrs Stout's arms crushed the breath out of her. 'What daft
lot of mischief have you been getting yourself into? Oh, bless your
little heart – I've been feared for you. Are you back with us, or is Mrs
Seward to look for two new nurses instead of one?'

'I in't coming back. I leave Chester soon and must take my things.
Do you mean Agnes is to go too?'

'Aye, but I'm sure she'll tell you about that herself.' Mrs Stout's eyes
became solemn and searching. 'Have you seen Anthony?'

'No.' That was all she could say.

'I thought as not.' The cook tilted her head in sympathy. 'Oh, perhaps
it's for the best, dear. Only tell yourself what it would have been like,
wed to such a fellow. It couldn't have been easy, could it now?'

Mary would not flare up, in front of Lara.

Easy? And it would be easy, would it, going back to the Infirmary?
Or going to London on her own? Or being Bryce's exclusive whore?

'Nothing can be easy. I rather have had it difficult with him than
without.' And she would not cry, either. 'But I've other plans now. May
Lara sit here while I go upstairs?'

'Of course she can.' Mrs Stout followed her to the door and put a
hand on her arm. 'Listen, you're not in trouble, are you, dear? Only,

you look so pale.' Mary held the cook's gaze for a moment. She wished Lara elsewhere. 'Mary—?'

Mary turned away and steeled herself for going up the stairs.

About halfway up, somewhere around the seventh or eighth step, her nostrils smarted with the sudden hit of an odour like a week-old pail of milk. Coughs and grumbles resounded against the walls. The odour strengthened and weakened – now the acid tang of vomit, now the sickly dullness of pus. Mrs Seward spoke loudly in the ward, reading a Bible passage, the verses straining through a throat contracted with bitterness. Now the gassiness of chamberpots left full, now the meaty warmth of used bandages. It must always have been like this.

The bedroom was as she had last seen it. Her bag still lay in the bottom of the cupboard; out of habit she put her hand into its folds, but there was nothing there. She packed up her quilted petticoat and her gown. They seemed shabby now, without the cleanliness and brightness she had become used to in Mr Barnston's house. Not sadness, this feeling. Not quite. Not regret, either. Just strangeness that she was severing the last link with Anthony. She half expected the click of the door latch, when it came.

Agnes looked different. Her chestnut curls were duller and straighter, her face whiter and her stance more weary. Stains smattered her apron and the rancid smell followed her into the room.

'I haven't come to forgive you,' she said. 'I don't need you as a friend. I thought you might want to know that William and I are to marry, that's all.'

For a second, Mary did not comprehend. 'You mean William Hartingshall?'

Agnes's expression darkened. 'Don't look at me in that way! Do you think any other man would want me now?'

'I said nowt. I'm glad—'

'What else am I supposed to do? Stay here until I die of some foul disease? Or dye my petticoats red and stand on the corner of Love Lane? Because they're all the choices left, so don't look at me like that.'

'I wasn't.' Mary smiled a rueful smile. 'I'm glad for you. I know it's what he wanted. He told me.' No use regretting the loss of Hartingshall's trust, or harking back to his reliance on her during his sickness. The future. That was what she must step towards now. 'He is recovered?'

'Almost. When he's strong enough – soon – we're to travel to London. He's to receive some money.' Her look showed she knew where it was to come from. 'That'll get us started. He says he loves me, which I'm thankful for, and I'm going to make damned sure I love him back.'

Determination hardened Agnes's face, but liveliness and optimism still played in her hazel eyes, and Mary remembered the strange feeling of almost permitting friendship. But what is friendship other than the period before giving someone reason to hate you?

'Are you sure? Are you sure you can make yourself love someone? I could not—'

'I am not like you, Mary – thank God – and I am sure. It is no less than most women have to accept, and I've no right to consider myself special.' Her hand curled into a fist. 'I will forget anyone else I have ever loved, will settle with William and have my own family, and I will be content.'

'I wish you well.'

They did not look at each other again as Mary left their room for the last time. Mrs Seward, leaving the ward, only stopped and glared at her silently, her mouth pursed, her whole face as solid and unforgiving as a prison wall, not built to keep things out.

'Goodbye, Mrs Seward,' she said. The door to the matron's room banged shut behind her.

Lara was terrified of the Northgate passageway. Mary could not dwell on anything for trying to persuade her to walk through it quickly, keep her eyes ahead and breathe through her mouth, as they had done on the way. But she was frightened. Frightened that the horses would trample her, frightened of beggars, frightened someone would take her pocket, or worse. Mary longed to break free from her.

At last they fled through into Northgate Street. Lara would not keep up, but the more Mary slowed, the more Lara lagged.

'What is it? Are you tired?'

'No.' Lara mumbled something about the smell of the street, and how noisy the carriages were, and then she picked at her fingernails. 'Were he a right proper drunkard, like that fat woman said?'

'What did she say?'

'She said he had a smile as bright as a knife, but was dreadful fond of gin.' Mary walked away without an answer. 'But, Mary, why did you get ruined by a porter? I know gentlemen do that sort of thing, but porters are no better than us. You might have told him to leave you alone.'

'He did not ruin me!' Lara stepped back in fright. 'I wasn't a rabbit blinking at a fox.' Lara's shrill apologies swirled round her head. 'I wanted him. Every time he looked at me, every time he smiled, I wanted him so much I might have burnt to a crossil if he didn't touch me.' Lara looked nervously about, her cheeks flaming. 'So call me ruined if you must, but don't make any mistake about who did the ruining.' They approached the cathedral. At the archway of Abbey Court Mary stopped, her heart fluttering. 'Will you take this back for me?' She thrust the bag-handle into Lara's hand. 'Take it back to Mr Barnston's. Don't worry about me – I'll come and get it later.' She ran through the arch, a wail rising behind her.

'Mary! Mrs Evans will kill me.' What if poor Lara did not have the wherewithal to get home? Guilt was as fleeting as the thought. She sped through the empty court, past the apple trees and into Cow Lane. There she stopped by the pump and caught her breath.

Cow Lane in the spring lay under a different kind of dirt from its winter slime. The ground had become solid and smooth, the peaks of hardened mud chipped off by the hooves of cattle on their way to market. Their manure crusted on the surface.

'Near get caught, did you?' A passing barrow-man chuckled.

'I'm not a . . .' But he did not mean any offence, and she did not take any. 'I got away.'

Mrs Starling's bundles of straw had darkened and shrunk. The old woman sat there again – the one who had rifled through Anthony's pockets that time.

What if she had walked past on that crisp January afternoon? What if she had just left him there, to make his own way home? Would he have found some other chance to kiss her? More fool him if he had.

Nebulous beginnings of cataracts filmed over the old woman's eyes. Her cheekbones protruded, round and wrinkled as walnuts, under leathery sockets. From her mouth upwards she seemed nothing but a skull with skin on. But under the toothless jaw weighed a tripey pad of fat, as though the years had caused all the substance of her face to drip to the bottom.

'Kill-grief! Tha'll take pity on a poor owd woman, willen thee? It dun't fill the hole, but it numbs the edges. It's all I ask. Take pity, lass.' Her palm was cracked and her long nails jagged.

'I've no money,' Mary said. 'Nowt.'

The woman gnashed her gums and hocked a cobbet of phlegm on to the mud. 'Damn ye, then, and I hope someone'll show more pity t' ye when it dies.'

Mary looked into the mist-threaded eyes, and shivered.

The gin shop's crooked door stood wide open this time. The room was emptier – bigger, it seemed, with the settles and chairs pushed back to the walls, and the fine tilth of sawdust brightening the floor. Two men and a woman lounged near the fireplace, which held only a dead mound of ash, and the smoke and heat of before had cooled to a calmer atmosphere.

'Mother Starling!' one of the men shouted. The other laughed at his difficulty in articulating the words. 'There's someone here as wants gin.'

'I don't,' Mary said. She could not want it. She had no money. Even if she did – want it, that is, which she didn't – she could not buy it. 'I'm looking for—'

'Your eyes.'

'What?'

Soft and fuddled, the man's laugh was too indiscriminate to cause offence. 'It's how everyone looks when they come here. Hiding and searching. Too sharp, too quick. Feel everything. The edges in't softened.'

'Will you tell me, sir, if Anthony Wells is here?'

'Ah.' The man slunk down in his chair and hunched his head into his shoulders. It was the woman, fubsey and kerchiefless, near falling out of her stays, who went to the kitchen door and called for the proprietress.

Mary made tight fists. Only a few moments more, then, of ignorance and, perhaps, of hope. Had that glimpse, in the Gallows Hill crowd, convinced him against her? Was he somewhere on the way to London, having pawned his watch to afford the fare? And who might he, on impulse, have taken with him?

No sparkle of friendliness enlivened Mrs Starling's face. Ridged and yellow, her thumbnail curved round the door as she reached to shut it. 'Not welcome,' she said, her eyes narrowing until there was nothing of the whites. 'And I think you've a fancy nerve, coming back here after what you did to that poor lad.'

'Is he here? I want to speak to him.'

'He's out. Now buy summat or get lost.'

'Then he still lives here?'

Mrs Starling's face filled the gap of the door. The old woman on the straw watched in silence. 'Might do. Might not. Might be in his grave.' The gap rushed narrower and Mary cried at her to wait. 'My God! Look at you!' Mrs Starling's lips parted in a skewed snarl. 'You lure an innocent lad into adultery, break his heart, and then come skulking back here before your husband's even cut down from the gallows. D'ye think Anthony had like to forgive you? I tell you, young madam, he does nowt but sit up in that room tinkering with that blessed watch and sending down for gin.' She raised a knobbly finger towards the ceiling. 'He's scarce ate. He's well-nigh a skellington, and it'll be your

329

fault if I find him lying dead as a dormouse one day.' The top of the door frame spat a piece of mortar.

Mary shambled through the Kelyards orchard, to the stones at the bottom of the city wall, where they had sat the time she had guided him home. It had been then that she knew. She might have pretended – even to herself – to be shocked, when he kissed her, but she already knew, from the way he looked at her while they sat on those stones.

Blossom petals, papery-brown with imminent decay, now covered them. Mary looked through the leaves to find the window at the back of Mrs Starling's. She counted the houses along and made out a large casement, its upper half smashed and boarded from the inside. The lower half showed nothing but a watery reflection of the cathedral Tower, clouds flowing behind it, hazy on the unwashed glass. She sat there a while, then smiled up as best she could, and followed the wall round to the Eastgate and on to the south of the city.

The unmarked mound of soil lay outside the churchyard of St Mary's, in a corner of the Castle grounds, crammed between the sunken green hollows of long-forgotten felons. On the other side of the city wall were the skinners' workshops: Mary heard distant coarse jokes and smelled the foul odour of the tanneries. Beyond them was the Dee, where the very tops of a ship's masts showed in front of a cornflower sky. Sweet and succulent, the spring grasses plaited easily. Mary formed them into a cross and laid it on the clods of earth.

I thought there was something more than our lives deigned to give us, and I near found it. You won't blame me, will you, if I don't come back?

The grass made a pattern of channels in her palm. She rubbed them absent-mindedly while she watched the shadow of the Castle stretch towards her in the late afternoon sun.

No man shall ever marry me out of pity again. There is something more and I'll keep looking, Selwyn. Don't blame me if I don't come back.

Water slurped at the keels of the ship. The masts swayed, at rest. Mary closed her eyes and pictured it gliding away round the sinuous course of the Dee, past the Rood Eye and the crane and the salt marshes, out beyond fields and farms until at last the river widened into the glittering estuary, the sails filled with blustering salt air and the ship burst on to the Irish Sea, the world before it.

You were not much of a husband, and I was even less of a wife. I take a different path now, and if it doesn't promise happiness at least it promises independence, of a sort. And that is not such a poor second.

She took out her gloves and pressed the soft leather to her cheek.

Forgive me, Selwyn, but I thank God it is not him under that soil.

Her limbs ached as she rose and brushed the grass from her petticoats.

'Goodbye, then,' she said. 'Forgive me, when I don't come back.'

She looked up at the city wall, where the ends of the masts drew circles in the sky; where the roofs of the mills jutted towards the clouds; where a lean figure stood and watched her.

Chapter 28

He was waiting when Mary reached the top of the steps, his face thinner and wearier, his waistcoat open for lack of buttons.

He opened the case of his watch and shrugged apologetically. 'It works,' he said, keeping his eyes down in examination of the face. 'Look.' When he held it out to her he seemed far away. But Mary moved closer, and watched the delicate numbers and hands. Her breath stopped; his fingers contracted round the case. And then, with a movement as fine as the quiver of a feather, the minute-hand trembled into life.

Mary smiled up at him, and he pressed his lips into a rueful line and shrugged again.

London, then. It could not be long now before he left. For all the pain that clouded her at the thought, the sight of the watch working – working because he had made it work – kindled a spark of happiness.

'Nothing I say will be good enough,' Mary said. 'I dreamt you forgave me, but I don't ask that. I only want to say I'm sorry. If you can't believe I mean it so be it, but I only want to say it before you go. I'm sorry.'

Anthony looked up the Dee to the seedy mill buildings and the bridge growing out of them. Boats passed under it, their oars tracing trails through the water. 'I keep meaning to sell this.' He ran one fingertip round the watch face. 'I need to, to raise the fare. It's hard to let it go.' He snapped the watch shut. 'I will, though, because it's what I'm meant to do. I don't need you. Don't need you at all. If this can't be our future then it'll be mine alone.'

She remembered moonlight, snaking and curling on the water, and the bridge's wall – high enough to stop her falling – grazing her hands as she stumbled against it.

The delicate gloves were not for hands such as those. What could some delusion of elegance be to her now? Not the tiniest part of her palms was unlined. Creases covered the skin. How long before they wormed up her arms and colonised her brow?

'I've no right to keep these,' she said, holding the gloves out to him. 'You might sell them instead, and keep your watch.'

Anthony looked straight at her for the first time. 'I bought them for you! Do you think you an't hurt me enough without flinging them back at me?'

Mary smoothed out the slender, empty fingers. 'They mean everything to me. But I didn't want you to have to sell your watch.'

'*Why didn't you tell me?*' Mary started at the force of his shout and two workers outside the tanneries looked up. 'You could have told me the truth at first. You could have trusted me.'

Anthony's fingers tightened around the watch as though he might hurl it into the river. Threads of copper burnished his hair; the sun lowered behind the Castle and put the river into a subdued light.

'It couldn't have stopped me falling in love with you,' he said.

'I was frightened it would, and that's why I didn't tell you.'

'You'd best tell me now, then, hadn't you?'

She nodded, and when he walked off she followed him.

They were silent at first, but when they reached the Eastgate he stopped, and said he had been to the infirmary but Agnes would not tell him where she had gone.

'I took bad and I've been recovering at Mr Barnston's house,' she said, but she did not feel much recovered. Still queasy, as if the gin had dissolved the walls of her stomach and made them thin as paper. She was glad when they reached the Kelyards and sat on the stones, where the scent of the apple blossoms settled the lightness of her head. Behind them the cathedral clock boomed a half hour, and Anthony looked at his watch and almost smiled to himself.

'Then I saw you,' he said. 'On the hill. I tried to get to you, and you were gone. Did you love him, as you said you loved me?'

'No.'

It was nearly dark when she finished telling him everything of the past two years. How the women of the village had rather do their hems themselves than pay Bryce Warbreck's apparent favourite to do them. How Selwyn had said to her, that evening when the sun had sent streams of fire to them on the shore, that he had better marry her, he supposed. 'And two days before the wedding – I was sitting at the table in our cottage – my ma lay asleep upstairs. Every snore cut through me; I thought it might be her last. I drank the end of my father's brandy. He died of a lump in his mouth that grew 'til he couldn't eat. That brandy sat there for a year, and I never touched it. Then I had to.' Anthony met her eyes and his hand brushed hers. 'At first I thought I could manage it. I would marry him, and we would have . . .' Mary faltered. 'We would have children, and I could love them, for all I didn't love him. The brandy got me, and I went to Bryce Warbreck's house. I'd pondered after him since I was – oh, I don't know – fourteen. And he'd kissed me that time, and I couldn't believe he didn't mean it. I made an idiot of myself. He was not long married, his wife already with child, and I begged him to run away with me. His wife – well, if you imagine what an angel looks like, that is her. His old servant took me out to the road and shoved me into the mud. There was a man there – a rich client, Bryce said. Some of them would come to pay their bills themselves, rather than be found out by their servants. He saw me, while I was bawling on the doorstep, and he looked so kind that I remembered him. It was Mr Barnston.' Anthony's eyebrows lowered. 'He buys goods from Bryce and no one knows. That's why he's been so good to me: he doesn't want me to tell anyone. And when I married Selwyn the women were behind me in the pews whispering about what I'd done.'

Twilight dampened the blossom petals that fell around them. At nine the man came to lock the Kelyards Gate, so they went in and sat behind the cathedral.

'Selwyn worked for Bryce, going to the Isle of Man to fetch beer and soap and brandy and such, and the money was good. He was rightly a labourer on the farms, but that was only a few weeks in the summer. We weren't poor. I ought to have been content.' She paused, and let her fingers rest in his. 'It's just I'm weaker than other women. I would have been happier with less if we had only loved each other.'

Anthony's eyes, grey and intense, seemed all there was in the world. 'Mary Jones,' he whispered. 'The name sits ill on you.'

'I've never got used to it.'

The clock struck the quarter hour. He checked the watch again, tilting it to catch the last streaks of daylight, and laughed.

'It still works,' he said. 'I'm feared to look at it sometimes. I think if it stopped my heart would stop dead. I think it would stop . . .' The breeze rustled the first leaves on the trees, and the scent of spring drifted over the city wall. 'If you said you wouldn't be Mary Wells.'

'That's what I want.'

Guarded, his lips sought hers. Then they found them, and the guard dissolved. It was like melting in layers; a heat like the first caresses of gin, but that it promised not to turn bitter.

When he walked her back to Mr Barnston's house it was near enough ten. He kissed her again and disappeared into the shadows; she smiled towards where he must be and knew he could see her in the light of the oil lamp above the servants' door. The footman, Mr Pettipher, answered – his wig off and his shirtsleeves billowing from the shoulders of his waistcoat.

'Ah!' he said. 'So there you are then, missy. Mrs Evans has wrung her wipe near to shreds over you. She's been nigh-on emptying the river wi' a ladle to see if you've thrown yourself in.' Mary took one last look behind her and saw a single glint of metal through the dark. 'You had like to get yourself up them stairs and start sorrying, lass.' The drawing room bell rang and Mr Pettipher clapped his peruke back on his head, swung his jacket on to his shoulders and buttoned up his waistcoat. 'More brandy, I reckon. It's always the way when Mr Warbreck's here.'

'He's here now?'

'Aye, like he is once a fortnight or more. Mr B. dun't see it, if you ask me. Apt to think too good of folk. It's the eyes, if you ask me.' Mr Pettipher adopted a tranquil expression and left Mary alone in the kitchen.

She rested her hands on the table, smiled down at her gloves and thought nothing more of Mr Warbreck. The sense of relief made gin seem as cold as the Dee-water the night of the wreck.

'Mary!' The way the voice made her jump set Mary to laughing, and then she could not stop. Mrs Evans's hair was close to being dishevelled, and the imperfection of it made Mary's giggles even worse. 'You don't know what an afternoon we've spent. Everyone is out looking for you. Lara has done nothing but bawl since she got home – and it's a wonder she did at all, she was so flustered when you abandoned her.' The housekeeper's voice, though full of concern, carried a tinge of anger. 'We have been frightened you might have done yourself a mischief.' Mary tried to calm herself. Her stomach ached with the effort. But when she opened her mouth to answer she burst into tears, and Mrs Evans rested her hand on Mary's shoulder.

'What is it? What has happened? Oh Mary, you haven't . . .' Mary breathed hard, and recovered enough to smear the tears away.

'I've found him,' she said. Mrs Evans's face fell to a smileless blank. 'He still wants to marry me and we're to go to London.'

She did not know what she had expected. Not jubilation and the sort of joyous hug she might have had from Mrs Stout, but if she had thought about it at all she might have hoped for a quiet word of congratulation, even a polite smile. The silence, therefore, disconcerted her. 'I know you don't approve of him, but we're to marry and you'll have to take comfort in the fact of getting rid of me.' It came out sounding unkind; she was ashamed at the glimpse of hurt in Mrs Evans's eyes.

'I suppose he fed you gin? After all we have done to try to turn you from this dreadful propensity to drunkenness?'

'No!' Offence did not dislodge her happiness. It was good to feel that fire of life in her veins; the dart of indignation that sparked her out of the stupor in which the house kept her. Who was this dreamy, sheltered woman – who had never had more than a speck of dust on the crystal to worry her – to tell her whom she might marry and whom she might not? 'I haven't touched gin, and I've no propensity to drunkenness – I only ever drank it when I felt like it, and would not—' She broke off when Mr Pettipher returned. The flop of his wig on to the table made powder wind up in a ghostly screen before the firelight. Mrs Evans sighed.

'Mr B. were askin' after you, Mary,' the footman said. 'So I said you were found, and if you ask me he'll be sending to see you once Mr Warbreck's gone.' Mr Pettipher fetched himself a pot of beer and sat down by the fire, putting his feet on the grate and exhaling contentedly. 'You know why they're always sending for brandy, says I? That Warbreck wants to drink it all to hasten the next order. He's a gafty sort, if you ask me.'

Did the servants know, then, where the brandy came from? Perhaps Mr Barnston was deluding himself that his reputation was safe.

'I tell ye – if I were a gentleman like Mr B. I'd not be thick wi' merchants and wasting good brandy on 'em.' Mary caught the housekeeper's eye, but could discern no knowingness about her look. Mrs Evans was now restored to calmness; she put a tender arm round Mary's shoulders and ushered her up from her chair.

'Go and wash your face, dear, in case he does send for you.'

Once she was in the stairway, its door shut behind her, tiredness overcame her. Not weariness, but a heady sleepiness that yearned for soft pillows and an open window letting in breaths of blossom-scented air. She trudged up and stopped at the turn of the stairs, where the door stood half open. The plain white wall backed directly on to the drawing room. Were they talking about her? Discussing how appalling it was for her to have absconded? To have been out of the control of one or the other for a few hours?

Out of their control. Mary sat on the stairs and put her ear to the wall, but she could only just hear the presence of speech, not the words.

Out of their mutual control.

Like Selwyn?

He was the beak Warbreck and his lads brought me to.

The remembrance of the words still filled her with unease. Was Mr Barnston the only magistrate in Chester? Did the men just happen to catch Selwyn within the vicinity of this house?

Smuggling violates the laws of man, but murder violates the laws of the Almighty.

What about the sale of body parts? Would that not rest in the latter class? And yet Anthony was free. Of no interest.

Mary, it's for your own good. He told me to lock you in . . .

So she would not commit perjury? Or so she would not jeopardise the conviction?

I swear I saw him smile at Warbreck when they took me away.

Candles illuminated the landing; someone hummed as they lit those downstairs. Light stretched upwards on to a portrait of another Trafford Barnston – perhaps his grandfather or great-grandfather – looking down over the stairway, with a voluminous wig, longer than Mary's own hair, and a cowering black and white spaniel, as spindly as a rat.

The voices were indistinct at first, and came to her in snatches.

'. . . run away . . .'

'. . .told me . . . manner of employment . . .'

There was a long pause; Mary pressed her ear to the drawing room door.

An uneasy laugh.

'Something fanciful, I assume? She always—'

'She said you offered to keep her as a mistress.'

The laugh again, and the sound of feet pacing.

'A mistress? Such a term implies affection. Wishful thinking.'

'A courtesan, then. A whore, sir. I am inclined to believe her.'

A glass being set down, the chink of the decanter stopper and – she brushed her ear to the keyhole – the glug of pouring liquid.

'Well, sir, I admit it. That is indeed what I offered her. What of it? Do you not yourself feel keenly the lack of a wife? But you might marry again, if you wished, whereas I must lie alone every night, with the most adored of women locking herself in the next room. What would you have me do? Mary's a pretty girl – I've never denied that. She's besotted enough with me to do as she's told, sufficiently sullied not to have anything to lose, and yet not such an inveterate trollop that she might be diseased – though I would get a physician to look at her before making any absolute bargain. And she's unlikely to produce any bastards. She is perfect for the purpose. Do you tell me you've not been tempted, while she's been lying upstairs? To see what you could make her do, eh, for a sup of brandy?' Humour hemmed Bryce's voice.

'Temptation, sir,' Mr Barnston said, 'does not require action.' Mary's eyes widened. 'What if she were to become troublesome? There might be a repeat of the behaviour I witnessed at your house.'

'Perhaps, but I don't anticipate her wanting anything more from me. She will always hanker after something other than what she has got. Occasional tears and what not I can manage with trinkets.'

'And you propose to reward her handsomely for her services? I beg leave to wonder where you will get the money, bearing in mind how you struggle to pay back the loan.'

'Sir, if you are not content with the Jones money and the profit on the silks—'

'It is a good start, but it is only a small proportion of the debt.'

'As I have said, the next trip goes out Friday.'

'My breath fails to be bated, Mr Warbreck. Does it not concern you that the longer you hold off paying the faster the debt escalates?'

'I am only too aware of that, sir.'

Someone – Bryce, she supposed – walked about the room. The firm unhurriedness of the tread was his, just as he had walked when he offered her the situation. He came close to the door and she shrank back, ready to bolt for the stair-niche.

'And yet, why do you encourage me to pay so promptly? Do you seek to forfeit your five per cent?'

A soft laugh. 'Promptly? It has been four years. I would rather forfeit future interest than lose my capital for good. Jones might have murdered someone just when it was becoming necessary to remove him, but we were lucky. He might have thought himself hard-done-by, but not a rich man or a poor one forced him to raise that hatchet. If someone else follows his lead they will play it with greater care. In the worst case the whole village could turn against you, and that would be the last I would see of my money.'

'I made them collect Jones's stash from Hilbre and bring it to me.' The rhythm of the tread grew a fraction faster, more urgent. 'Some of them came to Chester to see him off. They know what will happen if they try anything.'

'Perhaps. I only hope you do not underestimate their resourceful-ness. You need them. Or . . .' A pause; the gentle laugh again. 'Do you plan to don oilskins and row out to sea alone? Perhaps Mrs Warbreck would not object to standing on the shore in the rain, firing a signal.'

Mary smiled at the thought of her, shivering under the cliffs with the flintlock, smears of sand begriming her silk petticoat.

'I object, sir, to you talking lightly about Mrs Warbreck.'

Once, a pang might have flattened Mary's smile. Now she did not care. Poor Jessica, to be married to such as him.

'Another hundred by the end of June,' said Mr Barnston. 'I am not inclined to wait for the next Great Sessions in the hope that thief-taking proves more profitable for you than smuggling. The end of June, or I will require you to vacate the Watergate Street house. I am of a mind to sell it anyway; I have plans for a new building outside the Eastgate. I do not think I am being unreasonable. I could have you flung in gaol within half an hour if I were inclined to harshness, but I am prepared to give you a chance – yet another one. For Mrs Warbreck's sake.'

Impatience hissed in Bryce's sigh. He assured Mr Barnston of the security of the business, and Mr Barnston said he was pleased to hear it and would look forward to receiving the next hundred pounds very shortly.

'Ah . . .' Time stretched by and Mary heard nothing but the creak of the floor under Bryce's feet; she imagined him pacing past the looking glass and glancing into it.

'The problem, if I may be so blunt as to advance my true opinion,' said Mr Barnston, 'is that you do not compromise your way of living in order to accommodate your debts.'

'Neither do any number of gentlemen.' Bryce's proximity startled her.

'Very true. But I would take the liberty of reminding you that your claim to that status is at best precarious.'

'Sir—' Bryce's voice strangled, and he coughed.

The snigger that escaped Mary was not much more than a hush of breath, but she reddened and stepped back, and the sound of her heel on the floorboards rang loud in the amplifying length of the landing.

Time to leave. She was out of sight by the time the door whipped open, two steps up the stairway when he caught her.

'*Sneaking little bitch.*' Bryce bundled her back into the drawing room. 'What have you heard?'

'Nowt.' She glared back at his furious eyes. 'I only heard Mr Barnston say you in't a gentleman, and there's no news in that.' She fought away from him and clenched her fists.

'No violence in this house, please.' Calm as ever, Mr Barnston's voice belied the unease on his face. 'Mary, tell the truth.'

In silence she studied him. One of the best of men, she had thought him. Magistrate and philanthropist, governor of the infirmary.

'I heard that it's all your money. That you wanted Selwyn hanged because he bought a few barrels of beer.'

'Thank you,' Mr Barnston said. 'You may go to your room. I shall rely on your discretion until we can discuss the matter further.'

Mary lugged a chair from the servants' parlour and jammed it against her door while she changed into her own gown.

Cow Lane. Anthony would persuade Mrs Starling to take her in. What about the guinea she was promised – or more now, perhaps? Should she come back for it? Go back down to the drawing room and demand it?

What she did next almost made her smile with the strangeness of it. She thought about it. *Consider the options carefully. Do something that makes sense.* Stay in that comfortable bed, with its soft pillows and blankets, and a decent breakfast in the morning, and think about what to do. Curious, it seemed, that she had not just stormed out.

But she thought about it. Thought about walking through the dark streets with all her possessions, thought about arriving at Cow Lane to find that Mrs Starling refused to have her in the house after all. Or perhaps being admitted, and spending the night in the girls' room, on an infested bed, with loud women she had never met and who might laugh at her.

And then there would be the gin. Sometime it must happen. She could not go through the rest of her life safe from the chance. Not with Anthony. But the thought of its scrape in her throat, its grazing of her cheeks to redness, its sloshing in her stomach, its squeezing of her brain, frightened her.

Take pity on a poor owd woman.

That night, in the comfort of the cosy, clean bed, she touched her eye-sockets and thought them deeper, her cheeks and thought them hollower, and her chin, and imagined it swelling into a cushion of fat.

Clear-headed, she looked at the shape of the window – there was no moon at all tonight – and pictured what would have happened if Selwyn had made his profit on the beer. A few more trips, and perhaps others would have joined him. Adam Roberts and John Mobbett. Larger hauls, larger profits. Pulling away from Bryce's control. Finishing him.

CHAPTER 29

Half a crown towards Anthony's tab was enough to make Mother Starling admit Mary to the impermanent family of her Friendly House. The rules were painted on a piece of wood that hung over the kitchen door:

None to inquire into the origins of any person or property.

None to inquire what another knows, or knows not.

No thievery within doors.

One of the lads who pigged in the room with Anthony had left for Wrexham a week before, and the other thought a shilling good recompense for sleeping downstairs for a few nights. Mother Starling kept her own first rule and did not ask where Mary had got the money, but the truth was that Mrs Evans had handed her the coins amounting to a guinea that morning. A parting gift from Mr Barnston, she said. The housekeeper's tone conveyed her disapproval of the sum.

'I won't waste it,' Mary said.

Mrs Evans's fingers pressed into hers. 'I only hope we have imparted some influence.' The housekeeper's gentle eyes brimmed. 'Oh, Mary, I do fear for you. Please, Mary. Promise me you won't ever take gin.'

At that moment she would have promised anything to such a good person. Mrs Evans patted her cheek.

'I should like to say goodbye to the gold fishes,' Mary said.

The housekeeper and Lara exchanged looks, but Mary went to the courtyard and stared down into the water. Orange and white, silver and red, the fishes flowed tranquil paths up and down the pond. Sunlight bounced from their scales and she felt sad for them that they could not feel it.

Davy placed a letter into her hand before she left. In it, Bryce Warbreck requested a short interview at the warehouse room at eleven o'clock the following morning. Mr Barnston, he wrote – his tone curt – had asked him to convey to her something that would no doubt be of considerable use.

She had read it on her way up Bridge Street, then stopped by the pillory to put her bag down and read it again.

Once, she would have traced the tip of her finger over his name.

Noise and daylight sliced the floorboards in the casement room. Mary shook out the blanket, sending a downpour of mud-crumbs and straw through the cracks.

'Pray, Mrs Wells, don't smatter us!' Laughter swelled from below. Mary smiled.

Mrs Wells.

Mrs Mary Wells, wife of Anthony Wells, watchmaker, of . . .

She did not know any names of London streets.

Watchmaker of London. The whole of London!

But then, was it bad luck for them to have called her that? She smoothed the blanket down. If only there were no such things as banns and licences. Perhaps she ought to get her old wedding ring out of lavender and wear it for show while they travelled. The thought of it, though – that tarnished band Selwyn's grandfather had got cheap from a Liverpool captain whose wife died in the horse latitudes – dented her happiness, and she did not want to see it again.

A frizzle-headed cookmaid worked every night in Mrs Starling's kitchen, serving chops and chicken's legs at tuppence a time. One chop each night went gratis to Owd Widder Wiggins, out there on the straw. She wouldn't come in lest she got used to the warmth.

That evening Mary studied the chlorotic pallor of the lump of pork in front of her, and approached it hesitantly with her knife. The grey cat scraped a pile of sawdust in the corner by the fire. She gulped each mouthful down whole, and imagined her neck turning as green as the meat. Somewhere out in the street voices became louder and angrier.

'Now then, dears,' said Mother Starling, sliding along the bench and pressing her arm against Mary's like a bosom friend. Blotched red, her cheeks seemed swollen, as though gin found no room in her stomach and had to settle in her face. She wore short sleeves, and the bags of her upper arms hung empty as pieces of chicken skin. Whiffs of clary sage exuded from under them. 'A sup o' gin to wash it down with?'

Mary shrank into a veneer of calmness. She stroked the cat and made kissing noises while it rubbed its ear on her hand. Mother Starling went to the pantry.

'Anthony, I'm not sure . . .' He was talking to the maudlin fellow on the other side of him, who had his head in his hands.

'As I see it, either you love her or you don't . . .' He reached to squeeze Mary's knee, but did not turn to her.

The tin cup landed crooked on the table, its base dented, its rim veering to the side. Dull liquid half-filled it; its burden of sugar hung in a grubby fog. Here it was, then. Anthony downed his gin and swivelled his cup, his eyes grim.

'Some sort of doo-ment out there,' said Mother Starling, going to the window and smearing away the condensation. 'I wish they wouldn't brawl so, these fellers.' Mary feigned interest, leaving the gin on the table and joining Mother Starling to watch. A group of men milled around outside, encouraging a scrap. The participants could hardly stand, let alone fight. 'Silly sods,' Mother Starling said.

The distraction allowed Mary to pretend she'd forgotten the gin. She held up the cat to let it look out of the window, but it wriggled and slid from her arms. Mother Starling went about her business. Mary returned to Anthony, relieved but uneasy.

'Anthony,' she said, 'I don't want to—'

A kerfuffle in the main room made her break off. A bunch of people was supporting one of the fighters, guiding him towards the kitchen. He stumbled and grabbed at the door frame. Mother Starling reappeared from the pantry, shaking her head and muttering.

The man was big and scruffy, unshaven for several days and crowned by a mess of greyish curls. He held his nose tenderly between finger and thumb. He slumped into a chair, his eyes watery with drink and pain, and a fresh rivulet of blood drained down his upper lip. Mother Starling fetched him a dram, which he swigged down in one. 'Happen you'll be going to Mary's hospital in the morn, you silly old bugger,' she said.

Mary glanced at Anthony. 'It in't my hospital.' Then she offered the man her cup of gin. 'Here. You're in more need of this than I am.'

'Aye, well,' Mother Starling continued. 'What do you think? They'll cut it off, that's what they'll do, and for evermore folks'll be thinking he's had a dose of the French pox. In't that right, Mary?'

The man tipped his head back, and coughed as the blood went down his throat.

'They won't be able to do owt tomorrow,' Mary said. 'It'll be swelled as a beet-root. You might go now, if you like – Mrs Seward lets in emergencies. She wouldn't be happy, though.'

The injured man pitched his head forward again and snorted blood on to the table. The droplets soaked into the grain. 'I'm not going to any hospital.'

The nose was bent – pink and tender, not blackened and swollen like the ones Mary had seen before. She looked more closely. She could see the crooked line of bones beneath the skin.

'You'd be best to have it set now,' she said, 'before it puffs up.'

The man tried to laugh. 'Go on then, lass. You set it.' His voice was numbed, like someone with a cold. 'You set it, my love, and make me look as handsome a gent as ever promenaded around the walls. As handsome a bugger as ever subscribed to your damned hospital.'

Mary swung a chair out from beneath the table. 'All right then, I will.' The man's bushy eyebrows lowered. Mrs Starling put her flappy arm around Mary's shoulder.

'Little dear,' she said. 'I'm sure you're being very kind, but this is best left to a surgeon.'

Mary shrugged. 'Well, then, he may go to the infirmary and queue in the rain, and let them tell him he must come back when the swelling's gone, then they'll crack his nose to pieces when it's just stopping hurting.' She stared into the man's brown, bloodshot eyes. 'It's nowt to me what you do. I'm only offering.'

'Offering to stick your dainty little finger up me snout? I'll do without.'

Mary reached across to the other side of the table. 'No, I could use this spoon,' she said, and someone laughed. She held it up before him. Its straight, slender handle was just the right size. 'Now, will you let me take a chance?'

The man frowned. 'Will it hurt much?'

'Aye,' she said.

Anthony's maudlin friend pitched a lump of bread across the table. 'Let's see it, you daft beggar. Else all'll know you're feart of a girl.'

The man shambled round to Mary's side of the table and sat down in front of her. Mother Starling provided more gin, which he gulped back with a wince. 'If you make it worse I'll give you a nose to match it.' Mother Starling jabbed him in the shoulder.

'None of that, thank you, you great lout. I'll not have threats of hitting women in this house. This lot won't take kindly to it either.' The patient eyed the fascinated audience, then sighed and nodded to Mary to begin.

She ran her fingertips down the bridge, feeling the awkward roughness of the bone to the left side. There was an indentation against her thumb – the bones had shifted crookedly to the right. She placed the handle of the spoon at his nostril.

'Don't cry, will you?' she said, and a murmur of laughter went round the kitchen. People were calling others through from the main room. Mary eased the spoon-handle up into his nose, and the man repeated a catechism of swearing as she manoeuvred it against the displaced bone. Under her gentle fingers the bone creaked – more a feeling than a sound.

A satisfying snap made the kitchen's inhabitants raise a collective, horrified cheer. The man stifled a bellow. Mary withdrew the spoon and wiped its washy red tip on her petticoat, forgetting she hadn't an apron on.

'There,' she said, and returned to her seat next to Anthony. Mrs Starling fetched the man another cup of gin. The air hissed into his nose and he tentatively breathed deep, as if to enjoy a perfume. 'Don't touch it. I haven't any sticking-plaster to cover it. You must be guardful not to put it out again.'

The man nodded and gingerly wiped his eyes. Then he pushed through the gathered people and went outside, and rowdy laughter accompanied the sound of him being sick on to the mud. Mary wiped the blood from her fingers. Anthony's friend seemed to have forgotten his earlier anguish and was in fits of drunken giggles. He pushed tuppence along the table.

'For the entertainment,' he said. Mary smiled.

'It's kind of you, but I don't mean to take your money.' She tried to return the coin, but he waved it away. Another fellow followed suit, then another, and Mary found herself with eightpence-worth of people's gratitude for the diversion.

Then the patient came back, compelled by two friends, and handed her a shilling before staggering off into the night.

'Well, I think you deserve a little dram, *gratis*, dear,' said Mother Starling. Mary tried to protest, but a mug appeared before her and she smelled the familiar sharp fumes.

Almost four weeks, and she had not had a taste of gin. It hadn't, after all, been very difficult to give it up. Something began to swivel in her, like the turns of Anthony's cup between his palms. Wouldn't it be a mite dour not even to take one sip? Just a cupful, to be polite? Or would those women who slept in the room down the sloping landing

– the ones who looked, to be blunt, like hedge-whores – stagger into bed sniping over that snooty cat of Anthony's who thought she was too good for gin? Perhaps she could drink it while she was here, and resolve to have no more once they set off for London. London would be the turning point, the thick black line that underscored the ledger of her old life. Until then . . .

Her hand closed round the cup. She felt sick. *Mud streaming down her shift. Sweat cold as glass on her back.*

Eyes met hers in the liquid's cloudy surface. Eyes as sunken as rat-holes in a face of yellow straw, threads of mist nudging them to blindness.

Take pity . . .

The thud of the cup on the table made Anthony and his friend jump.

'I'm sorry, I don't drink gin any more,' she said. The people around the table went silent, looking at her in bewilderment. Mary mumbled that she was tired, and ran up the rickety stairs.

Light leaked up between the boards and wavered on the ceiling. Mary shifted and twitched, alone in the sagging bed. Something rustled inside the tick. Bugs pincered her back and the dusty scent of the straw made her sneeze. She traced the line of the plot of damp on the ceiling and counted the white furry spots of mould within its boundaries. No wonder you had to be drunk to live here. Mary scratched her head and wriggled her back against the bed, imagining the biting insects squashed to flat dabs of blood.

Then she must have slept, because she dreamt of fishes swimming to the brim of the water and continuing, unimpeded, through the air.

From the way Anthony crept into the room without stumbling, and how short a time it took him to undress and slink under the blanket with her, she could almost think him sober.

'Do they speak ill of me,' she said, 'for not supping the gin?'

Another burst of laughter rose through the floorboards, and she flinched.

'No,' he said. 'They don't. They're all talking about you, but it in't your lack of gin as excites them.'

'I don't want to drink it any more.' She was silent for a moment. 'If you saw us in London swilling gin together then I'm sorry for letting you down, but you can't make me raise a cup to my lips and I won't.'

Beyond the orchard the cathedral clock tolled ten.

'Mary—'

'People hated me for drinking gin, and if they hate me for not drinking it I am no worse off.'

'No one hates you for it. They're talking about what you did.'

'Anthony,' she whispered. He stroked her hair, and she listened to the voices downstairs for a time before continuing. 'I had this stupid idea – I thought I could work in an infirmary, in London – in the operating rooms. But they'd never take me, would they?'

'I suppose not. I can't say you look much like a surgeon.'

'I know. But what I've been thinking is, I could still treat people, couldn't I? I mean people who are feared of going to hospital. They could come to me instead. For wounds and things. I could stitch them up, or poultice or bandage them. Set bones. I'd charge only a bit of what doctors charge. Some folks don't care about societies and universities and such. They only want someone to help them get better.'

Anthony's arms tightened around her. 'Imagine us in London, eh? Me with my watches – you with your spoon. We'll make a fortune.' He laughed. 'It's a good idea. If that's what you want I won't object.'

Mary raised herself up on her elbow and looked down into the glitter of moonlight that caught in his eyes. 'You won't object?' she smiled. 'What makes you think I'd listen if you did?' She pressed her lips on to his.

Morning light spread underneath the board covering the smashed upper half of the window. When Mary awakened, with her head on Anthony's shoulder, she could feel the galloping of his heart. He clutched her to him.

Hung over, she supposed.

It was the first time they had spent the whole night together. She kissed him gently and he tried to smile.

'I've been awake all night,' he said.

'Too much gin?'

'Not enough.'

Only two cups, he said, and then he had stopped. He had made himself stop for her sake. He could do that sometimes, if he put his mind to it; if he closed his eyes and imagined the morning. Imagined waiting for it to get light, and yet growing frightened as the light grew, staring in dry-eyed terror at the patterns of grime on the ceiling. If he felt the vein pulse on the side of his head and thought of it pulsing so violent it burst; if he thought hard about rolling on to the floor and hugging the chamberpot, his brain wrung into a figure of eight, he could sometimes make himself stop. And that was what he had done last night, so he could wake up and kiss her without his throat trembling and a feverish pain hurting his limbs.

But it hadn't worked.

All night, he said, his heart rattled so fearfully he was sure it must wake her. Mary pressed her palm to his chest, and he smiled and said she was all that was keeping it in.

'I think Madam Gin has a plot against me, to trick me into letting her live.'

Did she remember, he asked, the night when they walked down to the salt marshes? Of course she did. She remembered how the night had ended too, but remained silent.

Did she remember the crack of the ice under their feet, and the old brambles stretching above them, and the marsh-grasses silvered by the moon, and the river so cold it ran as slow and thick as cream? Did she remember him shielding their faces when he kissed her, and how it made her giggle?

'I do.'

'So do I. Sometimes I think I want memories, and I want feelings. I don't know.' He hauled himself up and stretched his arms.

'Shall we walk there this afternoon?' Mary said. 'And see how it's changed.'

They would go there after meeting Bryce Warbreck.

Backed up to the alleyway next to the warehouse stood a waggon. Banter echoed in the alley and two men heaved a threadbare sofa into the yard.

'Ma Hodder's on her way, then,' said Anthony.

'Serves her right.' Sunshine fell on only the top third of the buildings. The ground was untouched by the light, near as wet as winter, the paving-stones still mud-plated and slippery. 'You will wait close by, won't you?'

He would rather go in with her, he said, but he would wait by the door and she must thump it, or shout for him, if she had even the slightest cause for unease.

'He won't hurt me.'

'No,' Anthony said. 'He won't.'

Since Mary had attended Hartingshall there the room had not changed. Slumped, beggar-like, on the floor, the mattress lay with its blankets shoved aside, a layer of dust blending into the grime of the pillow. It smelled of the infirmary, its fusty air cleansed by something familiar and metallic, like the quicksilver fumes around the apothecary's store. Bryce made an abrupt bow; she made no effort to return the courtesy.

'You have chosen a lifetime of diving for ha'pennies in an ocean of gin, I hear?' he said.

'Mr Barnston's quick to spread his opinions of other folk's circumstances.' The purse he clumped into her hand was disconcerting in its weight. Ten golden guineas strained the leather. 'He must be fearful scared for his own reputation to bribe me so.'

'Mr Barnston does not bribe. It is an advance reward for your discretion. He will not tolerate any further attempts at extortion.'

Mary kept her face indifferent.

Ten guineas! Ten guineas!

Then she couldn't help it. She took out one of the coins and tilted it to the window, and the way the light sparked off it made her heart give a skip.

It was easy now, to be in the same room as Bryce Warbreck. No blushing, no sickening disruption of her heartbeat. All she could wonder was whether that was it, whether she could leave now and get back to Anthony and tell him. Ten guineas!

But when she looked at Bryce again he held up a letter – the one she had hurried off to him on the hanging-day.

'This nonsense,' he said, 'about travelling to London alone and applying to a hospital – as a surgeon's assistant, for heaven's sake! You can't have meant it, surely? I thought it was nothing more than a counterfeit demurral to strengthen your bargaining position.' Then the terseness diffused from his voice. 'You need have had no fear of my provision being ungenerous,' he said quietly.

The coin made a pleasant chink when she dropped it back into the purse.

'That was what I intended at the time,' she said, 'but I've other plans now. I'm not going to be anyone's assistant – no one's servant. I've been under people's control long enough.'

Bryce leant back against the table, crossed his ankles and watched her thoughtfully. She returned the intensity of his observation, taking in the chunky silver of his watch chain, the harsh brightness of his shoe buckles, the way the sumptuous blue velvet of his jacket was betrayed by an imperfect hem.

'When do you leave for London?'

'Soon. Soon as there's a coach, I 'spect, now we have this money.'

'Go on the stage from The Feathers next Wednesday.'

Mary bridled at his presumption. 'Why should we?'

Bryce smoothed the folds of the letter and returned it to his pocket. 'There's a reason. I did not intend to trouble you with it. I have no wish to cause you distress. But the more I consider it, the more uneasy I become. You could be in danger from him.'

'Who?'

'Hartingshall.' Bryce gave a gentle half-smile of concern. 'In my opinion, it's simply a reaction to the hanging. Surprise, perhaps, that when all was over he found his brother still absent and his grief still present – that is not for me to say. What I do know is that Hartingshall's proportion of the reward has not been enough to console him. In short, he has asked me to dabble in thief-taking again.' Mary's skin chilled. 'He told me you could have stopped his brother's murder, but you looked away.'

'I couldn't have stopped it. How?'

'Then there is your involvement in the sale of his arm. I told him I truly believe you knew nothing of what Wells had done, but he still hates you for profiting from it.' She remembered Hartingshall clinging to her in terror. 'He asked me either to incite you to a felony, or to invent one with which to frame you.'

She remembered him begging her to go with him into the operating room, trusting her childish guesses about what would happen after his death. Another blow for that ephemeral notion, friendship. There was no such thing. Love or nothing.

'But you refused?'

'Of course I refused. You didn't think I would have agreed to such a plan?' She shrugged. 'Perhaps, had someone else been the proposed target, I might have been tempted to consider it. But not you.'

His eyes displayed kindness. Affection even – no dark thread of duplicity or violence. She fiddled with the string of the purse, twining it around her fingers.

'It is my great concern', he said, 'that Hartingshall will find someone else to help him, or recruit thugs to harm you without the need for too much strategy. That is why I suggest you embark on a particular coach – if next week's is not convenient you might send word to me which you take.' He smiled as though they shared a joke, his eyes crinkling. 'I have a few acquaintances who could ensure it is not robbed, at least within twenty miles or so of Chester. I don't think Hartingshall has the wherewithal to track you beyond that.'

'But he goes to London too. He's to marry Agnes. She hates me an' all. They might find me there.'

'Unlikely, in such a big city.'

'But Chester is a big city, and he had no trouble finding me, nor me him, here.'

Bryce laughed, and looked at the ceiling. 'If you call this a big city, I think you must prepare yourself for a shock.' Levity made an easy shift to sincerity. 'You will be careful, won't you? This Wells character – he will look after you?'

'He will.' After an awkward pause she turned to leave.

'Mary.' A strange air of diffidence overcame him; he fumbled in his pocket. 'You might as well have this. I meant to give it to you as a token of our arrangement. Take it anyway, and I hope you never find yourself in a situation where you are obliged to sell it.'

Vivid blue, changing and bright in the dull room, the handkerchief reflected hints of light with the clarity of a stream.

'Is this . . . ?'

'The rest is gone,' he said, watching her unfold the silk and take it to the window. 'Very profitably. But I knew how much you wished to keep it, and I beg you to accept it as a gift from a friend. I have wronged you in the past and have no wish to part on bad terms.' He returned her smile – with some sadness, she thought.

'Thank you.' She crammed the purse into her pocket and folded the silk as small as it would go.

When she looked up he was close to her. The white folds of his neckcloth were level with her eyes, the velvet-covered jacket buttons near enough that she might touch them. She remembered the strange evening light on the silver birches; the knowingness in his eyes. His voice came to her coaxing and gentle. 'Won't you kiss me goodbye, Mary?'

The quicksilver scent strengthened. She turned her face from his touch. 'No,' she said. 'I won't.'

He laughed gently as he drew her towards him. 'You will, Mary. Of course you will.'

Her shove made him stagger. She swung her fist at the door. 'I said I won't.'

Light rushed into the warehouse room, and the removers' shouts became clearer. Bryce raised his eyebrows and regarded Anthony's shabby suit.

'He tried to kiss me,' Mary said. Bryce sighed dismissively.

'So, you have settled for a specimen who wanders around looking like a madman because he can't afford a peruke.'

'You think I should have chosen a few tawdry gowns and a bed to put my back on? What's that, compared with someone truly loving me?'

'He'll love you until he's pissed that money against the wall, and—'

'Mr Warbreck.' Anthony spoke softly. So softly that Mary remembered the mist by the Northgate, the first time he kissed her. 'Mr Warbreck, you'll leave Mary alone.'

'Or you'll knock me down? I must be quick enough to move while you're working out which one of me to punch.'

Anthony looked at him narrowly, his cheeks hollowing. For the first time Bryce's gaze flickered away.

'She's told me everything about you, Mr Warbreck. She's told me how you laughed to hear her called a whore because of the lies you spread about her. She told me about you treating her like a dog pestering you for crumbs, and she's told me how you want a handy piece of flesh now your wife has more sense than to let you touch her. And now she scorns to be a wrung-out mop waiting for the chance to polish your vanity, you have to see if that smug gob of yours can kiss her back under your control.'

'Her imagination', Bryce said, 'has always been uncommon excitable. An innocent kiss between parting friends, and she sees it as an attempt on the virtue she would like to pretend she still possesses.'

'She told me how you claimed to have ratted on that old bawd for her sake. So fond of her, are you? So fond as to be revenged on Ma Hodder for bothering her? Do I believe you, I ask? Or do I believe them honest fellers out there?'

Bryce shot a look at the doorway, then at Mary. 'Who?'

'Their word is that you shopped her because her poisoned trulls have left you poxed to the gunnels. Do you deny it?' Anthony jabbed a finger at Bryce's chest. 'That's what you wanted Mary for, isn't it? You wanted someone who didn't matter. Someone you could use.' His knuckles paled against the lapel of the velvet jacket. Bryce tried to dislodge his grip. 'Well, she matters to me, Mr Warbreck. She's all that does.'

Bryce laughed; a powerless huff. 'You seek to make me drunk by breathing on me.'

The smack of Anthony's fist made Bryce's head hit the wall with a crack. Hartingshall's bed broke his fall and he lay across it, dabbing his fingers to the flow of blood from his nose. His peruke teetered upside down on the floor, revealing his scalp, reddened by a livid rash. Anthony prodded him with his foot, like a curious child discovering a dead animal.

'She in't yours any more, Mr Warbreck. She's mine, and I'm hers, and you're nowt to either of us.'

The sun had moved overhead, drawing shiny threads of vapour from the mud and turning the sky above the warehouses to a square of golden light. Anthony kept his gaze towards the ground as they walked in silence into Northgate Street. He shrugged when Mary looked up at him, but as she took his arm and pressed close to him the corner of his mouth twitched into a smile.

CHAPTER 30

'D'you think it's the night soaking through the day, or the day pushing back the night?' Anthony folded his hands behind his head and contemplated the unclouded sky. 'The blueness, I mean. Or do the day and night hang together, balanced one against the other?' Mary smiled at the sun on her face and the tick of insects in the grass. Contentment and unease battled in Anthony's sigh. 'I can't help thinking it's the night that's always there, and the sun only masks it for a time.'

A cloud of tiny birds dipped and rose over the marsh-grasses.

'Then enjoy the sun,' Mary said. 'We've just been given ten guineas. We're going to London next week—'

Anthony shook his head. 'We're not going on any coach he tells us to. I'd scarce be surprised if he meant to rob it himself and take back the money.'

'What about Hartingshall?'

'What can he do? He can't hold a knife and take the purse at the same time. He has nowt to do with it. Warbreck just wants you to do as he says, for the sake of it. For the sake of keeping you under his control. He's rotten as a turd.' He pulled the silk handkerchief from her stays. 'That's what this is about. Even when you're hundreds of miles away he wants to think of you weeping into it over him.'

Mary spread the silk out flat on her petticoat. Sunlight sapped the colour from it, paling the delicate threads, and when she held it up it formed a window of grey against the vibrancy of the sky.

'I should have thrown it back at him,' she said. 'Still, we can sell it in London. I won't weep into it – I don't know what I might catch.'

She smiled, but anger crossed his face and he stared out towards the river, biting the side of his thumb.

Thoughts were clear to her in such a quiet place. Bryce, from now on, would be nothing to her. No – already he was nothing. However much she tried to hate him she couldn't care enough to feel anything for him at all. Use – that was all he wanted from anybody. Some use.

Weariness made her lie back, sun seeping through her clothes. Gentle sounds lulled her. Cries of seagulls, larksong over the salt-grass, the surge of the water towards the sea. London had a river, too. There must be places there as peaceful as this. Dreams filled her head – a plain but respectable room or two at first, then a pretty cottage by the river. The Thames – that was it. Eventually a house like the ones in Abbey Court. Plenty of room for the children.

A tickle on her neck made her quiver; Anthony drew a blade of grass over her skin. 'You've been asleep for seventeen minutes,' he said. His eyes showed concern. 'You're terrible pale. You in't recovered properly, are you? You've never told me why you ended up at Mr Barnston's house.'

'Because of gin.'

He lowered his head to her chest. 'My fault.'

'No it wasn't. *I* drank it. I drank what Mother Starling gave me, and I went to the gaol and got more, and I drank that too. No one poured it down my throat but me.'

She sensed him wanting to say something. It took him ages. When at last he spoke he asked her to promise she wouldn't laugh. 'In London folk won't know I'm a drunkard,' he said. 'Since that night you told me about Jones I've drank a lot. A fearful lot. Sometimes it seems we've switched places, gin and me. I mean it drinks me, and keeps me handy for when it needs me, and it promises me things to make me drink it, and forgets the promises. Owd Widder Wiggins always says it numbs the edges, but that's just a trick, so you don't feel it eat them bigger.' He lay back and stretched his arms above his head. 'Here, drinking gin in't just something I do, it's what I am. But in London no one will know, and I won't have to drink it any more.' There'd be no one to laugh and say he couldn't do it; no snide crows to hunch and hop around him, waiting for the pickings of his failure.

'What if it follows you?'

'It won't, because I'm to leave it here. There's no point planning to stop – that'd only give it warning; give it time to work out how to keep me. It'll have to be quick – quick as a surgeon's saw. Madam Gin's going to wake up tomorrow and find herself severed. Powerless, like a dead arm, and I'll keep all the life to myself. It won't be easy. But Hartingshall lives, and so will I.'

Won't be easy. How many times had people told her that? Mrs Stout, Mrs Evans, Mrs Seward. Won't be easy. But why should it be? No one can climb a cliff-face if it's smooth.

'We will be married, won't we?' Mary said. 'As soon as we get to London?'

'When we've been settled enough time. Only a few weeks. Until then it's best to travel as Mr and Mrs Wells.'

A few weeks. But if they avoided the next week's coach and took the one after, that would make it quite a lot of weeks. Still, she would keep her suspicions quiet; tell him once they were married. Saying the words now must blight it. She stared up at the clouds.

'I think there might be a child.'

It sounded natural, once she said it. Just a progression of the scent of spring in the grass, another of the light-washed ripples of the river, another birdsong, a mote of blueness in the sky.

Colour sank and rose in his face, but what she would remember afterwards was the clarity of his eyes when he turned to her, and the way he smiled. She would always remember how he smiled.

They lay on the grass for over an hour, breathing the salt-threaded breeze and talking softly about the future, imagining what London would be like and how they would make their fortune.

'Wells and Son, Watchmakers,' he said, and laughed. Then he jumped to his feet and helped her up, excitement glittering in his eyes. 'Why don't we go tomorrow?'

Such a darned lot of trekking about at this time of year, said the keeper of the Pied Bull. Always one for biding at home, himself. Still, if folks must always be wandering who was he to refuse the profit? As far as he knew there were still places on the London coach, but they must engage with Mr Cavender to be certain.

Mr Cavender sat at a table looking out between the arches into Northgate Street, streaming ribbons of grey-blue smoke from a selection of orifices. Before him were ledgers and papers provided him by the coachmen.

Mary took a violent dislike to him, and kept silent while Anthony haggled over the price. She did not like the way his nose was broken in so many places that it curved like a spine; did not like the thick wires of blue-roan eyebrow that kissed at its bridge, or the nonchalance with which he riffled through the papers to find the one for the London stage. It had meant to set off today, but did not. No room inside, he said, and then added with a pointed *but*, he did not suppose it was inside seats they'd be wanting anyway.

And Mary did not like the way disgust scurried, rat-like, over his features when he wrote 'Mr and Mrs Wells' on the paper.

'A shilling,' he said. 'Each.' That would ensure them the seats in the basket and take them as far as Whitchurch. After that, he said, bringing the tufts of his eyebrows together, it would be sixpence a stage. Each.

Did she imagine it, or did he put an unpleasant emphasis on the word *Mrs* when he bid them goodbye, his lips tightening back over his teeth?

'Perhaps he did,' said Anthony. 'But you mustn't let anything distress you.' The protectiveness with which he put his arm around her made her laugh. As they walked past the window she smiled at Mr Cavender, and he blanked his face with smoke. 'Come on. When he sees us tomorrow, he won't think us such poor specimens.'

In a second-hand clothes shop in Werburgh Lane Mary bought a green cotton topcoat and a summer jacket, and a straw hat with a green ribbon. Anthony found a dark blue suit, with a russet waistcoat, and got them cheap because they had been there nearly two years, not fitting anyone else. Back at Cow Lane Mother Starling said they were as spruce a pair of swells as ever walked the walls, and if Anthony would only wear a peruke he would be handsomer than any other fellow in Chester.

'Mary likes me as I am,' he said, and smiled.

After they had paid off the rest of his bill she was aware of the purse hanging lighter between her skirts.

They exchanged a quick look when, after breakfast on Thursday, Mother Starling presented them with a free bottle of gin to warm them on the journey. Owd Widder Wiggins was not sitting on the straw when they left.

'We don't have to drink it,' Mary said, on their way through the Kelyards.

'No,' he said, his face white and tired. 'We don't.'

Sleep had been elusive for both of them in the cramped, slumping bed. Anthony had refused gin, and woken twice in such a sweat that he had to walk around the room, while Mary listened to the creak of the floorboards and the quickness of his breath, and the darkness intensified fears so distant from the tranquillity of their afternoon by the Dee. What if she was mistaken and there was no child? What if there was and it died? Or what if she died bearing it? What if there was some reason – some strange London law they had never heard of – that prevented them getting married before it was born?

Cultivated flowers bloomed in the borders of Abbey Court, and the clean scent of newly washed cobbles allayed the sickness she had woken with. In Northgate Street the smell was different – of dew lifting from horse dung, and the mingling odours of the detritus in the central gutter.

'Strange night,' he said. 'As if I could see from a distance how happy I am, and yet Madam Gin was there with her fist in my stomach, telling me I can't be without her.'

Rumour had it the coach would leave at about nine. Anthony's mood brightened as they sat in the Pied Bull observing the other passengers, guessing who was going all the way to London, and making up stories about what business they might have there.

The street became busy. The carriages of the gentry were not yet out, but waggons and a stagecoach already queued for passage through the Northgate. People on foot lugged country produce towards the Rows. She had done it once: brought bunches of rosemary and mint, and a few eggs, and sat on the boards of Lamb Row, too timid to shout, blushing at the slow winks of some of the men passing by, and wondering how quick she could make a shilling if she heeded them. Selwyn had put her off going again.

She expelled such hark-back thoughts, and was about to nestle towards Anthony when she noticed something.

Standing in a shop doorway on the opposite side of Northgate Street was a man. She had seen him before, or perhaps he just reminded her of someone. It was the shape of his chin she recognised – the way a dent in the middle divided it into two bulbs, like the cheeks of an arse. For a few minutes he stood picking at his nails or rubbing his foot on the ground, or scratching his head under his floppy country-style hat. Then Mr Cavender approached him, a bundle of papers under his arm, and exchanged a few words.

'That feller talking to Mr Cavender. Do you know him?'

Anthony peered through the window. 'Don't think so. Happen he was once a patient.'

'No.'

Mary looked out into the bright street. Mr Cavender dipped his head in a parody of politeness as he passed her at the door. She made a face at his back, and some of the other passengers laughed. Must just be someone she had seen around the city.

The Chester Tenacity was a monstrous machine, its unsprung body yellow at the top and black at the bottom, its wheels as tall as Mary. At the back was the large wicker basket where they were going to sit. Excitement built in Mary's stomach as the first pair of horses backed into the shafts. Sleek and shiny, their summer coats were full through, and a night in the stables had left them wide-nostrilled and fresh.

'Never been on a coach before, madam?'

She might have hoped it was not that obvious, but the sturdy gap-toothed fellow standing next to her was too jolly to have meant to ridicule.

'No,' she said. 'Only carts and such.'

'The worst of it is being overtaken, 'specially by folks on foot.' He laughed, and so did Mary, to be polite, but she could not believe that those strong horses wouldn't get to London fast as a dog to a chop. She clasped Anthony's hand and he grinned down at her, his earlier agitation dispelled. Sun cut off a few feet of the shade at the opposite side of the yard. By the time it flowed from overhead and draped the swept cobbles they would be on their way. All around, people chattered in excitement. The jolly man's luggage was next to go up; soon it would be their turn. The ostlers aligned another pair of horses, a grey and a bay, the muscles of their haunches sharply delineated. Even when someone jostled Mary by accident she was too happy to scowl at him.

'Have a care, friend!' Anthony spoke with more laughter than anger. 'My wife's in a delicate state.'

Mary's exhilaration stalled. 'Anthony!'

Thank God she had her gloves on; she imagined every pair of eyes flitting first to her belly, then to her left hand. She shot him a furious look. But then the way he smiled made her giggle, and when he kissed her the sturdy man's wife chuckled and said 'Ahh.'

'Mary.' Anthony lowered his voice. She followed his gaze down to the front of her jacket. A sliver of blue silk showed between the gentle white curves of her breasts. 'Keep it out of sight. Someone'll either take it or think you've took it.' Pushing it back down, she smiled, remembering Agnes's belief that Mrs Stout kept a whole larder of stolen food down her stays, and then she looked up and saw the man with the strange chin waiting at the entrance to the courtyard.

A single hard thump punched her heart.

She knew him. She might only have seen him once or twice before, but she knew him. 'Wait.' She spoke so sharply that Anthony's smile vanished. 'I know who he is. Don't look.' Anthony waved the next people to take their luggage on. 'He's one of Bryce's men.' Out of the corner of her eye she saw the man fold his arms, feigning incuriousness.

'You think they're after taking the money?' Anthony said.

She shook her head. 'The hanketch. And me.'

Four months 'til the Michaelmas Sessions. Dark, dirt, rats, maggots. Mangham flinging bread through the bars.

'Now wait.' Anthony's hands were firm on her arms. 'Don't fright yourself. You've done nowt wrong. You haven't stolen it and he can't—'

'Who would believe me?'

He gave it to me, your honour. Mr Warbreck gave me the silk only the day before. Because . . . because . . .

What say you, Mr Warbreck? Does the prisoner speak the truth?

I do not make a habit of bestowing silk handkerchiefs on servants, sir.

Strained composure veneered Anthony's face. 'We'll just walk quietly away. Pretend there's nowt wrong. Walk quietly out the other side of the courtyard and go back to Mother Starling's before anything happens. We'll lose the hanketch there.'

Come quiet now. We know it was you who took it.

Darkness spilled from the alley leading from the courtyard into Barn Lane. Shadows licked from it over the cobbles like a tide of tar.

They would turn left, Anthony whispered, and avoid Northgate Street. Turn left, and there were any number of ways they could disappear.

'What if I'm wrong?' Thoughts collided and spun. The inside passengers were in their seats, the sturdy couple heaving themselves into the basket, the wife watching them in concern. 'There's no other coach for near a week.'

'London will still be there.'

A slice of brightness parted the alley's black walls about twenty feet ahead. Silhouetted against it, one foot propped behind him, was another of Bryce's men.

Mary's breath came out in swathes, making her head spin. 'I know that one. Jack Joseph. Used to drive the cart. Used to . . .'

'Which is the weakest?' Anthony said.

'What?'

'The weakest. Which should we tackle to get away?' Mary tried to make herself calm.

Movement captured her eye. The one with the cleft chin nodded at someone, who stepped into the courtyard. Her legs juddered under her.

Bryce's top lip was swollen, and a bruise spread across his cheek. With him was a smart-looking man she had never seen before. His ruddy face and coarse walk belied the elegance of his clothes. His waistcoat was a vivid shade of blue. Blood pulsed in her ears.

Bryce looked straight at her, and his face was blank. Nothing. No evil, no delight in cornering her, no guilt. He just looked at her and then spoke to the man. As if he did not know her, and just passed her in the street, a plain girl beneath his notice.

'Through the inn?' Anthony spoke more to himself than her.

'Mr Cavender,' she whispered. There was no time to say anything else. The man in the blue silk waistcoat drew in a great breath and shouted.

'Sir, I see her. It's the very woman who stole it! The very woman, her hair as black as a witch's.' A stubby red finger jabbed towards her. 'There!'

Anthony clutched up his bag in front of him. 'Run,' he said. 'Cow Lane.'

Jack Joseph hadn't heard the shouts. He started up from his reverie, Anthony rammed the bag into his chest and all the air left his lungs with a grunt.

'Run!'

Turn left, he had said. She ran along Barn Lane. Was it the pound of boots behind her she heard, or her heart, or both? She ducked down a passageway and held her breath to silence it. Her ribs hurt under her stays.

Anthony was not with her. She could not leave him. If they were to go to the Northgate they would go together. If they were to end on the gallows they would jump from the cart hand in hand. She looked back. Jack Joseph's soil-speckled arms closed round her and lifted her feet from the ground.

Her instinct had always been that no one would fight for her, and she must do it herself. Her heels cracked Jack Joseph's shins; her fists thumped his thighs. He spun her round and she had a rushing glimpse of Anthony struggling with the arse-chinned man and the one in the waistcoat. Bryce could be anywhere.

Screams battled in her throat but she would not let them escape. They wouldn't help Anthony, and they wouldn't help her. She threw her head back, felt her hat hit Jack Joseph's face, and heard him swear.

But nothing she did could free his grip. Solid arms encircled her chest and she scratched for her life. She furrowed red lines in his hands, pulled his little fingers so far back it seemed impossible for them not to snap, kept flailing her heels at his shins, but he would not let go. An angry growl rumbled in his chest.

'It inna my bloody fault. I only do as he says.'

'Well, what if he says to stick a poker up your backside?'

Her limbs were getting tired. Jack's were getting stronger. The man in the blue waistcoat stood with his hands to his knees, a rope of blood and spit streaming from his mouth. Shouts echoed in the courtyard alley.

Mary's strength ebbed. Jack propelled her towards the Pied Bull. 'That's the way, Mrs Jones. Don't take it out on muggins – complain to *him* if you don't like it.'

More than ruefulness wove through his tone. Mary stopped struggling. Resentment. She knew the teeth-clenching bitterness of it, knew that if she could turn and look at him she would see a strand of grievance in his eyes.

'Aren't you sick of him, Jack?' Her voice was so solid, so unruffled. 'Aren't you sick of carting contraband? It's you who'll swing if you get caught with it, not him.' Bryce was still not in view. 'Where is he, then? Who gets their hands dirty and who takes the credit?' Jack stopped pushing her. 'All that money – it in't his. He's in debt. He can't pay it. If you left off doing the ghost walks for him he'd end up in gaol. He's got no power over you but what you let him take.' Jack Joseph's grip loosened and she spun to face him. There it was, that resentment. A speck in his eyes; a seed of rebellion. 'He's got the great pox, from spending that money on whores when it should be yours to spend on your family. You could tell everyone. You could smuggle goods for yourself – you have your boat. You have your banter with the Manx, who only know him through his coins.' Arse-chin landed on his face in the dust behind her. 'Let me go, and break free yourself.'

'Pike it then, you wily bitch,' he muttered. 'I'll see your friend gets away.' Mary clutched her petticoats and ran.

The passageway ended in an orchard, its blossoms decaying on the ground. Ahead, the backs of the Parson Lane houses rose bleak and black. Paths divided them – some dark and narrow, some washed in sunlight. She chose a dark one. Beyond, another alley, and beyond that, the Dissenters' Chapel. She skirted it and rested a moment, her lungs grinding each agonising breath in and out. Then anger seared her and she put her hand to her belly.

If this has harmed you, I'll hang rather than see Bryce Warbreck live another day.

Before her was a cross-legged figure, slumped against the chapel. Ragged clothes dripped off him and his fingers clasped his cloth-bound feet. She remembered Hartingshall, sack-like in a doorway, both arms intact, oblivious to the future. The beggar raised his palms, their cracked skin weeping and smeared.

'Have this.' Mary gasped for breath and pushed the handkerchief into his hands. 'It in't stolen.' Once it left her possession a new strength flooded her; a great deluge of relief. Bewilderment crossed the beggar's red-threaded eyes.

A thought darted through her mind. *He'll only spend it on gin. What a waste.*

He opened out the silk in front of him and looked questioningly at her, his lips widening into a gappy smile. Shame sunk in her stomach.

'Thank you,' he said. 'I know a feller as'll buy this. Thank you.' Mary hurried on into Watergate Street.

Not sure enough of her safety to risk the busy street, she hid in Dog-Breath Annie's, with a cup of filthy tea, dishevelled enough even in her new clothes not to excite much wonder, and then took a circuitous route back to Cow Lane. Mother Starling stood in the doorway, taking nervous swigs from a cup. She pulled Mary in with such a wrench that Mary staggered. Anthony was waiting to catch her.

'They walked away,' he said, holding her close to him. 'And he did nowt. His flunkeys walked away, and so did I, and he could only watch.'

They went to the Bear's Paw and sat there until a coach passed, and paid a boy a penny to ask the driver to stop before they ran out.

'Where does this go?'

'Through the city and to Warrington.' There was a coach from there to London, the coachman said, but they'd be daft to go that way, for they'd have to double back. Anthony opened the door and six alarmed faces turned towards him.

'Basket's empty,' said the coachman with a shrug. 'Shilling the trip, the pair of you.' They flung their bags in and scrambled up.

'Keep down.'

The basket was wide enough for Mary to lie flat on its carpet of straw, with Anthony cramped beside her. Sky filled her vision. Through her stays she felt the clamour of Anthony's heart. She clung to him, numbing her mind with the turn of the wheels. They passed through the middle of the city, stopping twice for what seemed like an hour, ready to spring up and run if they had to, but the coachman's grumbles didn't make anyone else get aboard.

Past the Pentice, turning up Northgate Street. Now they must be passing the Pied Bull.

The wheels stopped. The black turrets of the Northgate stabbed the sky. Minutes went by. Mary remembered looking out from the Blue Coat School at the queues of vehicles waiting to travel, one by one, through the passageway. Now it seemed forever before the basket at last began to rock again.

Under the Northgate the sound of the wheels echoed and the temperature of the air dropped. Odours of urine and stagnant moisture fingered the straw's scent away. Above, the ancient stones crumbled, their surfaces rough with decay. Deep grooves surrounded each block, nothing but the pressure of the structure itself holding them in. Below was the squelch of mud with no hope of ever drying; splashes hit the underside of the basket. Below that perhaps there were the cries of those in the dungeons, but they could not hear them.

Past the Blue Coat School, its row of square windows blanked by the sun. Its red-brick corner jutted out and, at the upper window facing the road, Mary glimpsed movement. She could not tell who it was. Opposite the lane to the salt marsh they made a sharp right turn, leaving its sunshine and grasses part of someone else's future. Past a quarry and a spinney, into the Gorse Stacks, past vegetable gardens, until the buildings became sparser and the road pressed on between hedgerows; and at last Anthony looked over the side of the basket, and said there was no one following.

They were silent for a mile or more, hand in hand, each overwhelmed by thoughts. Mary listened for the sound of hooves behind them, but gradually the rolling movement of the coach and the warmth of the sun on her knees calmed her.

Let Bryce flounder in his debt, let the villagers rebel, let Mr Barnston call in the money and send him to gaol till the pox rotted all pride from him. Sunlight glanced from the shiny black sides of the carriage and fragmented the thoughts to tiny, redundant specks. Let him sink without any help from her. It would happen soon enough. Useless hatred would not trap her as had useless love.

Anthony broke the silence, trying to smile. 'While we were running I didn't think of gin.' Everything about him showed he thought of it now. His eyes were deep and haunted, his hand unstill in hers. A film of sweat gleamed on his skin. He sat for another minute or two, strumming his fingertips over the wicker seat, and then he rummaged in his bag and brought out Mother Starling's bottle. 'She meant well, giving us this.' He pulled out the cork. Spirituous fumes ghosted up, playing on Mary's lips. She looked up at Anthony, her shoulder pressed close against his, and the hollows of his eyes were pearlescent and clammy. But a strange spark enlivened his gaze. Something that had always been there, masked. 'She couldn't have known I won't drink it. I won't pretend I don't want to.' He drew a long breath of the sugary scent and the bottle trembled in his hand. 'But that doesn't mean I have to, and I won't. For all our sakes. All three of us. I'll get rid of it.'

'Perhaps, once we get to Warrington, we can find someone to buy it.'

The road narrowed and the horses slowed, their harnesses jangling, the driver standing to see if the way was clear.

Anthony grasped her hand so tight that his knuckles paled to the shade of her glove. 'No,' he said. 'Now.'

The bottle spun and shed a crystal arc of gin that hung in the air for a fraction of time too small to count on a watch. Then it fell and lodged in the hedgerow, its corkless neck glinting at the road ahead.